No Law Against Love

Laws matter little - when love finds a way.

Highland Press
A Wee Dram Imprint

No Law Against Love

ISBN: 0-9746249-3-4
PUBLISHED BY HIGHLAND PRESS
A Wee Dram Book

Our Authors

Kristi Ahlers
Cheryl Alldredge
Rekha Ambardar
Susan Barclay
Leanne Burroughs
Cissy Hassell
Patty Howell
Deborah Anne MacGillivray
Victoria Oliveri
Jacquie Rogers
Jennifer Ross
M. J. Sager
Michelle Scaplen
Kemberlee Shortland
Jeanne Van Arsdall
Diane Davis White

This book is dedicated to all the brave women who have undergone treatment for breast cancer—and to the family and friends who have lost loved ones from this heinous disease. The seventeen authors in this book – all in various stages of their writing careers – have donated their time, talent and heartfelt blessings to all of you.

I wish to specifically thank my co-publisher, DeborahAnne MacGillivray. This endeavor wouldn't be possible without her help and support. Thank you, as well, to our associate editors, Cheryl Alldredge, Cissy Hassell, and Kemberlee Shortland. I couldn't have done this without your assistance! And to those editors who don't have stories in this book, thanks for taking the time to care and help with our first project!

~LLB

Table of Contents

Bad Cat

by DeborahAnne MacGillivray

• *Destin, Florida — Any dog or cat, which attacks and bites a person or another animal without provocation, shall be deemed a 'bad dog' or 'bad cat' and the owner or custodian of such animal shall pay a civil penalty of one hundred dollars...*

Present Day

"That is *not* a cat. That's a pit bull with fur!"

Ian St. Giles stood nose-to-nose with the sexy redhead, both of them leaning over the smiling cat. He never knew cats smiled. Actually, it wasn't a smile—the bloody beast *smirked.*

Ian enjoyed cats, but this one he could really grow to *hate.* Unfortunately, Katlyn Mackenzie adored the ridiculous creature, which was one-quarter Scottish Wildcat. Likely the only person on God's green earth—in this case Destin, Florida—who did. This *pony-sized* menace turned over trashcans, knocked-up half the female pussycats in a ten block radius, chased people down the sidewalk as they passed Katlyn's house and terrorized the town's dogs. From day one, after Katlyn moved into her great aunt's beachfront property, Destin hadn't been safe.

Just last week, Auggie Moggie shredded the ear of Molly Mays' toy poodle. Granted, he hated that dog even more, so he sniggered when the annoying poodle ran into Freddy Krueger in a fur coat...*hmm*...Katlyn's *darling.*

"There's a city ordinance against *bad* cats. You can be fined, you know," Ian warned.

Eyes flashing, the sexy woman in the black lycra bathing

suit fired back, "Is there an ordinance against grouchy neighbors?"

Ian pointed at The Cat Auggie. "That beast is a menace. I've been over here every day this week to complain about his antics."

As he stared at the longhaired, grey-striped tabby, with the half-white face, it finally hit him—Katlyn wore a swimsuit. It left *nothing* to his imagination. Evidently, she'd been tanning in the backyard before he interrupted with his latest complaint. She was sun-kissed pink and a sheen of perspiration coated her silken skin.

The black suit had a deep scooped-neck front and high, French-cut legs that went *all the way up* to her hipbones. He hadn't seen the back view yet, but figured it was barely there, close to a thong. The stretchy material may as well be spray-painted on!

His mouth watered and his groin achingly throbbed to life. A state he'd found himself in with increasing frequency since she'd moved into the house next door to his. Worse, it played seven kinds of havoc with his writing.

Her magnificent auburn mane hung in a braid over one shoulder and down to her waist. Hair like that sent a man into overdrive. Ian imagined it spread on a pillow as he drove his body into hers. Nearly groaning, he pressed back the urge rising within him to play caveman, snatch that long hair and haul her off to his cave—er, house.

Ian had been delighted to meet his new neighbor when he stopped by to act as *Welcome Wagon* three weeks ago. It was nice to hear another British accent in the midst of these Floridians. Gave them the first thread of commonality. Quite delightfully, the air crackled with sexual tension whenever they were near. The impact she had on his senses was electric, magic.

He'd rented the beach property for the summer to get a feel for the setting of his latest crime novel, an eye on his looming deadline. Only, every day that bloody beast sneaked into his house and stole something, dragging him away from his work. Today, the wee monster from Hell slipped inside while Ian carried in groceries. Auggie helped himself to a New York Strip steak and scampered off with it like a bandit.

How the hell was he to meet his deadline with the

distraction of mouth-watering Katlyn Mackenzie and her demon pussycat creating mayhem for his mind and libido?

While he *really* craved to lure Katlyn into his bed, this feline varmint saw Kat and he remained at loggerheads over Auggie's behavior. *Or lack of it.*

"Bad neighbor? How about turning that pony with fangs and claws loose on this poor, unsuspecting town? He just ate seven bucks worth of prime New York Strip. I think feeding the cat my supper goes beyond the call of being a good neighbor."

"Auggie," she put her hands on her hips, looking down at the cat with a frown, "did you steal the man's steak?"

The cat blinked up at her with an innocent face.

Ian expected a halo and wings to materialize any second. "Oh yeah, the little demon's going to admit his criminal ways. Look at him. He's *not* a cat. He should be playing Nose Guard for the *Chicago Bears*."

Katlyn sniffed disdain—at him. "Obviously, Mr. St. Giles, you're *not* a cat person."

"Auggie's *not* a cat," he repeated. "I don't care what he's told you. Will Smith and Tommy Lee Jones are looking for him."

"Well, follow me." She sighed, then turned on her heels.

The blasted cat sniggered at him. Ian balled up his fist and held it to the cat in silent threat, going into a Jackie Gleason imitation. "*Pow...zooooom, Alice!*"

"Auggie, ignore the bad man!" she called over her shoulder.

Ian had trouble drawing air as he caught the full view of that next-to-nothing swimsuit as Auggie and he trailed after Katlyn. With feline sensual grace, Kat crossed the yard and climbed the steps of the deck, heading to the backdoor. Auggie bounded behind her as if his legs were pogo sticks. Rather amazing considering his *tonnage*, but Ian spared little attention for the comical sight. His eyes were glued on the inch-wide strap that followed her spine and the itsy-bitsy, teeny-weenie, black triangle dead center on those two glorious orbs.

What an arse! His hands *itched* to grab it. He wondered what she'd do if he broke into a wolf howl. She'd certainly have divine tan lines—ones he'd loved to explore with his tongue.

So intent on watching those magnificent curves, he tripped on Auggie. The cat squalled as if Ian smooshed him flat. *Deliberately.*

"Oh, poor Auggie Moggie. Did the bad man hurt you?" she crooned, bending down to pet the feline on his head. The cat flashed Ian a look that said, *nanabooboo.*

Ian suspected Auggie tossed himself under his feet just to make sure he came across as *Snidely Whiplash* in Kat's eyes.

As he stared at her bent over at the waist, he just wanted to grab hold of those rounded hips and take her from that position. Blood left his brain in a whoosh, heading south. He rubbed his forehead in pain. "Aspirins," the dazed word came from his mouth.

Kat raised up and gazed at him with concern. "You have an ache?"

"Hmmm, yeah...I've got...*an ache*," he mumbled disjointedly.

Long, black lashes batted over the huge brown eyes, then they traced over his body and returned to his face. "Maybe too much sun? I wanted to tan, but the sun was making me woozy." She opened the refrigerator and took out a pitcher of lemonade. "This should do the trick."

She handed him a tumbler, then ambled down the hall. It afforded Ian another chance to view that perfect derrière as it moved with a dancer's grace and sensuality.

He leaned back against the counter afraid his legs wouldn't hold him. "Mercy."

Returning with her purse, she held out her hand. Like an idiot, he just stared. Her front view was as devastating. Oh, boy, how he wanted to yank down the top of that swimsuit and fondle those full breasts until she writhed and keened with a raspy need.

He realized she held something out to him. Opening his hand, she dropped two aspirins in his palm. Figuring they couldn't hurt, he popped them in his mouth and washed them down with the tart lemon drink.

Katlyn opened her purse and removed a five and two-ones. "Here. Auggie shouldn't have filched the steak. Auggie, tell the man you're sorry."

Auggie rubbed against his leg, almost contritely, then his tail vibrated as if he was going to spray. "Don't even think about it, you menace from Mars."

"You really don't like cats, do you?"

Her tone said, *such a shame, for otherwise I'd find you attractive.* Instantly, the urge possessed Ian to grab Auggie up and do nose rubs. "I like cats. Auggie isn't remotely like a cat."

She waved the bills under his nose. "Take them."

"What for?" Ian blinked blankly, drowning in her hypnotic eyes. He wondered what she'd do if he grabbed her and kissed her—*long and hard.*

"The steak."

"I don't want your money," he growled. *I want you.*

"Auggie stole your meat. If you won't let me repay you, permit me to cook for you."

Both his head and Auggie's snapped back. "You're offering to fix me supper?"

Her witchy eyes flashed. "Seems fair. I have a couple steaks." She wagged her finger at the feline. "And Auggie, Bad Cat, doesn't get a bite."

"When?"

"Tonight? Seven o'clock?" she queried, with a come-hither smile.

Ian nodded. "Done." He felt like sticking out his tongue and going *nanabooboo* at Auggie.

She put the bills back into her purse. "See you then."

Sensing dismissal, he sat down the glass. "Thanks for aspirins and the lemon squash."

His hand was on the doorknob when she called. "Bloody shame you hate cats."

"I don't hate them, just have...a *personality conflict* with that *thing* you call a pussycat." His eyes danced over her sexy body as she stood, leisurely unbraiding her long hair. "Why would it be a shame if I hated cats?"

With a mysterious smile, she shrugged her elegant shoulders. "Love me, love my pussy...cat."

Ian missed the step down onto the deck and nearly broke his ankle.

The woman was a bloody menace! *Mind out of the gutter, St. Giles. You've only been away from the British Isles three months. You haven't forgotten a pussy is a cat in Britain, not the* other *connotation Yanks used.* Since she was from Scotland, she used it in the Brit mien, though he judged she was perfectly aware of the American usage and did it just to push his buttons.

Well, they say pets take after their masters. *Bad Kat.* He struggled to hide the pole-axed expression as he slowly stalked to her. Invading her space, he let her feel his heat. And, oh brother, was he hot! The little witch had no one to blame but herself for playing with fire. Standing in that next to nothing swimsuit, unwinding that bewitching mane, she'd deliberately provoked him. The predator within him growled.

Realizing she pushed one button too many, she backed up.

Until she hit the refrigerator.

Putting a hand on either side of her shoulders, he grinned, pinning her. Playing Big Bad Wolf was entertaining. She sucked in a deep breath and held, shrinking back from him. That just lifted those perfect, grapefruit-sized breasts up closer to his face. It required all his remaining willpower not to gobble her up in three bites.

"Oh yeah, I figured if a man loved you, he'd just adore your pussy...cat." He leaned his body toward hers, yet not touching. His every muscle clenched as her tongue swiped her dry lips. "What's wrong? Cat got your tongue? Pity that, lass. Tongues...can...be...so...*useful.*"

He saw the pulse in her graceful throat throb, pounding out arousal. Wanted to feast on that vibrancy. As she stared, hypnotized by his scent, his closeness, he saw the skittishness shift. Deep hunger flared in her golden-brown eyes.

"Hmm...maybe we could...*discuss* that over supper."

Ian arched a brow. "Can we lock the tubby tabby terror outside? I'm sure he'll entertain himself menacing the Hood. After all, he's already eaten din-din."

"Oh, Auggie Moggie vets my dates. Weeds out the short-hitters." Her laughter was musical, something you'd expect to hear from a faery.

Ian chuckled. "Bet he does. Also weeds out the dog population and maybe small farm animals, too. Remember, if he bites me it's a hundred dollar fine."

She snaked her arms around his neck and nipped his lower lip. "And what if this Kat bites you?"

"Name your price, woman, I'll pay." His hands grabbed her waist and pulled her hard against him, relishing the perfection of how their bodies fit. Just as he lowered his head to kiss her senseless, the alarm on his Rolex sounded. With a groan, he bonked his forehead against hers. "We'll have to discuss *price* later. Sorry, lass, I have a conference call with my publisher and agent in five minutes. Gotta dash, luv."

He made it to the door, then jogged back, grabbed her and kissed Kat hard and quick. "To whet your appetite. I'd like my steak medium-rare and my woman as intoxicating as Highland Single-Malt Whisky."

Kat watched the sexy man dash across their yards to his house. She couldn't contain her sigh. Ian St. Giles was everything a woman could want. Precisely, what *she* wanted.

Not too tall—a shade under six-foot—he wasn't the bulky muscle of a jock that often lacked real strength behind it. Lean hard bodies really pack the power. Elegant men were deceptive, as people didn't notice just how strong they were. Ian St. Giles may be a writer, spending long hours at the keyboard, but there wasn't an ounce of flab on him. From her bedroom window, she'd often watched the black-haired man doing laps in the pool in his backyard. Those beautiful arms sliced through the water as if he could keep up that pace for hours.

Arms she kept seeing in her mind curved over her head as he pistoned his body into hers—as though he could keep up that pace for hours, too. Each day brought them closer to that reality.

Thanks to Auggie.

She sniggered, wondering when Ian would twig Auggie was horribly bright and fetched on command. A cautious lass, she didn't want Ian for a night, a week or a month—she wanted to bewitch him, sex him, drive him wild until they were old and grey.

"I think he likes us, Auggie. I like him. Oh, do I like him." She watched as Ian entered his house and the door closed. "Think we can make him love us?"

Ian sat listening to the two women nattering over the speakerphone. *That's what I get for having a female editor and agent.* After seventeen bestsellers, both these harridans wanted his hard-boiled, Sam Spade-style character to get *warm and fuzzy.* He listened to them reciting statistics, how sixty-five percent of all books sold were geared for the women's market. They had it in their mercenary little brains that he needed to buck the trend, and in a field dominated by women writers, pen his current crime drama with a heavy dose of romance and erotica.

"Ian, it's called *Romantica...*" Maggie Caldwell, his agent explained.

In a conference call with the two women, he was redundant.

"Leave it to women to muck up erotica with romance," he muttered to the fat cat, dancing in place on his desk and purring louder than a diesel engine. He swiveled in the chair to make sure he'd closed the door. Still shut. He wondered how the Moggie Monster slipped in again.

"Ian, you have asthma?" Jess Black, his editor, queried.

Ian frowned at the cat. "No, just a big furball."

"Furball?" both women echoed puzzlement.

"Never mind." He reached to pet the cat. The stupid thing tried to bite him. He shook a finger at Auggie and earned two more snaps. "Your mistress may bite me all she wants, Cat. You sink fangs into me, you're charbroiled pussycat."

He groaned, *pussycat* summoning images of his near brush at sex with Kat in the kitchen. He adjusted his aroused male anatomy, his black jeans suddenly too tight for comfort.

"Ian, do you have company? Are you listening to us?" Maggie demanded.

"I'm listening. You want me to change the book so it'll pick up women readers. You want hot sex, laced with romance," he repeated, glaring at Auggie who now gnawed on the mouse cord. He snatched the mouse away from him. "It's not a real one, Buster."

Jess asked suspiciously, "Who are you talking to, Ian?"

"A cat named Auggie."

"Oh, Ian, a cat! How delightful you got a pet. Now *that's* what we're talking about with your character. Tanner Descoin needs to stretch emotionally. He's been this freelance investigator for years. While the stories are sharp, Tanner's stagnant. He needs to grow."

"Did Archie and Nero *grow*?" Ian grumbled. "*I think not.*"

"Today, Ian, the big money's waiting for the man who delivers what women want. If you deliver a hot romance, from a man's point of view, we could push you into this new market. Double your sales practically overnight. Jackson's ready to shoot the cover. *Check & Mate* is the title—"

Ian snorted a small laugh. "Thanks for telling me the name of *my* book."

She went on as if he hadn't commented, outlining plans with the full-steam ahead of a runaway locomotive. "Descoin is in half-shadow, a sexy long-haired blonde just behind him, her arm around him, her long red nails stroking his chest. Descoin meets his match and tumbles hard."

"Redhead," Ian growled.

"What?" both women chimed.

"I said make her a redhead," he insisted.

"Okay, redhead. The cat is an interesting touch, too. Perhaps you can work a kitty into the plotline. Let Tanner mature. Find love, fall in love. Maybe she can help him on his cases, be an equal. You've got to have lots of steamy sex, Ian."

"Amen to that, sister." Ian chuckled.

Maggie's question carried a note of doubt. "Think you can do that, Ian? This is a new direction. Are the prose in you?"

Ian's eyes flicked to the computer screen. Auggie was on top of the monitor with an arm hanging over, batting at Ian as he leaned forward. His eyes scanned the words on the page.

> *...he trembled as he went down on his knees before her, an acolyte ready to worship at the altar of her body. Instead of the reverence that humbled him before her, he reached out and took, rolling her distended nipples until she moaned. Her head lolled back, the mass of auburn hair cascading down to her hips...*

Ian cleared his throat and shifted before his arousal had a zipper impression on it. "Um...well...so happens I started this little project. Perhaps the two can be... uh...*merged.*"

"Marvelous!"

"Wonderful!"

The two women carried on their discussion about marketing, release date, dare they advertise in *Romance*

Writers of America magazine? Their chattering faded into the background as he dodged Auggie's fat leg waving to swat at him.

The power of his words held him.

He couldn't sleep last night. Tossing and turning, two cold showers, and yet he still throbbed with the driving urge to mate with Katlyn. Obsession full blown. He'd stared at her bedroom window, willing her to come to it. When that failed, he ambled to the keyboard thinking to work. He couldn't write about Tanner. He could only see Katlyn before him. Him making love to her in every fashion imaginable. His fingers started typing and the words poured from his soul-deep hunger.

As he'd written the words, he understood he wanted more from this woman than just a hot affair for the next month while he stayed in Florida finishing his book. When he left come August, he wanted Kat to go back to England with him.

"Can you make these changes and still hit the target deadline?"

Jess intruded on his daydreams of Kat being in his bed, her body moving over him in a pagan rhythm. That mass of hair curtaining her shoulders and back, tickling him. He groaned as he realized with the length of her hair, it'd fan across his thighs, brushing in whispery, silken caresses as she rode him hard.

He choked on his parched throat. "Um...deadline...yeah ...it's doable." He needed to shower and shave. Glancing at his watch—just enough time if he hustled.

"You'll get a couple of the love scenes roughed out and fax them to us next week so we can see if you're hitting target?" Jess suggested.

"Um...certainly." His eyes caught the light come on in Katlyn's upstairs bathroom.

"Super!" Maggie and Jess chimed like magpies.

Ian wondered if Kat knew her bloody bathroom was about 50% visible from his bathroom. *Time to move location, St Giles. Showtime.* "Uh...maybe make that...two weeks."

Kat appeared dead center of the window and peeled out of that black suit. The witch did a striptease for him. *Someone shoot me quick and put me out of my misery!*

"This is...a new direction...I'll need time...get in tune with ...*things*. Catch you two later. Don't do anything I wouldn't do."

Which left everything under the sun. He smiled at the cat. "I'm a man with plans, Auggie."

Ian and Auggie pulled up in the midnight blue Jaguar XJ to find the Destin police parked in Katlyn's drive. Ian and the cat looked at each other, silently asking what the other knew about this development.

After Ian had hurriedly showered, he grabbed his keys to the Jag, knowing he could reach the florist before they closed. Auggie had trailed right behind him. He nearly knocked Ian's legs out from under him as he bounded into the car, clearly going with him. Ignoring the command to decamp, Auggie sat in the passenger's seat as if he rode in cars all the time. "You claw my leather bucket seats, I'll hogtie you and let Mrs. Mays' poodle chew on your ear."

Ian had reached the flower shop as it closed and purchased a gorgeous bouquet of two dozen yellow long-stem roses. Stopping at the liquor store, he intended to buy a bottle of blush Chablis. Instead, he spotted a three-hundred-dollar bottle of Glenlivet Scotch. Anyone could bring wine. He figured the straight path to his Scots lass' heart would be with a wee dram of Scotland's finest. Confident his choices would please Kat, he rushed back, arriving fifteen minutes early.

"Auggie, appears this is one of those occasions where being early won't ruffle the hostess." The cat sat innocently. "What say, pal, you stay safely in the car while I suss out what's up with Destin's finest..."

Auggie dashed across his lap as he opened the door and beelined for Katlyn on the deck. Ian saw Kat waving her arms at the policemen, her expression riled. One of the uniformed men swiped at Auggie as if to grab him. "Uh oh, *not* good," Ian muttered, as Katlyn stepped between the feline and the officer.

Ian approached in cool fashion, though he was anything but. Katlyn stood shaking and wore the expression of a mother lioness defending her cub.

"Evening, Officers. Anything I can do for you?" Ian moved to stand beside Katlyn, hoping she'd calm now that he was here.

"We came about the cat—" one started.

"Ian, they want to take Auggie with them. He'd be terrified. They can't have him." She trembled worse.

"Auggie's not going anywhere." Ian fixed both men with a level stare, silently telling them he *meant* what he said. "What seems to be the problem?"

"Mrs. Mays filed a complaint. Said that cat," the taller man pointed at Auggie who'd gone into his cherub-with-halo-and-wings routine, "bit her."

"Unless Miz Mackenzie can produce proof the cat had rabies shots he'll have to be quarantined," the man's partner clarified.

"Auggie doesn't have rabies," Ian stated, daring either man to contradict him.

"We need papers proving that. Auggie has been deemed a *bad* cat."

Kat swiped away a tear. "I don't have papers. I misplaced them in the move. If they call the vet's office, he'll confirm Auggie has all his shots. It's just until morn."

"I'm sorry, Miz Mackenzie, but a complaint has been lodged."

"When did Auggie *bite* Mrs. Mays—the lady with the poodle that *attacked* Auggie last week, I presume?" Ian challenged.

The two exchanged glances. "Yeah, she has a toy poodle."

"Irritating thing," the shorter one chimed.

"Something we can agree on, Officer. I believe if you check the ordinance you'll note it says, '*Any dog or cat, which attacks and bites a person or another animal without provocation, shall be deemed a bad dog or bad cat and the owner or custodian of such animal shall pay a civil penalty of one hundred dollars.*' I judge that stupid poodle gnawing on Auggie's hind leg would fall under *provocation*."

Ian put his hand on Kat's back and gently rubbed, hoping to soothe her fears. Auggie twined against the back of Ian's legs, peeking around his left calf. Silly feline knew Ian stood as his champion, ready to do battle for him.

"So when did Auggie bite the biddy?" he pressed. "Maybe we should take Auggie to the vet and have him examined. Might make him sick."

The shorter one sniggered, only to fall silent at the glare from his by-the-book partner. When the other man quieted, he answered Ian. "About forty-five minutes ago. Said she was walking the toy dog near the end of the block when Auggie jumped out and bit her."

"Did you see the bite marks?" Ian disputed.

There was a hesitation. "Well, no...but her hand is bandaged."

"I'd go back and demand to see her hand. Then I'd inform her it's against the law to file false charges. Auggie was with me for the last four hours. He was here with us until four p.m. Then I went home to take a conference call from my agent and editor. They can attest to the cat making noises and purring in the background. After that, I showered. He rested on the bathroom floor and shredded a box of Kleenex. When I drove into town, Auggie rode with me. We stopped at the florist's before six. The florist will recall. She commented on Auggie following me about. About a half hour later we stopped at the liquor store. Jake Wilson laughed at Auggie in the car window waving his paw. Pray tell, how was Auggie supposed to bite some dried up troublemaker when he was in the car with me the whole time?"

Auggie wiggled as if he knew he was off the hook. He'd abandoned his angel mode for his *nanabooboo* face.

"Officers, if that's all...Kat, Auggie and I are grilling out this evening. Sorry, you had a trip out here for nothing."

The two officers nodded and started to turn.

"I believe you meant to say you're sorry for upsetting, Miss Mackenzie," Ian prodded.

Both mumbled an apology, then shuffled off. Auggie started pogo-ing around the deck sideways and hissing at the officers. Ian reached down and grabbed him by the scruff of his neck. "Don't push it, Auggie-nator."

Katlyn threw her arms around his neck and planted a noisy kiss on his lips. Giving a small hop, she wrapped her legs around his waist and proceeded to kiss him senseless. Dropping Auggie, Ian put one hand at the small of her back and one on that sexy derrière and shifted, so she didn't pull them off balance.

With one foot, he pushed Auggie into the house, then swung Kat and himself inside and kicked the door shut.

He'd wanted to give her yellow roses and share a toast of Glenlivet under the moonlight. He planned to make the night special, then he'd let Kat lead him inside and welcome him into her bed, her life.

Scratch plan A. They'd *never* make it to midnight, doubted they'd make it to the bloody bed. Kat already lost the playful euphoria, and downshifted into rabid arousal with the force of lightening striking. Spiraling pheromones now blinded them with need.

With his remaining vestige of sanity, his poor beleaguered, bloodless, male brain searched *desperately* for the nearest safe spot to land. Kat yanked at his shirt, breathing as hard as he. Buttons popped and ricocheted against the walls as she tugged it from his slacks. Kat's legs loosened. She slid slowly down him, ending with her long nails raking over his painful erection and then along his thighs.

So much for looking for a convenient spot—his last sane thought as she pressed her face against his thigh, rubbing like a cat. He barely undid the slide hook on his black pants before she had the zipper down, raking her long nails down the turgid length of his flesh.

He about lost it—then and there.

Damn woman! She was out to torture him. Ian's blood thundered through his body as he fought to keep from passing out. "Yes...damn..." he panted. "Oh Kat...my Kat...my *bad* Kat."

Shaking, he grabbed her arms and pulled her up, as he went down, unable to stand. On his knees—and still mostly in his pants—he slid his hands up those smooth thighs, then under the skirt to those globes of her firm arse. He smiled wickedly as he felt she wore thongs. "*Bad Kat.*"

He spread her legs, pulling her to straddle him as he rolled to his back. Shifting the panties aside, he smoothed his fingers over her sensitized opening, drenched with her body's arousal. She was so wet. The scent clouded his brain. Shifting the thong aside, he yanked her down hard on his aroused flesh, filled her with one, hard stroke. Damn she was tight, fisting around him with a power that blew his mind.

He shifted her so her knees straddled his hips, but that movement sent her to shuddering. Kat came apart with a force that saw her internal ripples vice around him, the shudders snaking down his flesh in waves.

Unable to hold back, Ian shattered in a thousand red-hot pieces.

Head spinning, he tried to focus. Shaking, he rolled them over and pulled her to spoon against him. "Well, bugger. Sorry, lass, don't think I've ever been so out of control. I bought yellow roses and thirty-year-old Glenlivet. Wanted tonight to be special."

"It *is* special." She turned and kissed him softly. "You rescued Auggie. My hero."

He laughed, full of joy. "Well, this promises to be a happy life. My agent and editor want me to write Romantica, though they feel I need help with my *research*."

She rubbed her head in the curve of his shoulder. "Um...I can *help* with *research*."

"Since Auggie is continually in one bother or another, I guess I'll be playing hero on a regular basis."

"And I'll be *rewarding* you regularly."

She rolled and planted a kiss to his chest. "Ian..."

"Hmmm."

"I have a confession. Auggie is a very bright cat. Brighter than any cat I've ever seen. Watch." She raised up on one elbow to see Auggie sitting on the chair. "Auggie, fetch."

When Auggie just looked at her, Ian laughed. "Teach you."

"He's being Auggie." She snapped her fingers. "Auggie, go get my car keys."

He sat, unmoving for a minute, then scampered off. Bouncing on his pogo-stick legs, he returned, the keys jangling from his mouth. He dropped them on the center of Ian's chest.

"Auggie, fetch my hair brush," Katlyn commanded.

Again, the cat dashed off. After a small wait, he came in with a brush, dropping it next to the keys. He sat and pushed out his chest, proud of his accomplishments.

Kat leaned over Ian to give Auggie a pat. "Good Auggie."

Ian caught the wrist of her arm and towed her across his body. "You're telling me when Auggie stole things he wasn't being a general pain in the arse, he was on a mission?"

"Sorry. In a way Auggie has been playing cupid for me."

"So you just *happened* to be in that sexy swimsuit after Auggie stole my steak."

"I have to admit what Auggie stole each time was his

selection. I didn't say steal your steak."

"What did you say?"

She leaned forward and nipped his chin. "I said, *Auggie fetch Ian.*"

He shifted, rolling her under him and pinning her arms over her head as he drove himself into her slick, welcoming warmth. "Hmmmm, *Bad Kat.*"

She arched up, meeting his every thrust, sending him out of control. His body splintered from a force he'd never experienced. He smiled ferally as he figured this was the first of many new experiences with this woman. Gasping, he tried to keep his heaviness from pressing Kat into the hardwood floor, but she snaked her arms about chest and pulled him against her, obviously relishing his weight.

"You're not angry with Auggie and me?"

Panting, he laughed. "What can I say?" He reached up and patted Auggie who danced just above Kat's head. "I love you, love your pussy...cat—and will for the rest of my life."

Auggie meowed, seconding that.

DeborahAnne MacGillivray is the author of four books due out in 2006—
A RESTLESS KNIGHT, RAVENHAWKE, INVASION OF FALGANNON ISLE, and RIDING THE THUNDER.
Be sure to visit DeborahAnne's website
www.deborahmacgillivray.co.uk

Chocolate in the Afternoon

by Leanne Burroughs

• *Great Britain - It's illegal for a lady to eat
chocolates on a public conveyance.
- It's legal for a male to urinate in public, as long it's on the
rear wheel of his vehicle and his right hand is on the vehicle.*

London, England
June, 1820

Stephen Webber raised his glass of port in salute to his tablemates. He was foxed to the gills and couldn't have cared less. His brother needed help, and timing was bad for Stephen to assist financially. What else could possibly go wrong?

Weaving his way out of White's front door, Stephen stumbled a time or two as he departed the Gentleman's Club. He reached his right hand out to steady himself and held fast to his carriage. Bloody hell, he had to piss. That's what happened when a person tried to drown their sorrows in port all night. He should have used the necessary room before he left the club. Glancing around to ensure no one was about, Stephen unfastened his breeches, braced himself with his right hand, and relieved himself near the rear wheel.

He'd just released a long sigh of relief when a head popped out of the carriage's window.

"You there. Get away from this vehicle or I shall summon the authorities. How dare you do something so disgusting in public?"

Stephen found himself staring into the face of a woman—
a beautiful young woman. One he'd never seen before.

What the bloody hell was she doing in his carriage?

After refastening and adjusting his breeches, Stephen
opened the carriage door and entered, sliding into the seat
opposite the young woman. He felt a dip in the carriage and
knew his driver was back in the driver's box. Stephen tapped
three times on the roof and the carriage moved forward.

Lady Elizabeth MacNairy's eyes widened in surprise. She
moved to reach for the door, but a long leg stretched across the
carriage and settled on the seat beside her, effectively blocking
her exit.

She panicked. "Get out of my carriage, sir, or I shall
summon the authorities."

Through the moonlight seeping into the carriage,
Elizabeth saw a slow, lazy smile spread across the man's
countenance. His deep brown eyes never left her face.

"You do threaten to summon the authorities a good deal.
Feel free to do so."

Elizabeth's eyes widened at his audacity, but before she
could make a rebuttal, he continued, "And then, perhaps, you
can inform them what you are doing in *my* carriage."

"Y...your carriage?"

Brown eyes twinkling with merriment, they moved lazily
down her body before returning to her face. "Yes. Might I
enquire what you're doing here?"

"I...I was...I am..."

"For someone so quick to threaten me with our
upstanding authorities, the cat seems to have gotten your
tongue, *mademoiselle*. However, I repeat my question. What
are you doing in *my* conveyance?"

Elizabeth swallowed, trying to rid herself of the lump
threatening to clog her throat. Could she push his leg aside
and jump from the carriage? Possibly, but she'd more than
likely kill herself in the fall. Her circumstances might be dire,
but ending her life didn't seem a palatable conclusion to the
situation. She hadn't risked running away from her uncle to
die at the hands of a stranger. *Albeit a very good looking
stranger.*

"Although it is none of your concern, sir, I am trying to
avoid someone."

A smile spread across his face.

Had she just thought him good looking? No, this man was more than handsome. A lock of his black hair fell over his forehead, making him look like a tousled boy. Elizabeth curbed the urge to reach out and brush it off his face.

"Ah! I incorrectly guessed your marital status. Perchance you try to avoid a husband. Why? Did he catch you dancing too many times with another man at one of the *ton's* parties? Or perhaps he caught you in the garden, wrapped in your lover's arms? Lips locked in a kiss? His body pressing against yours?"

Elizabeth felt a blush creep up her face. How dare this drunken sot suggest such things?

"Let's see, who near St. James Square had a large bash tonight—one I made a point to avoid?" He paused in thought, then his eyes brightened. "Lady Ashforth? She and her husband live in the area. Is that how you came to be hiding in my carriage?"

Angered, Elizabeth leaned forward to slap his face. He easily blocked her hand.

"How dare you suggest I would do something so—"

"Daring? Improper? Risque? Come now, do not try to protest innocence. Do you always secret yourself in a stranger's conveyance?"

"Of course not," she bristled. "If not a matter of life and death, I would never—"

Stephen immediately sobered. "Someone threatened your life? Who? Where is he?" He leaned forward to peer out the window. "Why did you not immediately say so?"

"I did not say my life is in danger. I merely—"

"Woman, are you in danger or are you not? Cease with your prattling and give me a straight answer."

Stephen watched the anger seep out of the young lady seated across from him. She slumped against the seat. The most ridiculous urge swept over him. He wanted to reach out to draw her into his arms and comfort her. He didn't even know her. For all he knew, she could be here to rob him.

He felt a smile edge across his face. As if this wisp of a woman could rob anyone. He doubted she'd even come to his shoulders. Whatever made him think such a thing? Perhaps the panic in her big, blue eyes that made her look willing to do whatever it took to stay alive?

Her sandy blonde hair was fastened in a chignon at the base of her neck. A dark blue hat matching her dress sat askew on her head, a few stray tendrils working their way free of the pins. She looked a lady of means, not a common street trollop. So what was she doing out unescorted in London? It just wasn't done.

A lone tear slowly crept down her cheek.

She raised her eyes to meet his. "After Father died last month, my uncle arrived from Scotland. To gain control of my estate, he insists I wed my cousin. A loathsome man." She shivered at the thought.

"My sympathies for your loss."

She nodded in silent thanks.

"You don't sound Scottish. You have no brogue."

She shook her head. "My father was Scottish, but I was born in England. My uncle hates me for my English upbringing." She sighed and shifted in her seat. "Though barely more than a lad at the time, Grandpapa survived Culloden's bloody battle back in '45."

"When King George's forces crushed the foolhardy prince's ill-equipped men?"

Elizabeth shot him a frosty glare. "Grandpapa said they fought bravely, but had no chance of winning. The king's brutal son, Cumberland, gave the order all be put to death."

"I know English history well. I need no history lesson. The Scots never stood a chance. It was a mooncalf's bargain to support the prince in the first place. But you digress. What does this have to do with someone threatening you?"

Elizabeth clenched her hand into a fist. Why was she bothering to tell this man anything? He was obviously too arrogant to listen to the truth. Yet there was something about him. She couldn't quite put her finger on it, but he seemed to want to protect her. She just didn't understand why. Deciding not to bash him over the head, she chose to give him one more chance.

"I'm trying to explain, if you will quit interrupting."

He smiled, but nodded for her to continue.

"Grandpapa was injured, but fortunate enough to escape. He ran, knowing he had to flee the country. My grandmother, an Englishwoman, found him near death in a forest on her family's estate. She took Grandpapa home and tended his wounds." Seeing the man's arched brow, she glared and added, "She was a very caring young woman. To make a long story short, they fell in love, left her country home in the Borders and returned to her family home in St. Albans, north of London. My father was their first born."

"So, you've lived in England all your life?"

"I have. England is the only home I know—and now my uncle tries to take it from me. He never forgave Grandpapa for having an English wife. Never forgave Papa for living in England. As soon as he was old enough to leave, my uncle went to Scotland to live. He blames everything wrong in his life on the English—takes no blame for anything himself. I don't know why he hates everything English."

She stopped when her stomach growled. She reached into her reticule, drew out something small and unwrapped it. She placed a piece of chocolate into her mouth and let it melt on her tongue. The smell of chocolate wafted throughout the carriage.

Elizabeth closed her eyes, savoring the small treat. "Forgive me for not sharing, Sir. It's the only piece I have, and I fear I haven't eaten this day. Uncle brought me into town to get the license necessary for me to wed my cousin. I ran away when they both stopped at that establishment to celebrate their cleverness in forcing me to wed."

"White's?"

At her nod, Stephen again reached up with his walking stick and tapped on the roof once. The carriage immediately turned the corner, changing direction.

Stephen smiled. "For one so ready to summon the authorities, you really should learn more about the local laws."

"Whatever do you mean?"

"Well, you threatened me with that when I was...outside my carriage."

"When you were in the middle of that disgusting act?"

Stephen laughed. "Yes, then. I do apologize. Truly. Had I known anyone was around, I never would have..." He stopped.

"Relieved yourself?" she supplied.

"Again, I apologize. However, I do feel the need to tell you I could have you arrested now as well."

"What?" She looked appalled and her blue eyes rounded

in fear.

Stephen nodded. "For two things, actually. Trespass—and now for eating chocolate."

"Has your mind gone feeble, sir? You cannot have me—"

"Ah, but I can. Though ridiculous, the law states a lady may not eat chocolate in a public conveyance."

"But, I never—"

"Never ate chocolate? Or never trespassed on my property? In truth, I fear you are guilty of both."

"This is *not* a public conveyance."

"It *is* a conveyance, is it not?"

"It is."

"And we are out in public, are we not?"

"Yes, but—"

"I rest my case."

"You, sir, are drunk!" she said, indignation rife in her voice.

The horses slowed, and soon came to a stop.

Elizabeth turned to look out the window. "Where are we?"

"My townhouse." He leaned forward to open the door, then stepped down. He reached his hand out to her. "Come."

"Never!" she shrieked. "I would rather—"

"Return to your uncle? Shall I arrange for my driver to take you back?"

She looked quickly over her shoulder as though afraid her uncle might be conjured up just by mention of his name.

"Come," Stephen said again. "I guarantee your safety."

"How—"

"Woman, I tire. I drank too much and I need to go into my home. If you wish my protection, come with me. If not..." He shrugged. "Well then, I wish you well."

Elizabeth bit her lower lip. Dare she trust this man? Surely, were he going to ravish her, he could have done so in his carriage. But to go into his home? Could she—dare she—go with him?

She sat for a moment, staring at him. Tall and lean, he looked very much a rake. His eyes met and held hers. They drew her in with their intensity. He had an air of authority about him, yet seemed to be a man she could trust. Why she couldn't say, but Elizabeth trusted her instincts. Father always called her a good judge of character. *Well, Father, I truly hope you're right.*

Casting her lot to Fate, Elizabeth reached for the man's extended hand and stepped down from the carriage.

Soon she stood in the front entryway to a grand townhouse. An elderly, grey-haired woman who'd appeared after the doorman allowed them entry, now stood before them frowning. Her eyes raked over Elizabeth before returning to her employer.

Elizabeth's eyes swept the richly appointed hallway, the floors graced with Connemara marble. She could see into the nearby salon and drew a sharp breath of the beauty of the Aubusson rugs. Her mind snapped back to the present when she heard the man say, "That will be all, Mrs. Brown. I'll need no further assistance tonight."

"And the young lady?" Mrs. Brown queried, her disapproval apparent.

"Miss...my wi..." He stopped, stumbling over the words. "My wife, the new Viscountess, and I shall retire to my bedchamber."

Elizabeth stifled a squeak. Her head turned quickly to stare at him. A wide grin spread across his face as he looked at her. Why had he said something so ridiculous?

He took her arm and started to move her toward the tall, winding staircase. Elizabeth held back, unwilling to go upstairs with him, but he tightened the grip on her arm and pulled.

Not wanting to make a scene, she followed. She glanced back to see the housekeeper standing at the foot of the stairs, the woman's eyes clearly wide with surprise over the unforeseen announcement.

As soon as they entered his bedchamber and he closed the door, she rounded on him.

"How dare you make such a ludicrous statement? Hell would freeze over before I would ever agree to become your wife. I'm trying to avoid a marriage, not jump into one!"

He laughed. "Nor do I wish to wed, but my busybody housekeeper rushed out as soon as she heard a female voice. While speaking with her, it dawned on me I had no idea who you are. You never got around to introducing yourself, and I blurted out the first explanation I thought of."

Elizabeth blushed. "Oh, well, I...ah, my name is

MacNairy. Lady Elizabeth MacNairy." She turned to take in her surroundings, wondering if her uncle's actions had finally driven her to madness. She stood in a man's bedchamber and had no idea who he was either! Despite the situation, she didn't fear this gentle man. She turned back to face him and drew in a breath when she saw him removing his waistcoat. "And you?"

"Webber. Stephen Webber." He moved to sit on the bed and began removing his boots. "Viscount Linden at your service, Miss MacNairy."

He motioned to a chair beside a small table with a decanter on it. "Please, have a seat."

Elizabeth sat, glad for the distance between them. Though she felt an instinctive trust in the Viscount, the realities of the situation were just beginning to sink in. "You said you could help me. Pray, tell me how."

His boot thumped to the floor before he turned to her. "Later this morn we'll head to the bank to withdraw and protect your funds. For now, I am too tired to talk further. I need to sleep."

Elizabeth's eyes widened as she glanced about the room.

"I know there is not much left of the night, but you mean to have me sit in this chair whilst you sleep?"

"Rubbish. You shall sleep with me."

Elizabeth jumped to her feet. "I shall do no such thing! You said I would be safe. I should have known you would—"

"On the far side of the bed," he said impatiently. He swept his hand toward it. "It's quite large, a bloody parade ground, actually. Place the pillows between us if you do not trust me. And unless you have other clothes hidden somewhere on your person, I suggest you remove your dress and sleep in your chemise. It would not do to appear at the bank garbed in wrinkled clothes."

Grumbling, he slipped into bed and pulled the covers over him. "It has been a long time since I've slept with any clothes on. Come to bed, woman. I am far too tired to ravish you."

What a lie! Stephen closed his eyes, pretending to sleep.

He heard the rustle of her clothes as she removed her dress. His manhood immediately hardened. The bed moved under her weight as she edged under the sheet, remaining near the rim of the bed. Bedamned! Why was he putting himself through this torment? All he had to do was roll over and slake his needs with her body. Her reputation had been ruined the minute she entered his townhouse, though he'd been too intent on playing the knight in shining armour to consider the repercussions. Pushing aside his conscience, his mind conjured images of creamy white skin and his hands filled with her full breasts.

Gads, he had to stop these thoughts. He'd promised her she'd be safe, and one thing he never did was renege on his word.

But it was going to be a *long* night.

Stephen woke with his arms wrapped around something warm and soft. The *something* snuggled closer. His eyes opened wide as his crotch rubbed against her very firm derrière.

With a groan, he considered rolling to the far side of the bed. But the thought of removing his arm from her waist and losing the sweet sensation of his manhood pressed against her bottom was more than he could bear. He wanted to hold her a little longer.

Wanted to wake up like this for the rest of his life.

Where had that ridiculous thought come from? He'd slept with many women since coming of age. Not once had he thought of keeping one. He hadn't earned the reputation as a rake for nothing.

Gritting his teeth, Stephen moved away before she awoke. He didn't want to frighten her. She had to trust him or he wouldn't be able to assist her. And he definitely wanted to help her—although he had no idea why. Wanted to protect her from the uncle she told him about, even though he'd never heard of the man before. Wanted to protect her from everyone—everything—*always.*

Elizabeth hadn't slept this well since her father died. Suddenly, she sat bolt upright.

Papa! Uncle Fergus! Cousin Horace. Oh, dearest Heaven, what had she done?

She looked around the room and saw the decanter had been moved. In its place sat a tray of food. Her stomach grumbled as she inhaled the tantalizing scent of eggs. Rising, she approached the table.

Eggs, bread, marmalade, and fruit were piled high on a plate she found under a silver warming cover. She was so hungry. She'd not eaten at all the previous day. Her only thought, as her uncle dragged her around town, was to somehow escape him.

She'd done that, but at what cost? She'd spent the night in a man's bed! Albeit the situation had been innocent, she was ruined. Why hadn't she thought of that last night? Now she'd have to marry her disgusting cousin, Horace. What had she been thinking?

While her mouth was full of bread and orange marmalade, the bedchamber door opened.

Stephen Webber stood in the doorway, clad in fawn colored breeches and a white linen shirt. His wide shoulders practically filled the doorway. Elizabeth had trouble swallowing her food at the sight of him.

Had he done anything to her as she slept? A blush tinged her cheeks.

He broke her reverie when he said, "It is time for you to dress. We must reach the bank before your uncle has a chance to get there first. We should be there when it opens."

He didn't sound as if he had a hangover. The man had been totally foxed the night before.

"All right, I will." She raised a glass and took a sip of juice. "Thank you for the breakfast. I was famished."

"I remembered your stomach growling when you broke the law last night." A smile crossed his face and his brown eyes glinted with merriment.

"Broke the law? I did no such thing. I—"

"Ate chocolate in my carriage. Have you forgotten so soon? I've been debating if I should turn you over to the authorities."

"You wouldn't! You promised you would—"

"Take care of you," he finished for her. The impact of those words made him pause. "I remember quite well. I'm just not certain why I made such a promise."

She stiffened.

"Well, you certainly do not have to keep it. I can care for myself."

She turned her head away, but not before he saw her lower lip quiver—that luscious, shapely lip.

"If you will excuse me," she said, rising from the chair, "I will freshen myself, dress, and be on my way." Her eyes met his and held. "I thank you again for the breakfast. And the place to sleep."

She stammered before continuing, and Stephen saw a blush rise to her cheeks. "Did we...did you...?"

He burst out laughing. "Merciful Saints, you are an innocent. Trust me, had we done anything scandalous, you would *definitely* know it."

"Oh, well, I didn't know." Her cheeks were now crimson.

"Obviously," he teased before motioning to her clothes, laid neatly across the settee at the foot of the bed.

"Dress. We must hurry to the bank."

Elizabeth stiffened. "Thank you, but I can go by myself. I—"

"Get dressed," he repeated impatiently. Blast, this woman could be irritating. "I said I would accompany you, and that's the end of it." He turned to leave the room. "I shall await you at the base of the stairs."

He left before she could protest further.

When she came down the steps, Stephen's breath caught in his throat. Her sandy blonde hair cascaded in curls down her back and over shoulders. Her blue dress was slightly wrinkled, but he doubted many people would notice. No man would be able to tear his eyes away from her face. Well, okay, maybe they'd make it to her breasts, but they'd freeze there before going back to those full lips and blue eyes. Eyes that seemed to beckon him whispered promises of what could be. Blue eyes that allowed him to see tomorrows, happiness...*the future. Ah, what a wicked sense of humor Fate has.*

Stephen found himself drawn by them—by her. He wanted to know everything about her, wanting those tomorrows.

Taking her arm, he nodded to the doorman and escorted her outside into the bright morning sunlight.

It didn't take long for them to arrive at the bank. He knew everyone quite well, often accompanying his friend, Trevor, there after an evening of too much gambling.

"Let me do the talking," she told him.

He nodded, stopping paces away. He didn't want to complicate the transaction.

Several moments later he was startled when she shrieked, "What do you mean I cannot have any of my funds? That money belongs to me. Father left it to me. Uncle Fergus has no right to it."

"Lady MacNairy, I'm sorry, but that's the stipulation placed on it. Your uncle is your legal guardian, and until you wed he controls the money."

"But...but..."

Stephen couldn't stand to see the tears streaking down her cheeks. This woman made him feel emotions he'd never had before. He moved forward to place his arm around her. Knew he shouldn't, but couldn't stop himself. Something about her made him want to protect her—*forever*.

"Is there something wrong, my dear?"

Elizabeth turned toward him, eyes pleading. "This m... man refuses to give me my money."

Stephen pretended he'd heard none of their conversation. Turning, he looked at the bank manager, a man he'd seen many times on his visits with Trevor. Drawing her close, he spoke before he had time to consider the consequences. "Good day, Turner. Is what my wife tells me true? You are refusing to release the funds her father left her? I do not believe your patrons will be pleased to hear such a thing if I choose to inform them. Neither will the authorities."

Elizabeth stiffened and looked up at him, but held her tongue.

The bank manager gaped at Stephen, but quickly gathered his composure. "You and the young lady are wed? I'm sorry. I had not heard the news."

The Viscount's attitude indicated he found this conversation boring.

"My wife and I came to close her account so she could join her money with mine. It's easier to handle investments that way." His eyes narrowed. "I'm quite certain you've taken good care of my wife's money since her father's death. Now, my good man, is there some reason you refuse to release it?"

The manager flushed. "Her uncle came here and told me he'd be in charge of her affairs. Assured me he was her legal guardian. I fear...he's made some large withdrawals during the past sennights."

"I see," Stephen said, drawing Elizabeth closer still. This had to come as a surprise to her. "Is there any money left?"

"Of course. Of course. Certainly. A sizeable sum. It's just that...well, it matters not. Terms of the account say the money is hers when she weds. If she is your wife, then it's all hers."

"If?" Stephen's icy voice indicated if the man uttered one more word, a challenge would be forthcoming.

The man swallowed hard. "I shall have someone count it for her now."

"Splendid," Stephen said with a smile. "I am sure you do not mind if she sits while you gather it for her."

"Oh, my, well of course. Forgive my manners. Please have a seat, Viscountess Linden. And forgive my earlier confusion. Had I known you and Viscount Linden were wed, I never would have argued with you."

Stunned, Elizabeth merely nodded.

Stephen helped her up into his carriage and seated himself on the opposite side. "You need to invest this in a safe place. Somewhere your uncle won't be able to touch it."

"Why did you do that?"

"Get your money? I thought you wanted it." The left side of his mouth twitched up in a half smile.

"Why did you say you were my husband? You didn't have to do that. Now my uncle will probably come after you, too. I never meant to involve you in his hatred."

"I can take care of myself. I am worried about you. Where do you plan to go now?"

"I hadn't thought that far ahead. With Uncle Fergus taking my home, this money is all I have."

"It is a tidy sum."

"Yes, but it will have to last me a long time. At least until I can find some way to invest it." She seemed to eye him carefully before speaking again. "Could I put the money in your bank?"

"That would do no good. No matter where you put it, your uncle would have claim to it."

"Even if I were to put it in your account?"

"Of course not, but..." He drew up short, realizing what she'd just said. "I cannot allow you to do that. My brother is in trouble right now. Financial trouble. Unless our family can figure a way to get him out of this bind, I fear he might run away to the colonies."

"America?"

"Yes, and it's something our family would rather not happen. He likes his life in England and Mother likes having him close."

"But certainly the colonies aren't that bad." She stopped a moment, lost in thought. "Surely Uncle Fergus would not follow me there. He'd have all my land to dispose of as he chose."

The thought of her getting on a boat traveling to a far away land didn't settle well with Stephen. Who knew what sort of men she'd find there, although many of his friends had already moved there, appointed to government positions by the Crown. But for all he knew, others could be heathens, and the thought of her with them didn't settle well with him.

"No, you shall stay here." Bloody hell, why was he insisting she remain? She was nothing to him. She was— everything he'd ever wanted in a woman. Strong and courageous—and beautiful. Most women would simply fall apart and let the men walk over them. His *wife* didn't do that. She went after what she wanted.

He'd marry her. Keep her safe from her uncle, from the world. Perhaps it wasn't the usual manner one obtained a wife, but obviously Fate had smiled upon him. In truth, he'd cast his lot the moment he took her to his home.

He tapped on the roof of the carriage, indicating he wanted the driver to stop. He opened the door and stretched up to speak with the man. Soon he was seated again and the carriage resumed motion.

"Where are we going? Back to your house?"

"No, we must pay a visit to the Bishop at my parents' church and request a license. We have a busy day ahead of us, *wife*."

"We cannot wed today, sir. Even were I to agree, banns must be called. My uncle would never allow that to happen. Have you lost what little sense you had?"

"Quite possibly." He smiled at her, the cat after the canary expression. "However, although we could request a special license from the Archbishop of Canterbury's local representative and be wed immediately, anyplace we so choose, I can request an ordinary license from the Bishop at Hanover Square since my family has attended church their for years. Now, do you wish to escape marriage with your cousin or do you not?"

"I do."

"Keep practicing those words, my love. You shall put them to good use shortly. Odd you didn't notice—Hell's about to freeze over."

Dazed, Elizabeth walked out of Saint George's Church. How had she let this man—almost a total stranger—talk her into getting married?

Why had he done it? His brother—he'd said his brother needed money. It had nothing to do with her, he just wanted her money. Well, he couldn't have it. She needed to keep it safe in case she had to run for her life. After all, what did she really know about this man—other than he'd just made her his Viscountess?

He seemed kind, had certainly protected her so far, but could she take that at face value?

In bed that night after he'd made love to her, Elizabeth hoped he'd never come to his senses or think he'd made a mistake marrying her. Though she'd been nervous, he'd made her feel things she never imagined. She hoped morning would never come. Surely he'd change his mind then.

He reached over and pulled her close. She complied easily, wanting to be as close as possible. His warmth comforted her, and his scent enveloped her. When his fingertips again began skimming over her skin, Elizabeth moved closer on her own.

He reached over and pulled her on top of him, then ran his fingers up and down her spine.

"Are you sorry for what we've done?"

Resting her cheek on his chest, she ran her fingers lightly over the soft whorls of hair. "I know not what I feel yet. It's all too soon—too fast."

"Yes, you are right, yet part of me thinks we've made a good choice." His manhood stirred to life as she moved her fingers lightly over his nipple. "A *very* good choice."

Elizabeth couldn't help herself. She wanted him to hold

her all night. Wanted him to make love to her again. "Let me see if I can find which *part* you are talking about."

It didn't take long for her uncle to discover where she was. Less than a week after their marriage, he stormed into Stephen's house right after breakfast, knocking the doorman aside as he entered.

At Elizabeth's gasp and the man's angry face, it wasn't difficult for Stephen to conclude this was *the* uncle.

"Welcome to my home, Lord Fergus. My wife and I are *pleased* you have come to pay your respects." He swept his arm to a nearby chair. "Would you care for a seat—or will this be a short visit?"

"Ye bloody thief! Ye think tae take my money? I'll have this *marriage* annulled. Marriage my arse! 'Tisnae legal—ye dinnae even ken each other."

A smile slowly crossed Stephen's face. "Oh, I assure you, Lord Fergus, our marriage is completely legal, and I know my wife *very* well."

MacNairy blustered, "Well, I never."

"Really? Sorry to hear that. So you're saying your son— the one you tried to force on Elizabeth—is not really your heir? Hmm, I'm sure the authorities would be interested in knowing you planned to steal her money by wedding her to a man not related to you. We have all sorts of silly laws to cover every occasion. I am quiet certain we can find one or two to suit you."

"Of course he's my son. Ye know verra well what I mean."

"Yes, I do. And now I want you to understand me. Elizabeth is my wife. There shall be no annulment. I plan to protect this woman from you for the rest of her life. Now, if you do not wish me to contact the authorities and have you incarcerated for theft of her funds, I suggest you leave my house and never darken its doors again. Nor will you have any further contact with my wife—ever."

When the large man didn't move, but continued to glare, Stephen stressed, "If you've heard anything at all about me, MacNairy, you know my word is my bond. Do I make myself clear?" His eyes narrowed and he rose to his feet, his hand protectively on Elizabeth's shoulder.

MacNairy backed to the door, never taking his eyes from Stephen, anger etched across his face. "Aye, *Viscount Linden*. I understand perfectly." Without another word, he turned and left the room. The door slamming on his way out made a few of the expensive vases wobble and the windows rattle.

While they sat and ate lunch, another visitor came to call. Stephen's brother, Christopher, came through the dining room door.

"It's good to see a smile on your face again. Christopher, may I introduce my wife, Lady Elizabeth Webber, Viscountess of Linden? Elizabeth, this is my brother, Christopher."

"The one you...told me about?"

"The very one. Some day soon I shall have to take you to meet my entire family. Had they not been out of the country, you would have met them already." He said the last to Elizabeth, his eyes alight with happiness.

He turned to his brother. "And what has you smiling?"

"Thanks to your help, there is no threat of my having to leave London. I know not how you came up with the money, Stephen, but I thank you. Just wanted to come tell you in person."

He rose and started to walk toward the door. "It is a delight to have you in the family, Elizabeth. I can't remember the last time I saw my brother look so relaxed and happy. It seems you are very good for my brother. Mother shall be delighted to hear someone's finally made an honest man of him." His lip twitched upward as he shot Stephen a look of pure devilment. "I believe she and Father are due back home next week."

As soon as he left the room and they heard the front door close, Elizabeth turned to Stephen. "You gave him my money after all?"

He saw the disappointment in her eyes.

"No, I did not. I invested a good deal of it for you, but would never use your money without telling you."

Her look clearly revealed her disbelief. "Then how did you help your brother?"

"Sold some securities. I took a big loss on them, but Christopher's welfare was more important than my making money."

He rose and pulled her into his arms, brushed his lips against her forehead. "I would never do something to hurt you, Elizabeth. I promised you when we first met that I would protect you."

"Yes, but—"

"But nothing. I didn't fully realize I meant it at the time, but I know it now. I plan to protect you the rest of your life. I meant what I told your uncle, but I didn't just mean I'd protect you from him. I'll protect you from everyone."

Elizabeth stood on her tiptoes and wrapped her arms around his neck. "When I was little, Papa was always nearby. I've missed having him around. Missed his loving me. I know Papa's watching me from Heaven, but it's nice to have someone else watching over me now."

Stephen reached under her knees and lifted her into his arms. "Ah, that I shall, wife. I plan to watch, and touch—and taste."

"Stephen, it's still afternoon!"

His smile was the only answer she got.

He opened the door to his chamber and kicked it closed with his booted foot. He carried Elizabeth over to the bed and dropped her negligently in the middle before heading away and rummaging through his desk drawer.

When he came back, he handed something to her, then began to remove his clothes.

Elizabeth looked at him quizzically as he drew the drapes over the window to block out the afternoon sun.

"Enjoy the chocolate, my love. Our bedchamber may not be a public conveyance, but I guarantee before this night's over, you'll have enjoyed the ride of your life."

Leanne Burroughs is the author of two books,
HIGHLAND WISHES and HER HIGHLAND ROGUE,
both currently available at Amazon.com.
Be sure to visit Leanne's website
www.leanneburroughs.com

A Second Chance at Forever

by M. J. Sager

• *Multiple States – It's illegal to have oral sex*

Ethan Jackson's blood thrummed through his body as he waited for Jennifer Shelton to answer his knock. Her short note, *The Regency - room 1635 - any time after seven,* had taken him by surprise. Jen wasn't due to visit for another two weeks. Pleased she was early, he still wondered at the unexpected visit.

The door opened and he let out a pent-up breath. His gaze flickered over the woman he planned to marry as soon as she said yes to his as yet unasked question. Jen hadn't changed much since he last saw her a few months ago. In fact, but for a few gray steaks in her short cropped brown hair and some tiny laugh lines, she looked much the same as she had when he first fell in love with her thirty years ago.

His gaze slid over her body once again. Clingy red silk dress, black stockings and two-inch stilettos. *She never dressed like that back in high school!* His mouth watered.

Jen raised a brow. "I believe the note said anytime *after* seven."

Ethan checked his watch. Six fifty-six.

She grinned, her hazel eyes sparkling. He smiled back, stepped through the doorway and glanced around the hotel room. An expensive, well-appointed suite, this was one hell of a step-up from their normal meeting place. What was Jen up to?

She brushed past him. Her perfume tickled his nose as the gentle sway of her hips beneath the red silk enticed him. He drew in a ragged breath and turned away before his jeans became unbearably tight.

A possessive hand on his arm sent tingles through his body. He turned to the woman he loved.

She beamed a smile at him. "Surprised?"

Hell, yeah, he was surprised. His gaze flicked over her naughty attire. *Man, oh, man.* His mouth went dry.

She licked her lips nervously and stepped back.

Ethan gripped her by the shoulders and hauled her against his heated body. She gasped at the contact. *Damn.* Her sensual red lips begged to be tasted.

It was hard to breathe, much less talk. "I'm surprised—and pleased."

He moved his hands down the back of her slinky dress until he came to the swell of her buttocks. *Ahhh,* he remembered the feel of these mounds under his fingers. He splayed his hands over them and pulled her wickedly against his arousal. "I didn't think you were coming for a couple more weeks."

Jen grinned, her eyes mischievous once again. A dimple showed itself in her right cheek. Her hands slid up and around his neck to caress his sensitive nape. "I haven't *come* yet, Ethan."

An image of her naked beneath him, arching up to meet his thrusts flashed through his mind. Lust pooled hard and heavy in his groin. He lengthened, thickened and pulsed against her. The evil seductress wiggled her hips.

Jen guided his head down and softly brushed her glossy lips over his mouth.

"I've missed you." Her breath mingled with his.

Unable to take her teasing a minute longer, he crushed his lips to hers. His tongue swept into her warm, soft mouth, running over her teeth to caress the ridges of her palette and parry with her tongue. Minutes passed before he released her so they could both breathe. The gasps for air did little to fill his chest.

Her fingers brushed his lips and he playfully nipped their tips.

"I missed you, too, Sweetheart." Desire deepened his voice. "I'm glad you decided to visit earlier than planned."

Her gaze dropped from his face to the hollow of his throat. She pressed her lips together and he felt her body tremble.

"Well, the truth of the matter is," she said as her cloudy gaze lifted to meet his once more, "something's come up and it was either visit now or put it off for God knows how long." She ground her pelvis against his. "I chose to come early."

In spite of her teasing tone, Ethan knew she was hiding something. She'd been an open book since reentering his life two years ago. He'd been in the midst of a messy divorce and she'd been caring for her husband, Tom, who'd had end-stage colon cancer. She'd found him on a high school reunion website. It was the first time he'd heard from her in nearly twenty-five years. Seeing her name and reading her message had opened a floodgate of feelings and memories of the relationship they'd shared as teenagers.

When he needed someone to turn to after the devastating end of his twenty-two year marriage, she'd been there with encouragement and support. He could do no less when she needed someone during Tom's long illness and subsequent death.

"What do you have to do?" he asked softly.

She shook her head and gave a wan smile. "Nothing important."

She stepped out of his embrace and turned away. He wanted to prod her into telling him what was behind her haunted look, but she'd put up a wall and he knew she'd tell him only when she wanted him to know. Instead, he yanked her backward and pressed his groin against her buttocks. His hands slipped around her waist and moved up to cup her breasts.

"Jen," he groaned. "I want you."

"Yes."

He swept her up into his arms and carried her into the bedroom. Laying Jen on the bed, he followed her down and covered her with his body. Her palms smoothed down his back as her legs locked around him. He nuzzled her neck and breathed in her soft, unique scent. His hips snuggled between her legs and he rocked gently against her.

Jen bucked and twisted. Ethan found himself flat on his back. She straddled his hips and her dress hitched up to her waist. He lifted his head until he could see the triangle of her black lace thong. Fingers gripped the hem of the red, silky confection she wore and in one fluid movement it was up her body and over her head. His regret over not being the one to remove it fled as soon as he saw what she wore beneath it. Black lace corset, garter belt, thong and silk stockings. His gaze swept her from neck to thigh. He'd forgotten how damn good she looked in lingerie. His fingers twitched as he lifted a hand to touch her thigh.

"You are so beautiful," he whispered, feeling the heat of her skin beneath his palm.

She shook her head.

"Yes, you are, Jen. Inside as well as out," he added. "You always have been. You always will be."

Something passed behind her eyes so quickly he thought he'd imagined it. Then she smiled wickedly. Her red-tipped fingernails trailed up his stomach, scorching him through his shirt.

"For that, you may have anything you want," she teased.

Anything I want? Does she know how vivid my imagination is? Of course she did. Twenty days of love-making in the past fifteen months had allowed them to do just about everything they'd ever dreamed of doing to each other. But being given *carte blanc* made his heart race. He jerked beneath her. She smiled, as if in acknowledgement, and moved against him, teasing him without mercy.

Still straddling him, Jen helped him undress. Once he lay naked beneath her, she slipped off the bed.

"Move." She pulled on his legs until his buttocks rested on the edge of the mattress and then she knelt between his legs.

"That's illegal, you know," he said as she kissed him in a most intimate way.

Eyes twinkling, she lifted her head and looked up his body to meet his gaze. "Is it? That's one of the silliest laws I've ever heard of. Do you suppose the cops will bust down the door and arrest us?"

He regretted teasing her, regretted the fact her mouth no longer pleasured him. "No, I don't suppose they will."

She shifted between his legs. "Well, silly law or not, I'd hate to be hauled into court wearing this outfit. Perhaps I should stop."

He lifted his head and looked at her. Her breasts

threatened to slip out of the black lace corset. She licked her lips as she watched him. Ethan groaned and reached out a hand to guide her head back to his straining member. "Perhaps you shouldn't."

She grinned at him—a grin he knew meant bliss beyond imagination. Then she was doing just that.

He closed his eyes, drowning in the riot of sensations she made him feel. He pulled a pillow from the top of the bed, put it behind his head, and opened his eyes so he could watch her.

When he couldn't take the intense pleasure any longer, he pulled away from her.

"Come here." He helped her onto the bed and slowly removed her lingerie.

With tender fingers, he traced the faint scar on her left breast. The first time they'd been together after their twenty-plus years of separation, she'd told him she'd had a benign tumor removed several years before. It chilled him whenever he thought of how he could have lost her before she'd re-entered his life, filling it with a love that had been missing for so long.

Aching with a need he couldn't remember having before, he rolled on top of her and slipped between her legs with a groan.

Jen's fingertips caressed his face and chest. Her legs snaked around his hips and she arched against him, taking him completely inside her body.

"Oh, Baby, you feel so good," he whispered. It had been four months since they'd last been together and he'd forgotten how good it felt to be with her, to hold her. She held nothing back and met him with as much enthusiasm as he had.

He pulled back slightly and watched her face as he moved in and out of her, watched passion darken her hazel eyes, the flare of her nostrils, the way she bit her lip to keep from crying out. She shuddered under him, cried out his name and touched his soul with her acceptance. He loved her and he gave as much as he got. He strained against her and spilled himself into her. To his surprise, a lone tear escaped her eye and slid down her face. Wondering at what caused it, he kissed it away.

"I love you, Ethan," Jen whispered.

He collapsed against her, his body spent. "I love you, too,

Jen."

Awareness dawned slowly as Ethan awoke several hours later. For a few moments he lay still, gathering his bearings. Conscious of a warm, satisfied feeling thrumming through his body, he remembered where he was. He and Jen had made love two more times before finally falling into an exhausted but sated sleep. And yet, he could feel his need for her rising again.

He reached for her. His hand continued to move across the empty bed until it came to the edge. Blinking away the sleep in his eyes, he sat up and searched the room. She wasn't in it. Where was she?

A noise in the outer room caught his attention. A glass door slid open. He realized she was stepping out onto the balcony. *Why?*

The answer would have to wait a few minutes. He needed to pee. Ethan shuffled to the bathroom. After washing his hands, he pondered the freshness of his mouth. Lord only knew what his breath smelled like. Jen's leopard print cosmetic bag sat on the countertop. He unzipped it and searched for a tube of minty toothpaste. His hand brushed some folded papers. Curious, he pulled the forms out and glanced over them. *Medical reports?* He frowned. *Why would Jen have medical reports?*

He knew he shouldn't, but he couldn't help himself. He read the first page—and wished he hadn't.

"Oh, my God," he whispered.

His heart sank to his stomach. His knees buckled. His bare ass landed hard on the cold ceramic edge of the tub. He flipped through the pages in disbelief. He closed his eyes, opened them again and refocused on the words. No, they didn't disappear. And they didn't change.

Ethan drew in a ragged breath and stood. Now he understood why she'd moved up their visit. In ten days she would be in the hospital, undergoing surgery. When did she plan to tell him?

He grasped the papers in a fist and quickly moved into the bedroom to slip on his jeans. He stepped onto the landing, his bare feet curling against the icy concrete.

"Jen?"

She whirled toward him, clasping a hand to her throat.

"You scared me," she whispered, taking in a deep breath.

What he felt must have shown on his face. Her brows knitted. "Ethan, what is it?"

A cool morning breeze brushed against him, chilling his skin. At least he felt as cold on the outside as he did on the inside.

Her hand fingered the lapel of her robe.

Realization struck. From the way she shifted her gaze from him, he knew she hadn't meant to tell him. He rubbed the back of his neck. Damn her. Had she only come for one last quickie? Is that all she wanted from him, three or four weekends a year of sex? The thought stung.

Ethan stared down at her, silent until she looked at him again. Did he really know her at all? He thought of the ring he planned to buy in anticipation of asking her to marry him.

Damn! If she couldn't trust him with this news, how could he trust her with his heart?

"Ethan?" she asked again. "What is it?"

He didn't answer. Honestly, he didn't know what to say.

Her gaze darted to the papers clutched in his hand. She gasped. "What did you do?" She didn't wait for an answer. She didn't need to. Jen knew what he'd done, what he'd found. She pushed past him. Ethan followed her into the suite.

Her body shaking, she planted her palms on the table's glossy veneer and choked on her sobs. Her hands balled into fists as she whirled on him. "You had no right to snoop in my things!"

"I didn't snoop, Jen. I was looking for some toothpaste."

But she didn't seem to hear him. She drew in a deep, sobbing breath. "I wanted this to be perfect. I *needed* it to be perfect."

"It was." God, it had been more than perfect. It had been everything he'd ever dreamed of.

She shook her head. "No, *you* ruined it, Ethan."

Anger flared in him. "Answer me one question, Jen. Were you planning to tell me?"

She stared at him through the early morning darkness, tears streaming down her face. He wanted to take her into his arms and soothe her. But if she didn't trust him enough to tell him her most grievous news, what right did she have to his compassion?

There was a long pause before she answered. "Yes."

"*When?*" he bit out.

She shrugged. "I don't know. Later, I suppose."

"After you'd left?" He dragged a hand down his face. "Would you have sent me an e-mail saying, 'Oh, by the way, I'm having a breast removed tomorrow'?"

She sobbed. "I don't know, Ethan. You—" she raised a finger, pointing it at him "—don't know what it's like to watch someone die from cancer." She ripped the papers out of his hand.

His heart splintered. He couldn't, wouldn't think of her dying. God could not be so cruel as to give her back to him only to take her away so soon. "I know what it's like to watch something die, Jen. True, Sally didn't die of cancer, but our love, our marriage died a long and painful death."

"It's not the same," she countered.

"Yes, it is." He gripped her by the shoulders, wanting to shake some sense into her. "It *is* the same. And you had no right to keep this from me."

"No, no. You're the one without the right. You had no right to read these." She waved the damning papers in his face. "Who do you think you are?"

A cold, brutal hand squeezed his heart. He released her. "I thought I was the man you loved. I thought I was the man who was going to marry you."

She gave him a quizzical look. "What? What are you talking about?"

He laughed without humor. "I already had the ring picked out, Jen. I thought we'd go look at it tomorrow and see if you liked it as much as I do. I planned to ask you to marry me. I felt we'd both grieved our losses long enough and that we were right for one another. I guess I was wrong."

She lifted a hand and touched his forearm. "I can't marry you, Ethan. I couldn't put you through the hell I went through with Tom."

His skin burned from her touch while the remainder of his heart broke into a thousand unrepairable pieces. "Shouldn't I be given the chance to decide, Jennifer? Doesn't what I feel count for something? Don't you love me?"

Silence stretched between them.

Christ. Had he been wrong about her feelings for him? Could she have pretended all these months when she told him she loved him? He couldn't believe she was as heartless as his ex-wife had been. His bitterness rose like bile.

At the end of their marriage, Sally told him she hadn't loved him for years. Though she'd been plenty able to lie and say the words to him up until she asked for the divorce. Ethan couldn't believe Jen was just as callous. He clamped his teeth together so tightly his jaw began to ache.

She shook her head, tears clumping on her eyelashes, and he could almost see her erect an invisible wall around herself.

"No, I don't love you that much, Ethan. Not enough to marry you, even without this...medical problem." She drew his gaze with her hard voice. "I enjoy my freedom too much to want to be tied down again to...anyone."

Her touch scorched his arm.

"Are you screwing someone else?" He knew his words were cruel, but he couldn't help it. She *had* been lying to him all these months!

"You know me better than that."

"Do I?"

Her hand dropped away. "I'm going back to New Mexico tomorrow. I have a five p.m. flight."

"So, I was just one last quickie." *Damn her to hell and gone.*

For a second, surprise and hurt crossed her face. Then she shrugged. "Think whatever you like, Ethan."

He heard the weariness in her voice, but pushed aside his sympathy for her. She hadn't planned to tell him at all. *Goddamn it.*

He stared at her, the dripping of the kitchen sink the only sound in the suite. "I'll get dressed and leave."

She didn't move for several seconds. Then she nodded. "That's probably for the best."

It had been hell, those first days after he'd left Jen. Ethan wanted to kill someone, but the woman who'd betrayed him was eighteen hundred miles away and out of reach. He tried destroying the e-mails, notes and letters she'd sent to him over the months, but he couldn't bring himself to do it. Instead he read her words over and over. And they convinced him Jen had been lying about *not* loving him.

Christ. She loved him *too* much. He realized that now. Too much to let him watch her die of cancer.

Feeling ten shades the fool for not realizing it sooner, he now understood what she'd done. She'd moved their scheduled visit up to allow her to be with him one last time—to share the best night of their lives—while she still considered herself a whole woman. How foolish of her not to trust their love or to believe he'd ever think her anything less than beautiful.

How could he let her go through this alone? If she truly had only a few months left, he wanted to be there beside her, supporting her, loving her. But she did have a lot of explaining to do before they could move on.

Five days after the most incredible night of his life, Ethan caught the red-eye to El Paso. He didn't call before he packed his carry-on luggage and purchased his ticket. He didn't plan to give Jen a chance to refuse his offer. And he knew she was stubborn enough to do just that.

He'd been to her house once, but she'd picked him up at the airport and had driven him to her home in Las Cruces. If it hadn't been an hour's drive away, he would have taken a cab. Instead, he rented a car, pulled out the computer-generated directions and arrived at Jen's house before noon.

As he waited for the door to open, he recalled the last time he'd stood in anticipation of Jen answering his knock five long days ago. The longest five days of his life. On that evening he'd been filled with rampant lust. Now anger and a bit of trepidation churned inside him. What if he was wrong? He didn't think he could take another rejection.

Jen's twenty-six year old daughter, Maddy, opened the door. Her jaw dropped open when she recognized him. "Ethan, Mom didn't say you were coming."

"*Mom* didn't know I was coming." Ethan's heart thudded in his chest and his stomach juices roiled in an acidic jumble. *Please, don't let me be wrong.*

Maddy, who looked like a younger version of her mother with the same hazel eyes and brown hair, broke into a grin.

"She's being real stubborn, isn't she?" she asked in a conspiratorial whisper. "I knew something was up when she came home two days early."

That was news to Ethan. She'd told him her flight left the next day. "Your mother came home early?"

"Uh-huh. She wasn't supposed to be back until Tuesday," Maddy explained. "When she arrived on Saturday night, I immediately knew something was wrong. She refuses to talk to me about it. Though, she did say she wouldn't let you go through what she did with Dad."

Ethan looked past Maddy to gaze into the house. He didn't want to think about Jen dying. He wanted her in his life for years, not months. He settled his gaze back on her daughter.

"She wouldn't tell me anything either, Maddy." He swallowed the lump in his throat. "How bad is the prognosis?"

It seemed she suddenly realized they still stood in the doorway of the house. She gasped, then opened the door wider. "Ethan, I'm sorry. I guess I was so shocked to see you standing there that I lost my sense of good manners. Please, come in."

His gaze darted into the interior of the house again.

"She's not home just now." Maddy laughed. "She went to get her nails and hair done."

Ethan recalled the red-tipped nails that had raked his body only a few long days before. His stomach clenched at the memories.

Maddy glanced at her watch. "She should be home in about half an hour. Come, *sit*." She led the way into the house. "Would you like something to drink or eat? I was just going to fix myself a sandwich."

Ethan's stomach growled, reminding him he hadn't eaten since the night before—except for the bagel the airline called breakfast. He followed Maddy into the kitchen and sat on a barstool.

Maddy answered his questions as she made sandwiches, pulled out bags of chips and filled glasses with tea.

"Good Lord, she told you she didn't love you?" Maddy exclaimed when he relayed how she'd turned down his marriage proposal. "I knew she was being irrational, but I didn't think it had gotten that bad."

Ethan quirked a brow at her. "What do you mean?"

"I mean my mom loves you, Ethan."

Ethan laughed. "I know, Maddy. I reread all the letters

53

and e-mails she sent me over the last months and finally came to *my* senses. She doesn't want me to see her during her illness. I suppose it's some silly notion that I should remember her the way she was, not the way she'll be after she—" He swallowed the lump again, unable to say the word.

Maddy's hand caressed his with a gentle touch. "Ethan, my mom isn't going to die. Yes, she has a lump and yes, the biopsy showed it was cancerous. But, it's a small tumor and it hasn't metastasized. The surgeon is positive he can remove it all. She'll need a round or two of chemo just to be safe, but Mom's situation is nowhere near the same as Dad's. His cancer wasn't diagnosed until surgery was no longer an option."

The girl's eyes clouded with sorrow.

"Maddy, I'm sorry. This must be hard on you. And then to have me trying to step into your father's life..."

Maddy shook her head. "It was hard when Mom first told me the diagnosis. I had visions of Dad's death; I'm sure the same as Mom did. But we soon learned the prognosis wasn't as serious as his." Her hand squeezed Ethan's. "But as far as trying to step into my father's shoes...well, Dad was a hard man to live with. Mom loved him and he loved her, in his own way, but it wasn't the fairytale love women always dream about." She smiled.

Ethan nearly choked on his tea. "You think that's what she'll have with me?"

"Don't you?"

He thought about their last night together. He wasn't sure how fairytale it was, but it was certainly the most fulfilling night he'd ever spent with a woman. More than he'd ever hoped for with the woman he loved. And he did love Jen. He knew he wanted more nights or days—he wasn't picky—just like that one with Jen.

The sound of the front door slamming shut kept him from answering. Maddy met his steady gaze. She nodded slightly, then picked up the empty plates from their lunch and put them into the sink.

"Maddy?" Jen called from the front of the house.

"I'll make myself scarce," Maddy whispered, then louder, "in the kitchen, Mom."

As Jen walked through the door from the hallway, Maddy left through the door to the dining room.

"Maddy, do you want—" Jen stopped short when she spied Ethan standing beside the bar. Her newly manicured hand flew to her throat. Her gaze darted around the room nervously. "Where's Maddy?"

Did she think he'd locked her in the cellar? He thumbed his hand over his shoulder. "She said she was making herself scarce."

Jen worried her lower lip. She drew in a deep breath and exhaled slowly. "What are you doing here?"

Well, what had he expected? That she'd throw herself in his arms and demand they get married before the sun went down? Now that he thought about it, that's exactly what he hoped she'd do. Meeting her eyes, he said, "Did you really think you could drop a hot potato like that in my lap and leave it there?"

She hadn't moved into the room and he refused to take a step toward her. He'd already come eighteen hundred miles. She could walk the last ten feet.

Clearly nervous, her hand fluttered at her throat. "I...I don't know what I think."

What the hell did that mean? Anger rose anew. He bit out, "Jennifer Shelton, I want an answer. I've come a long way to get it and I want it now! Do you love me or not?"

Her hand dropped to her side. Her hazel eyes filled with pain and she nodded. "Of course I do."

He exhaled loudly. The pressure squeezing his heart eased considerably. "Then why did you tell me you didn't? Why are you shutting me out?"

She moved across the room then, but not to him. She pulled out the barstool Maddy had just left and plopped down on it. "It wouldn't be fair, Ethan, to ask you to go through—"

"You have no right to make that decision for me, Jen. You should have enough faith in our love for each other to know I would never let you go through this alone. It's unfair of you to push me out of your life when you need me the most." He resisted the urge to reach for her. He still needed her to come to him.

She fidgeted with her hands on her lap. "Yes, it was. I...I just..."

"What?" he asked when she trailed off.

Jen lifted her gaze to his face. "I just didn't want you to

suffer."

"What the hell do you think I've been going through for the past five days? I love you, damn it. I want to marry you! You kicked me out of your life that night. Do you really think I've not been suffering? These have been the most miserable days I've ever spent. Far worse than anything I experienced when my marriage dissolved." He wanted to reach out and grab her arms, wondered if he'd get away with shaking some sense into her.

Tears welled up in her eyes. "Ethan, I'm sorry."

"For what?" He wasn't letting her off that easy for the hell she'd put him through.

"Ethan—"

"Don't you dare tell me to get lost again."

She slid off the barstool. "No, no. I wouldn't do that." Finally, she reached out a hand to touch his arm. "Can you forgive me?"

His skin burned where she touched him and the tightness in his chest abated. "Not for a really long time. You're going to have to make it up to me for years to come, you know."

Vaguely, he heard the sound of a door opening and closing. Maddy really *was* making herself scarce.

"What do you say I start right now?" With a tentative smile, she slipped her hands around his neck, then moved her hips against his. "I love you, Ethan, more than words can say."

He placed his hands on her hips. A hint of a smile tugged the corner of his lips. For the first time in days, he could inhale a deep breath. "Then maybe you should show me just how much."

She gave him that wicked grin he remembered so well and reached up to kiss him. He pulled back.

"What?" she asked.

"First you have to answer the question."

"What question?"

He slipped out of her arms and dropped down to one knee. He hadn't even gone on bended knee when he'd asked Sally to marry him. He pulled the ring box out of his shirt pocket and flipped the lid open. A solitaire diamond, with his birthstone on one side and hers on the other, winked at them.

"Jennifer Elizabeth, I love you. Will you do me the honor of becoming my wife?"

A tear streamed down her face. This time, he knew it was a tear of joy. She nodded and held out her left hand. "Yes, I'll marry you."

He slipped the ring onto her finger and stood. She flew into his arms and smothered his mouth with hers. The kiss was deep, sensual and sent blood surging to his loins. His hands clamped down on her hips and pulled her against his thickening sex.

Ethan broke off the kiss and nuzzled her neck. "Jen, I want you—now."

"Yes," she breathed.

"If we get married in the morning, your children won't be here," Jen told him as they settled into the restaurant's booth for dinner. Tucked in her purse was Tom's death certificate which they'd picked up an hour ago from her safety deposit box, since they needed to present it before they could apply for their marriage license.

"I talked to Jeremy and Denise before I left. They know I'm marrying you."

Jen eyed him over her glass then took a sip of water. Had he been that sure of her that he could tell his children of the wedding before she'd said *yes*? He smiled as if he could read her mind. His warm hand clasped hers.

"I wasn't a hundred percent sure, of course. But I knew you'd lied to me. I knew you loved me and I was *fairly* certain of my powers of persuasion." He wagged his eyebrows at her. "I told them I wasn't letting you go and I wouldn't be back until we were wed." He lifted her hand and kissed the engagement ring she wore. "They're happy for us and wish you the best of luck with your recovery, Sweetheart."

Jen blinked back the sudden tears and swallowed hard. She smiled at him. "You should know Pete might be a little taken back by the suddenness of it. As the only boy in the brood, he was closest to his father. Besides, as a man, he doesn't necessarily believe in romance."

Ethan raised a brow and drew her toward him by tugging on her arm. "*This* man believes in romance." He brushed his lips over her mouth.

Fire spiraled through her. It had always been this way with Ethan. One touch from him and she quaked with desire.

She pulled away before things went too far. They were in public, after all.

"How bad do you think he'll take it?" Ethan asked, twirling one of her short curls around his finger.

"I'm not sure. Since he's in the middle of the Pacific on his carrier, we won't be able to tell him until after the fact," she replied. "They just deployed last month and he's not scheduled to return for another four months. So, we don't have to worry about his reaction right now. We can cross that bridge when we come to it." She gave a slight shrug. Lord knew they had enough worries as it was.

Ethan picked up her hand and kissed the ring again. "Do you know how pleased I am that New Mexico doesn't have a waiting period? By this time tomorrow, you'll be my wife."

Her muscles clenched as his tongue licked between her fingers.

The waiter appeared and took their order. The talk turned to other things, like how they would manage their cross-country marriage until the doctor certified her well enough to move.

"I'm just glad it's summer, Sweetheart, and school's out. I can be here for you for the next few months. Besides, I've been thinking. I might apply for a teaching position here," Ethan told her.

"Are you kidding? You just made head of the department there. Do you think I'd ask you to give that up? You worked long and hard to get that job. I won't let you throw it out now without a second thought. We'll discuss it later. No snap decisions, Hon. I can rent my house out until we decide what we want to do. In the meantime, as soon as I'm able, I'll be moving in with you. You better clean out a closet for me."

"Closet? Hell, I've seen how many clothes you have. I better convert the spare bedroom into a walk-in."

She laughed, tickled by his teasing. "Yes, and you should see the pale pink number I bought at the same time I bought the red dress and black lingerie. Of course, if you think I have too many clothes, I can always leave those items here."

His eyes turned a darker shade of brown, passion filling the orbs. "I don't think so, Sweetheart." He leaned over and whispered in her ear, "As a matter of fact, I think I need to see that dress and lingerie again. Soon."

She squeezed her legs together at the sudden heat that spiraled through her. Ethan nibbled her earlobe, sending shivers down her spine. She didn't know if she could wait until dinner was over to be alone with him.

He must have had the same notion, because the next minute he called the waiter over and told him to make their order to go. As soon as they got the meal, Jen happily left the restaurant arm-in-arm with Ethan. She knew just where in her room the black lace and silk lingerie was, but she wondered if he'd give her time to put it on.

In the end, he didn't.

The pale pink outfit she'd referred to was now packed in her overnight case, the one going to the hotel with her where she and Ethan would spend their wedding night.

Maddy and her younger sister, Kate, helped Jen put the finishing touches on her hair and make-up. Ethan was in the judge's chamber with Maddy's husband. Steven would stand with Ethan while the girls stood with her. She drew in a deep breath and turned away from the mirror.

"Come. I've made him wait long enough."

Maddy grinned. "Yes, you did. I can't believe you turned him down when he asked you to marry him last week."

Taking each daughter by the arm, she walked out of the small restroom lounge. "What can I say? I wasn't thinking straight."

"Well, it's a good thing you came to your senses. I can't believe he flew all the way over here and demanded you marry him." Kate always had been the dramatic one of the group. "Ethan's going to make a wonderful husband."

"Yes," Jen replied as she opened the chamber door and spied Ethan beside the judge, waiting for her. As his eyes bore into her, familiar heat coiled through her. "I know he will."

A smile lighting her face, she stepped toward the man she'd loved for thirty years and a second chance at forever.

59

M.J. Sager

M.J. Sager's short story, HAPPILY EVER AFTER,
was published in the
Bay Area Writer's League Anthology.
Be sure to visit M.J.'s website at
www.mjsager.com

A Love to Remember

by Cheryl Alldredge

• *Florida - If an elephant is left tied to a parking meter, the parking fee has to be paid just as it would for a vehicle*

John rubbed his forehead as he stared down at the stack of reports. They were only halfway through and he'd already asked himself what he'd gotten into at least a half dozen times. He leaned back in his chair and stretched his long legs, crossing them at the ankles. He studied the two men fidgeting nervously in the chairs facing his desk. Together, they represented the entire city police force. Two part-time officers and himself—one full-time, first day on the job, Chief of Police. If the reports were any indication, he could well understand why the Mayor had hired from outside the city. He'd assumed the Mayor had been exaggerating when he'd warned John the combined IQ of the current staff probably didn't amount to his bowling average.

"Well, it appears to me our top of the 'Most Wanted' list is some woman who doesn't like to put a quarter in the parking meter."

Officer Brown laughed, but Officer Cain straightened and leaned forward in his chair.

"That's right, Chief. The woman's a damn menace." Cain spoke earnestly, as if describing an axe murderer.

Brown reached over and swatted Cain with his hat. "Oh shut-up, Cain. You're just holding a grudge, that's all."

John waited patiently for the two to return their attention to him. "If I'm not mistaken, there are only two parking meters in the downtown area and plenty of parking. How does one woman rack up twenty tickets?"

"She uses the space in front of Thompson's market once a

61

week," Brown supplied. "Been doing it for near onto six months."

John looked to Cain. "And you ticket her every time?"

"And she *never* pays." The twenty-something Cain spoke the words through a clenched jaw. Clean-shaven with a crew cut, he looked like a high school JROTC cadet in his city uniform. Officer Brown was likely three times his age. Brown reminded John a bit of an aging Charlie Brown, round and frowning.

Brown slumped further into his chair. "You ought not to be bothering Miss Smith that way. She's a sweet little lady, never done nobody no wrong."

A picture of a petite, blue haired grandmother formed in John's mind. That many tickets really had to be addressed. Grandmother or no, she needed to pay the tickets or contest them. John might be young to be Chief of Police, but that didn't mean he was wet behind the ears. His job might not be political like a sheriff's could be, but he knew the people of his new home town would be watching him closely his first week on the job. He'd have to handle things carefully. He tipped back his chair, and drummed his fingers along the wooden arms.

"Okay, Cain. Tell me about your menace."

"Thinks she's above the law, she does." Cain vibrated with something akin to anger. "Rides that damn elephant into town like she's queen of the jungle or something."

John shot forward in his seat. "Elephant? That better be some kind of metaphor." His scowl had Brown squirming in his chair, but Cain was too caught up in the excitement of relating Miss Smith's sins to pay him any mind.

"Nope," said Cain. "It's an honest to God, Asian elephant and she rides it into town and ties it to the damn parking meter."

John was too stunned to speak. He looked to Brown for confirmation.

"She owns an animal refuge, just outside the city limits," Brown explained. "They take in old circus animals and such. Been there long as I can remember."

John turned back to Cain. The emotion that had been simmering had become clear. Excitement. The fool was excited because he thought someone was finally going to take his parking tickets seriously.

"You idiot." Furious, John fought not to shout. "She ties an elephant to the parking meter and you write her a parking ticket?"

A much deflated Cain nodded.

"And I suppose," continued John, "she goes into that market to do her shopping?"

Again Cain nodded.

John shook his head with dismay. "Don't imagine she builds a fence around the elephant or leaves a handler to watch over it?"

Cain's brows furrowed and Brown sat straighter in his chair.

"You do know this state has laws about handling wild animals? Specifically, laws about elephants—to protect innocent bystanders who might unknowingly spook one and get trampled in a charge." The fool had been issuing the woman a parking ticket when she could be hauled in for leaving an exotic and potentially dangerous animal unattended in a public parking space. It was reckless and irresponsible and it didn't fit with John's image of a blue haired, shrinking Mrs. Smith.

An hour later, John rolled the city cruiser up to the gate of Smith's Animal Refuge. The fence was high and sturdy, with warning signs clearly displayed. A cattle guard stretched across the ground beneath the locked metal gate. John left the car to idle and stepped out of the cruiser to look for an intercom system. Movement in the distance caught his attention and he stepped over to peer through the wide bars of the gate.

At the end of the drive, several barns and corrals flanked a typical ranch style house. Several fenced enclosures dotted the surrounding area, but the movement came from the yard directly adjacent to the home. A brightly colored beach ball flew into the air in an elegant arc. Before the ball could make its way to the grass below, the orange and black striped tiger that had been crouched on the green lawn bounded into action, patting the ball with one wide paw. The woman who'd thrown the ball laughed at the animal's antics as if she played with a house cat. She stood in the grassy expanse, long golden hair blowing in the afternoon breeze—yards away from the safety of the house. Long limbed and willowy, she moved with casual grace as she walked to the rolling ball and plucked it from the ground, heedless of the power of the animal rolling on the grassy carpet at her feet.

John's muscles tightened with icy worry even as the heat of anger rushed up his neck. How could the woman be so reckless? Though something about her confidence struck him as more than arrogance. She clearly lived side-by-side with exotic animals every day of her life. He'd looked up the records on Smith's Animal Refuge and found the operation was legitimate. Still, she'd broken the law when it came to the elephant. He needed to speak to the woman to find out if she had any sense in her sun-streaked blonde head.

He didn't see an intercom, and he really didn't want to risk startling the tiger by honking his horn. He was just about to go to the car and radio someone to call her by phone when the tiger's playful attitude gave way to alertness. Perhaps the wind had changed, he couldn't be certain, but suddenly the tiger and the woman both stared at him with intensity and curiosity. After a moment's hesitation, the woman lifted a hand in a wave, then turned and led the tiger around the corner of the house and out of sight.

Returning alone, she began the long walk to the gate. He watched her move closer with fascination. The white cotton threads edging her cut-off blue jean shorts drew his eye to tanned thighs. They were the thighs of a swimsuit model, he thought. A light layer of perspiration made her skin glow. Yes, he could definitely enjoy a little touch football on the beach with Miss Smith. Knowing his eyes were hidden behind the mirrored tint of his sunglasses, he allowed himself a long leisurely look. Her generous breasts were veiled behind a tight fitting cotton shirt that only served to ignite his imagination. When he managed to move his scrutiny up to her face, he found a sparkle in her big blue eyes and her wide lips quirked in a welcoming grin. Would she wear that expression to welcome her lover to her bed?

Calliope Smith studied the lawman at her gate as she went to meet him. He appeared lean, yet powerfully built in his dark city uniform. His jawline was firm and tanned. His sandy brown hair, just long enough to tussle in the breeze, showed no signs of gray. She'd guess his age at mid thirties. Young for a Chief of Police. But chief he must be. As far as she knew, it was the only position the city had open.

She had no idea why the man believed he was standing at her gate, but she knew beyond doubt the reason he'd appeared in her life on a warm summer day. She'd always known certain things without question—since she'd been a small child. Her mother had said she was blessed by God. Her father had assured her she had fairy blood. She grinned, wondering what her future husband would think. Imagine being married to her hometown Chief of Police. She'd only been home six months and hadn't been sure she'd stay until that very moment. It was for the best. She couldn't abandon the refuge and she'd had no luck finding someone qualified to take over the responsibility.

Without hesitation, Calliope fitted the key to the lock and opened the gate. She stepped close to the man whose name she didn't know, the name she fully expected to share, and stretched her hand out in greeting. "Good afternoon, Chief..."

He clasped her narrow hand in his much larger one. "Gage. John Gage. Pleased to meet you. Miss Smith?"

"Calliope," she said with a nod. His eyebrows shot up. It wasn't an unusual reaction. Most people expected a 'Smith' to have an equally common first name. Her parents had gifted her with something a little more unusual and, she thought, it probably fit far better than they ever expected. "Chief Gage, do you believe in love at first sight?"

She had to give the man credit. He didn't flinch at her use of the *L word*. She liked that he actually thought about her question, or seemed to. It was hard to read him behind those sunglasses.

"Well," he said, giving her hand one last gentle squeeze before releasing it, "my grandmother once told me she knew she was going to marry my grandfather the day they met. She never lied to me—that I know of, so...yeah...I guess I'm willing to consider the possibility."

Calliope beamed. It was a very good answer.

Chief Gage cleared his throat and directed his gaze toward the house. "I'd like to come in and look around."

The refuge was firmly outside the city limits, so he really didn't have any right to barge in, but he was her future husband and it seemed like a good way to get to know him.

"We don't do public tours, Chief, but for you I'll make an exception."

Calliope pushed the gate across the drive and held it open. Curiosity ate at her as she watched him drive forward, clear the gate, then wait for her to close it behind him. She pushed it closed, then walked to the passenger's door, promising herself she'd be patient about his reason for being there, just as she'd be patient about falling in love. Even when you know you've just met the love of your life, it still takes time for the feelings to grow.

When she slid into the passenger seat, John's hands tightened on the steering wheel. "I don't see anyone else around. Are you alone out here, Miss Smith?"

"I have a helper, but he's off this afternoon. That's why I let Tasha out to play. I can't give her any freedom when Barry is around. Tasha isn't too fond of men. I think she was mistreated by a male handler at some point in her past."

"Tasha? The tiger?"

"That's right. Even Father had to be careful around her." She still remembered the day her father brought the Bengal home as if it were yesterday. At the tender age of fifteen, Calliope had been awestruck by the beautiful animal. A feeling not so dissimilar to the one she'd felt when she'd looked out and seen Chief John Gage standing at her gate.

"I assume this is a family run operation. Where's the rest of your family?"

"They died in a car accident earlier this year."

"I'm sorry. That must have been rough on you."

"Yes, it was..." As the car stopped, Calliope looked at her childhood home and realized, sometime in the last few months, the sorrow in her heart had become manageable. "But here, everywhere I look I see them—always happy. They loved the refuge, the animals, and the work they did here. It was a wonderful place to grow up."

She turned to look back at John and although his eyes were still hidden, she was certain he studied her from behind them. The only question—whether he thought her a nut or just attractively original. Slowly he reached up and removed the mirrored sunglasses. His eyes devoured the features of her face—lingering, she thought, on her lips. The very notion compelled her to study his sensual mouth, to wonder how he'd taste.

After a long moment he got out of the car. He was half way around to open her door before Calliope recovered enough to comprehend. The gesture tugged at her heart, so she let him play the gentleman. The hand he offered to help her out felt warm and strong. She stepped out of the car and pushed to her feet, then led him around the edge of the house. She was just about to launch into her slightly rusty, guided tour mode when Tasha appeared in the window with a roar. John nearly jumped out of his skin.

"You keep the tiger in your home?" He sounded outraged.

"No, not normally. She has a very safe enclosure on the other side of the house, but I didn't want to keep you waiting. It's okay. She's house broken and very well behaved. I'd be happy to introduce you to her."

"No!"

She was startled by the strength of his reaction. Most people were wary, but fascinated by big cats like Tasha.

"You don't like animals?" She couldn't marry a man who didn't like animals.

"Of course I do, but you've already said she doesn't like men. What are you trying to do, get me eaten?"

Calliope laughed. "She doesn't like men, but she's not liable to attack you with me handling her either. None of the big cats are ever completely tame, but Tasha's very well behaved."

"I didn't come here to meet your tiger. I came about the elephant."

"Dolly? I know..." Calliope, held up a hand to forestall any jibes at the name. "It's a stupid name for an elephant, but it's the name she came with. Why would you be here about Dolly?"

"I've heard you've been riding her into town."

"Oh, my. This is about Jethrow's silly tickets, isn't it? I can't believe it. That man has hated me since kindergarten. You couldn't possibly have come here to arrest me because Jethrow, for some unknown reason, can't stand me?"

Just then Tasha chose to roar and paw at the window. Chief Gage swore under his breath. "I came here to decide if you needed arresting. So far the verdict is still out."

Despite John's hesitation, he did end up meeting Tasha. Before the tour could begin, Calliope insisted on taking the tiger back to her enclosure. After a brief set of guidelines on interacting with Tasha, she'd opened the back door to the house and the big cat had cautiously approached him. Together the three of them had walked to the tiger enclosure. To John's amateur eye it looked both secure and comfortable. In fact, the entire property seemed well maintained. According to Calliope, all the enclosures had been designed with the animal's comfort in mind.

Calliope acted the tour guide with good humor and obvious love for the refuge. Her earthy sensuality combined with a clever, if quirky, wit appealed to John more than he cared to consider. Yes, he found her sexy, but it went beyond that and that made him wary. She'd saved Dolly the elephant for last and John followed her to the large barn, surprised to realize he was in no hurry for the tour to end.

"Here we have the largest of our barns. Dad insisted it be built high enough to house a giraffe, though we've never had one here." Calliope laughed as she waved John into the shaded interior. "We have an assortment of stalls and work areas. At the moment, Dolly has the place to herself."

John saw the large gray beast through the top half of two giant doors that had been opened in a wall that divided the far end of the barn, creating an elephant sized stall. He could also see sunlight through large exterior doors that stood open, allowing Dolly to move in and out of her shelter.

"Do you always leave those doors open?"

Calliope's lips tipped in a grin. "Only on Tuesdays and Fridays."

"Today is Wednesday, and why the—"

"I was only kidding." Calliope shook her head. "I'm certain you have a sense of humor, but I'm beginning to think it might take some work to find it."

John refused to give in to her tendency to stray from the subject at hand. "The elephant?"

"Oh. Yes. Dolly. There's a fenced area beyond the barn. It isn't nearly enough space, though. She really needs more exercise. That's why I ride her to town—for exercise."

John couldn't believe she thought exercise a sufficient motivation to break the law. He wondered if it didn't have at least a little to do with irritating Jethrow. He suspected the trouble between Officer Jethrow 'Jay' Cain and Calliope Smith had a long and colorful history. The fact she knew his full name had to eat at Cain. The man hated being called Jethrow.

John watched as Calliope walked over to the elephant. "You break the law so the elephant can get her exercise?"

Calliope frowned. "I'm perfectly well qualified to handle her. I'm trained to handle all the animals we keep here. I wouldn't have them here if I weren't. The refuge is fully licensed. I know what I'm doing, Chief Gage."

"Then you also know it's illegal—and dangerous—to have an elephant out of an enclosure with no protective barrier between her and the public. You must know the dangers and still you leave her unattended—"

"I don't leave her unattended. Dolly is virtually harmless, but I know there are always risks with wild animals. Why do you think I tie her to that darned meter?"

"I have no idea."

Calliope continued, barely taking a breath. "It's not as if Thompson's has the best prices in town, but it has huge windows directly in front of those two metered spaces, so I shop there to ensure I can keep an eye on Dolly. She's never out of my sight and I only ride her during the day when children are in school. Any adult with half a brain would know to steer clear of her."

"So you tie her to the meter?" John should have been outraged, instead he found himself admiring her passion. Standing with her back to the big elephant, Calliope's cheeks were flushed pink. She was a spitfire and he had a weakness for fiery women.

At that moment, Dolly reached her long trunk over the barrier to give Calliope a little shove—right into John's arms.

She felt good there. She made no effort to extricate herself, he noticed. John could feel her hands pressing warmly against his chest. Looking down into her face, he found her staring back at him with an air of expectancy. The opportunity was too golden to let pass. He leaned down and pressed his lips against hers. When she leaned into the kiss, he pressed the advantage, pulling her closer. Close enough to feel the softness of her breasts and the heat of her body. Damn he wanted her. He deepened the kiss and luxuriated in the press of her against his hardening erection. Her hair fell over his hands, making him think of how it would form a curtain around them as she rode him.

Riding. There was something about riding... Damn. Her tumble into his arms tempted him to give in to distraction, but he fought it.

"You can't ride Dolly into town anymore. It's just not safe."

She blinked her big blue eyes as if coming out of a trance. "Then what am I going to do? She needs her exercise."

To restore his concentration, he looked over her shoulder at the large elephant. Dolly raised her trunk in a salute. Giving her a wink, he returned his gaze to the woman in his arms. He'd been on the verge of telling Calliope she needed to get rid of the elephant, but he owed the big girl. "It sounds to me like you need a bigger enclosure."

"Well. Yeah. But it's a lot of expense and work to put up that much fencing. Fencing that will keep in an elephant, don't forget."

It occurred to him the refuge had no visible means of support. "Can you afford it?"

"Maybe the materials, but not the labor. Our budget is a bit tight at the moment. I'm going to need to do some major grant writing now that I've decided to stay."

"You were thinking of leaving?" Why did that idea distress him so much?

"I left a fabulous job at a very prestigious zoo to come back here when Mom and Dad died. I've been trying to find someone else qualified to take on the refuge, but I recently decided this is where I belong."

John gazed at her long and hard. He had to be nuts to be glad she'd be sticking around. She and her animals would probably turn out to be nothing but trouble. A final look into her blue eyes pushed aside any doubt. Crazy or not, he wanted a chance to get to know her. "If you can purchase the materials, I'll round up the workers. Deal?"

Her answering smile punched him in the gut. He shook off the hunger eating at his concentration. Maybe Cain was right. The woman really was a menace. John set her away from him, trying to regain his composure. "If you're going to keep her, you need to bring in extra help. It's dangerous, you being here alone with all these animals."

"I take precautions. I even have tranquilizer guns on hand for worst-case scenarios. They're right over here."

This, John had to see. She led him to a small office. Sure enough, she had two tranquilizer guns and a shotgun in a locked case. Having them seemed smart, but could she handle them? Calliope unlocked the case and lifted out the shotgun. Curious, he watched her as she hefted the large gun. Her face had gone pale and she had an unfocused look in her eyes.

"Hey, you okay?"

She jumped at the sound of his voice and backed away from him.

"Calliope, what's wrong?"

"Nothing. Uhh....I think you should stay here for a short while."

Belatedly, John realized she was backing straight out of the door. Stunned, he watched her slam the door shut. He heard what sounded like a crossbar falling into place—locking him inside.

Panicked, Calliope ran toward Tasha's enclosure—the sound of John yelling through the office door still ringing in her ears. The man certainly knew his curse words. Standing in front of the gun case, she'd had a flash of premonition. She'd known instinctively the scene that had filled her thoughts wasn't very far into the future. Heck Jones, her nearest neighbor, planned to let Tasha out of her cage. He hated the tiger and he probably hoped, free and unsupervised, she'd get into enough trouble to require her destruction. Unfortunately, chances were good she'd do just that. Tasha was a sweetheart, but she was, after all, a tiger. If she didn't attack Heck, she'd be chasing down goats. That wouldn't win her any friends.

Calliope slowed as the enclosure came into view. If Tasha had already been released, running past her wouldn't be a good idea. Cautiously, Calliope scanned the enclosure and the surrounding area. She couldn't see Tasha. The gate stood open—she was too late.

Where was Heck? Calliope crept from tree to tree like some great African hunter. Only her prey wasn't the tiger. She stopped and scanned the pasture that lay between Tasha's enclosure and Heck's property. Nothing. She turned back to the enclosure and there he was, making his way around. But why? She'd just started toward the gate when a muscled arm closed around her waist, lifting her off the ground.

"Where do you think you're going?" John's voice was soft and menacing in her ear.

"Oh, no. John, you shouldn't be here."

"Why the hell not?"

"Tasha's loose. It isn't safe."

She felt him tense behind her.

"Are you planning to shoot her?"

"Of course not!"

"Then why the gun?"

"For Heck...my neighbor. He let her out." Calliope pointed to where the other man was still creeping around the enclosure. "See?"

"You planning to shoot *him*?"

She squirmed, tempted to kick his shins with her heels. "I had hoped to scare him off before he opened the cage."

Still pressed against his chest, she felt him exhale with a sigh. "First things first. Let's go get that gate closed."

"But Tasha—"

"Is in her enclosure. I'm beginning to think she's smarter than her keeper. At the very least, better behaved."

Heck must've planed to get behind Tasha and use his gun to startle her out of the enclosure. Feeling like an idiot, which only served to make her furious, Calliope couldn't speak. The moment John set her on the ground, she started toward the gate only to be caught up short as John snatched the gun out of her hand.

"I'll take that."

Calliope released the shotgun and set her sites on the gate. She had to get it closed before anything terrible happened.

The instant the gate clanged shut, John went into action. Heck ran, but he didn't have the speed to outpace him. She didn't even try to hide her grin as John cuffed him and marched him back to the city cruiser.

With Heck tucked neatly in the back, John returned his attention to Calliope. She shivered under the force of his scrutiny. Would he take retribution on her for locking him in the office?

"You want to explain how you knew what he was up to?"

She sighed. "You wouldn't believe me."

"Try me."

He'd have to know eventually. "Okay. I...sometimes I *know* things before they happen."

"Women's intuition?"

She could imagine instinct and intuition were something an experienced cop could understand. The easy answer tempted her. She could agree, but her future husband would have to deal with the reality sooner or later. She decided to offer the truth, hoping it wouldn't take him too long to get over the shock.

"No," she said. "More like...premonition."

Two weeks later, John stood in the hot afternoon sunshine, checking over the last touches to the new fencing. He'd organized work crews to help and they'd finally finished. He'd spent his day off working side by side with Calliope's helper, putting up the last stretch of fence. Squirting the last bottle of water across his face and chest to cool off and clean up, he turned toward the barn in time to see Calliope and Dolly headed across the field.

Woman and elephant appeared completely comfortable with each other. Calliope rode the elephant with the same earthy sensuality she did everything else. Her hair blew free in the breeze and a mischievous grin lit her face.

With the fence done, he'd no longer have an excuse to come out to the refuge. He'd been there, to work on the fence, as often as possible over the past weeks. In the evening, she always had lemonade waiting. When he managed to put in a whole day, she brought him a picnic lunch that they shared under the nearest tree. He'd come to look forward to spending time in her company.

She was sexy as hell, but he reluctantly acknowledged it was something more that drew him to her. He wanted her, but he couldn't afford to get involved in a serious relationship with her. She had a tendency to ignore the law. They might've made a deal about her elephant riding, but as of that morning, she still hadn't paid those tickets.

He could arrest her. He grinned. That would ensure he'd see her again, but it would be hell on their relationship. Oh hell, he was *already* thinking of her in terms of a relationship. He'd known all along, with her, it would take more than a brief affair to satisfy him. Acceptance settled over him as he watched her slip off Dolly's back with surprising grace.

"The fence looks great. Dolly and I can't thank you enough for all you've done."

John shrugged off her gratitude. "What can I say? I'm a sucker for girls with weird names."

Calliope laughed and he felt it right down to his toes— and other more interesting parts of his anatomy. She stretched out her hand. A small slip of paper flapped in the breeze. "Here. I thought you'd like to see this."

He didn't need to take it. He recognized it instantly.

Calliope waved the paper in the air. "Here take it. It's a receipt."

John nodded and accepted the small slip—proof she'd paid the tickets, all of them. "You turning into a law abiding citizen?"

"Of course. I assure you all this lawlessness is *not* my usual style."

He reached out and pulled her closer. "No, your style is more the free spirit-gypsy." Despite his damp state, he tugged her into his arms. His intuition told him his earthy, free spirit wasn't likely to complain. "Have any more premonitions lately?"

She worried her bottom lip with her teeth. "I...I have them fairly often, I'm afraid."

"Any about us?"

She hesitated for a long minute. "Are you sure you want to know?"

John nodded.

"The day we met, I had a premonition that we would... be...um...married."

John threaded his hand through her golden hair and tipped her head back so he could meet her eyes. "I had a feeling you were going to say that."

John watched the smile light her face as she realized he wasn't going to be scared off by her answer. Then he did what he'd wanted to do since he'd seen her riding her elephant out to meet him. He kissed his future wife with all the passion he could muster.

A Love to Remember

On her lips he tasted his future and knew...theirs was going to be a love to remember.

The silly law that inspired this tale is widely circulated on the Internet and attributed to my home state of Florida. We do have a surprising number of elephants here—the Ringling Bros. and Barnum & Bailey® Center for Elephant Conservation is located here—but I'd be very surprised to see an elephant tied to a parking meter in my home town. Of course, I've always loved surprises! If you're ever lucky enough to see one in your town, be sure to let me know—cheryl@cherylalldredge.com.

Be sure to visit Cheryl Alldredge's website
www.cherylalldredge.com
http://ladycharlie.livejournal.com/

Jeanne VanArsdall

The Woman in the Window

by Jeanne VanArsdall

• *It's against the law to dress/undress a mannequin without
pulling the blinds*

I fell under her spell while I stood watching her dress the
blonde woman. She fluffed the scarf, and then adjusted the
neckline of the dress—meticulously it seemed, in every detail.
Her movements were magic, like a soft beautiful melody.

She removed the pins she'd held firmly between her lips,
then glanced up and caught me staring at her. She was
adorable, and I was smitten. We continued to stare, until she
raised her brows questioningly.

"Cute, really cute," I said.

"Sorry, she's taken." She laughed, and I could have
drowned in that laugh.

Determined to be macho, I nodded slowly, pursing my
lips. "I was referring to you."

"Well then, thanks," she said cheerfully. She stepped out
of the window and extended her hand. "I'm Carli. Welcome to
CJ's."

"Thanks," I muttered. "I'm glad the store was still open. I
saw the blinds pulled and thought you'd closed early."

"Oh, no. We never close early." She smiled again. "But it's
against the law to dress or undress a mannequin without
pulling the blinds."

"You're kidding me, right?"

"Nope, absolutely true. It's to keep all the men out there
from stampeding the store." She laughed and moved on
quickly before I could respond. "I like to keep a fresh new

76

window scene for my customers."

She lost me there, so I just kept rambling...anything to keep her talking. I didn't want to make my purchase and leave. "How often do you do this window dressing thing?"

"When the mood strikes, mostly. But I try to encourage the mood every week or so."

Sometime during the conversation, I'd moved nearer to her to continue this magnetic exchange. "Looks like a tough job to me...stepping around and between all that stuff."

"I've broken a few things, but eventually you get used to walking in tight spaces. You seem very interested. Are you in retail by any chance?"

"No, not even close," I said, shaking my head. "I'm the new football coach at the university."

"Oh, Jason Block." She raised both hands in front of her. "I'm sorry. I should have recognized you. I read the article about the new super coach in our paper. Sounded very promising."

"Yeah, your publisher was pretty flattering. I hope I can live up to all that praise he dished out."

She propped both hands on her hips and looked sternly at me. "Well, you'd better or you might get tarred and feathered around here. We're desperate for a winning season." She shook her raven hair back and grinned. "Just kidding. Here," she said, extending her hand, "let me ring that up for you."

I surrendered the sweater I'd been clutching like a football. "That'd be great, and save my hide, too. We're having a birthday dinner for my sister at my parents tonight. I just remembered on my way home that I hadn't bought her a gift yet. And believe me, she'd never let me forget it. So I'm really glad you were still open."

"Me, too. Did you find everything okay? I mean size, color, everything?" Now she was stammering.

"I know the color's good and she's just about your size. I think it'll look great on you...er her. I mean, I don't know what size you are, but it looks pretty close."

Carli smiled, took the sweater and checked the size. "You're good," she said, walking toward the register.

Jason followed along, pulling out his wallet. "How much is this little beauty going to cost me?"

She removed the tag and folded the sweater. "I'll go easy on you, since you're new in town," she said, looking up with green eyes sparkling. "I want to make a return customer out of you."

It wasn't what she'd said so much as the way she'd said it. Or at least the way I'd heard it. I drove on to my condo and lightheartedly bounded up the stairs. I stripped my clothes off and stepped into the shower. I tried to think of plays on the field this afternoon, but my mind kept leaping back to the raven-haired image that had burned into my mind at CJ's. I finished showering, dressed and headed out to my parent's home two and a half hours away.

I flipped on the radio, determined to get her off my mind. A Christmas song was ending and immediately led into a commercial. "Don't forget to stop by CJ's for all your Christmas gift needs. Carli says she has a nice sample of just a few of the beautiful gifts in the new window display she just finished today. Come by soon and let Carli or her helpers assist you with that perfect gift selection."

Good grief, I couldn't get away from her. What was it about her anyway? She wasn't all that special. Oh no, she wasn't special—how about wonderful? I slammed my fist down on the steering wheel. This wasn't like me at all. I like pretty women, sure, but they don't usually hang around in my head like this. I pressed search, located a ball game on the radio and listened until I pulled into my parent's drive.

My sister, Ellie, came running down the sidewalk and jumped into my arms. "Hey, bud, I'm so glad to see you! Guess what? I've been accepted at Georgia. Now, we'll be living in the same town. How great is that?" She was all excited and hyper as usual. An honor student, a cheerleader and a very pretty girl, I figured I'd probably be spending half my time keeping the boys away from her.

"That's fabulous," I said, grinning and detaching myself. "Just for that, I brought you something."

"Oh, no you don't," she said, hands on her hips. "This is for my birthday. I want something really, really special for this big accomplishment!"

I put my arm around her and pulled her close. "What makes you think this isn't really special?

"Oh, I didn't mean that, Jason. Honestly, I didn't. Can I

open it now?"

"Don't you think you should at least include Mom and Dad in this celebration?" I asked, tousling her hair.

We reached the door, walked in and everyone hugged. Ellie immediately began tearing into her package. "Ohmygosh! Ohmygosh!" she squealed. "This is the most fabulous sweater I've ever seen. I love this, Jason. Wherever did you find it?"

"A little shop over in Athens, called CJ's."

Ellie held the sweater up, preening and dancing around. "Look, Mom, won't this be divine with that new skirt you guys bought me?" Before they could answer, she rambled on. "Hey, Jason, I've been in that store before. A friend and I went over there a couple weeks ago looking around. The woman in there was a knockout. I think she owns it. Did she help you?"

"Well, Sister, I don't know. What did she look like?"

"She had this really dark brunette hair, lots darker than mine, and longer, and sort of greenish, gold eyes. It sounds weird, but it was the coolest color of eyes I've ever seen. And, of course, she had this fabulous figure. I think she must work out or something. Was that the one?"

"Yeah," I sighed, "I think that was the one."

"Ohhhhh," she teased. "You liked her, didn't you?"

"Ellie, I just met the woman."

Silence covered the room like fog. And it seemed like everyone was staring at me. "What's not to like?" I commented, raising both hands in the air.

Mom quickly jumped in. "Okay, okay, who's hungry? I've got roast beef and mashed potatoes to start with."

I answered. "Mom, I'm always hungry when you're cooking."

"Me, too," chimed the rest of the family, moving towards the dining room.

We sat at the table, said grace, and the food started making the rounds. "So, Jason, are you staying a few days with us?" Dad asked.

"I'm not sure about the whole weekend, Dad, but I'll stick around for awhile tomorrow for sure. I've got to work on some strategy and plays for the team—see if I can pull out at least a few wins before the season ends."

"I hope you can, Son. Seems to me that quarterback's pretty good. Just can't get any protection 'til he can get the ball off. He's got a hell of an arm if you ask me."

"Yeah, I think he's got a lot of potential. That's one of the things I'm working on. I need to get some wins. I'd hate to get tarred and feathered."

"Where'd that come from?" his mother asked. "It's not that bad."

"I was just kidding," I laughed. "That's what Carli told me the townspeople might do if I didn't pull out a winning season."

"Carli who?" they all asked together.

"Oh, uh, the woman at CJ's," I said quietly as I ran my hand through my hair.

"The hottie?" Ellie queried, smiling and cocking her head.

I inhaled deeply and blew out my breath. "Yeah, Ellie, the hottie."

"Well, I'll be darned," she said, digging into her potatoes.

"Let's change the subject," Mom said. "Tell us about your condo, Jason. What's it like?"

I described my condo and chitchatted with the family through dinner, but the word that hung heavy in my thoughts was 'hottie.' Yeah, Carli definitely fit that description. But she was more—thoughtful, sensitive, and...damn, I had to stop this right now.

I went back to Athens around four, Saturday afternoon. I was hungry and didn't have much to cook at home, so I headed to a little pub that has outdoor seating and good food. I'd planned to eat outside, but saw on the TV that the game I'd wanted to see was in full swing and in the third quarter. I pulled up a chair in direct view of the television and ordered a beer and pasta.

"Excuse me, ladies," Carli said. "I have to go speak to a friend." Clearly Jason hadn't seen her and a couple of her girlfriends at the booth on the opposite side of the room. She wasn't going to let that stop her.

"Who is that?" they whispered.

"Control yourselves. I've got dibs on this one," she said shaking her finger at them and scooting out of the booth.

"Well, don't hurry back on our account," they chimed in, smiling broadly.

The thought crossed Carli's mind as she started toward

him that he just might be meeting someone. Maybe that's why he hadn't approached her booth. Well, if that was the case, she'd speak politely to him and return to her friends.

"Well, hi there, Coach."

She caught me off guard, and I thought I must have been thinking about her. But then I heard her again.

"Coach?"

I turned, nearly knocking over my beer, and saw her...an absolute vision in tight jeans and a turtleneck sweater. *Good golly, that law ought to be against her, not her dressing some damn mannequin.*

"Hey, how are you?" I said, pushing back my chair and standing.

"Great. You here for dinner or the game?" she asked, rocking back on her western boots.

"Both, I guess. I just got in from my parent's and didn't have much to cook at home." Then I looked down, finally getting all the way down to her feet. "Pretty fancy boots you got there. Been riding today?"

"Nah," she smiled, shrugging. "I just like boots."

"I see," I said, nodding my head. I shifted my stance, took a deep breath and asked, "Are you alone?"

"No," she said, turning and motioning to a booth across the room. "I'm with a couple of girlfriends, but they won't mind if you're inviting me to join you." She smiled that million-dollar smile and I felt like I'd just won the lotto.

"That would be nice." I pulled out a chair for her and asked what she'd like to drink or eat.

She leaned her elbow on the table and looked directly at me. "What are you having?"

"Pasta with garlic, mushrooms, and broccoli. Very healthy and very strong. Oh, and of course, a beer to even things out," I said, laughing.

"My kinda guy," she said. "I'll have the exact same thing."

Slamming my beer bottle down on the table, I almost choked. *I couldn't believe she'd just said that.*

While eating, we talked and laughed and watched a little of the game. She understood the plays and even yelled a time or two. Before we knew it, the evening had passed and it was after eleven.

"I'd better get going," Carli said, looking at her watch.

"I've got a salesman coming early in the morning. I'll need my power sleep."

"I thought buyers went to markets and that sort of thing."

She grimaced. "Believe me, I do enough of that. But this guy comes by the shop between markets, in case I'm running short. It really helps me a lot."

"Sounds like you like your work. That's good."

"Yeah, I do. But you know what, it seems like we talked a lot about me tonight. Maybe next time you can fill me in on what makes you tick," she said with a grin.

"I'm on." *What really sounded good was the fact there could actually be another time.*

"Tell you what," she said, with that hand on the hip pose again. "Now that I know you're a pasta man, maybe I'll whip you up one of my fabulous dishes. Do you have the nerve to try my cooking?"

Did I ever! I'd try anything she cooked. "Sure. If you're willing to slave away in the kitchen, I'm sure game," I said, grinning from ear to ear.

I swear, I didn't remember feeling this deliriously happy in high school lust. Could this possibly be love? I'd always been deathly afraid of the 'L' word, but if this was a sample, man was I ready to tackle it.

I walked Carli to her car and then drove to my condo. I had a hard time falling asleep. Every time I closed my eyes, her face appeared.

Sunday morning came bright and shining. I'd found a nice little church nearby and after services I went by the grocery and then home for gourmet sandwiches and chips. I worked all afternoon on plays and viewing videos from opponents' games I'd picked up from the athletic library. I showered and turned in early. I slept soundly and headed for the office early Monday morning.

I'd only been at the office about thirty minutes when a police officer knocked on my door. I invited him in and he quickly informed me I was being arrested in the name of the Jaycee's Jail and Bail Charity Drive.

"What does that mean exactly?" I asked dubiously.

"Well," he laughed, "it means you get to sit in jail 'til somebody comes and bails you out."

"Why me?" I asked, trying to control my temper.

"I don't know. Could be some of your players. Somebody volunteered you. Don't matter. Fact is, you got to find somebody to get you out of there. You get three phone calls. Least that's better than real jail rules. Come on now, don't give me no problems, okay?"

I was suspicious, to say the least. "Does this happen to a lot of people?"

"Oh, yeah," he laughed. "I've already picked up about ten people this morning." He obviously thought this more humorous than I did.

I snatched up my jacket and followed him out. When we arrived at the jail, I saw several other people from the university—all in the same predicament. It all became clear after talking with them and I got into the swing of things. They told me over $45,000 had been raised for the Jaycees last year. I decided being stuck here wasn't too bad. But I still needed to find someone to bail me out for $150. The bad part was I had to stay put until I came up with the money and, they informed me, I couldn't pay it myself. However, they smiled and said I could match it, if I felt so compelled.

I walked up and down the cell, thinking how awful it would be to really be incarcerated. Who could I call? My parents would comply, of course, but they'd have to wire money or drive two and a half hours. Suddenly, a thought hit me. I would test my newest friend. Or whatever she was. At this point I really wasn't sure. Anyway, I got the guard to look up CJ's and dialed her number.

"Good morning. CJ's. How may I help you?"

"Hi, Carli, it's Jason. Jason Block."

"Well, hello. How are you?"

"Actually, I've been better. I have a favor to ask. If you can't do it, just say so. I'll understand, really. I mean—"

"Jason, for Pete's sake, what is it?"

"Well, I'm in jail."

"Jail? What happened?"

"It seems some local yokel had me arrested so someone could go my bail to raise money for the charity drive the Jaycees are hosting. Have you ev..."

She was laughing so hard, I couldn't finish my sentence.

"I'm sorry, Jason, they don't usually get the newcomers."

"I'm glad one of us can laugh about it. You know, it's pretty awful in here, even pretending. Look, I know I don't know you very well...yet, I mean. But would you consider coming down here and bailing me out of this place?"

"Well...I guess I could do that, but you'll owe me...big time."

"Uh, oh. What does that mean?"

"Ummm, I don't know yet, but I'll think of something worthwhile. Just how valuable are you?"

"Not very. A cool hundred and fifty will do it."

She laughed that sultry laugh that lit my fire. "I'll be right down."

And she was. I was out and back at the campus within the hour and she returned to her store. She refused to let me pay her back, declaring she'd rather me be indebted to her. Somehow, it made me feel real good.

When Carli arrived at her business and saw the police car, she wondered what the problem was. As she walked in the door, she saw the officer, whom she knew quite well. "Hello, Jake. What's going on?"

"I'm sorry, Carli. Old lady Pearson called in on you. Said you were dressing your mannequin without pulling the blinds. I'd like to help you out, but it looks like you're guilty." He jerked his thumb in the direction of the mannequin.

"Good gosh, Jake. They picked up a friend of mine on the Jaycee's bail and jail drive and I went to bail him out. Can't you just let me pull the darn blinds?"

"I would in a minute, but you know how mean that ole woman is. I'll have to take you in. It's just routine. Get someone to go your bail and you'll be out of there in a heartbeat."

Carli picked up her handbag and headed for the squad car with Jake. She'd get that ole lady back if it took a hundred years! She'd tried to be nice to her, but she was just impossible! And this certainly proved it.

I was sitting in my office going over paperwork on a new player when my phone rang.

"Hi, Jason?"

"Yeah, this is Jason."

"It's Carli. Carli Jenkins."

"Oh, how are you?"

"Well, not too good at the moment. You got $100 you can spare for awhile?"

"Sure, what's up?"

"I'm in jail."

"They got you, too? That's double teaming," I said disgustedly.

"Not exactly," she sighed. "Listen, I'll tell you about it when you get here, okay?"

"Sure, Carli. I'll be right there."

I wondered what the heck could have happened. The bail was pretty low, so it couldn't be really bad, could it? I drove like a maniac getting there. I had to get Carli out of that place. It was horrible. I pulled in front of the police station and went inside.

"Where is Carli Jenkins?" I asked the desk clerk. I signed the paperwork and waited until they brought her out. She looked okay, but very perturbed.

"I'll tell you when we get in the car," she whispered.

We got in the car, put on our seat belts and I started the engine. "Now," I said, "what happened?"

"When I got your call, I was in such a hurry I left the store without closing the blinds. Unfortunately, I wasn't finished dressing the mannequin." She smiled, a wicked gleam lighting her eyes. "I left her naked from the waist up. While I was gone, one of my competitors from across town apparently drove by and saw her. It was just the opening she needed to complain about me."

I frowned. "Surely the police didn't take her call seriously."

"They had to," she continued. "It's the law, and I did leave a naked woman in my window."

She continued to tell me the story of the old lady who apparently no one liked and whose business was practically nonexistent. She was just a bitter old lady.

"On the other hand, I really feel sorry for her," Carli said. "I think I'll go over and visit her and see if I can help out some way."

"Carli, the old bag just cost you $100. And you want to help her?"

She threw her head back and laughed. "Oh, no, she just cost you $100. But yes, I think I do want to help. I was very angry with her at first, but I don't think she has any family left and not many friends. Besides, it's Christmas. Would you want to be alone?" A gleam lit her eyes. "You want to help me out with this project? If you do, I won't charge you the extra fifty bucks you owe me, and we'll be even-Stephen. What d'ya say?" She sat there, with brows raised, grinning, and looking innocent.

What could I say, but yes. "Carli, do you see this as some sort of long-term commitment? Me bailing you out...you bailing me out? This sort of thing?"

"Absolutely, Coach. I knew the first day I met you, we'd be on the same team."

*Be watching for Jeanne VanArsdall's
future website.*

A Toast to the Bride and Groom

by Victoria Oliveri

• *Pennsylvania - A couple cannot legally marry if either participant is inebriated.*

Downingtown, Pennsylvania 1839

Dreadful. The only word that came to her mind in view of her current situation was *dreadful*. Maryette Browning sat at the table clutching the napkin in her lap until her fingers felt they would bleed as her father paced the room around her like a slobbering wolf. Her mother, pillar of society that she was, sat implausibly silent across from her as her father rattled on.

"Master Westbrook is a prominent businessman. He has over two hundred acres in Coventry and purebreds at New London. I see no reason why you shouldn't accept his proposal."

"Father, I know nothing of this man. Do you expect me to marry a complete stranger?" Eyeing her mother, she hoped she would come to her defense, but her father silenced her.

"You have no other choice. Tell her, Mother."

"Your father is right, dearest. Marrying Westbrook would be a coup for you. You would finally come into society the way you always should have."

"Society? This is about society? Is that all either of you care about? What of love, Mother?" she asked, looking from her mother and then back to her father, who rolled his eyes wildly before he threw himself into the seat at the head of the table, his corpulent face flushed and sweaty.

"You're being childish, Maryette," her father said as he

cut into his steak. "The man has offered for your hand, I've given my permission and that's the end of it."

"Father," Maryette pleaded, but it was useless. Her father's adamant look was all she needed to see. She bowed her head, admitting defeat.

"You'll see, dearest. Master Westbrook will be a wonderful husband. You'll have a beautiful new house in the country. It will be brilliant for you."

"Yes, Mother," she answered dully. Folding her napkin, she placed it on her plate. "May I be excused? I wish to take a turn to get some air and clear my head."

"Yes, that would be fine, my dear," her mother said.

"Be sure to return before candle-light," her father barked as he looked up at her, juice dripping from his chin. "One thing this family does not need is scandal."

Maryette stood and smoothed out her skirts. Disgusted, she headed for the door where she pulled on her fichu and checked herself in the mirror. Earlier that morn, her long, chestnut hair had been pulled back into a chignon and circled with a string of braids that ended with a soft cascade of ringlets down her neck. Turning her head from side to side to ensure everything was still in place, she thought to wear a hat, but decided she would do without and grabbed her parasol instead, before heading out into the afternoon sunshine.

She opened the fanciful sunshade as she stepped onto the porch and a strong, autumn breeze caught the fragile Battenberg lace and tore the handle from her grip, sending it spiraling through the air. With a yelp, Maryette leapt down the stairs and up the dusty street chasing the parasol as it tumbled overhead in the breeze. As the wind died, the parasol dove to the ground. Catching her off guard, she tripped over it and found herself embarrassingly sprawled in the middle of the street. Before she could come to her senses and quickly brush her skirts back down over her petticoats, a leather-gloved hand had reached down to help her to her feet.

"Are you all right, Miss?" The deep, resonant tones came to her as she looked up, shielding her eyes with one hand to peer up at the man through the bright sunshine.

"Yes, quite," she said, a bit humiliated as she stood and brushed the dirt from her dress, then turned to watch her parasol roll down the street. "Oh no!"

"Not to worry," the man called over his shoulder as he dashed down the street, catching it moments before it tumbled into a nearby stream. He unfurled the lacy umbrella and shook the dirt from its delicate fabric as he made his way back to her.

"A bit worse for wear, I fear, but I believe it is still usable," he said, handing it back to her.

Maryette took the parasol thankfully and gave the man a quick curtsy. "Thank you, Sir. That was most kind of you."

"'Tis the least I could do to help a damsel in distress." He nodded politely, moving to where he'd hastily dropped the reins of his horse.

Maryette smiled up at the man, realizing quite unexpectedly how striking he was, not only in action but in style and countenance. His well-fit trousers were tucked neatly into his smart riding boots and his tailcoat displayed his muscled, broad shoulders and slim waist in a most appealing way. It was then she wished she'd worn her hat, so she could hide the blush flaming her cheeks as she gazed at this handsome and effortlessly charming stranger.

"I wish there was some way I could repay you, Sir, for a gesture so kind." She immediately wished she hadn't said a word as he turned to meet her gaze and the smile he gave was surely her undoing.

"Perhaps there is a way," he offered, his voice smooth as silk as he stepped closer, sending an uncontrollable shiver through her. The way his eyes made a wicked sweep of her body was indecent, but she could not turn away from him. Instead, she stood her ground, no matter how her knees quivered.

"I assure you, Sir, I am a respectable young woman."

The man chuckled wryly and tipped his hat to her.

"No doubt you are, Miss. I thought nothing less. What I would request of you is your assistance, nothing more."

"My assistance?" she asked curiously, swallowing the lump growing in her throat.

"I am new here in Downing's town and though I do not plan to remain here, I will need a place to stay. Would you be able to direct me to a respectable establishment that might put me up?"

Maryette let out a relieved sigh and turned to look up the street.

"Certainly, Sir. Downingtown has some of the finest establishments one can find along King's Road, the best being Hammond's, there on the left."

"And is it an honorable business?"

"Most assuredly, Sir. I know the Hammond's well and there is no finer family in the county. You will find no gambling or other debauchery there."

The man rubbed his chin thoughtfully and gave her a scowl.

"Shame," he said, cracking a sly smile. "I could go for a bit of faro."

Maryette gasped and covered a giggle with a delicately gloved hand. "Sir!"

"Johnathan..." he said, offering her a broad, genuine smile and a formal bow, removing his hat to reveal a head full of lush golden curls.

"I beg your pardon?" She gasped again at the sight of him.

"My name is Johnathan."

Maryette could feel the heat rise up her neck as he smiled proudly, expectantly. When she did not respond, he tilted his head, his sapphire blue eyes twinkling devilishly.

"And would I have the honor of *your* name?" he asked.

"Maryette," she offered beneath timid lashes.

"Well then, Miss Maryette, would you do me the added honor of accompanying me to Hammond's for a touch of tea?"

"I – I do not feel 'tis proper, being I have no chaperone." She averted her eyes from him diffidently.

"'Tis the middle of the afternoon. We are in full view of the town, Miss Maryette, and I have no mind to do anything untoward to damage either of our reputations."

Maryette gave him some consideration and looked about the street. After a moment's pause, she nodded to him.

"Very well, I shall accompany you." She smiled demurely as Johnathan offered his arm, which she took gladly.

Walking up King's Road on the arm of such a fine looking man made Maryette feel regal, as though everyone in town *should* be looking at her with astonishment. Her manner, her posture, her very air changed as they rambled toward the inn at the end of the street. She felt beautiful, important—and just a bit scandalous for being so brash in broad daylight. She also wished she were dressed in an amazing gown, her hair topped with a fine Parisian bonnet of velvet and feathers. As it was, she was mortified she'd stepped out in one of her duller walking dresses instead of something more tasteful. Still, her escort didn't seem to mind.

He'd been rambling on about his travels and how weary he was from them. She smiled and nodded up at him decorously as her mind continued with its daydreams. How deliriously happy she would be to have a man such as Johnathan in her life. They could attend the theater, be invited to high society balls – they would be the talk of the county. And then her smile suddenly faded as her father's voice came crashing through her fanciful thoughts. "The man has offered for your hand, Maryette. I've given my permission and that's the end of it."

She was to be married in three days to some stodgy businessman who was probably old, fat and more concerned with his wealth than her happiness. The mere thought of having to be coupled with such a man made her stomach lurch. She suddenly felt ill.

"Are you quite well, Miss Maryette?" Johnathan asked as they stepped off the street. "You are looking quite piqued."

"I shall be fine once we sit. I suppose I have taken too much sun," she offered weakly, looking away from his concerned gaze. She could never tell this stranger what was really wrong.

Without a word, he took her elbow and, placing a hand at the small of her back, helped her up the stairs to the inn. The feel of his warm touch made her gasp and she bit her lip to conceal her quickening breath. As he ushered her around to the veranda, she thought for sure she would swoon. He smelled so wonderful standing so close to her, a mix of saddle leather and lavender, his breath warm against her neck as he helped her sit.

"I shall be just a moment," he said with a nod as he turned and strode purposefully into the inn. Maryette was finally given the opportunity to catch her breath and she blotted her forehead with her handkerchief as he left her. Her father would be furious if he found her in the company of a strange man when she was, for all intents and purposes, engaged.

Johnathan rushed inside to find the innkeeper. He'd hoped to make this a quick stop, deal with his pending business and be on his way in but a few days, but after running into the enticing Maryette, he wondered if his life wouldn't soon be fraught with some huge complications. Making his way inside, he rang the bell and was met at the desk in short order. A tall, lanky man with wire-rimmed glasses approached him, quite eager to serve.

"How may I help you, Sir?" he asked, smoothing his thinning hair across his brow.

"I shall need a room for the next two or three nights, if you will. I would also have some refreshments brought out for myself and my companion, and quickly if you will, as she is feeling a bit ill from being in the sun overmuch."

"As you wish, Sir. Do you have baggage that needs to be brought up?"

"I shall bring it in later. For now I should go out and tend to the young lady."

"Of course. We'll have some refreshments brought out to you at once." The man quickly disappeared through a door and Johnathan could hear him shouting orders for what he'd asked. He nodded, knowing they would be taken care of quickly, so he made his way back out onto the porch. Turning the corner, he stopped for a moment to take in the scene before him.

Maryette had removed her modest fichu, baring a delicate expanse of neck and shoulder for him to view—and he was more than happy to partake of such a vision. She seemed to be quite flushed, and his eyes followed the rosy glow down over her gracefully swelling bosom, where it disappeared beneath the fabric of her pale yellow dress. At the sudden thoughts that rushed through his mind, his mouth went dry. He took a deep breath and adjusted the fabric of his trousers, thankful he'd worn his broad-falls rather than the more fitted breeches he normally wore on his travels. Gaining some composure, he stepped toward her and offered a broad smile, removing his hat as he took a seat next to her.

"And how does the beautiful Miss Maryette fare?" he asked as he removed his gloves and placed them in his hat.

"Please, Johnathan," she said with yet another intriguing blush.

A Toast to the Bride and Groom

"Please?" he asked as his brow rose quizzically. The sound of his name on her luscious, rose-tainted lips sent a jolt of passion to his groin and he fought to control his demeanor as his fingers itched to touch her velvety skin. If only he could hear her beg for something more, he would be a happy man, but he knew all too well what women were about these days. All modesty and propriety, without a hint of mischief—and once married, they became confined and dreary. In view of the woman before him, he considered that to be quite a waste.

"I am here strictly as your guide and nothing more. I do not care to draw any more attention to us than has already been managed," she offered in hushed tones, nearly a whisper, which sent yet another jolt through him. He shifted in his chair, hoping she didn't notice his discomfort.

"I apologize for my impropriety, Miss Maryette. I meant no indecency with my words, though I must admit to beauty when I see it." He gave her a coy smile and leaned back in his seat as an older woman approached their table with a tray of drinks and pastries.

Maryette grimaced at Johnathan's forwardness, knowing she should be appalled by his rudeness, but she couldn't help the flutter in her heart knowing he thought her beautiful. His blue eyes watched her vigilantly and she fidgeted with the folds of her skirts nervously while their tea was poured for them. Once the servant had left the table, she took up her cup and saucer, ignoring his previous remarks.

"What brings you to Downingtown, Sir?" she asked as she sipped her tea.

Johnathan, not missing her formal address, dipped a biscuit into his cup and brought it to his mouth with some enthusiasm. After devouring the small pastry, he licked the tips of his fingers and gracefully dusted the crumbs from his lap.

"Business, mostly," he offered, taking up the small cup and taking a sip. "I have some investments in town and need to take care of them before I return home."

"And where is your home, if I may ask?" she placed her saucer and cup neatly in her lap as she awaited his response.

"'Tis hard to say these days, as I have been abroad, though I hope to build near Philadelphia soon enough."

"That must be very exciting, traveling as you do.

Although, do you not miss having a home to return to?" she asked curiously.

Johnathan nodded. If only she *knew* what he wanted to return to when his travels were completed. Having the means to build houses in every county was a luxury, but having a woman like Maryette waiting for him would make him never want to travel again.

"I do miss not having a home, but I hope to resolve that soon enough," he offered with a kind smile. "And what of you, Miss Maryette? What does your future hold?"

Maryette's gaze dropped to her lap as she toyed with the handle of her cup. She feared telling him the truth, else he would flee and leave her sitting there wallowing in her own pity. This was her last chance for folly and she wished to enjoy herself while she could. If her father meant to saddle her with a pompous lout of a man, then she saw no flaw in taking some liberties with what time she had left to herself. Lifting her gaze to Johnathan's once more, she gave him a shy smile while she patted her lips with her napkin.

"My future?" she asked, cocking her head. "Much like your own, I suppose...uncertain."

"You must have some desires for your life, no?"

"I assume I shall be like every other woman, married off and asked to serve her husband's needs," she said despondently.

Johnathan choked on his tea at her response. Having her serve his needs would be a dream, but he did not have needlepoint and cooking in mind for this alluring woman.

Throughout their tea they covered topics ranging from fashion to politics and Johnathan grew more and more intrigued by Maryette. When their refreshments were depleted, he shook out his napkin and stood.

"Would you accompany me for a stroll about the park?" he asked, offering his hand to her. "I hear it is lovely this time of year."

"That is true. The leaves have taken on their autumnal hues and they are afire with color." She took his hand and came to her feet, allowing him to lead her off the porch, across King's Road to the strolling path.

They ambled for what seemed like hours, enjoying the views and one another's company. All thoughts of impropriety fled Maryette's mind as the handsome Johnathan escorted her along the meandering path to a secluded gazebo in the far corner of the park. He'd laughed at all her jokes, listened to her thoughts and offered his opinion as though she was his equal. Quite a refreshing change from what she was used to in her father's care. Once seated beneath the confines of the gazebo, Johnathan gave her a wide smile.

"I must say, Miss Maryette, you have been a most agreeable companion this afternoon. If only I had met you earlier, I daresay my travels would not have been such a bore."

Maryette stifled a giggle behind her hand.

"Johnathan, you flatter me overmuch."

"Do I?" he asked, moving closer to her on the narrow bench. "I daresay I could praise a woman of your splendor incessantly."

Maryette flinched as he placed his arm across the bench behind her. She wanted to flirt with him, giggle and be girlish, but the very thought of it made her weak with anticipation even as his daring words set her blood on fire.

"Please..." she begged, her voice nearly inaudible.

"No need to beg," he said, placing a warm hand on her shoulder. "I shall do anything you ask of me, Miss Maryette."

She gasped breathlessly, biting her trembling lip.

"What is your deepest desire?" His eyes were a shade of beguiling blue now as their gaze wandered to her lips. "Please tell me, Maryette."

She felt she would surely swoon as his gentle fingertips traced circles on her shoulder as he spoke. She had never felt anything so delicious in all her life.

"I daresay, Johnathan, we should not be—" She made to move away, but his hand grasped her shoulder tenderly and turned her into his arms as his kiss took her words from her lips. His mouth was soft and inviting and she could not deny the heat that spread through her body as he pulled her closer, deepening their kiss into something desperate and searching.

"Maryette," he moaned into her ear as he nibbled there, "how you make my blood rush through my veins."

"Oh, Johnathan." His name left her lips in a sultry sigh that nearly cost him his composure. Their kiss had turned from innocent to sinful in mere moments as Maryette slowly wrapped her arms about his neck and clung to him wantonly.

The swelling in his groin was growing agonizingly painful as her soft moans drove him to the edge of madness. He pulled away from her abruptly before he could no longer stop himself.

"Miss Maryette, I cannot begin to describe my hunger for you and I pray you do not disrespect me for what I have done or said."

"I do not," she said breathlessly. "I only wish I could speak my heart to you after what we have shared."

Johnathan blinked at her answer, half expecting her to slap him for his forwardness.

"I implore you then, please speak your heart, for I am eager to hear it."

Maryette shuddered, her words stuttering on her lips as Johnathan kissed her hand. As panic slowly closed in on her, she could think of nothing more to do but run. Offering one last, feverish kiss with every ounce of her being, she touched his face tenderly before dashing out of the gazebo, down the path to her father's house where she rushed to her room and locked the door tightly against a world she would never know again.

"What am I to do, Hannah?" Maryette sobbed into her handkerchief as she sat at her vanity. Her dearest friend, Hannah, had come to help her prepare for her wedding, which was to be held at St. James Chapel in only an hour.

"I do not know, dearest," she offered as she worked on Maryette's hair, placing the combs high on her head to hold the veil which her mother had loaned her. She'd carefully placed several tiny, pink rosebuds around the crown of her head and though she looked every bit the beautiful bride, she did not feel the part at all.

"Was there no word of Johnathan? Have you not seen him about town?" she asked, her tears streaking her face.

"No, dearest. I went to Hammond's, but there was no Johnathan lodged there and I have seen no man of your description. Perhaps he completed his business and already left town."

"Perhaps he has," she said, her words stuttering through her sobs. "Dear God, Hannah, he is lost to me."

"All you can do is make the most of this match and move on. It is what is expected of us all," Hannah offered sorrowfully, brushing her own tears from her cheek.

"I cannot, Hannah, I tell you truly. I love Johnathan deeply and I must find him before it is too late. We must delay this marriage until he is found. I am sure he will offer for my hand without fail. He is an affluent businessman and I am sure more than adequately moneyed to appease my father. We must delay this wedding, Hannah...but how?" Maryette stood and paced the room, wringing her hands against the beautiful cream damask of her gown.

Hannah paced with her, biting her lip and then she turned abruptly.

"Wait!" she said excitedly. "Wait here!" Hannah rushed from the room and after a few moments returned to Maryette and slammed the door, locking it behind her. When she turned, she held out a bottle and a glass to her friend.

"Hannah, this is no time for a toast." Maryette threw her hands in the air exasperatedly as she continued to pace.

"No, dearest, drink! Drink the entire bottle. 'Tis the law, you know. The minister cannot marry you if you arrive at the altar inebriated."

Maryette caught her breath in her throat and her heart skipped a beat.

"You are aright! Oh, my dear friend, how brilliant and devious you are. I shall love you forever for this." She took the proffered bottle, removed the cork and drank as much as she could in one breath. Feeling immediately dizzy, she sat, and over the next several minutes, finished off the bottle. After nearly a half hour, her head was spinning and she began to giggle uncontrollably.

"I do believe, Hannah, that I am right and thor...thor... thoroughly inedibated..." she said with a hiccup.

Hannah giggled, taking the empty bottle from her hand.

"Good girl, Mare, now let us get you to the church so your nuptials may be suspended, hopefully indefinitely."

Hannah helped her to her feet and they made their way out of the house and down the block to the chapel where her father and mother waited impatiently on the outside stairs.

"Please, go inside," Maryette announced rather exuberantly. "I want to make a grand entrance."

Her parents nodded dutifully and went inside as Hannah fixed Maryette's veil and fluffed her gown to make her more presentable. When all was readied, Maryette gave her a wink and the two stumbled up the stairs and entered the church with wide smiles. Maryette stood, wavering, at the back of the church while Hannah made her way down the aisle. When she reached the end, she turned and gave her a nod.

Maryette walked slowly, trying her best to keep even footing as she made her way down the aisle, a grin spreading across her face at the secret she kept hidden. When she finally made her way to the altar to face her new husband, she nearly fainted.

"Jo...Johnathan!" she cried, her voice slurred. She blinked her eyes several times trying to ensure he was really there. She reached out a hand to his arm in effort to steady herself.

"Maryette?" he asked, his brows furrowed as a look of happiness, then confusion crossed his face. "Maryette, are you drunk?"

Maryette stifled a burp and felt the sudden wave of nausea as she swayed. He caught her shoulders to steady her.

"Johnathan, why did you not tell me?"

"I suppose I could ask the same of you."

"What is the meaning of this?" Maryette's father shouted as he approached the altar, grabbing Maryette by the arms, pulling her from Johnathan's hands and shaking her brusquely. "You already know each other? By the saints, you know one other intimately enough to use your Christian names?"

His tirade instantly brought her to tears and she began sobbing uncontrollably.

He pushed her away in loathing. "Daughter, you are a disgrace! I cannot believe how you have dishonored your mother and I before this entire congregation."

"I cannot marry this woman, Master Browning," the astute minister barked as he slammed his bible shut in disgust and turned away from Maryette and Johnathan and faced her furious father. "As anyone with any morals knows, not only has she sullied the sanctity of the church, but it is against the law for me to do so in her condition."

"But I love him!" Maryette sobbed aloud, reaching out and imploring to the minister. "This has been a terrible mistake. You must marry us! Give me a moment and I shall sober. Please!"

Johnathan pulled her into his arms and kissed her soundly as the congregation looked on and gasped audibly.

"'Tis quite all right, Sweeting," he chuckled in spite of himself. "To know you will be my wife once you have sobered is well worth the wait."

The journey to their newly built manor near Philadelphia was a long one, but an amazing experience for Maryette Westbrook. She beamed joyously as she sat beside her dashing husband and the look he gave her as he edged his horse forward made her smile.

"I'm sorry for the scandal I caused on our wedding day, Jon," she offered, clutching his well-muscled arm as she laid her head on his shoulder.

"'Tis I who should apologize for my behavior, Maryette. If only I had known who you were, it could have been avoided, but I am glad you consented to marry me in the end."

"Consented? How could I not?" she asked, smiling up at him with such love in her heart she was brought to tears. "You were so gallant and endearing the day we met."

"I probably should have admitted this sooner, but I couldn't. As much as I hate to confess it, Sweeting, I had the same reluctance as you to the marriage. Had you not shown up in the state you had, the minister would have soon found I was just as inebriated as you—and for the same reasons."

Maryette looked up at him, stunned, sniffing back her tears as a grin spread across her lips. "You hadn't!"

"I had. The thought of leg-shackling myself to a homely farm girl didn't seem very appealing after meeting you," he said with a chuckle. "I suppose we should both thank our stars our worst nightmares became a wonderful dream after all."

He leaned down and kissed her deeply as they pulled onto the long driveway that wound its way to their new home. Turning serious, he brushed his thumb lazily over her lips. "I vow, my dearest, in view of what happened at the church, I believe neither of us should ever again drink another drop—"

Smiling, Maryette cut in before he could finish, "A long as we both shall live."

Victoria Oliveri

Be sure to visit Victoria Oliveri's website
www.victoriaoliveri.com

Bare Feet and Cherry Pie

by Cissy Hassell

* *Alabama - You may not drive barefooted*
* *Kansas - It's illegal to put ice cream on cherry pie*

Simone gritted her teeth in annoyance as she heard the siren. She checked her rear view mirror, knowing what she'd find. A police cruiser. A helluva place to get pulled over by a cop, she grumbled. She was just passing through, for heaven's sake. The darn town probably didn't even have red a light!

She grimaced in distaste at her bad humor. All she wanted was to get across the Kansas state line. And she had miles to go. She should've waited until she reached Wichita and hit I-135 north. From there it was a straight shot to I-70 that would take her to Colorado. But she'd been listening to music, not paying attention to where she was going and made a wrong turn somewhere. Then she'd become hopelessly lost. The town she'd just passed through wasn't even on her map— Climax, Kansas. A really dumb place for a romance novelist to get caught.

Caught for what, she wasn't sure. Definitely not speeding. She'd been driving slow as molasses in January, trying to get her bearings. The lay of the land, her grandmother would say.

What law of this Podunk town could she have broken? Going *too* slow, maybe? She wasn't even in the city limits, if you could call this dusty old place a city, she thought snidely. She eyed the cop in her side mirror as he stepped out of his car, took note of her tag number and called it in.

Not bad on the eye. A body like his could be written into her next novel. Muscles bulged from his short-sleeved shirt.

His broad chest strained the front buttons. And when he leaned through his window to get something out of the car she got a good look at his firm backside. It was too bad she couldn't afford to spend any time in this town.

Better get this over with, old girl. Time's a wastin'.

She opened the car door and stepped out into the heat of the day, a blast of hot air smacking her in the face. Massive heat waves rolled off the black asphalt, shimmering in the air like ghostly images. She covered her eyes with her right hand to shade them from the blinding sun. Her throat felt dry and raspy, making her wish for a cold bottle of water to slake her thirst.

She took a moment to study the area, taking note there was nothing but dust, rock and scrub brush. She brought her attention back to the man who was just another irritant in a long day and her body thrummed.

Lincoln Hayes stopped his forward movement, staring at the vision that stepped out of the car that had been driving along at a snail's pace. His mouth went dry. Her hair was dark, short and curly. Impatience drifted across her face. A face with unbelievable features. Arched brows formed to perfection. Eyes, thickly lashed, a mysterious shade of green. A short pert nose that he was sure could rise in disdain. Lips, luscious and shapely, beckoning him to walk right over and have a taste. And a come-hither body that had his own body flashing spasms of heat that matched the waves rolling off the pavement.

He placed both hands on his hips, taking a moment to clear away the images that had planted themselves in his brain. He was a police officer. There was no place in his line of work for this type of thing. Judging from the way she was dressed, she could be anyone, he thought tiredly, maybe even a hooker making her way to Nevada to ply her trade in the anything-goes city of Las Vegas. He knew he was being unfair, judging her simply because he was irritated at the day he'd had and she was the closest person to take out his aggravation.

He gave her one last thorough examination from head to toe.

Bare feet? Hmm. Toes? Tasty!

Glancing again at her features, he reached deep into his old academy days and sought for something. Her bare feet triggered a dim memory of an old and ridiculous law still floating around. Driving barefooted in this state was illegal, and if she gave him any trouble—and she looked like the type that would—he'd slam her pretty ass in jail so fast the polish would blast right off her toenails.

He drew in a breath at the idea of doing such a ridiculous thing and brought his gaze back down to her bare feet. Even her toes looked scrumptious. Toes that were indeed brightly polished a glaring red.

The woman—Simone Beauvais her registration had indicated when he called her license number in—seemed amused at his perusal and lifted a brow. Link cleared his throat and moved closer, his right hand resting on his weapon. These days you didn't take any chances, no matter how good they looked.

"I wasn't speeding," she began as he approached.

Damn. Her voice had to be sexy, too. It was throaty and dreamy, with a hint of mystery. And fantasies. Fantasies of sultry nights and silk sheets.

He shook his head, trying to clear away that vision, too. Trouble. He knew she was going to be nothing but trouble. It was in her entire demeanor. The way she stood. The way she held her head to the side in a provocative manner. Damn, he cursed again. What was taking him so long to get to the heart of the matter?

"I know you weren't speeding, ma'am. That's why I stopped you."

She just stood there, nibbling on her bottom lip.

"You all right, ma'am?"

He was looking at her strangely, Simone noted, opening her eyes again, a little put off by his lingering gaze.

"Yes, Officer, I'm just fine," she snapped, annoyance clearly riding her like a cowboy on a bronc with a burr under the saddle. "Will you tell me what my offense is so I can be on my way?"

He knew it. From the moment he got out of bed this morning, something told him this was going to be a bad day. Trouble with a capital T.

He put on his official face and stepped forward. The aggressive movement caused her to take a step backward. "First, ma'am, you need to change your tone of voice. You're bordering on insolence. I don't know where you come from—the big city, no doubt." He paused for effect, letting his words sink in, and then raked her body with a brazen glance. "But around these parts, law officers are respected. Second, I stopped you to see if you needed assistance. You were going so slow I though something might be wrong with your car."

Fire flashed in her eyes. "As you can see," she huffed, not paying the least bit of attention to his warning, "there is nothing wrong with my car. I've lost my way, ended up in this nothing place and can't find my way out again. It's not even on the damn map, for heaven's sake!"

Losing his patience, Link had had enough. He was hot, tired, and hungry to boot. And, he wasn't about to let this pint size scrap of dynamo put his town down, let alone speak to an officer of the law in such a disrespectful manner.

"Step away from the car, ma'am," he ordered. "I need to see your driver's license."

"How the hell am I supposed to step away from the car and get you my driver's license at the same time when my purse is in the car?" she all but shouted.

"Turn around and place your hands behind your back," he commanded in return.

"I will not!"

"Are you resisting an officer of the law?"

"You're arresting me?" She seemed bewildered by the very idea.

"Yeah, lady, I'm arresting you."

"But I haven't done anything. What's the charge?"

"Driving barefoot while operating a motor vehicle." Oh, Link knew he was stretching the truth, but so what? She was way out of control. Well, that was stretching the truth a bit, too, but what the hell, she needed a place to cool down. And he had a big desire to bring her down a peg or two.

"What are you talking about? There's no such law as that," she sputtered. "I'm not taking another step until you prove it to me!"

"Have it your way, ma'am."

Link picked up her petite frame like she weighed nothing, slung her over his shoulder and moved to his patrol car, ever aware of where her hands were so she couldn't get his gun. He opened the back door as she beat his back with her small fists, shoved her inside, and slammed the door before she had a chance to protest.

He slid into the seat, grateful for air conditioning, and gunned the motor. Their eyes met, locked and clashed in his rearview. She was fuming and he didn't realize until this moment how much he was enjoying this encounter.

"I'll have your badge, mister!" she vowed vehemently. "You won't get away with this."

His smile was deadly. "You better stop while you're ahead, little lady. You're racking up charges every time you open your mouth."

"Like what?"

"Oh, I don't know. The bare feet, for one. Resisting arrest. Threatening an officer of the law."

"You've got to be kidding me! All that because I was going too slow?"

"No, ma'am. I stopped you because I was concerned. You're the one getting defensive," he told her.

"Defensive?" She was sitting behind him and her screech in his ear was like he'd been hit on the back of the head.

"You've been warned, ma'am. If I were you, I wouldn't say another word."

He glanced in the rearview mirror to see her muttering a litany of what he was sure were expletives. The muscles of her jaw worked fiercely trying to keep her mouth shut.

She clamped her jaw tight when she caught his glance in the mirror.

Link laughed quietly to himself. She was so pumped full of rage, keeping it inside had her face glowing with the effort to keep it at bay. He could only imagine the tirade of names dancing on the end of her tongue—just waiting to spew out. He had to admit, though, she was a handful. And he liked the challenge. It had been a long, dry spell between women in his life and this one intrigued him. Idly, he wondered how much trouble he could get into with this trumped up charge. He wasn't even sure it was still on the books in Kansas. Other states, yes—definitely in Alabama.

Simone kept quiet—trying to contain her rage at the moron calling himself a lawman. Maybe this was for the best, she thought. She'd been riding a whirlwind lately and was feeling the pressure. If she could keep herself from killing the arrogant sheriff, this might give her nerves a much-needed respite from the day. She longed for somewhere to go, someplace to be where no one knew her and there'd be no demands made on her. She never thought it would be like this when she embarked on a writing career. All she wanted to do was write, but there was a lot of baggage that went along with it. Still, she was doing what she wanted, what she loved, she just needed to slow down and take things at a slower pace.

And, right now, it seemed she had no choice. She glanced out the window as they came into town, taking note of the shops and stores along what she perceived to be the main street. She spied a small café and realized she hadn't eaten in a while. She wasn't really hungry, but needed something to put in her stomach.

Link took one last glance in his rearview as he pulled into his designated parking space. She'd calmed, he noted, more accepting of her fate. He felt a surge of guilt hit him as he pushed on his door. What had gotten into him? She hadn't really done anything to deserve being arrested and put behind bars. He'd made it personal, he knew that without a doubt. She'd gotten to him, under his skin, into his head, fast and furiously. It irritated him that she'd done it so swiftly without even trying. Yet, it made him want to know more, see more. He wanted to touch, to taste, to explore.

"Look, Officer," she said, as he opened the door for her. "This isn't really necessary. I apologize. I was out of line. I'm just frustrated I have so far to go and so little time to get there. Then of all things, I lost my way. You understand, don't you?"

He didn't answer, but nudged her forward through the door of the sheriff's office. Once inside, he seated himself at his desk, and gruffly told her to be seated, wondering how far he was going to take it.

"Hey, Link, how's your day going?"

"Hey, Charla. Mine's fine, how's yours."

Simone took measure of the leggy blonde that had come through the door. She had a badge on her chest. Another cop. Great, just what she needed, but couldn't stop the personal assessment of the new arrival's attributes anyway. She was a beauty. A face to die for. All porcelain skin and absolutely blemish-free. From where she sat, Simone knew there was little make-up on that face to speak of. And that hair. She'd kill for that hair. Long and blonde, pulled back in a ponytail at the neck. You couldn't get *that* color in a bottle.

A spurt of envy washed over her. Probably bed mates, she thought snidely, then was brought up short when they were introduced.

"Charla, meet Simone Beauvais. Simone, Charla. She's my sister."

Yeah, she could see the resemblance now. It was the eyes and the way they looked you over. They could find you wanting—or not.

"Hi, Ms. Beauvais. Speeding, were you?"

"No, I can definitely say I wasn't speeding."

Charla chewed on her lip as she stared at her brother, noting the tell-tale flush of red stain his cheeks. Hmm. So, that's the way the wind blew.

"Okay," Charla continued. "What great crime have you committed that the big bad wolf dragged you in on?"

Simone glanced over at Link. "I guess you better ask the sheriff here. I'm a little vague on the charges."

Charla waited a heartbeat then sat on the edge of Link's desk. "What's her crime, Sheriff? Shall I throw her in the slammer?"

Link raised his head and gave Charla an icy glare. "I'll need you to retrieve her car, Deputy. It's at the city limit sign."

Charla rose slowly and glared right back at Link, not liking at all the way this was going down. "Just what's the charge, Sheriff?"

"Operating a motor vehicle while driving barefoot."

"What?"

"There are other charges as well, Deputy."

"Simone, would you mind if I spoke to the sheriff alone?" Charla said, keeping her eyes trained on Link. "Why don't you go down to the café, have a cup of coffee or something and I'll meet you there in a moment."

"You can't tell her to go, Charla. She's under arrest, and she isn't your collar. Besides you have to go bring her car in."

Simone opened her mouth as if she had something to say, then shut it, pressing her lips tightly together. Charla frowned as she watched Simone make her way to the door.

"Did Link say your name was Simone Beauvais?" Charla asked before Simone opened the door. She knew that name from somewhere.

"Yes, I'm Simone Beauvais. Why?"

Charla looked her over. A long appraisal, probing, a committing to memory of features. "No reason, really. Your name just sounds familiar."

Simone's eyes flashed wide, then quickly looked away. "I can't imagine why."

The minute Simone was out the door, Charla was on Link like a bear on honey. "What the hell do you think you're doing, Lincoln Hayes! That's a trumped up charge if I ever heard one. What's gotten into you? Driving barefoot? You've got to be kidding! You *are* kidding, right?"

Link blew out his breath and sat heavily in his chair. He scraped his hand over his face and heaved a weary sigh. Women. They were going to be the death of him yet.

"You haven't answered me, Link. What'd she do to get you going?"

"Hell, if I know," he finally admitted. "She stepped out of her car, all dark hair and compact body and I felt like I'd been hit in the gut with a sledge hammer." Color rose to his cheeks at his admission to his sister.

"Ah. Attractive woman. Testosterone. Raging hormones. Understandable."

"I just lost my mind," he told her, grasping for any explanation and failing miserably. "I saw those painted toes of hers and lost it."

"I guess that explains it, then," she teased. "You better let her off the hook, though, before she decides to sue your ass. Wouldn't that be a scandal for our little burg?"

"Have Randy take you out there and bring back her car."

"While I'm gone, Link, you better be thinking of a way to get out of this before she finds out there's no such law. Let her off with a warning or something."

He nodded and watched her go, deciding her advice was sound and the best course of action to take. He was getting a headache and rubbed between his eyes. Other parts of his body ached, too. With a groan, he rose and adjusted his pants. They'd become too tight—ever since he'd met that little baggage down the street. Every time thoughts of his prisoner entered his head, his body reacted. From the moment she'd stepped out of that car, he didn't have a brain that would function. Other body parts were functioning quite well, however.

He'd better go see what she was doing. No telling what trouble she'd get herself into next.

Simone wandered into the café near the sheriff's office and sat in a booth by the window. From this view she could see everything going on in town. Not much to see, though. People walking about, stopping on the street, chewing the fat. She picked a menu out of the slot behind the catsup and looked it over. Homemade cherry pie. That and a cup of coffee would hit the spot, for sure. Maybe ice cream, too.

"Hi. Know what you want?"

Simone glanced up at the waitress—a teenager chomping on a wad of gum. "Yes. A cup of coffee and a slice of cherry pie with a big scoop of vanilla ice cream on top."

"Coming right up."

The café door opened, the tell-tale ringing of the bell attached to the top the only sound it made. Simone knew without raising her eyes that Lincoln Hayes had entered. She refused to acknowledge his presence. She was still put out with him for using his caveman tactics on her. Throwing her over his shoulder, indeed!

She didn't want to think of him now. He infiltrated where he didn't belong. If she let her thoughts wander on their own, they'd be on him before she could blink and she couldn't have that.

"Hey, Sheriff," called the waitress. "The usual?"

"Sure thing, Becky."

He didn't wait for an invitation, just plopped down in the same booth and faced her. She didn't look up, pretending to read the menu. She was still angry with him, among other things. She could feel his eyes on her, but kept right on reading. If she let herself admit it, he intrigued her. The way his mouth curved, the way those dark eyes flashed and assessed her. By the multitude of inky lashes. And that voice. She closed her eyes for a moment, mentally filing the velvet smoothness of it away to be taken out when she got ready to use it for her book.

She'd seen him before—well, not in the flesh, of course— but she dreamed often of a man with dark hair, dark eyes, tall and sexy as hell with a velvety voice to match, one that raised goose bumps on her flesh the size of boulders. A man who'd made her weak in the knees and breathless.

And, she'd written about him, she confessed. He was there in *One Enchanted Evening*, his long lean body sprawled across the rug in front of the fireplace. He was there in *A Time for Loving*, curled around her heroine's body after he'd seduced her and loved her until she begged for mercy. Then again in *Just the Thought of You*, as he'd made love to her heroine under a harvest moon, held in the circle of his arms as they'd listened to the rhythm of the surf kissing the shoreline. And in *Your Loving Arms* as she'd been beneath him on a secluded beach, moving with him in the night, the taste of salt on his skin as her lips brushed his neck, the moonlight streaming down on them. Even now she could feel the gentle rasping stroke of the beaded grains of sand on her back just the way she'd written it in her book.

Good Lord, she was a sick puppy, fantasizing about this backcountry sheriff just because he resembled the man of her dreams, the man she couldn't help writing about in her books. She frowned and gulped as she suppressed a shiver of excitement. She forced herself to set all that aside. She didn't want or need another distraction in her life. She was going full speed the way it was. She wanted him to go away. It was unsettling having him sit across from her and not saying a word. She had to do something, though. He was unraveling her like pulling a wayward thread from a sweater.

"There's no reason to keep tabs on me, Sheriff. As you can see, I'm not going anywhere. I don't even have a car," she told him, instilling all the ice she could muster in her voice.

"Don't go all frosty on me, Simone," he advised. "Your rap sheet's just gonna get longer."

"I don't have a rap sheet, Sheriff, unless you're going to charge me with all those ridiculous allegations of yours."

She finally glanced up. A too-handsome face with a pleased smile on his lips awaited her. She could cheerfully commit murder, she decided, imagining her hands around his throat. She leaned forward, bent on giving him another piece of her mind, then decided against it as she felt a flash of heat shoot down her body. This was ridiculous. She shouldn't... couldn't be this attracted to a strange man.

A hint of her perfume drifted toward Lincoln, tantalizing

his nostrils. His body reacted, wanting more. He saw a flicker of desire light her eyes before the shutters went down and banked the fire. As he stared at her, he was shocked to realize this was the woman who'd been his constant companion for years. He carried her in his mind. She came to him in his dreams.

Of course, in his dreams, she was wildly erotic, willing to please him in any and every way, and always had a ready smile—far removed from the vision that sat across from him with a talk-to-me-at-your-own-risk glare in her eyes.

He needed Simone, he realized suddenly. Needed her more than he ever needed anything in his life. Needed to keep her here so he could explore his feelings. He had to find a way to accomplish that goal.

"Here you go, Sheriff. Hot and black. And for you, miss, your cup of coffee and cherry pie with a scoop of vanilla ice cream on the top, just the way you ordered it."

It couldn't be this easy, he thought, trying to suppress the surge of glee that sprouted wings and took flight. She'd probably brain him with something if he tried that. He was already stretching the realm of the law the way it was. But what the hell, he'd give it a shot anyway.

"Sheriff, if you don't mind, could you take your coffee elsewhere? I'd like a moment to enjoy my own coffee, pie and ice cream alone."

He kept a straight face. "Well, I would if I could, Simone, but you see, you keep breaking our laws."

"What have I done now? All I'm doing is sitting here trying to eat my cherry pie and ice cream, for heaven's sake."

"Exactly."

She could swear the air sizzled. She could feel it snap along her skin. She felt his hand on her arm burning the flesh, then felt something cold on her wrist and a resounding click. She glanced down in horror. She was wearing a silver bracelet. Well, actually, she was handcuffed.

"You son-of-a-bitch," she shrieked. "Get these idiot things off me now!"

"You're under arrest, Simone—again. Come with me."

She jerked her arm, bucked against the restraint, but the dangerous glint in his dark eyes kept her from doing what she'd planned to do—giving him a good swift kick in the family jewels the first chance she got.

"Don't even think about it, Simone," he warned. "And, you better come along peacefully or I'll throw you over my shoulder again."

"This is so ridiculous," she fumed. "Do your thing, Sheriff. I'm not going another step until you tell me what you're arresting me for!"

"In this state, it's illegal to put ice cream on cherry pie."

"That's the most absurd thing I've ever heard in my life!"

"Come along peacefully now and there won't be any more charges."

She didn't want to come along peacefully. She wanted to rant and rave, to kick and bite, to pull his hair. But she didn't dare add assaulting a police officer to her ever-growing offenses. She followed peacefully.

Once inside the sheriff's office, Link escorted her into a cell. Back in the coffee shop, the murderous gleam in her eye shot a bolt of satisfaction right through him. He'd had trouble stopping the smirk that curved his mouth upward, but now he was guilt-ridden. He shouldn't be doing this. He could lose his badge over nonsense like this, abusing the law for his personal satisfaction. But it was the only thing he could think of to keep her close to him until he could figure out what to do. He couldn't allow her to leave. He'd never see her again if he let her drive away.

Still, he was within his rights. The ordinance was clearly written that it was *illegal to put ice cream on cherry pie*. Of course, if you came right down to it, she hadn't been the one to actually *put* the ice cream on the pie, but she'd ordered it. Sure, that was splitting hairs, but what else could he do?

If she would only give him a chance, get to know the real Lincoln Hayes, she'd see he was no fly-by-night backwoods law officer, that he was a man of real substance. A man who'd spend long nights loving her into the wee hours of the morning. A man who'd be there for life. Bring her coffee in the morning. A rose on her birthday. Tissues when she watched one of those girlie movies.

God, help him. He had it bad. How in the world had this happened? He didn't even know the woman. Yet, he knew her. He knew enough. He wanted her, not just for a quick lay. He wanted her...forever.

Bare Feet and Cherry Pie

Gramps was right, he commiserated. That old man and his predictions. He said it would happen like this. That he'd be blind-sided by a dark-headed sweetie one day. He'd never believed him. *Until now.*

Simone didn't know what to make of all this. Her skin was still burning from his touch. She reeled from everything that happened. First, from the fact she was behind bars for putting ice cream on cherry pie. And, second, because in a short amount of time that black haired, dark-eyed, walking dream had her hormones raging out of control. Even the humiliation of being arrested hadn't touched her. Not really. Not the way she'd been touched by him. Well, she hadn't actually been *touched* in the physical sense. Just caressed from afar. Caressed by those dark eyes that reached deep into her soul, caressing like a lover.

The squeak of hinges had her whirling around. Link stood in the doorway.

"Hold out your arm and I'll take the cuff off."

Reluctantly, she followed his instructions. What else could she do? He unlocked the cuff and walked away, leaving the cell door slightly open.

"Is there anything I can get you?"

"A soda would be nice—since I didn't get to finish my coffee when you so rudely told me it's against the law to put ice cream on cherry pie."

His smile was sheepish, he knew. He moved away, went to the soda machine, put in a dollar and extracted the Coke when it fell down the chute. He dropped the cuffs and keys on his desk as he passed by.

He stepped cautiously inside the cell. There were things going on here that had him taking deep breaths and trying to slow his heartbeat. He set the Coke on the small table and made his way back to the door. He needed to get himself outside where he could breathe.

It had suddenly gotten way too hot inside the small cell, the room smaller. He ran a hand through his hair in frustration, searching for relief. When he did, his elbow hit the bars on the door triggering the mechanism to slam it shut.

It only took a moment for him to realize what happened—the door was locked and the keys were on his desk. He was locked inside with the woman of sultry nights and silk sheets and no way out.

Simone saw the shock of surprise run across the sheriff's—Link's features. It was readily apparent from the slump of his shoulders and the shaking of his head that something indeed was wrong.

"What is it, Link?" she asked, her voice barely a whisper. "Are you okay?"

Frustration, along with a boatload of embarrassment, swept through him like a raging storm. What a damn fool thing to do! He sighed deeply, crossed his arms, and relaxed his body against the bars.

Her fingers were warm against his bare arm. A streak of energy rippled upward as they settled more firmly where she touched him. She felt the zap in her fingertips, dropped her hand and swallowed.

"Link," she said again, concern lacing her voice.

"I'm fine."

"Then what's the problem?"

He pursed his lips, mulling over in his mind what to tell her. How to tell her she was locked up tight with him, the arresting officer.

"Try the door."

Simone frowned, then stepped up to the cell door, took hold of the bars and pushed. It didn't budge. She tried again. Nothing. She spied the keys on his desk and the absurdity of the whole situation hit her.

The laughter bubbled out before she could stop it. She made her way to the bunk and fell into it. She laughed so hard, tears streamed down her face. She nearly lost her breath, then the hiccups started, coming out in little squeaks.

"I fail to see the humor in the situation," Link snapped.

"Well, I do," she gulped. "The big bad wolf of a sheriff locked in here with a hardened criminal who puts ice cream on her cherry pie!"

In the blink of an eye, Link strode forward and yanked her off the bunk, her body meeting the heat of his. His eyes glinted dangerously, warning of a threatening storm approaching. It only added fuel to an already raging fire.

"Careful, there, Sheriff Hayes. You're just about to lose your cool," Simone taunted.

He dropped her as if he'd been burned. The sense of

disappointment that slipped through her was a surprise. Their lips had been so close and she'd wanted to feel his on hers. Then her eyes widened as he ripped the badge off his shirt and threw it over his shoulder through the bars of the cell. It landed with a clink on the tiled floor.

"Without the badge, Simone, I'm just an ordinary citizen. Just a man."

He pulled her gently to him this time, showing her another side of Lincoln Hayes.

The kiss was hot. Wild. Hungry. Shattering. Needy.

Simone forgot all the declarations of denials, forgot everything but the sweetness of his taste against her mouth, the heated pressure of his body against hers. With a low moan deep in her throat, she pressed against him, submitting to the heat of his kiss.

Link couldn't stop. He hadn't meant to come on like a sex-starved maniac out of control—as wild and hot as his kiss. Yet, he felt control slipping away with the answering call of her body as his reached out to her in one voice. He trembled, shaky from need, starving to have her. He wanted to make love to her, to hold her gently, give her a part of himself he'd never given another woman before.

Simone felt the hunger driving him, felt the strength of his hard-muscled body straining against her. She matched his hunger, his passion, his need and wanted more. The urgency to feel his skin against her own was overwhelming. With another low moan of want, of need, she moved against him.

He whispered her name, soft, low, husky. A soft caressing sound that fueled her desire. He ravished her mouth, gently, tenderly, yet there was a sweet savageness to it that called to her.

As if he wanted her to know him, remember him, leave his imprint so any other would be wiped from her mind.

Heat pulsed inside her, uncurling in agonizing slowness that sent a rush of yearning spiking through her.

Oblivious to their surroundings, aware only of their hunger, Simone thought nothing could drive them apart.

Nothing—except being slammed with a reality brick.

The office door opened and Charla marched inside. Her jaw dropped from shock. Catching her brother in a lip-lock with a hot mama was something she'd wanted to do her whole life. She'd caught him and here was her chance to never let him forget it. But she drew blanks, had a brain freeze!

Simone and Link jumped apart at the intrusion, embarrassment heating their cheeks.

Finally, Charla moved forward. When she did, her foot connected with Link's badge and sent it skidding across the floor. She frowned in its direction. When her brother made no move to leave the jail cell, she paused and looked around, a little confused. Then she saw the keys lying on his desk. Serves him right, she decided.

She arched a brow. "Problem, Sheriff?"

"Don't get cute. Unlock the door, Charla."

"Oh, so it's Charla now. Not Deputy?"

"Unlock the damn door, Charla," he growled.

At a snail's pace, she moved over to the cell and rattled the barred door. "Hmm. Locked yourself in, did ya', Sheriff?"

"I swear, I'll turn you over my knee when I get out of here if you don't open this door right now."

Irritation etched itself over his face and Charla understood he knew she'd never let him live this one down. It was bad enough to get caught locked in his own jail cell, but to be caught putting the moves on the prisoner was humiliating.

She looked at Simone and grinned. Simone grinned back. "So, you're Simone Beauvais. *The* Simone Beauvais?"

"Guilty as charged, Deputy."

The look Link gave Simone was one that said *so?* "Is she supposed to be somebody?"

"Simone Beauvais."

"I know who she is," he shouted. "Just *who* the hell is she?"

"Simone Beauvais," Charla told him. "She writes novels. *Romance* novels."

Link groaned.

Charla couldn't stop herself. She laughed. "Yep, Link, she writes *girlie* books. Another thing in a growing list I won't let you live down." She couldn't keep the *gotcha* smirk from spreading across her face. Knew from the look on his, he definitely was going to do her bodily harm the minute she opened the cell door.

He gritted his teeth. "Open the door...please."

"Actually, I've got rounds to make. You know, to keep our

fair citizens safe from all those criminals running around driving barefooted."

"Charla!"

"That's not the charge anymore," Simone teased, a broad grin crossing her face. "He arrested me for cherry pie and ice cream."

"What?"

"Yeah, seems it's illegal to put ice cream on cherry pie in this state."

"It is not!" Charla glared at Link thinking he had truly gone insane.

"Check it out yourself, if you don't believe me."

Charla went to her computer, logged on, brought up the state ordinances and searched for illegal laws. First she typed in driving barefoot but nothing came up under that search. Next, she typed in cherry pie and ice cream. Within minutes, it popped up on the screen. *Illegal to put ice cream on cherry pie.*

"Well, I'll be damned."

She grabbed the keys, unlocked the cell and swung the door wide. Link stormed out, stalked to the office door and exited without a word. The girls looked at each other in amusement.

He barged back in a few minutes later and barked, "You're free to go."

"Well," Charla commented after he'd left again. "I don't think I've ever seen him in such a snit." When she looked over at Simone, she found her frowning and biting her lip. "Got to ya', did he?"

She nodded. "He does have a way about him."

"Better get going before he changes his mind. When he has a mad on, he's stubborn as hell. Your car's parked out front. Come on, I'll walk you out."

Charla held the car door open as Simone slid behind the steering wheel. Out of the corner of her eye, she saw Link standing off to the side. She turned her head and saw the indecision in the gaze that fastened on Simone like super glue. She pushed the door closed and walked away.

Link walked up to the window Simone had just closed and tapped it. She hit the button and it glided downward out of sight.

"What is it now, Sheriff Hayes?"

He put both his hands on the top of the car to keep from cupping her face, to taste her again. "Do you really have to go? I'd like you to stay. Get to know you. I mean, well, why were you in such a hurry to get to Colorado anyway?"

"Truthfully?"

He nodded.

"I was running away. I just wanted time to myself for a few days. Somewhere quiet. Peaceful."

"You could have all of that here, Simone. With me."

"I can't, Link. My plans are made."

"Plans can be changed. We started something, Simone. Something good. I'd like you to stay awhile. See where it leads."

"I can't."

He couldn't ask her again. If he did, he'd look foolish.

She started the car, backed out of the parking spot, then drove away.

Charla came up behind him as he stood watching. "You're letting her get away?"

"I asked her to stay. She said she couldn't, her plans were already made."

"And you're just gonna let her go?"

"It's what she wants."

"Brother, did I ever tell you that you're a dickhead?"

"On numerous occasions."

"Well, I'm telling you again."

Link opened his mouth for a quick retort, but she'd already walked off. He continued to watch Simone as she drove away with his heart. He sighed, his chest tight as the taillights of her car vanished from view.

Simone passed the city limit sign going the opposite way she'd come in. She needed to put this place behind her. *Far behind her*. But she couldn't seem to make herself go any faster. She pulled over to the side of the rode, leaned her head back against the seat and closed her eyes. Before she'd left, she'd let her eyes gaze across his features, filing away every angle, every curve. She wanted to count his lashes but knew she didn't have the time. Damn!

Link had been right. There was something brewing under the surface. And, none of it made sense. She was drawn to him more than she'd been to any man. He made her feel things she only wrote about. Things she herself had never had the opportunity to experience. Maybe now *was* the time to put on a new skin. Instead of writing about love, she'd test the waters for herself.

Then, in a flash of enlightenment, she knew what she was going to do. Nobody said it had to make sense!

♥

"Sheriff, this is Becky, over at the café. Can you come over here for a minute? I have a slight problem."

She smiled mischievously, dished up a big scoop of ice cream and placed it atop a slice of cherry pie.

Link hurried over to the café, unsure what he would find. Becky hadn't sounded scared, so what was going on?

The fork was sliding out of her mouth as he entered. That was just as erotic as the kiss had been. He sauntered over to the booth and sat down.

"You know, ma'am," he drawled. "It's illegal in these parts to put ice cream on cherry pie."

Simone slowly lifted her heavily lashed green eyes, licked the white ice cream from her lips and gazed at him seductively. Holding out her hands, she throatily whispered, "Take me in, Sheriff. I'm all yours. Do with me what you will."

Cissy Hassell is the author of
THORNS, A KNIGHT THIS WAY COMETH, THE SAME
LOVE TWICE,
NOWHERE, THE BRINGER OF RAPTURE, and
DECEIT TIMES TWO.
Be sure to visit Cissy's website at
www.cissyhassell.com

Sadie, the Shady Angel

by *Diane Davis White*

• *Idaho - It's illegal for a man to give his sweetheart a box of candy weighing less than fifty pounds*

Somewhere Above the Rainbow and Far Behind the Clouds

Sadie, the Shady Angel ran her tongue over her freshly painted lips. "There, that ought a do it. I'm gonna find me a rich, good looking angel-man tonight."

"Sadie, you know you can't vamp Angels. These righteous, upstanding men wouldn't be here if they'd taken up with the likes of you. No wonder you're still a fledgling angel. Your behavior is absolutely plebian at times."

Sadie stared at her mentor. "Ha! Who knows what *that* means, Miss Prissy? I'm just trying to get my kicks. You and your 'blah, blah, blah' about goodness and moral rectitude. As if you never did it! How'd you get those three kids of yours? Immaculate conception?"

"Enough! We have an assignment we need to concentrate on. Not your promiscuous past."

"Promiscuous? Did you just call me a slut?" Sadie's narrowed eyes glittered with anger. Her chin thrust at a belligerent angle. Hands on hips, she glared at the shorter, rounder angel.

"Not in so many words, no." Pricilla looked almost remorseful.

"Yeah? How many words does it take?" Sadie wasn't taken in by that phony look of contrition.

"Hush up and let's get on with this assignment before we

get shuffled over to statistics. If there is anything I hate, it's counting a bunch of worthless statistics," Pricilla huffed.

"Yeah, only because the ones attributed to you are so boring." Sadie mocked her huffiness, chest stuck out, chin high, nose in the air.

"There is nothing boring about winning seventeen blue ribbons at the County Fair for my Delightfully Dark Fudge Bonbons. If you had an ounce of decency, you'd stop badgering me about my homemaking skills. Ha. Like I hadn't accomplished anything in my life. Now, let's get on that cloud heading for Earth! The next one doesn't come for a week!"

"Are you kidding? That's a thundercloud. I get a real headache when those things go off! Not to mention seasick when they rumble and roll around."

"You'll have to make do. The fluffy white ones with the silver linings have already departed and we don't have time to waste." Pricilla lifted the hem of her white robe and started running toward the already departing cloud. "*Now*, Sadie. Let's go!"

Following reluctantly, Sadie didn't bother to lift her hem—the gown was too short to touch the ground. Flipping her middle finger at the departing Pricilla, she shuffled along, half-hoping to miss the cloud.

No such luck. Just as Sadie reached the edge of the cloud, the thunderous roar of its take off pulled her off balance, sucking her in. She fell, face first onto the cloud's damp, musty surface. Right at the feet of her ever-smirking mentor, Pricilla. "Well, help me up, for Go...goodness sake!"

"Watch it. I heard what you almost said." Pricilla stuck out her fat hand and tugged the taller angel to her feet. "You've been in more trouble for your language than anybody I've ever taught."

"Yeah? Well, you ain't heard nothin' yet." Sadie mumbled something unintelligible about the other angel and looked away toward the lightening strikes below them. "What do you suppose it would be like to ride one of them down?"

"Probably quite painful." Pricilla wasn't about to enlighten her charge with the tale of her experience with lightening. She'd just come out of Angel 101, such a novice that she'd believed her joke-happy mentor and jumped onto a bolt headed straight for a tree. The tree had caught fire. The limb

Pricilla clung to broke, dropping her onto the pavement. And because she hadn't gotten her full-fledged wings yet, it hurt—a lot.

Sadie, clinging to the edge of the slippery cloud, leaned over and lost her lunch—then sat moaning as the deafening noises and hot flashes of light speared straight through her brain.

"Where are we going?" she moaned to Pricilla.

"I told you—Idaho. Do not be obtuse!"

"Did you just call me stupid?" Sadie lifted her face, annoyed and feeling rather greenish. She eyed Pricilla's delighted smile sourly. "Well? Did you?"

"Not in so many words, no," Pricilla repeated her favorite phrase.

"Why do you always say *'not in so many words'* like that? Either you called me stupid or you didn't. Either you called me a slut or you didn't. Which is it?"

"Both, actually." Pricilla folded her hands at her waist. Pulling her chins as high as she could, she tried her best to look down her nose at the taller Sadie. "You were assigned to me because you've been...well...incorrigible. No one wants to bother with you anymore. I'll venture if you had not saved that little girl's life, you would be somewhere else right now, wishing for some ice water and a cool breeze."

"Are you saying—?"

"Yes, I am," Pricilla interrupted Sadie with a smug twist of her mouth. "Everyone knows this is your absolute last chance to get your wings. Now, let's get to it."

The cloud master shouted over the howling wind. "Jumping off point ladies! Get ready, get set...GO!"

Sadie felt the cloud dissolve beneath her feet, and suddenly, she plunged through space, surrounded by swirling white stuff. "Snow! Wow! I ain't seen snow in years." She stuck out her tongue, catching a few flakes. An act that cost her dearly as she bottomed out on a hilltop, biting down hard on her tongue. "Outh! Thath hurths."

"Oh, stop your whining and wipe the blood off your chin before it gets all over your clothes." Pricilla—who'd landed most gracefully—struggled to get her left wing tucked back in. "I have problems of my own, you know."

"Yeah, like that silly wing that never wants to stay in

place. Maybe you should put some superglue on it." Sadie snorted a laugh in a most unladylike manner.

"Do you want to know about our assignment or not?" Pricilla made one last effort to tuck the unruly wing. Finally it disappeared beneath her robe. "There, that should do."

"Okay, tell me then." Sadie leaned against the tree, cleaning her nails with a sliver of bark. "I'm all ears, boss woman."

"That's *boss angel*, to you." Pricilla rolled her eyes to the heavens and spread her arms as though beseeching someone to help her. "There is a young woman that wants to fall in love, but hasn't the courage to go for it. And we have just the right man for her. He's a widower and has a sweet little boy. Now in Idaho, there is a law about bringing candy to your sweetheart—"

"I'll go for it if you'll let me." Sadie grinned widely. "Where do I go to go for it?"

"Stop the nonsense, Sadie. I could send you back for insubordination, you know."

Sadie answered by sticking out her tongue and swirling her skirts. "I don't think so, Miss Prissy. It would mean you'd failed—and you don't want *that* on your record."

She watched Pricilla turn red, then purple in her anger. Sadie loved to push the Senior Angel to the limit. The woman was positively stuffy and unbending. She walked around as if she was perfect and everybody else was an underling. It grated on Sadie, who in life had been a kindhearted—if slightly wild—woman. Sadie thought what Pricilla needed was a good roll in the hay, but of course, she couldn't say that. *Well, I could,* she thought with an impish grin, *but I'd suffer for it, for sure.*

"What's my role in this?" Sadie asked as she trudged along beside her companion. "What are you going to ask me to do? Teach her to vamp?"

"Hmmmm. Not a bad idea," Pricilla mused aloud. "The girl has no skills in that area from what I understand. Of course, your idea of vamping is a little...well, a tad...shall we say—"

"What? Are you planning to insult me again?" Sadie sashayed and danced in a circle around Pricilla, doing an impromptu bump and grind. "Go ahead. Do it. You're just jealous because you had such a boring life...while I—with my beauty and passionate nature—"

"Behave yourself. We need to get going," Pricilla admonished with a menacing shake of her middle finger—the one with the power-zapping, built-in butt-swatter.

Sadie, ignoring the command, gazed around at the beautiful countryside. "So, this is Idaho. Never been here before. Pretty, but kinda cold, though."

"You cannot feel cold, and you know it," Pricilla admonished in her uppity voice.

"Yes. I can. Maybe you don't feel anything because you lack soul." Sadie ran her hands down her sides, outlining her flamboyant figure. "You lack other things, too, I'll bet."

"I have more soul in my little finger—"

"Ah, put a sock in it, Prissy." Sadie was getting fed up with her so-called teacher. "So, what's her name? What's she like? Do you have a plan?" She figured if she hit the old gal with too many questions, she'd shut up for awhile.

"Sarah," Pricilla said succinctly, ignoring the outburst, "is a very tidy young woman. I have been given to understand she is almost compulsive in some of her habits. It's up to us to help her relax...give her a little boost so she can fall in love."

"Yeah, I get it. Loosen her up a bit. Give her some pizzazz." Sadie wrung her hands together in anticipation of such exciting fare. "I can teach her all sorts of tricks—"

"Enough!" Pricilla stopped in the middle of the lane. "We don't need to teach her about your...*ahem*...former profession. A few delicate hints about what attracts a gentleman will be sufficient."

"Hey, what era were you born in anyhow? Delicate hints? Gentleman? Oh, geeze, what an air bubble you've got between your self-righteous ears."

Seconds later, Sadie found herself flat on her back in a huge pile of leaves—among other things. "Ugh!" She lifted one hand and sniffed, nearly gagging. "That's shi—"

"Do not say it!" Pricilla leaned as close as she could and handed the underling a tissue. "Use this and hurry. We're late."

"Why'd you zap me?" Sadie rubbed her backside where she'd landed, and eyed the other angel with resentment. "I got a right to my opinion."

"Not when it undermines the moral fiber of a *Fully*

Winged Angel Superior." Pricilla drew her ample body to its tallest posture and stuck out her considerable bosom. "I'm your superior and you must follow my lead in all things. Never question my decisions. Above all, do not disparage or impugn my character."

"Your what?" Sadie began to laugh. "I wouldn't dream of it, sister. Hell, I can't even spell those words."

"You are being impertinent and I shan't have it!" Pricilla lifted her arm, aiming the middle finger of her left hand at Sadie. "You know what this means, don't you?"

"Yeah, it means fu—"

"Do not say it," Pricilla warned. "This is my power finger and I'm going to zap you again if you keep up this foolishness. Do you understand, Sadie?"

Sadie threw up her hands in surrender. "Whoa! If you're going to spout gibberish at me, I'll shut up. I don't understand half what you say, and you want me to obey your every whim? Ha!" She flinched as Pricilla gave her another warning look, pointing her power finger. "I was just kidding," she said in what, for Sadie, was a meek tone.

"I somehow find that unbelievable. However, I'll let it pass. Oh look, a farmer with his wagon. Quick, we'll catch a ride."

"Catch a ride on that thing? I'd rather be boiled in oil."

"That could be arranged. Here we are. Oh, good fellow!" Pointedly ignoring the comment, Pricilla moved into the middle of the road, standing in front of the prancing horses, causing the poor farmer to almost lose control of the animals. She raised one white-gloved hand, palm upward. "You there, farmer! Stop. We'd like a ride please."

The farmer sawed back on the reins, stopping the horses just in front of them. He wore a look of shocked surprise. "Scarin' them animals like that'll get ya trampled. Get outta there."

"Are you gonna to give us a ride?" Sadie took instant control, looking the driver up and down in her sassy manner. "We need to be somewhere in a hurry. I warn you, if you don't do what she wants," she jerked her chin at Pricilla, "she'll zap you right outta that seat."

"You tryin' to threaten me?" The farmer lifted the reins. He started to urge the animals around Priscilla with a click of

125

his tongue. Instead, he found himself flying through the air. Seated in the middle of the road, he looked up at the Pricilla, and scratched his head.

"Told ya." Sadie nodded sagely at her companion. "That's just half of what she'll do. Now, give us a hand like a good boy."

Pocatello Idaho—Somewhere beneath the rainbow

Sugar jumped from the window seat and crawled across the floor, stalking some small insect, no doubt. Sarah watched her favorite companion in morose silence. *A pet is wonderful, but a human being—specifically a nice man—would be so much better.*

As though sensing her thoughts, the Persian came to her and jumped in her lap. Playfully, Sugar batted at the fringe on the couch pillow behind her head.

"Oh, a man around the house would be so nice, wouldn't it, Sugar? I don't quite know what to do," Sarah Tuttle said to her kitty. "I wish we had a boyfriend."

Sugar meowed in sympathy. Her yellow-green eyes glittered with what seemed to Sarah like pity. It hurt when your own pet felt sorry for you.

"It seems like every time I meet a nice man, he just...goes away. I guess I'm boring."

The Persian jumped down and walked herself around her feet, rubbing against her ankles and purring softly.

"Oh, I know you love me and you think I'm perfect. Truth is, I'm not. I don't have a clue how to get a man, much less hold one."

The cat jumped back into her lap and settled comfortably, bathing one dainty paw.

"How I wish that wishes *did* come true," she said on a little sob. "That shiny nickel we threw into the wishing pond didn't get our wish, did it, Sugar?"

Her doorbell chimed. She jumped to her feet and headed for the door. "Who could that be? I never have company. Now be nice, Sugar. No hissing!"

Sarah looked through the apartment door's peephole and let out a gasp. There were two women, one short and chubby, the other tall and rather rag-tag looking. The short one had what looked like a silver wing sticking out of her cloak. The other one, a redhead with too much makeup on, had a brand new pair of Nikes peeking out from under her too-short, slightly-soiled garment.

"Angels? Here?" Sarah, never giving a thought to just how she knew they were angels, opened the door quickly. She drew them inside, looking up and down the hall, lest one of her neighbors see her unusual guests.

"Hello," she said politely, adjusting her glasses to peer at the two disheveled ladies. "What can I do for you?"

"It's what we can do for you, girlie. First, get rid of those horrid glasses. You need a makeover really, really bad." Sadie jumped right in, earning an elbow in the ribs. "Ouch...you had no call—"

"Be quiet," Pricilla admonished in an aside. Smiling angelically at their hostess, she asked, "You are Sarah Tuttle, aren't you?"

"Yes, but—"

"We are your wish come true," Pricilla said in her most virtuous tone, then looked askance at her underling. "Well...at least one of us is."

"What's that supposed to mean?" Sadie stepped forward, a belligerent look in her eyes.

"Ah...ladies...er...angels? Won't you sit down, please?" Sarah waved an arm toward the small couch. "Would you like a cup of tea or coffee?"

"Coffee...hot and strong...just like I like my men."

"Enough!" Pricilla rolled her eyes at her hostess. "You'll have to forgive Sadie. She's a novice in many things....polite society being one of them. I will have tea, and so will Sadie."

"If you'll excuse me for a minute, I'll go brew some." Sarah turned, but not quickly enough to miss the tongue sticking out of the redhead's mouth as she glared at her counterpart.

"And coffee!" Sadie chimed in, looking daggers at Pricilla. "Strong and hot."

Sarah smiled to herself as she bustled into her little kitchenette. She liked these angels, though she thought them completely unusual as far as angels went. At least, she thought so, having had no previous contact with heavenly beings, and knowing only what she'd read. *They're here to grant my wish,* she thought happily and began to hum.

"Ready to go, son?" Lean, well-muscled Reed Carter jumped down from the porch. "We've got to hurry or we're going to be late."

"Daddy...I wanna stay home," Reed Campbell Carter Junior whined in his four-year-old-almost-five voice. "I don't wanna see Nana. She makes me eat those green things...what are they called?"

"Vegetables, Camp." Reed laughed and gently nudged the boy into the van and his safety seat. "They're good for you...make you grow strong. If you try really hard, you'll learn to like them."

"You don't eat 'em."

"Well," Reed fished around for an answer and grinned. "I'm grown, so I don't need to eat veggies anymore, son."

"I wish my momma hadn't gone off to Heaven. I don't think she'd make me eat them old slimy vet-stables."

"Veg-e-ta-bles," Reed corrected slowly. He closed the sliding door then got behind the wheel. He sat quietly a minute, contemplating how to answer his son's comments. The boy hadn't said a word about his mother until he'd started preschool and saw the other boys had mothers.

"Well?" Camp piped up from the back seat. "Can we get her back? God don't need her. Mary Ellen Stubs says God has everybody where he wants them, can put anybody anywhere, so can we get Mommy back, huh?"

The lump forming in Reed's throat kept him from answering right away. He still mourned and missed Camp's mother, though she'd been gone three years. He wished he could do as the boy asked. His job as a parent was to keep the boy grounded in reality. After a lengthy pause, he said, "Camp, you're mommy isn't coming back. She can't...because—"

"Because God won't let her," Camp shouted. "I hate that old man!"

"Camp! No! Don't *ever* say that. She can't come back, because God needs her."

Reed pulled the van to the curb and cut the engine, then turned to face his son. Being a single parent to a precocious little boy wasn't easy. He didn't have all the answers. Hell, he didn't have most of them. All he could do was reason with the four-year-old and hope something would sink in. "Let's go feed the ducks."

Seated on a park bench close to the water, Reed handed a bag of breadcrumbs to Camp. He leaned back and watched the sky darken. The clouds kept shifting and reforming into large masses that might bring rain.

"What are we going to do about Mommy?" Camp wasn't giving up. "Can we send God a letter? You know, like we do Santa Claus. Hey, we could ask Santa to give her back. I'll bet Rudolph knows 'xactly how to find God's house."

"Camp, Santa Claus is only for toys and gifts. Not even God can bring back Mommy now that she's in Heaven."

"Then what about one that's not in Heaven...you know? We could look for a new mommy, couldn't we?"

Reed was saved from answering as two little old ladies in strange looking white garments swooped—literally—down from the tree above. Rubbing his eyes, Reed thought he might be hallucinating. He blinked and looked again. Now they were walking toward him. Strange, very strange.

"Hello, young man," the short one said to Camp. "Are you feeding the ducklings?"

"Yeah."

Reed saw his son was sulking.

He eyed the little woman in the white gauzy gown and satin cloak with amusement. They must be going to a costume party. Then he saw the silvery wing tip. Some outfit...must have had a good seamstress.

Camp saw the wing, too. "Are you a angel?"

"Actually we are..." Sadie began, only to stop as the other one pointed a finger at her. "That is...we're dressed this way—"

"You're going to a party!" Camp piped up, grinning. "Can I come?"

"Camp! You don't ask people if you can go with them." He smiled apologetically and shrugged as though to say, what the heck, he's just a kid.

"Actually, we're here to invite you both to a party," Pricilla said, smiling benignly at the boy.

"A real costume party?" Camp jumped off the bench and danced from one foot to the other. "Can we go, Daddy? Can we?"

"What kind of party is this?" Reed, despite his

misgivings, was intrigued. Though they were strangers, he felt pulled toward these women somehow. "If it's a fancy party, we're hardly dressed for it."

"No...that is, Sadie and I are in fancy dress because... well..."

"We just came from rehearsal for the church pageant," Sadie chimed in and preened a little at the look of surprise she got from Pricilla. "We didn't have time to change. It's a party to cheer up a young lady who needs...cheering up."

"Yes," Pricilla chimed in—getting the hang of adlibbing, "she's dear to us...and her parents were recently taken to Heaven."

Camp spun to face his father. "Like Mommy. Oh, Daddy, can we go? I know just how the lady must feel."

Reed looked at the shining joy in his son's eyes and couldn't resist taking them up on it. "What time shall we be there?" What the heck, if there was something wrong, he'd simply leave.

"Now. We're already late, actually." The short one practically danced on her toes, she seemed so excited. "Do you have a vehicle handy? We were going to take a cab..."

"No problem," Reed said as he took Camp's hand. "Follow me, ladies."

Reed felt as though Fate had stepped in and taken a hand. Lighter of spirit than he'd been for days, he followed their directions, only getting lost twice before he managed to pull up in front of the correct house. And that bit about stopping for a fifty-pound box of bonbons! Now *that* was strange.

"Hello," Sarah said, extending her hand to the cute little boy who stared up at her with such worshipful eyes. "My name's Sarah. What's yours?"

"I'm Reed Campbell Carter, Junior." Camp glanced up at his father before spinning his gaze back to her. "You'll do nicely."

"Do what nicely?" she asked, puzzled.

"Ah...he's just joking. My son, the jokester." Reed smiled nervously. "He's always saying crazy things. You know how kids are."

"Actually, I don't know very much about children at all." She smiled at the man. He smiled back. Sarah knew—just knew—he was the one. His light blue eyes were gorgeous, full of warmth and intelligence, brimming with humor and curiosity. He possessed every quality she'd written down for her ideal man. "But I do like them," she added quickly.

"I'm glad you like me." Camp stepped closer and stepped on her bare toe. "Sorry."

"Oh! I forgot my shoes," Sarah said, hurrying into her bedroom. She could feel the heat of a blush rising on her face.

Oh my gosh, don't let me blow this opportunity. Please, please let him like eccentric, absentminded, and slightly bookish women who do stupid things like go barefoot to a party in their honor.

"Hey, a cat!" Camp knelt on the floor and ran his hand over the cat's back. It arched and purred, visibly enjoying the attention. "What's his name?"

"Her name is Sugar," Sarah supplied, walking into the living room. "Looks like she likes you."

"I like her, too," Camp said enthusiastically.

"Ah...let me introduce everyone." Sarah led them through the small gathering. Introductions didn't take long. There were only a few neighbors present on such short notice. Sarah still marveled at how quickly the angels had put this together. And just so she could meet the man of her dreams. Sarah glanced at Reed out of the corner of her eye just to be sure he was real.

"Ah, and of course, you've met Sadie...ah...Sadie?" She reached for the last name, mortified she couldn't produce it.

"Angelino," Sadie said with an impish smile. "Just call me Angel if you forget my name."

"Sadie Angelino is an unusual combination." Reed smiled politely. "Very nice, though."

"My father was an Italian railroad worker. On my mother's side, which is Irish, I was named for my great grandmother. She was in the trade."

"What trade is that?" Sarah looked at Sadie with wide, curious eyes.

"Ah...she means her mother was an actress," Pricilla said a little too quickly.

"No, I did not." Sadie gave a sly smile. "I meant what I said. She worked the docks in London after they threw her out of Dublin."

"You never told me that!" Pricilla glared, huffing her

chest out. "I don't believe a word of it, Sadie. You make up these...these horrid tales to entertain people."

"Never mind. It's not important," Sarah interrupted, seeing another spat coming. For friends, these two didn't seem to get along well.

"I have to be going, Sarah. Thank you for inviting me." Elderly Miss Emma Bridger, retired schoolteacher, barely came to the middle of Reed's chest. She looked up at him, smiling. "You have a handsome young man here. Looks like a keeper to me. Did he bring you the requisite box of bonbons? It looks very large...just like the law requires."

"Law? I...ah...that is," Sarah began, not daring to look at Reed. "Miss Bridger, so glad you could come. Let me walk you up the stairs."

"I'll do that," Reed offered gallantly. "Any lady who thinks me handsome deserves special treatment." He held out his arm. Miss Bridger laid her gnarled, arthritic hand on it, allowing herself to be led from the room. He looked back at Sarah and winked.

Sarah melted. *If I were a candle, I'd be a puddle of wax at this very second.*

"Camp, would you like some cake?"

"Yeah...I mean, yes, please." The boy was obviously a scamp trying to stay on his best behavior. She liked that. A child without spirit was destined to lead a dull life. But a child without manners would find misery along the way.

"We brought you fifty pounds of bonbons. Can I take some home with me?"

"Fifty..." Sarah looked at the angels. "Why?"

"Because it is the law," Pricilla answered. "If a man is courting a lady and he arrives with less than fifty pounds of candy—minimum—he'll go to jail."

"He's here to court me?" Sarah blushed, her thoughts jumbled. "I've never heard of such a law."

"Well, believe it, Honey," Sadie injected. "Pricilla don't know much about a lot of things, but she knows her laws. Now *I* can tell you all about courting."

Reed let himself back into the apartment, shaking his head and chuckling to himself. He looked into Sarah's sweet gaze and his heart thumped hard.

"What are you laughing about?" she asked. "Share the

joke with us."

"Ah...Miss Bridger tells me the fifty pounds of bonbons will be sufficient to keep me out of jail." Slightly bemused, Reed felt odd. He had ever since the two strange ladies approached him by the lake. "Says now that I'm officially courting you, I won't have to bring more than forty pounds the next time."

"Oh," Sarah said, her lips pressed together, stifling a giggle.

Lips Reed wanted to kiss. The thought startled him. She looked away, blushing from his blatant staring. He pulled himself together with some effort, knowing he couldn't stand and stare at her all day, no matter how much he wanted to.

A loud giggle on the other side of the room caught his attention. Eager to be distracted, Reed looked over at Sadie. He couldn't stop grinning as she wiggled her eyebrows and batted her eyelashes at the elderly gentleman upon whose knee she was seated. Very strange old gal, he thought. Very strange, indeed.

"Would you care to have a seat?"

Sarah's soft voice instantly brought him back to her. Nodding, he followed her across the room and sat at the small dinette. Sarah sat across from him, and Camp followed, carrying the Persian like a grand prize he'd won at the fair.

"I ah...know this sounds incredibly forward, Sarah." Reed felt nervous. His palms were sweating. "But I'd like very much to take you to dinner sometime. Do you think that would be alright?"

"Ah...well..." Sarah stalled, wondering if there was some magic spell on him. If so, she didn't want him. It wasn't right to trick a man into romance. He should want to take her to dinner because he wanted to, not because angels put an enchantment on him.

"Ah, come on, Sarah." Camp took one of her hands in his, the cat clinging precariously to his shoulder. "You 'en me 'en Dad could have a great time. 'Sides, if you're gonna be my new mommy, you'll have to get used to eating dinner with us. Right, Dad?"

Sarah nearly choked on the boy's statement, but she was saved from answering when her door swung open suddenly, revealing a pot-bellied police officer. His nameplate identified him as Deputy Sniffle. He marched across the room, eyes staring hard at Reed. His hand clutched the butt of his gun.

"You Reed Carter?"

"Yes, what can I do for you, officer?" Reed knew he must look as astounded as he felt.

"Gotta weigh the bonbons." The deputy looked around the room, spied the huge box, and headed straight for it. "Hope it weighs in okay."

"Well, that was fast," Pricilla whispered in an aside to Sadie. "I only conjured him up a few minutes ago."

"Sniffle? Where'd ya get a name like that?" Sadie sniffed in disdain. "I could do better than that."

"Hush and watch." Pricilla seemed terribly excited.

"You got a bathroom scale?" Deputy Sniffle hefted the red and silver box. "It feels like fifty, but I gotta be sure."

Sarah—as though in a daze—brought out her bathroom scale and set it on the coffee table. She watched the deputy carefully set the box on the scale, saw his face scrunch in concentration as he peered at the needle on the scale. Then he straightened, his face wreathed in a huge smile.

"Done and done, Mr. Carter. You've got yourself a courtship license."

Sarah stood numb as Reed thanked the deputy, escorting him to the door. No one spoke. Sugar jumped out of Camp's arms and curled her body around Reed's legs, nearly tripping him as he made his way back across the room.

"Well, it looks like I'm not going to jail," he lamely joked.

He stared at Sarah so intensely she wanted to melt right into his arms. The sounds of chatter began to pick up around the room, the music played softly on the radio. The angels stood to one side, arm-in-arm, finally appearing to be comrades.

"Let's go," Camp said, tugging on his dad's pant leg. "We gotta get married."

"Ah...son, it's not done quite like that," Reed said, never taking his eyes from the sweet smile Sarah bestowed on him.

"Okay...then let's go to dinner first...then we'll get married," the boy responded, looking at the adults with a big grin.

"Well, Sarah?" Reed asked softly. "Do you want to go out with us?"

"I certainly do, Reed." Sarah squeezed the little boy's hand that had crept into hers. "But I have company right now."

"Where?" Reed looked around the empty apartment. Sometime during their idle of staring into each other's eyes, the room had cleared.

"Well, then just let me get my coat," Sarah answered, virtually floating toward her closet.

"I think we did a good job, don't you, Sadie?" Pricilla was puffed up again, like she was very important.

Somehow, that didn't bother Sadie as much as it had. She looked at her mentor with new eyes. "Yeah...guess you knew what you were doing after all."

"We, Sadie," Pricilla corrected kindly. "You did your part very well. It wouldn't have been such a successful mission without you."

"Well, thank you, Prissy." Sadie was astounded at the sudden change of attitude and the gracious praise.

It didn't last long.

"Okay, let's get moving. We have three more assignments in this town alone." Pricilla moved off, her misshapen wing flapping wildly as she took flight through the open window.

Sadie followed, lifted on the draft of Pricilla's wings. "When will I get my own?" she asked in a rather whiny voice.

"You'll get your wings when you earn them. In the meantime, watch where you're flying. Stay in my draft and for goodness sakes, keep your skirts down, Sadie! We need to stop at the confectioners for another box of chocolates. This time let's go for caramel centers, alright?"

"And just who gets to carry that fifty pound box, huh?" Sadie knew the answer, but was too light of heart to care. After having brought true love into the lives of Sarah and Reed, she thought she could really get into this.

Now if I could just get that damned prissy Pricilla to lighten up, this could be fun.

Be sure to visit Diane Davis White's website
www.dianedaviswhite.com

Tutti-Frutti Blues

by Kemberlee Shortland

• *Carmel, California - Ice cream may not be eaten
while standing on the sidewalk.
(Repealed when Clint Eastwood was mayor)*

From the moment she woke that morning, Dr. Maisie Daniels' day had been a series of comedic blunders bent on destroying her sanity. It started the moment her alarm went off.

Scratch that.

The alarm failed to go off because its batteries died during the night. Waking late, Maisie was forced to cancel her morning appointments, informing her secretary, Pam, she'd be in after lunch.

Maisie always tried to look at the bright side of things and decided a stroll through town would be just the thing to clear her head.

That theory held true until she closed the door behind her. It wasn't as if the weather was bad. The day dawned with the typical mist rolling in from the Pacific, but it had burned off once the sun came over the Santa Lucia Mountains. By the time she left her little Comstock cottage on Torres Street, one of Carmel's gingerbread cottages, it was so warm she'd left her sweater at home, wearing little more than a white t-shirt and denim cut-off shorts.

What irked her was that her sweater sat on the sofa

beside her purse. She distinctly remembered the location of her purse because it contained her house keys. The same keys she'd left the house without. The same keys she'd need to get back in again!

"Well," Maisie sighed aloud, "a stroll through town doesn't require keys. I'll go to the office, get the spare set then come back to get ready for work." Headed toward town, she set off down Sixth Street, crossed Junipero Avenue, and then cut through Devondorf Park.

The park encompassed one square block. Surrounded by trees, the center of the park was lush green grass. Flowerbeds in bloom dotted the park with vibrant color.

At one side, poles flew the flags of the town, state and nation. On the three remaining sides were signs that simply read: No dogs, playing ball, skateboarding, kite flying, climbing trees, picking flowers, eating, drinking, littering. Keep off the grass.

And Maisie's favorite: No loitering.

The town designed an attractive, fragrant and peaceful park, then made it an offense to loiter. Maisie wondered about the logic of the town counsel sometimes.

With the threat of prosecution, Maisie hurried through the park lest she be cited for dallying.

Midway across the park, her mind on getting to the office, she stepped in something that shouldn't have been on the path, let alone in the park. When she looked down, two things crossed her mind. The first of which was how thoughtful the dog had been to stay off the forbidden grass.

But that thought was pushed aside when her gaze slipped down her bare legs and saw what else was on her feet. Her slippers. Not just any slippers, but her pink bunny slippers!

She shot a quick glance around, suddenly panicked. Had anyone seen the town's therapist traipsing through the park in bunny slippers?

The answer was a resounding yes. One of Carmel's finest stood on the sidewalk staring at her with his mouth open. She might have been attracted to his handsome dark features if she wasn't so damned embarrassed! The quicker she got to the office the better.

Without thinking, she rubbed her foot in the grass to remove as much of the mess as possible, then raced for Ocean

Avenue. She paid little attention to the stares she received and prayed she didn't meet up with anyone she knew.

On his walk down Ocean Avenue, Officer Jake Hennessey spotted a woman in the park. She was tall and slim with a heart-shaped face surrounded with dark curls. Drawn to her long, sexy legs, he raked her with his gaze. His mouth popped open in appreciation. While his imagination ricocheted with lascivious thoughts, his groin tightened uncontrollably.

Then he spotted her bunny slippers. The brakes in his brain screeched to a halt, pushing his lusty thoughts aside. Was this one of Carmel's notorious eccentrics?

He decided to follow her to be sure she was all right. It wasn't such a difficult task. Eccentricities aside, he'd never seen such sexy legs, and she was hot in her tight shorts. What *was* difficult was keeping his erection under control. He just hoped none of the citizens noticed one of their officers walking around with a hard-on.

The woman turned onto Dolores Street, stopping at an office window. The sign read M. Daniels, Ph.D., Family Therapist. He wondered what the woman was doing here. Glancing at her footwear he had some idea.

She was obviously agitated to find the door locked and mumbled something about walking home for keys. Could this be *her* office?

He busied himself looking into a shop window and let the woman pass by. Her stride more purposeful, she practically ran up Dolores Street to Ocean Avenue. He swore he heard her bunny slippers squeal in protest as she rounded the corner onto Ocean.

By the time Maisie reached Mission Street, she was tired and fed up. A fine sheen of perspiration covered her body and her feet ached. Normally, Ocean Avenue's steep hill wouldn't have bothered her, but today in slippers and high anxieties, she considered telling Pam she was taking the whole day off. If her afternoon went anything like her morning, she'd much rather climb back into bed. Tomorrow had to be better.

Then she spotted it. Swensen's Ice Cream Parlor. There was nothing she could do to stop her feet from carrying her through the doors.

Her mouth watered as she ran her finger along the long glassed-in freezer compartment, looking for her favorite. Her pulse sped up when she spotted the brand new tub in the freezer. The fruity mixture glistened, daring her to buy a scoop. The compressor fan blew warm air on her legs, intensifying her hunger for the icy treat.

Then she remembered her wallet was in her purse. Undoubtedly, the wallet was cozied up to her house keys, the two laughing at her.

Her eyes stung with frustration. She looked down the counter, which suddenly seemed a lot longer. Since she'd entered, several people had come in and were waiting for their turn.

Her heart pounded with embarrassment. All their gazes wavered between her face and her bunny slippers. She couldn't just walk out after drooling all over the glass freezer. How could anyone wearing bunny slippers in the middle of an 80-degree day keep her pride as she left an ice cream store without a scoop in her hand?

That's when she saw the police officer again. Her stomach tightened when his gaze met hers. He stood on the sidewalk at the shop window, staring at her. This close, she could tell he spent his free time on the beach. He was lean, tanned and his hair was sun-kissed. Even from this distance, she could see the golden tones of his eyes.

She nervously pulled her gaze from his and glanced back at the young man behind the counter, her thoughts back on the problem at hand. Praying silently, she thrust her hand into her pocket. There had to be some change. Just fifty cents was all she needed.

Her heart pounded when her fingers grazed the edge of a wad of paper. She extracted a dollar bill. One single dollar bill was wadded at the bottom corner of her shorts pocket.

"Thank God," she whispered and kissed George Washington's image square on the face.

"Are you ready to order, Dr. Daniels?" asked the clerk impatiently.

Maisie cursed the intimacy of a small town. The young man wearing the silly paper hat behind the counter was unfamiliar to her, but he knew her. She had no doubt he'd rush home tonight and tell his family and friends about the crazy therapist in her bunny slippers. Her career would be ruined by morning.

Maisie squared her shoulders and said, "Yes, I am. Tutti-Frutti, please," and slapped her dollar on the counter. "Two scoops. I need it." She murmured the last under her breath.

Her moment of panic gone now that she had her double-dip in hand, she stepped through the shop door and prepared to take her first bite of the creamy delight. All other thoughts were pushed aside. Her mouth watered, taste buds worked overtime, stomach grumbled at the delay.

Finally, her lids fluttered closed as she brought the cone to her lips. The sweet fruity smell mixed with cream assaulted her senses. The chill tickled at her lips the instant before they made contact. She moaned aloud but didn't care. She was about to lose herself in the best flavor ice cream ever created. Her lips parted …

"You could get arrested for that," came a deep, sexy voice beside her.

Maisie's eyes snapped open. Her body jolted from the start and the ice cream went flying through the air to land on the hot pavement.

"I'm *so* sorry," Jake was instantly embarrassed for having startled the woman and sorry for her loss. He took the naked cone from her trembling fingers.

He'd continued to follow her through town and was thankful when she stopped at Swensen's. He needed to catch his breath, and get control of his erection. Her ass would be his undoing.

He saw her agitation while he watched her in the shop and wondered again what a beautiful woman like her was doing wandering the streets of Carmel in her slippers. She seemed perfectly normal otherwise.

Their gazes met suddenly and his heart hammered a hole in his chest. Even through the frustration that worried her features, she was certainly a beauty. Her green eyes were dazzling. He wondered again if she was a Carmel eccentric, or if she was M. Daniels. That still didn't explain the bunny slippers. Maybe she was eccentric after all. He meant to find out. And her walking out of the ice cream parlor with a double dip was just the motive he needed.

Tutti-Frutti Blues

Ever since Carmel's ban on eating ice cream on the streets had been passed, it had been the bane of the police force. There were criminals out there. Like jaywalkers and people who'd parked over their 30-minute limit! There were more important things to do than hunt down offenders of the ice cream ban.

Okay, so Carmel was a boring town to police, but after ten years on the San Francisco force, he deserved a hassle-free job. This woman was the most exciting thing he'd come across since moving here six months ago.

When she emerged from the shop, he waited a moment to see what she'd do. He expected her to continue on to her destination. But when she stopped in front of him, oblivious to his presence, he could only watch.

The cone had her hypnotized. She drew the cone toward her, lips curving. Her eyelids shut, her full lips parted, the tip of her pink tongue darted out. He wasn't sure if it was his groan of arousal or hers.

They both watched the double scoop fly off the cone. He heard her whimper at the loss and instantly felt apologetic for startling her.

"I'm sorry," he repeated. "I'll buy you another."

She slowly lifted her gaze to his. He saw disappointment in her eyes, her lips trembling. "It's okay. I didn't need it anyway." She glanced back at the melting glob between their feet.

"There's a difference between need and want," he said. Like, while he didn't *need* the complications of a woman in his life, he found he *wanted* to pull her into his arms and console her. "This was my fault. Let me buy you another cone."

She took a deep breath and when their gazes met once more, he noticed she'd relaxed. "No, honest, it's alright. I don't really have the time for it. I'm already late."

"Can I walk you to wherever you were going?" he offered.

She crossed her arms. Jake couldn't help notice how it made her breasts swell against her t-shirt. He swallowed hard.

"Why would I let you do that?" she asked, lifting a single, beautiful eyebrow. "I don't even know you...Sergeant Hennessey, is it?" He saw her glance at his nameplate, forgetting he was in uniform.

He grinned, thrusting out his hand. "Please, call me

Jake."

She hesitated before taking his hand. He felt a jolt race through him at her touch.

"Dr. Maisie Daniels."

"And your friends?" he asked, glancing down at her feet.

Maisie's eyes squeezed shut as she muttered, "For the love of God!"

Jake chuckled at the instant flush of Maisie's cheeks, reluctantly releasing her hand. "It's okay. I've met a lot of the local eccentrics."

"You don't understand," she said. "This has been the day from hell." Without prompting, she proceeded to tell him about her day, which ironically, answered a lot of questions.

"I think we could both use a double-dip," he said. "Please, let me buy you another cone."

"Thanks for the offer, but if I'm not in the office after lunch," she said, looking at her watch, "I'll be looking for another job."

She pulled the tissue from around the cone in his hand and bent to pick up as much of the melted ice cream as she could, then tossed it in a nearby litter can.

"Are you going to give me a ticket for eating ice cream on the street?" she asked.

"Technically, you didn't eat the ice cream. Though I suppose I could cite you for intent." The corner of his mouth quirked.

Maisie must have caught his teasing intention. Her brows drew together seriously, but he could see humor lighting her eyes. "I suppose you're right. Had you not startled me, I'm sure you could've also charged me with willful disregard of the law."

"Which law is that, Dr. Daniels?"

"The one about eating ice cream on the streets."

"Oh," he said with effect. "I thought you meant the one about staying off the grass and not loitering in the park."

"You saw me?" she gasped.

"I saw a woman in bunny slippers in the park, muttering loudly about a dog. Naturally, I was concerned about her safety—"

"—and followed me though town to the ice cream parlor," she finished for him.

"Well...yes." Caught! He omitted the fact that he was following her legs and ass more so than being worried about her mental stability.

"I appreciate the police force's desire to keep me safe," she said, grinning and laughing lightly.

What else could he say but, "You're welcome."

"If you'll excuse me. Work calls, no matter how much I wish I could start this day over again."

Maisie moved to step away from Jake, but he caught her elbow with his fingers. A jolt shot through her body, releasing a riot of butterflies.

"If I can't buy you another ice cream," he said, "would you let me buy you dinner? Tonight?" His unexpected invitation caused her to hesitate. "It's the least I can do. And...I'd like to see your friends again." He flicked a playful glance at her slippers. Rightfully, she punched him in the arm. "Hey, I can get you on assault, too, if you're not careful," he said, laughing and rubbing his arm.

"Serves you right," she told him. He *had* to know how embarrassed she was.

"Seriously. Please. Come to dinner with me. We'll meet in a public place so you won't think I'm some weird stalker bent on molesting your bunnies. Please," he repeated, giving her a pleading look.

She couldn't stop the laughter that bubbled up suddenly at his reference to molesting her bunnies. "With an appeal like that, how can I refuse?" she replied.

"Great. How does The Forge sound? Seven p.m.?"

She wasn't sure he could grin any wider when she agreed. She'd only just met Jake, but her heart pounded with anticipation at seeing him again.

Jake watched Maisie walk across Ocean Avenue and cut through the park. He could have followed her to find out where she lived, but he knew where she worked. If she stood him up, he'd know where to find her.

When she'd disappeared through the thick of the trees, Jake turned and strode along Ocean Avenue, whistling contentedly.

When he woke this morning he would rather have been

spending such a lovely day on the beach instead of going to work. Then he met Maisie and was instantly thankful for drawing foot patrol duty today.

He still had to finish his shift, but he could feel the new pep in his step.

And now that he had a date, he wanted to buy a new shirt before the end of his shift. He'd have to shower at the station so he could be on time.

Maisie looked at her watch the moment she saw Jake walk through the arch cut into the hedges. Seven p.m., on the dot. Her heart flipped as he scanned the patio, his eyes lighting on her almost immediately.

She'd been a nervous wreck since their meeting. Her day had started off with one disaster after another, and it hadn't gotten any better by the time she got home. Her neighbors were all out, so she had to appeal to the nearby market to use their phone. If she hadn't wasted her dollar on the ice cream she could have used a pay phone.

Pam brought the spare keys, then Maisie hurried to get ready for work while Pam waited. By the time they got to the office, Maisie kept dropping things, even once bumping into the desk and sending a stack of files sailing onto the floor. She heaved a sigh of relief when the day finally ended.

Finding something to wear for dinner proved a challenge. After pulling out half the garments in her cluttered closet, she finally chose a light summer dress. Unable to decide on a hairstyle, she just ran a brush through it and left it down.

Jake stepped up to the table and kissed her cheek before sitting beside her at the raised fire pit. That simple kiss ignited the fire of desire. His aftershave assaulted her senses and sent heat shooting through her belly. His whiskey-colored gaze burned a path down her body as she moved. And his sun-kissed hair waved casually around his clean-shaven face. He'd dressed in curve hugging jeans and a white shirt opened just enough to reveal a tuft of hair on his chest.

Her nerves fluttered wildly.

He signaled to the waitress for a beer and a refill of her

Diet Coke. She tried to relax by shifting to cross her legs.

Jake erupted into a fit of laughter. "You're certifiable. You know that, don't you?" he asked, wiping the tears from his eyes.

She lifted a foot and wiggled the bunny ears at him. "I don't know what you mean." She couldn't help laughing with him. She'd been right to bring the slippers with her. They helped break the ice.

The evening passed well with friendly conversation, delicious food and easy-listening background music. At sunset, tiny fairy lights came on, romantically lighting up the hedges and trees.

After dessert, a silence fell between them. Maisie knew the evening would soon be over. She wasn't ready for it to end.

"I've had a wond..." they both started.

Laughing, Maisie said, "You go first," waving her hand in Jake's direction. Her fingers caught the edge of her glass sending the remainder of her cola into his lap. He leapt back with a startled yelp, overturning his chair.

"Oh, my God! I'm so sorry." She dropped to her knees, blotting the dampness on his jeans with her napkin. He said nothing as she worked, but she felt the tension in the air. When her hand brushed the firmness in his jeans, she gasped. "Oh!"

Jake slowly removed Maisie's suddenly frozen hand from his erection and assisted her back into her chair. He righted his own and reseated himself. Neither of them spoke until after the waitress brought the bill. Jake paid, then turned back to the still silent Maisie. He didn't know her well enough to read her thoughts, but with her gaze focused on the fire, she appeared more startled than upset.

He took her hand in his and said, "I'm going to walk you home." She didn't protest when he stood and helped her to her feet. After her discovery, he didn't think it was any great secret how he felt about her, so he slipped his arm around her and pulled her close.

As they crossed the road to Sixth Street, Maisie missed the curb and tripped. Jake caught her before she hit the ground, but she twisted her ankle anyway.

"I don't know what's wrong with me today. It seems like I can't do anything right."

He thought she was crying by the way her shoulders shook, but she surprised him by laughing.

"It could be worse. You're lucky you twisted your ankle in the company of a knight-in-shining armor." He bent and lifted her into his arms. "Just give me directions and I'll have you at the castle gates before you know it."

She laughed, then put her arm around his neck and pointed up Sixth Avenue.

During the short walk, Jake wondered what it would take to get another date with the destructive Dr. Daniels. He loved the feel of her in his arms. Her body felt right against his. She was sharp witted and intelligent to talk with. And he had to admit she was damned sexy in pink bunny slippers.

He chuckled to himself as he set her on the porch. He took the keys from her to unlock the door. Her sense of humor appealed to him. He hadn't expected her to wear her slippers to dinner, but the moment he saw them, he thought he could love her. He didn't necessarily believe in love at first sight, but after spending the evening with her, he knew his feelings were moving in that direction.

Maisie watched Jake step through the door, flip on the light and glance quickly around. "Habit," he told her. "Just checking to make sure everything's okay."

Stepping inside, she offered, "Coffee? It's the least I can do to thank you for dinner, and for carrying me home." She hung her head, laughing lightly. "I'm such an ass sometimes."

She felt his fingers on her chin, lifting her gaze to his.

"You have a beautiful ass," he said, winking. "Sure, I'll stay for coffee."

She felt her cheeks flame at his comment, but said nothing. How could she after a statement like that?

He helped her into the kitchen and sat at the tiny table while she made coffee. She set a kettle of water on the stove to heat, then scooped grounds in the coffee press. It was when she reached for the cups that she stepped wrong on her foot, sending pain shooting through her ankle. She fell backwards. Jake caught her for the second time that night. The cup in her hand shattered on the floor.

"Sit. I'll make the coffee." When she'd settled in a chair, he asked, "Do you have any peas in the freezer?"

"Peas?" She lifted an eyebrow at the question.

"For your ankle." He went to her freezer and found the small sack and, after folding a kitchen towel around it, sat down across from her and gently pulled her foot into his lap. He placed the package of frozen peas over her ankle and held it in place. "The cold will help bring down the swelling. You use peas because they're small and curve around your ankle better than broccoli."

His wink made her laugh. She appreciated his effort to make her feel better. It worked.

While he had her foot in his lap, he boldly stroked her calf. She didn't protest, but relaxed with his ministrations. His fingers were firm yet tender. She tried convincing herself the pain radiated up her leg and the massage was helping, but in reality she wished he'd stroke the rest of her body as he was her calf. Her heart thrummed at the thought.

"I can't remember a day in my life when so many things have gone wrong," she managed to say, trying to shift her thoughts.

"We all have off days."

"A couple things going wrong are normal. I think I've won the lottery on bad luck today," she told him.

"It'll be better tomorrow."

"Are you always so nice?"

He smiled. "It got me a date with a beautiful woman, didn't it?"

She flushed again at his comment but held his gaze. Her heart thundered, making it difficult to breathe.

His gaze smoldered, captivating her. Then he raised her leg. He brushed his lips across her ankle, instantly relieving the pain. He didn't stop there but moved along her leg, placing tiny kisses as he went. When he reached her inner thigh she squeaked with both surprise and pleasure.

Jake looked up as he lowered her leg to the floor, then dropped to his knees between her thighs. He cupped her face in both hands. The warmth of his palms sent shivers rushing through her body. Her breath caught as he leaned into her.

The instant their lips met she was lost. She wrapped her arms around his shoulders and clutched his shirt. The scent of his skin mingled with his light cologne, intoxicating her. His lips did everything to her that his gaze promised.

Jake knew it was a mistake to be so forward with Maisie, but he couldn't help himself. Touching her skin enraged his senses. At this moment, need and want melded into one and he found he needed Maisie in his life and he wanted her to himself.

Grasping her hips, he pulled her forward on the chair and ground his erection against her. Her legs went around his hips and held him while she scored his back with her nails. He arched at the pleasure-pain, groaning into her sweet mouth. She still tasted of apple and cinnamon from dessert and he wanted to eat her up.

God, how he wanted her!

His heart pounded in his ears at the thought of ripping off both of their clothes so he could feel her naked body on his. He smoothed his hand up the center of her belly and between her breasts until he found the tiny buttons at the top of her dress, intending to get her naked first, but the moment his fingers popped the first button, the kettle whistled on the stove.

Reluctantly, he pulled away and reached over to turn off the gas. The whistle died, leaving the kitchen quiet as a tomb.

Sitting back on his heels, he looked into her passion-filled eyes. He finally said, "I'm sorry. I shouldn't have done that." What had he been thinking? He'd only just met her and here he was, on his knees in her kitchen trying to take her clothes off. He couldn't explain it, but he desired her more than he'd ever wanted any other woman.

"Ever since I met you this morning, you're all I can think about. You're the most amazing woman I've ever known, and after tonight I don't think I'll ever be the same again."

Jake's confession knocked the breath out of Maisie. How was it possible he felt the same things as she? One date and she was ready to let him throw her on the floor and strip her naked.

Her heart squeezed into her throat and she barely got the words out. "I can't stop thinking about you either. When you look at me, I feel things I've never felt before. I can't explain it. We've only just met, yet..."

"...it's like we've always known each other."

That was exactly what she felt.

"I really like you, Maisie. I don't want to scare you off by being too aggressive. But, there's something about you. I want to get to know you better. I'm just not sure how long I can keep my hands off you."

Maisie's heart soared. "I want to get to know you better, too. It feels right between us. How could we go too fast? And after everything that's gone wrong today, being with you is the only right thing I've done. Don't spoil it for me now." She felt like she was pleading, but she spoke from the heart. She knew she was falling for him.

"I was wrong about you."

"You probably still think I'm certifiable," she said, resting her uninjured foot on his chest, stroking his chin with the bunny ears.

"Yes, you are that," he said, chuckling. He leaned forward and stroked the hair from her temple. "What I mean is, I thought I really liked you. Now...I think I could love you."

Maisie's heart flipped and she pulled him back into her arms, wrapping her legs around his hips once more. "I think I could love you, too."

After looking for so long, she'd finally found him. Jake wasn't just Mr. Right. He was her hero. He'd rescued her from more than a twisted ankle and endless nights alone in her house. He'd saved her from the Tutti-Frutti blues. If not for him, Maisie was sure she'd drown her frustrations in ice cream, trying to convince herself the fruit was good for her, while her ass grew to the size of a melon.

Hmmm, she thought, *Jake said he likes my ass, so maybe the bigger the better.*

"I'm taking you to bed. Our first time won't be on the kitchen floor." He rose, scooping her into his arms.

"Don't forget the ice cream," she said, and leaned into the freezer for the carton. She wiggled her eyebrows, grinning wickedly. "We won't need spoons."

Be sure to visit Kemberlee Shortland's website
www.kemberlee.com

A Lover's Serenade – Almost

by Rekha Ambardar

• *Kalamazoo, Michigan - It's against the law to serenade your girlfriend*

She sat on a high mahogany stool, framed in the pink adobe archway that led onto the balcony with golden sunset radiating behind it like a gigantic halo. She'd have been pretty if she weren't so plump, and if her sleek, glistening hair hadn't been pulled back in a severe knot. He thought her probably in her mid-twenties.

The moment she caught his eye, Garrod Tyler edged away from his Kane Products colleagues and turned his ear toward the woman, trying to hear what she was saying. She spoke in Mexican, and his Mexican was sketchy. He hadn't wanted to come all the way to Monterrey, Mexico when Kane's Corn Products had sent him here from Kalamazoo.

"I'm dyslexic," he'd told them. "I don't know Mexican and never will."

They told him they'd give him a test to determine how dyslexic he was, but he finally relented, saying, "No, no need for that. I'll go."

So, here he was in Monterrey, homesick, and at a business party.

"Who's that?" he asked Juan, one of Kane's sales associates, nodding toward the woman on the stool.

Juan turned to look in the direction Garrod indicated. "That's Inez Lujan. She wants a job at Kane Products. She just got a degree from an American college. She was thinking of applying for your job, but by the time she decided, they'd already hired you."

Garrod's interest peaked. "You know her well?"

Juan nodded. "We were in school together as children, and kept in touch now and then. As you can see, all the attendees here aren't from the company. Some are friends of friends and others are here because they heard of the party and just wanted to come have a good time."

"Hope she wasn't too disappointed when I was hired," Garrod said, watching the movements her mouth made as she talked rapidly to a man and a woman standing nearby.

"She did say maybe you wouldn't like it here and might go back to the States. I'll introduce you to her and then she won't be such a formidable competitor. Then you can tell me what you think of her." Juan threw him a wink and a grin as they moved to where she sat.

She stopped talking to her companions as they approached. Garrod was meeting her to stop any idea she might still harbor of angling for his job. One thought stuck in his mind, though – she knew Mexican and he didn't. But he could learn, couldn't he? For the sake of his job? There was no going back now, not after Jessica had broken off with him.

"Inez, meet our new sales associate, Garrod Tyler. He's new in Monterrey and could use an introduction to our fair city," Juan said. "Would you consider taking him on a short tour? I wouldn't ask you if I didn't know how much you enjoy showing people our local sights."

"What's in it for me?" A slow, lazy smile careened across her face. "A job?" Her English was good, but heavily accented.

Juan shrugged. "Who knows? If something opens up, I'll let you know." He turned and left them together.

"So, you are intimidated by our city?" Inez watched as Garrod pulled a wickerwork chair near her and sat down.

"Intimidated, no. It's just different," Garrod said. "Juan said you just got a degree from the U.S. Did you like it there?"

"Yes," she said, but sounded unconvincing. "I missed my mother and extended family. How about you? How do you like it here?"

"Okay so far. But the food's a little too spicy. I'll get used to that in time, though."

Inez laughed. "And I carry salsa picante in my purse when I go out to eat."

Garrod grinned. "That's different."

Somebody came by holding a tray of glasses with punch. Garrod helped himself to one, wondering if it was spiked. He turned to her. "Like one?"

She shook her head. "I had mine."

"Juan tells me you're looking for a job at Kane's, "Garrod said.

"Anywhere. I need a job."

He glanced at the fashionable leather calf-length skirt and gold jewelry she wore. She didn't appear destitute. "Take it easy. The first thing to getting a job or a loan is to look like you don't need it."

He looked up as his boss, Manuel Munoz, strode over. "Hope you've met everyone here, Garrod. We want you to feel at home."

"Don't worry. I'm doing okay. Inez might even be my tour guide in Monterrey," Garrod said.

"Hello, Inez." Manuel smiled at her as if he knew her. She might have been to these parties before, and if so, she'd be working at Kane's Monterrey branch before too long—if that was how the hiring was done around here.

"Well, enjoy the party," Manuel said and disappeared to greet a group of people just coming in.

Garrod's gaze strayed to the picturesque opulence of the hall, with its polished red floor tiles, pink adobe archways and large splashy oil paintings. It had the illusion of space.

"So, will you show me around Monterrey next weekend? I don't have a car yet, so it'll have to be the bus or hitchhiking."

"We won't have to do that. I'll show you Barrio Antiquo by horse drawn carriage. It's a delightful experience, and I think you'll enjoy it. Monterrey has soccer and bull fights, if you like that sort of thing."

"One of these days I want to participate in bull running." Garrod turned to see her reaction.

"Are you loco? Why?"

"The excitement."

Garrod had decided it was time he took an interest in the fabric of life in Mexico. If anything could pull him out of his lassitude, something like bull running would. Talk of a brusque introduction to Mexico and its attractions. Maybe it would be just what he needed.

By ten o'clock the party dwindled to a straggling few and he got up and said his goodbyes. As he walked out to the portico and went down the stone steps, short footsteps hurried behind him. He turned and saw Inez.

"How did you get here?" she queried, a tote bag slung across her shoulder.

"I walked. It's just around the corner from my apartment."

"I'll drop you." She motioned toward a chili pepper red Jeep by the crowded curb, and he got in on the passenger's side.

She started the Jeep and turned sharply onto the road. An irate cab driver shouted and pumped a fist at her. It didn't seem to affect her. "Mexican stock car racing drivers learn by driving through our traffic."

"I'm finding that out." He leaned inward automatically as vehicles came dangerously close to them and then veered away in a split second.

"This Saturday, how about I pick you up and show you Barrio Antiqua. You'll like it."

"Barrio Antiqua? What does it have?"

"Many cultural attractions. There's even - how you say – wild night life there," Inez said with a laugh.

"That would be great." He pointed to a cream colored apartment building that shone in a mellow glow in the mix of moonlight and city lights. "That's where I live."

She dropped him at the curb and swerved off into the inky darkness. Watching as she disappeared around the corner, he silently bet it was all just a strange dream.

For the rest of the week, Garrod was lost in his work at the office making calls to local clients. Now and again the thought that on Saturday Inez would show him Barrio Antiqua pushed itself into his mind as he thumbed through the contact list on his cell phone. At least now when he called folks at home, he could honestly tell them he was seeing the place and pretend he was enjoying it.

For lunch, he bought an enchilada from one of the outdoor stands and took it to the Plaza where a fountain played on the cobblestones encircling it. Kids played in the water from the spray. As his gaze strayed to the vibrant colors and noise around him, another thought clubbed him. He wasn't attracted to Inez, possibly because he wasn't over Jessica yet. How did you get over the only girl you ever loved since high school and were all set to marry when she threw you over just because he'd been laid off from a job?

"Garrod!" A voice called from behind. Turning around, he saw Juan waving as he got out of his car and walked over to him. "You could have come to The Cantina with us for lunch."

"It's okay. I'm just enjoying the scenery and the enchilada."

"Here all by yourself? What you need is a girlfriend," Juan said grinning. "My plan failed, my friend."

"Your plan?"

"Introducing you to Inez. I invited her to the party to introduce you to her."

"You mean she wasn't really looking for a job?"

"She may be since she has friends at Kane's, but for now she's lined up a job at Phizz Soft Drinks."

"Sorry your little plan didn't work, buddy." Garrod chuckled conspiratorially. "But...we are supposed to go to Barrio Antiqua on Saturday." He raised his forefinger to make the point.

"That's a good start." Juan checked his watch. "See you at the office." He sprinted back toward his car and was gone.

A twinge of annoyance prodded him. Now everyone was worried about him – his dislike of the place and his loneliness were clearly showing. Monterrey was beautiful, so were the people, but his heart wasn't here. He missed Jessica, like a captive used to his captor. Go figure.

On his way home later that evening, he saw posters about the weekend of Sanmiguelada – the running of the bulls – which was this coming Friday. He hadn't missed the signs – visitors pouring in from all parts of Mexico to participate.

He stared at the poster on the wall outside the office building. Hundreds of bulls stampeded behind runners who wore blue jeans, white shirts and red bandanas tied around the neck. What a way to kill yourself.

Yet the more he saw the posters each day, the more they intrigued him. The picture haunted his soul and wouldn't let him be. It filled him with a desire to be one of the runners, too. Then he made his decision. He would run with the bulls. He wanted to prove to himself he could do it. Butterflies kicked in his stomach at the thought. He'd do it. It would be a story to tell his grandkids someday—if he ever got married.

After work on Friday, he took the bus to San Miguelada de Allende. By the time he reached it, the bars, restaurants, and cantinas were ringing with activity. The aroma of corn tortillas, onions, and chili peppers sifted through the sun-baked air, making him ravenously hungry. He stopped at a small stall and bought two beef tacos smothered in onions and tomato ketchup and wolfed them down, then chugged down a can of pop.

The event would begin Saturday morning. Part of him knew he should call Inez and cancel their date, but he didn't want to scare her by telling her why. Would she think him a fool for wanting to do this?

In an effort to quell his guilty conscience for not calling Inez, he stepped into a nearby bar.

"Good thing you came today, my friend. Tomorrow, there'll be a ban on alcoholic sales. Being chased by a bull and being drunk to boot is a bad combination, amigo," the bartender told him, scrutinizing him. "I sell drinks. I should know. Are you here to watch the bull running?"

"No," Garrod said. "I'm running with the bulls."

The man shook his head. "Be careful." He walked away as if washing his hands of Garrod's foolishness.

Garrod checked into a box-sized, red-tiled motel for the night.

At nine o' clock the next morning, he arrived at el Jardin, San Miguel's central plaza, which began to fill with people. The streets around the Jardin were blocked off with barricades, inside of which a dozen or so bulls would be let loose.

He saw some onlookers perched on the balconies in restaurants – for a fee of $150, he overheard someone say. Such madness.

He tried not to think of his own craziness. Why was he doing this? He was doing it on a dare – by himself to himself. He'd lost Jessica and had been laid off from his job, only to be shipped off to Mexico. He had to win at something! Surely he could take part in bull running and survive. He was up to it. He'd run track in high school and had worked out every other day back in the States. He was in good shape, much better than many of the runners he saw nearby.Men in cowboy hats, and even a few women, piled into the plaza. He suspected the women would leave as soon as the bulls were let loose. Some of them, he'd been told, would just stay to taunt the bulls and make them madder than ever, and then would escape to safety.

The day grew hotter and the sun blazed down. Finally, at noon, the bulls that were trucked in from the ranches were let loose through the barricades. Garrod was ahead of the crowd, at the front of the mass of runners. If the bull stampeded over him, they'd have to get through the others behind him first.

A horrendous noise resounded through the square as the bulls started charging to the taunts of the bloodthirsty crowd— and Garrod ran for all he was worth. He ran, his heart pounding, as the sounds of the bull's hooves grew closer, ever closer. He thought only that he wanted to survive this, not end his life gored by a bull, a loco Gringo annihilated by one of the massive beasts. What was he doing running with the bulls anyway?

He ran as he'd never run before. He could almost feel the hot breath of the raging animal behind him. He shifted to the left, away from the bull's path, and felt a brief respite, even as sweat dripped into his eyes, making it difficult for him to see. He ran on, and as he did, he felt his energy being quickly sapped in the sweltering heat. To his relief, he realized the bull wasn't on his back, although another quickly gained speed behind him.

Garrod sprinted as fast as he could to stay ahead of many of the runners. Faster, faster he ran, rapidly out of breath. How long could he keep at it? He dashed on ahead, just barely able to reach out of the enclosure. He spotted a small space in the crowd of runners, glided through it and out of the barricade, and climbed up a small tree outside a cantina. He coughed and caught his breath, panting, hot and sweaty. He'd only just escaped. But the thrill of running was not to be believed.

Back at the motel, he saw the angry red bruises and scrapes, and remembered he'd fallen and called out to Heaven when he heard the snort of the rampaging bull behind him.

Despite the approaching night, Garrod took the last bus back and at midnight he stumbled into his apartment, sank onto the bed, and slept the sleep of the dead.

He awoke to a loud knocking on the front door. He glanced at the bedside clock. Eight in the morning. Who'd be knocking on a Sunday? He dragged himself out of bed.

"Who is it?" he called out.

"Inez."

Here she was. Somehow he'd have to explain his escapade with the bulls instead of going to the Barrio with her yesterday. Would she forgive him? A part of him hoped so. He opened the door.

"Inez, I'm sorry. I wanted to call and tell you about yesterday, but didn't know how. I went to the bull running." He stood aside. "Please come in."

"You did *what?*" she squealed in obvious disbelief. "You could have killed yourself."

Garrod nodded gingerly. "I discovered that very quickly. I didn't tell you in advance because I feared you wouldn't approve."

She peered at him. "You look terrible." A worried expression crossed her face. Then she looked around. "Where's your kitchen. I'll make coffee. You *do* have a coffee pot, don't you?"

He pointed in the direction of the small space on the far end of the living room. "In the cabinet above the counter you'll find the coffee grounds. The coffee maker's in there, too. Give me just a minute. I'm going to wash and make myself presentable."

By the time he showered and grabbed the towel to dry off, and pulled on shorts and a T shirt, the welcome aroma of freshly brewed coffee floated his way.

Taking mental inventory, he figured Inez was here to find out why he wasn't around yesterday to go to the Barrio. Yet now she stood making coffee and looked worried over his plight. Couldn't be that she was interested in him, could it? Because it wasn't going to help. He was still carrying the torch for Jessica, when he should have thrown that torch out the window long ago, especially after the way she dumped him.

When he reached the small table near the kitchen area, his only piece of furniture, Inez had two steaming mugs of coffee on it. He pulled out a chair for her. "Have a seat."

She took the seat, her eyes raking over him as she did.

"So," she drawled, "how was the bull running? You must have run very fast. There are more casualties than victories in that sport."

Did her words convey a feeling of relief, or was he reading in more than was there? He wondered why her thoughts suddenly mattered. "I'm a good runner. I just wanted to see if I was still good at it."

"Tell me about yourself. Do you have a girlfriend back in the States?"

"Did. We were engaged to be married, but she decided not to go through with the wedding when I was laid off from my previous job."

Garrod saw the obvious question in Inez's eyes. "I don't want you to think it was all about my job. It was more complicated than that and Jessica had problems at home."

"What problems?"

"Her father was ill and she had to help her mother take care of him. So I couldn't force her to make a decision – any decision." Garrod shook his head. "When I got this job, I thought she might come back, but she didn't want to come to Mexico." As he spoke he felt the familiar choke in his throat. Jessica still hadn't left his psyche.

"In truth, it seems she didn't really want me after all, just the prestige and salary she thought my position held." He wanted no pity even though it was still a sore point. "It was funny, because, on her birthday, I thought I'd go her house and serenade her."

"Serenade?" Inez looked interested.

"You know. Men go to their girlfriend's window and sing a song. You do that here in Mexico a lot, don't you?"

"Oh, *si*. I know what you're saying. Very romantic, no?" Inez smiled, and her face lit up.

"Romantic, yes, but it didn't work. I got busted for singing under her window."

Inez looked puzzled again, and Garrod realized he'd have to explain about American slang. "Well, where I used to live—in Kalamazoo—it was against the law to serenade your girlfriend. At least, that's what the policeman told me when he threatened to haul me off to jail."

"What did he do?"

"Gave me a warning, but said if I was caught again, I'd be

arrested the next time." It sounded silly even to Garrod.

"Then a lot of people would be arrested here in Mexico, because serenading is our lifeblood and pastime."

"I guess I was in the wrong place then."

Inez sipped her coffee, seemingly lost in thought.

"How about you? Is your family here?"

"I have a large family of uncles, aunts and cousins. I live with my mother and younger brother." She seemed suddenly distant, for all her vivacity. "My father and an older sister died in a car accident when I was six years old. My mother had my brother and me to take care of."

"Sorry to hear that. What happened then?"

"My grandfather said he'd take care of us if my mother moved in with them and took care of the household. Like a housekeeper." An edge of sarcasm slipped into her tone. "But Mother wanted none of that. She took us both and went to college in the States to get her degree, then opened a photography studio. I help her with it. She's tough, that lady."

And intriguing, like you, Garrod wanted to say, but wasn't sure how she'd take it. He took several sips of the coffee. It was strong and refreshing, and it cleared his head just as if he'd given it a good shake.

"You've been through a lot. Your mother, especially."

"Yes," Inez agreed, watching him closely. "What about you? What brought you here?"

"My job—but mostly Jessica. She's now engaged to the president of an important company."

"You are sad?"

"I was." He paused for a moment and just looked at her. "Now I don't know."

Sympathy and understanding showed in her gentle smile. "You deserve the best."

Something in her smile warmed him. It was the first time he'd allowed himself to feel anything since he'd come to Monterrey. Still, he didn't want pity, hers or anyone else's.

He shrugged. "It isn't the end of the world."

"But I can see it has affected you plenty, as you say in America."

Garrod chuckled at her use of American slang.

Inez finished her coffee and washed her mug in the sink. "Actually, I came to invite you to my grandmother's house for the comida."

"Comida?"

"Lunch after church. Every Sunday, after church, we meet there – my mother, brother and I, and all my aunts, uncles and cousins. In Mexico, we're always surrounded by our relatives."

"That's a nice custom. So you're never lonely." Did she miss growing up without a father? He wondered.

"That is true. Though sometimes our houses get very crowded and noisy." She laughed. "Anyway, there's plenty of food and nice people."

"Thanks, I'd like to come." Here was a chance to see how families lived in Mexico, and there couldn't be a better way to spend the day. He'd only been to bars so far.

Garrod went into the bedroom to change into a pair of jeans. He had to look presentable at the very least.

"My car is parked outside, when you're ready," Inez called from the living room.

Minutes later, they were pushed along by the tide of traffic honking behind them. The glare of the morning sun hurt his eyes.

He saw the contrasts he'd heard about in the houses and the people and the array of small dwellings. Hills and vegetation in the distance looked starved for water. But the dull glaze had a soothing effect on him and he was glad it wasn't a working day. If it were, he'd be on his way to meet the distributors of Kane's Corn Products and he'd have to have all his wits about him, not half dozing.

They came to a hacienda-style house and Inez pulled into the curved cobbled driveway and parked. "This is my grandmother's house."

She led the way around the back to a large stone patio, where a group of people stood chattering or sitting on white wickerwork chairs. A large man was barbecuing meat on a grill, and children ran around, playing a noisy game of tag.

A plump elderly woman with thick white hair walked toward them. "Inez!" She grabbed her in an embrace.

Inez spoke to her in Mexican, then turned to Garrod. "This is my grandmother. She's very happy you could come. She says you are very handsome."

Embarrassed, Garrod laughed. "That's kind of her. Please

tell her I'm honored to be here." It sounded stilted, and he wished he knew Mexican enough to converse with the old lady.

A long table was laid out with every delectable kind of food, exotic and colorful, and Garrod's mouth watered, wondering when they'd be eating. He didn't have to wait long. The man at the grill finished his chore and carried an enormous platter of steaks to the table.

There was a sudden whisper of interest as a tall man dressed in a dark suit walked toward the gathering. He seemed to know everyone and smiled his way through them and approached Inez.

"How lovely you look."

"Thank you, Mateo."

"I see you have a guest." The man's statement was formal, his manner deliberate.

"This is Garrod. He works at the big company in Monterrey."

A thin, petite woman and a slender youth came out of the house.

"Come and meet my mother, Anya, and brother, Julio." Inez waved to them and they walked over.

"Glad to meet you," Garrod said, shaking hands with both of them. It was obvious they didn't speak much English, so they smiled at him a lot and then turned their attention to Mateo.

"Mateo seems like a person of great interest here."

Inez sighed. "He's very well known and respected, owns landed property." A cloud flitted over her face.

"I get the impression you don't much care for him."

"He's a family friend and I'm expected to marry him."

Garrod jerked his head toward her. "What? I thought that sort of thing didn't go on anymore."

"It still does." She played with a big silver ring on her finger thoughtfully. "And I have to make a decision soon."

"The decision to marry him?"

She nodded, then looked up and gave him a wry grin. "Romantic, no?"

"Very," he said sarcastically.

"Let's try to forget all that for now. Why don't you let me introduce you to everyone?" She took his hand and went around groups of people who obviously had a lot to say to one another, even though they probably saw each other just the day before.

The food was ready and they all sat at the long table which had been spread with enchiladas and dip of every color, roast beef, chicken, and meat wrapped in tortillas. Garrod had never seen so many meat dishes. He probably couldn't taste all of it, but throwing caution to the wind, he decided to give it his best effort.

Inez was quiet on the ride back, and Garrod didn't want to pry.

"I enjoyed the lunch a lot. Just thought you should know. And your relatives are very nice." He glanced at her, at the faraway expression on her face.

The revelation that she was expected to marry had unsettled him, and he wasn't sure why. She was only just becoming a friend and she certainly was free to do what she wanted – or had to do. He was no modern-day Zorro to rescue her from the wealthy guy. She wasn't going to discuss him, Garrod could see. He settled back in his seat and tried to enjoy the ride back. A breeze filtered through and he felt drowsy from eating too much. When she didn't say anything, effects of all the food he'd stuffed himself with began to take hold and he dozed off in the car. Inez shook him awake when they reached his apartment. He got out and waved and watched her drive away. As he turned to enter his apartment, Garrod wondered why the thought of her possibly marrying another man so bothered him.

On Monday, when he was closing a wholesale shipment deal to Tijuana, his office phone rang. It was his supervisor, Dave Kemper, from the Kalamazoo Home Office.

"We want you here for a meeting with the boss as soon as you can," he said.

Garrod's heart thudded in his chest. He swallowed and said, "Anything wrong?"

"No, no. We just have several new options to discuss." Dave sounded friendly and matter of fact.

It was probably something to do with some deals, Garrod thought, and they wanted him there. He phoned his mother and told her the good news.

She was ecstatic. "That's wonderful, dear. You know, Jessica has been asking about you."

"Jessica?"

"Yes. Don't know why."

Garrod hung up thoughtfully after talking to his mother for a few more minutes.

When Inez called to say hello, he told her about his upcoming trip to the States.

"Are you happy to be going?"

"I sure am." He should have toned down his enthusiasm, or she'd think he was ungrateful for all her help. He couldn't help it. He was just happy to be going home, even if just for a week.

On Friday, he was ticketed, checked in and seated on his Air Mexico flight to Houston. From there he switched flights to Kalamazoo.

He had never been so happy to breathe the clear crisp air of autumn. The late afternoon sun glowed through the glass tunnel as he stepped off the plane and then picked up his luggage.

His mother met him at the entrance to the secure area and gave him a long hug. "You look thin. You've been gone only two months and you've lost weight."

"I missed you, too, Mom." He hadn't lost weight, but if she thought so, it didn't bother him.

"Now, what's this about Jessica?" Garrod asked as she drove the ten miles to her house in the suburbs.

"I don't know. She asked about you and if you'd be visiting sometime." His mother took a turn on the long circular road that culminated at a dead end where a mid-sized red brick and beige-washed house stood serenely near a willow tree. Garrod felt a leap of happiness to be home. That and a good home-cooked meal were worth everything to him. "I told her you'd be home today, dear, so don't be surprised if she calls."

After a chicken casserole dinner and coffee he helped his mother clear and wash the dishes. When the phone rang he went to pick it up. It was Jessica.

"Well, this *is* a surprise," Garrod said.

"How are you, Garrod? It's so nice you're home. How's Mexico?"

"It's okay. I'm getting used to it." Not – but he wasn't going to tell her that. In fact, he had no intention of telling

Jessica anything. He just planned to listen. "How are you? And when is the wedding?"

"There is no wedding, Garrod. It's off."

"What?" So that was why she'd been so eager to contact him. He should have known. "What happened?"

"Marrying money isn't all it's cracked up to be. He was a control freak. I'm just glad I found out before we got married."

"Sorry to hear it didn't work out." He could have told her about the marrying money part, if she'd cared to listen to him. "You'll meet the right guy some day and everything will work out."

"That's just it, Garrod. I was wrong to break up with you. I realize that now."

"It's nice to hear that—but it's a little bit late."

"I'd like us to get back together."

Jessica's remark hit him between the eyes like a sandbag. He should have guessed she'd think along those lines. She'd lost her ticket to money, so now she was looking for a second chance. She'd get another chance, but not with him. Images of a pair of sultry brown eyes crept into his memory. In that instant he knew he wasn't the guy for her.

"That's not possible, Jessica. I live in Mexico now. You wouldn't like it there."

"Yes, that's true. But you could get a transfer back to the States, couldn't you?"

"I wouldn't count on that. These things take time. Besides, you and I have different lives now."

She sighed. "I was wrong to think we could go back to where we were."

"Where we were? You're the one who didn't want to give us a chance." He tried to keep his tone level.

"I was in between jobs then, too. Two of us with uncertain futures—what would we have lived on?" Disappointment seeped through her tone, and it surprised Garrod to hear it.

It was no use. He'd used all he had to get over Jessica and now it seemed he had. He was surprised to learn he'd actually moved on.

"You'll be fine, Jessica. I want you to be happy. Something tells me I'm not the guy for you."

"Wish I thought differently. Goodbye, Garrod," she said,

and hung up.

At eight o' clock the next morning, Garrod drove his mother's car to the home office of Kane's Corn Products. It was good to see Dave and all the other guys, but the meeting was with Dave and his boss, Kyle—a man Garrod had never particularly liked.

Garrod followed Dave to Kyle's office.

"Have a seat. You look good. Mexico must agree with you."

Garrod grinned. "Thanks." He wanted to keep chitchat to the minimum to get to the point of the meeting.

"Let me cut to the chase," Kyle said. "We have a new job percolating here, sales manager for our Midwest territory, and we need someone to spearhead that. We've heard great things about you from our Mexico office and thought we'd give you first dibs on it. Would you like to move back to the home office and take charge of that?"

Garrod took a moment to let it sink in. "This sounds good and is just the sort of job I would have liked before. But I've changed since I left here. Grown up, I hope. I'd like to think over it, if that's okay with you."

"Sure, it's okay. Think it over for the week you're here." Kyle rose, went to the coffee pot and filled three mugs. He brought two mugs to where Garrod and Dave sat and handed them out.

When Dave and Garrod left Kyle's office, Dave said, "We'd love to have you back."

Garrod nodded.

At his mother's house, while in the shower later that evening, Garrod came to his decision. He was just carving out new experiences for himself. Sure he'd been homesick, but with some luck, that would disappear when he made more friends. Besides, there was Inez. He'd only known her a short time, but he had to admit there was something special about her.

He'd never have the same feelings for Jessica again, so what was the point of going back to square one? He now accepted they'd never been right for each other. He was a romantic, she only seemed interested in money.

The next morning he gave Kyle his answer. Though surprised, Kyle wished him all the best.

At the end of the week, Garrod's flight touched down at Monterrey and Inez was there, again framed in the golden light of the Mexican sunset. She ran toward him as he disembarked the plane. He caught her in a tight embrace and planted a kiss on her full lips.

There were no words between them. It had taken awhile for him to come to his senses, but this was one serenade he was sure about – for once.

Rekha Ambardar is the author of
HIS HARBOR GIRL and MAID TO ORDER
Be sure to visit Rekha's website
http://rekha.mmebj.com

A Frightful Misconception

by Jennifer Ross

• *Canada - It's illegal to scare someone to death*

Mitch hummed as he boiled water to make some tea for his neighbor, Mrs. Fairfax.

He prepared a tray with two of those dinky little cups and saucers—the ones she was so fond of and he couldn't get his finger through. He fixed her tea the way he knew she liked it, then buttered some toast and added it to the tray. Cream, sugar, the teapot, and he was ready. Pushing the door open with his foot, he brought her the cup and plate of toast.

"Good morning, Mrs. F," he said as he set the tray down on the dresser.

Mrs. Fairfax's voice was frail and reedy. "I was afraid you didn't have time for me this morning, Mitch. I'd hoped you'd come early today, as I had a most distressing night."

"Here, let me help you sit up. Where's that extra pillow I bought you? Ah, here it is, it slipped under the bed a bit "Yes, ma'am, sorry to be late. You can tell me all about it while you drink this. I made you toast, too, and I hope you'll eat it this time." He returned to the dresser to pour a cup for himself, then sat on the chair next to the bed.

"Now, what happened last night to disturb you?"

"It was the noises again. You remember, I told you about them yesterday? They were far worse this time! The banging and the creaking, so loud and—"

"Now, now, don't get all upset. Remember your heart."

Obediently, Mrs. Fairfax nodded and sipped her tea.

When Mitch was satisfied she was calmer, he asked, "Could you tell where the noise came from?"

Mrs. Fairfax took a deep and shaky breath. "From right in

167

this room. The noise was everywhere. Bang, bang, creak, creak."

"Have you talked to that old nurse lady, what's-her-name, about it?"

"Her name is Meghan, young man, and she's far too lovely to be called 'old nurse lady.' As a matter of fact, I have. She said she'd tell the doctor, but I don't know what she expected *he* would do about it. I do wish you and Meghan could meet. I know you'd hit it off."

Oh, great. Another old biddy to look after. God, the stress and worry of one is more than enough. "Well, maybe today I'll stick around and wait for her. I think it *is* time we have a talk."

Mrs. Fairfax's expression brightened considerably. "Could you really, Mitchell? I'd hate to keep you from your job. I know they aren't easy to find these days."

"As it happens, there's no work again today, so don't fret about keeping me from it."

"Another lay-off day? But that's the third one this month, isn't it? Oh Mitch, you must let me help you with some money."

"Now Mrs. F, we've been over this before. I'm not a charity case yet, but if I find I'm short on the rent next week, I'll let you know, okay?"

Mrs. Fairfax smiled and nodded her approval. "It's such a shame. A nice, caring, helpful boy like you shouldn't have to worry about making ends meet. You don't take expensive holidays, and you only have that small apartment, it's just not right. Well, I've taken care of everything. You'll see."

"Please, Mrs. F, don't wear out that heart of yours worrying about me. I'll be fine. Now, tell me more about this noise you keep hearing."

Mitch nodded over the rim of his teacup as Mrs. Fairfax nattered on. Finally she grew weary, and Mitch helped her lie down for a nap.

"I'll take these dishes, then wait for that nurse, Meghan, in the other room. Feel free to call out if you need anything."

It didn't take long to clean up, and Mitch wandered through Mrs. Fairfax's living room. He admired the antiques and knickknacks. He didn't turn on the TV for fear the noise would disturb her, and he quickly grew bored.

A Frightful Misconception

He opened the door to Mrs. Fairfax's room and observed the steady rise and fall of her chest in deep sleep. Now was his chance to get some stuff from his place.

His apartment was across the hall. It was a small one-bedroom—not a huge three bedroom like Mrs. Fairfax had. It didn't take long to gather some electronics, and he was back in her apartment within two minutes.

She still slept.

Mitch decided to make a call while he waited for the home-care nurse to arrive.

"Long time no see, man, how's the 'big smoke?' Have you played the new Resident Evil 4 yet? Nah, I just rented it. Want to buy it and more wireless speakers for my system, but it doesn't fit into the budget right now. So, how's it going at the bar? Wait, did you say RadioDive was coming? Sweet! Man, I would love to see them live. Any chance you can snag me a ticket? Yeah, I hear you. Good times, yeah, I know. Yeah, I'll have to put that at the top of my wish list and see what I can do."

He heard the key in the lock of the front door. "Listen, buddy, I gotta go. There's someone coming I wanna talk to. Later, man."

He hung up the phone as a woman made her way into the living room.

Mitch stared in astonishment. *THIS is Meghan? She's the same age as me!*

Meghan was startled to see someone else in the apartment.

She appraised the young man as he introduced himself. Tall and a bit overweight, with short wavy black hair, he wasn't a handsome guy, yet there was something compelling about him. Perhaps it was the piercing blue of his eyes, or his open, trusting gaze. He looked to be two or three years younger than her.

She knew he was Mitch before he mentioned his name, simply because Mrs. Fairfax never spoke about anyone else. *Classic computer geek.* She smiled as she spied the cell-phone and one of those gaming toys on the coffee table. Still, it was awfully good of him to spend so much time caring for a woman who was nothing more than an aging neighbor.

"Mrs. Fairfax is asleep. She had a bad night," Mitch

explained, trying to keep his mind off Meghan's great body. "I wanted to talk to you about the noises she says she hears." He motioned to the couch, then sat beside her.

"Yes, she mentioned them," Meghan said. "Are they getting worse?"

"Yeah, I think so. They're really upsetting her. Look, I know the door is always locked in the mornings, and apart from the building Super, you and I are the only ones with a key. I gotta believe she's imagining it, but her mind seems sharp as a knife. Could it be a side-effect from some medicine you're giving her?"

"I spoke to the doctor and he said hallucinations aren't known side-effects with any of the drugs. There's always a chance it's so rare it's never been recorded, but these aren't new drugs she's on. So I think that's unlikely."

"I don't get it then. It could be someone doing something in one of the units around here, I suppose, but I know most of these people, and none of them have a bed-time past ten o'clock. Besides, I haven't heard a thing, and I'm a very light sleeper."

Mitch got up and went to stare out the window, jamming his hands into the pockets of his baggy pants.

Wow, he's really worried about her. "Could it be the Super, then? How well do you know him?"

Mitch gave a short bark of laughter. "Nah, sounds too much like work for him. I can't believe he'd come up here to repair anything—never mind do it in the middle of the night."

Meghan felt sorry for the poor guy. She suspected Mrs. Fairfax's mind was starting to go, yet he was having trouble accepting the possibility. She could see why Mrs. Fairfax liked him so much. Despite his tough guy act, he seemed genuinely sweet and, well, *nice.*

"How long have you known Mrs. Fairfax?" she asked, as she pushed her long, brown ponytail over her shoulder. Her interest was more about him, and she hoped it wasn't obvious.

"Not that long. I had what I thought at the time was a great job offer." Mitch tried for a wry smile, but it came out a grimace. "So I came to Waterloo from Toronto just over a year ago. We chatted in the elevator a few times. Then, another time I saw her struggling with some bags, so I helped her. After that, she'd bring me cookies and stuff and I'd help her with things around the house. It's only been since she got out of the hospital we've grown to be what you'd call friends."

He felt uncomfortable admitting to a friendship with a woman old enough to be his grandmother, but something about Meghan helped him to talk. He sat beside her—a little closer than he had before—and waited for her reaction.

Meghan placed her hand on his knee and gave a light squeeze. "Well, I think it's wonderful—"

"MITCH! Mitchell, are you still there?" Mrs. Fairfax's voice was a high-pitched squeal.

They both rushed to the bedroom.

Meghan took one look at the white, strained face, and prepared a needle while Mitch helped the trembling woman to a sitting position. Her eyes looked huge in her face, and she had trouble breathing.

Unceremoniously, Meghan pulled back the covers and stabbed the needle into Mrs. Fairfax's hip. Immediately, the woman's color returned and her breathing eased.

"What's the matter?" Mitch asked.

Mrs. Fairfax grasped his hand. "I was so frightened," she murmured.

"What happened?" Meghan asked as she watched Mitch place a protective arm around the old woman's shoulders.

"I heard it again. The banging and the creaking, but this time..." She closed her eyes for a moment, then opened them again. "This time, I heard a voice."

Over her head, Meghan and Mitch's eyes locked.

"We were talking in the other room," Meghan said slowly, her brow furrowing. "Maybe you heard our voices?"

"No, no, it wasn't you."

"Well, I called an old friend earlier. Could it have been me talking on the phone?"

"No. It was a man, but it wasn't you."

"Are you sure, Mrs. Fairfax? Coming through the walls like that, Mitch's voice could take on some eerie sound effects."

"No, I tell you, it wasn't Mitchell!"

"What did the man say? Could you make out the words?"

Mrs. Fairfax's breathing grew labored and her arms started to twitch, and the two young people did their best to calm her again before she could continue.

"He said, 'Belinda. Belinda, I'm waiting.'"

"Oh, wow," Mitch said and sank onto the chair. "Do you think it might have been your husband calling from beyond the grave?"

Meghan looked hard at him to see if he was hiding a smile. Guys didn't believe in that stuff, did they?

The wrinkles on Mrs. Fairfax's forehead took on additional creases. "Well...no, I don't think that can be right," she said after a moment.

"Look, Meghan and I were in the other room. We didn't hear any banging or anything, and the only voices were ours. There are only two choices, don't you see? Either you're being called from another dimension or you're losing your mind. I don't think you've suddenly gone crazy, so..."

Meghan glared at him. *I like thinking about the supernatural, too, but we're supposed to be calming her, not making her more frightened.*

She took a slow, deep breath. Sometimes she hated her job. Mrs. Fairfax was a dear, kind old lady, and it would be a shame if senility set in. But it *was* the rational explanation. "Actually, Mrs. Fairfax, it could be your mind helping you to come to grips with your situation. You know, to make it easier to leave this life and move on. A coping mechanism."

Mrs. Fairfax looked at Meghan. "Oh no, dear, I'm not imagining it. No, I think Mitch is right and someone is calling me from the other side. But I don't believe it would be Mr. Fairfax, is all."

"Why not, Mrs. F? Who else would be calling?" Mitch glanced over at Meghan. "Or who else would your mind imagine is calling?"

"I just don't believe Mr. Fairfax would care enough to wait. Stan was a ruthless, unfeeling man, I'm afraid. Those qualities did well for him in business, but they didn't make for a good husband. In the last years of his life, we barely spoke to one another. Besides, I would like to believe I'm not going to the same place he deserved to go." She managed a feeble smile.

Mitch leaned over and took Mrs. Fairfax's hand. He looked deep into her eyes. "I'm so sorry," he said.

"Oh now, Mitch," Mrs. Fairfax said with her best attempt

at a laugh. "I didn't mean to upset you, and I don't blame all men. You're a sweet, sensitive boy, and I thank you for your concern. In fact, I'd like to thank both of you for the care and friendship you've shown me. You look good together, too. I knew you'd be perfect for each other."

Meghan was too embarrassed to look at Mitch, so she missed the way his face reddened. She attempted to gain control of the sickroom by bustling around with her syringe and medications, and said in her best no-nonsense voice, "I have other appointments today, Mrs. Fairfax, so I'll go prepare your sponge bath." She gazed pointedly at Mitch. It was time for him to go.

He took the hint and stood. God, he was grateful for the chance to escape. He didn't know how he could look at Meghan after *that*. "I'll be by at the usual time for your supper, Mrs. F. We'll talk more then."

Mitch dumped the contents of the can into one of Mrs. Fairfax's pots and put it on the stove to heat. He knew she wouldn't approve of stew from a can, but what the hell—he was no gourmet chef and she ate like a bird anyway. He couldn't talk himself into trying to make stew from scratch just to watch her leave it in the bowl.

While it heated, he cut and buttered some slices from the fresh baguette he'd bought. He should have made a salad, but simply sliced a tomato. Once everything was ready, he prepared two trays and tried to stifle the guilt he felt at the sorry effort.

"Here you go. That didn't take me long, eh? You start eating while I get mine."

He returned to the bedroom and took his seat on the chair, balancing the tray on his knees. "How're you feeling now? Did you have a good afternoon?"

"Yes, I think so. Meghan gave me something to help me sleep before she left, and it must have worked because I was dead to the world until you came in."

"Good." He frowned at her and pointed his spoon at her tray. "So, why aren't you eating?"

"Oh, I'm sorry, dear boy. I don't have much of an appetite tonight." She looked at his face—was that worry or frustration—and took a mouthful of stew. It wasn't very good, and its heat made her nose run, but she chewed and swallowed to make him feel better. "What did you do this afternoon, with the day off?"

"Oh, you know. I went grocery shopping, and I fooled around on my computer a bit. Nothing special."

"So, what did you think of Meghan?"

Mitch sighed and shook his head. "Look Mrs. F, she seems very nice, and I'll admit I wouldn't mind knowing her better, but you're wasting your time. Girls aren't interested in me. They can't see past the 'computer geek' label they saddle me with the moment we meet. Believe me, I tried hard enough in college."

"But you're not in college anymore, Mitchell, and besides, I think Meghan is different. She can see the worth of a man, and I think she likes those electronic gizmos, too."

"Yeah, well, whatever," Mitch said before he lapsed into silence and concentrated on his meal. He mopped up the last of his stew with the bread, then rose with his tray.

"I'll take this into the kitchen and then come back for yours." He looked at the almost untouched food. "Please try to eat some more while I'm gone, will you?"

Mrs. Fairfax sighed and nodded. He asked so little of her, the least she could do was *try*.

Mitch frowned as he dumped the majority of her meal down the sink. Then, with the kitchen clean and the dishwasher humming, he returned to her bedside.

"I think we'll probably finish the book tonight," he said, as he took his seat and picked up the paperback he'd been reading to her. It was one of those romance novels he'd always thought were so trashy, but it had sci-fi elements, too. To his surprise, he was thoroughly enjoying it. *I even like the romantic parts—as long as the guys in T.O. never find out.*

"I never realized how the story could be enhanced by having a strong, young man's deep voice read it to me," Mrs. Fairfax said. She smiled and batted her eyes at him in an exaggerated flirting manner.

They both chuckled as he found the page and began to read. This was her favorite part of the day, and she closed her eyes and let her imagination follow his words into the scene.

All too soon the story was finished and it was time for

him to go back to his own apartment. "I'll see you in the morning, as usual, Mrs. F."

"Thank you, Mitchell, for everything. I don't know what I would do without you. Do you think you could call Meghan and let her know I'm alright? She was a little worried about me when she left this afternoon. Her number is on a pad by the phone in the living room."

He looked at her overly bland, innocent face. *There's no way in hell I'm calling Meghan. God, she'll think I'm desperate.* He remembered the feel of her hand on his knee—he'd thought of little else all day—and felt the heat rise in his face. Disgusted with himself, he tried to change the subject. "Let me take this extra pillow away so you can lie down properly. There, that's better. Have a good night, Mrs. F."

Mitch felt his heart sicken the next morning as he entered Mrs. Fairfax's bedroom with the laden tea tray. He'd known it was likely he'd find her lifeless body one day and had imagined the scene and what he would do. But he'd never imagined the wide, staring eyes, the gaping mouth, and the hands clutching and clawing her chest.

He didn't need to go any closer to know she was dead.

He went into the living room and tried to pick up the phone, but realized his hands still held the tray. With a quiet oath, he set it down on the coffee table. Only then did his hands start to shake. The 911 operator promised to send an ambulance immediately. Mitch thought that made little sense. There was no need to rush.

He sat briefly after he hung up the phone, then picked it up again. He needed Meghan.

Two weeks later, Mitch pushed his chair away from his desk. He'd been playing for hours and the room had grown dark.

With Meghan's help, he'd handled Mrs. Fairfax's funeral arrangements. It had gone well, although the mourners consisted solely of himself, Meghan, Mrs. Fairfax's lawyer, and three old biddies who volunteered with the Library Foundation. Mitch hadn't known Mrs. Fairfax used to volunteer to keep the shelves stocked and neat, but he wasn't surprised. It sounded just like her—thoughtful.

175

After the service, he met with the lawyer, who informed him he was Mrs. Fairfax's main beneficiary. He still found it difficult to believe how rich she'd been. Even with the substantial donations she made to several charities, he'd be able to live comfortably off the interest alone. He'd been surprised she hadn't left anything to Meghan, since she thought so highly of her, but the attorney had explained she couldn't be a beneficiary since she'd been one of the witnesses. And Meghan hadn't seemed the least bit upset. Said she'd known that when Mrs. F asked her to witness her signature.

He'd enjoyed the time he'd spent with Meghan over the last few weeks. She was a tiny little thing, a bit mousy-looking, but her body was definitely filled out in all the right places. She was also fun to be around—so friendly and really smart. She seemed to like him, too, but he couldn't come up with an excuse to see her again now that everything was taken care of.

The first thing he'd done was arrange a line of credit. Then he'd quit his job and gone shopping. The third thing he'd done was join a gym, and he'd spent the last two mornings working out. Every muscle in his body ached, but it was a good feeling. He wanted to be ready on the off chance he ran into Meghan again. After all, the town wasn't *that* big.

Mitch got up to go to the fridge for a beer and groaned as his muscles protested. He took his beer into the living room, sank onto his new leather couch and sighed with relief when his muscles stopped straining.

He reached for the remote control and looked at the TV. He could afford to buy a bigger one, but he'd have to wait until he moved out of this small apartment. Actually, his TV was plenty big enough—he was slightly embarrassed at how much money he'd spent on his home theater system and his computer when he first moved in, but he'd had fourteen months before he had to pay, and he'd been full of optimism at the time.

"Mitchell O'Keefe? Waterloo Regional Police. We'd like to talk to you. Please open the door."

The voice and accompanying knock startled Mitch out of his musings. He groaned as he rose from the couch. *How did they get into the building without buzzing me?*

He opened the door to find two plain-clothes detectives and two uniformed officers behind them. One of the detectives held out a sheet of paper. "We have a warrant to search your premises."

Mitch took the paper and saw it was, indeed, a search warrant. He saw his address, the date and approximate time, and saw they were looking for 'electronic audio and recording equipment.' His hands began to sweat and he stared at the cops in bewilderment as they pushed past him and into the apartment. Mitch stood at the door, looking dumbly down at the paper in his hand. His heart felt like it had moved into his throat, where it thumped fast and loud.

It didn't take the police long to find what they came for—his stuff was in plain sight, after all. "Wireless speakers, recording equipment and a computer program for manipulating sound. It's all here, ma'am. We've even got a remote control for the stereo," one of the officers said.

"Mitchell O'Keefe, you are charged with the first degree murder of Belinda Fairfax," the lead detective said as she pulled his arm back to handcuff his hands behind him. Mitch gasped at the pain in his arms as the detective continued to read his rights from a small index card.

"I didn't touch her! We were friends!" he shouted, completely disregarding his rights.

The other detective smiled as he took his arm to lead him away. "Of course you didn't. Didn't think we'd search the building's dumpster, right? Didn't need a warrant for that. We found the old pillow with the strange hole in the foam. It looks just about the right size for one of these speakers." He motioned to equipment a field officer was preparing for transport. "We've also gone over your recent financial situation. You benefited more than anyone else from her death. You couldn't wait any longer for the money, eh?"

"But she was sick!" Mitch tried to explain.

"Yes, but her doctor was surprised by how quickly she faded. Apparently, he thought she should have lasted for months in her condition."

"But...you can't do this!" Mitch panicked, and he tried to twist out of their grasp as they herded him into the elevator.

"Relax, we can and we are. You were very clever, but you didn't do your homework," the lead detective said as she pushed the button for the lobby. "In Canada, Mr. O'Keefe, it's illegal to kill a sick person by frightening them. It's been tried

Jennifer Ross

before. Did you believe we'd never catch you?"

Meghan nodded in satisfaction as she folded the newspaper and turned to smile at Mitch. "Of course you were acquitted. Even the reporter thought the evidence was a joke," she said as he sat on the couch beside her. "So they found a pillow in a dumpster. Big deal."

"But it might have convicted me if you hadn't testified about how Mrs. F asked you to dispose of an old pillow for her." Mitch wrapped his arms around her and placed a soft kiss on her temple.

"And it explains why she asked you to buy her a new one." She snuggled against him and enjoyed the stroking caress of his fingers on her arm.

"Yeah, but I did benefit from the Will, and I did have all that electronic stuff. What if people think I killed her and got away with it?"

"What people? Mitch, look around. I probably have most of that stuff myself. Nobody our age will think it proves murder."

Yes, Mitch benefited from the Will. She'd had to testify about that part, too. How Mrs. Fairfax had asked her to witness her signature. There was nothing strange about it—Mrs. Fairfax knew what she was doing.

Meghan remembered the thrill she'd felt when Mitch used his one phone call to contact her. He needed her! Of course, he'd ruined it by saying she was the only person he knew in town, but he couldn't deny he'd memorized her number.

She'd managed to arrange her schedule to be in court throughout the trial, and had spoken with him most days. She knew he'd come to rely on her presence. He didn't have anyone else there to root for him. The thought of such a strong, self-sufficient man needing *her* filled the void she'd attempted to ease by nursing.

She smiled as she remembered his relief yesterday as the verdict was handed down. *Not guilty.* Afterwards, they went to a downtown bar to celebrate, just the two of them, and they'd shyly admitted their feelings. She looked at him, now lean and fit, and thought how the time he'd been remanded in lockup had done wonders for him. She itched to feel that strong chest,

bare against hers.

Life sure is strange, she thought with a smile. How one person's death could bring two people together. Tonight, they were supposed to be going to dinner and a show, but she wouldn't mind if they stayed in. She fitted her head more snugly against his shoulder and breathed in his masculine scent. She'd much rather make out.

Mitch couldn't get over her. She was far too good for him, of course, but she didn't think so. Now that he was rich, he at least had something to offer her, but he was positive the money had nothing to do with her feelings for him. *She liked me when I was an alleged murderer. Maybe Mrs. F was right and I am worthy.*

Tilting her head up to receive his kiss, he brushed his lips lightly over hers. It only made him want her more.

She responded immediately, and her lips clung to his until he parted them to plunge inside. His tongue swirled against hers, tasting, taking. He moved his mouth to rain little kisses along her jaw line and down to her throat. As he nibbled his way to her ear, he whispered, "I love you, Meghan."

Meghan moved her head to look at him. "I love you, too," and she pulled his lips down for another long kiss.

The heat rose within them both until they were frantic with desire. Breathlessly she pushed him away. "Would you like to see the rest of the apartment? It's only a one bedroom."

Mitch smiled and took the hand she held out, allowing her to lead him to her bed. As they walked, he glanced up at the ceiling.

You planned the whole thing, didn't you, Mrs. F? Are you up there, proud of your accomplishment? He squeezed Meghan's hand.

You are one sneaky, sweet ol' lady. Thanks!

Be sure to visit Jennifer Ross' website
www.jenniferross.ca

Getting It In The End

by DeborahAnne MacGillivray

• *York, England - Excluding Sundays, it's perfectly legal to shoot a Scotsman with a bow and arrow*

Present day, York

"*Why don't you shoot me? It'd be more humane!*"

James Douglas Kinloch heard those words echo in his brain the past two weeks, though most writers would insist a brain couldn't echo. Still ticked, he was prepared to argue the point of creative license. He'd meant those words when he tossed them at his boss Murray, editor-in-chief for *Money & Trends* magazine, after he'd been assigned to cover a Writers' Renfaire in York, England.

As he surveyed the pandemonium around him, he saw *no* reason to retract them.

These were writers, he should feel at home with them. He penned a monthly column on books and contributed to *M & T's* reviews section. Nevertheless, in this case misery did *not* love company.

These were Romance writers. *Another breed of wordsmith entirely,* he'd learnt.

Amazingly, women were responsible for sixty-five percent of books sold in the world, virtually financing publishing houses to stay afloat on their efforts alone. He understood why *Money & Trends* sent someone to cover the gathering. *Only why him?*

Getting It In the End

Accepting there was no reversing his boss' edict, he'd done his homework and learned a lot about the power these females wielded, how often the male bastions of fiction writers—jealous of the higher incomes—mocked them. He'd come prepared to have a male ego adjustment and accept these women for the dynamos they were, give them their professional dues. Having sampled dozens of the genre since taking up *M & T*'s bookbeat, he admitted they were as talented in their craft as their male counterparts. Maybe more so. He approached the forth-coming article, planning to portray them in the professional light they fully earned.

Then he landed in the middle of this weeklong madness.

First Annual York Historical Romance Writers Renaissance Faire.

He glared at the huge banner strung across the fairway entrance, then sighed. "What a mouthful."

These mothers, wives and lovers—even grandmothers —seized the chance to kick loose and let down their hair. *Oh, mama, did they ever let down their hair!*

His tush was tender from the grab-arsing going on. Any good-looking male became a target for their *turnabout's-fair-play*. Male models, historians, re-enactors and servers were ogled, teased, tormented— and pinched—as the ladies fair let it rip. They were having a high time and it was only the first day!

This week was going to be a *long* one. He considered putting in for hazardous duty pay.

Getting into the spirit of things, most wore period dress. Queens, scullery maids, Scottish lasses and even female warriors flooded the grounds of the two-thousand-acre *Majestic Park Hotel*. Once, William Wallace had laid siege to York. While he wasn't a descendant from Wallace, James began to feel he now paid for all Scottish transgressions against the ancient city.

The faire was a chance for the women to meet their fans, but it was also an opportunity to do hands-on research. They could learn to buckle their swashes, try a hand at jousting, handling a claymore or give the English Longbow a go to strengthen their writing.

So far, the only *hands-on* he'd experienced was on his arse!

Gaggles of giggles alerted him to the approach of

marauding females, so he darted around a huge tent to dodge another gauntlet of bum-pinching.

Peeking around the edge of the canvas pavilion, intent on hiding from the bawdy wenches, James backed up as their voices neared. Focused on saving his tender backside, he failed to pay attention where he was going. Turning another tent corner, he crashed into a body.

Putting hands out to stop his fall, one closed over a full, round breast, the other on a curvy hip. *Female.* As he attempted to prevent himself from crashing to the ground, their feet caught on the pegs of the tent. Spinning around the taught lines, they went down in a tangle of arms, legs and a mass of honey-coloured hair.

He landed on his arse—hard—with her on top of him, air whooshing from his lungs. That sweet curve of her pelvis rode perfectly over his groin as she straddled him, a white-jeaned knee on either side of his hips. He'd enjoy the position if he hadn't been nearly writhing in agony.

Vision spun as he fought the urge to puke. With her planted on top of him, he couldn't raise up. Blawing wasn't an option! He'd end up drowning in his own vomit. His mind could see the headlines in the papers now—*Man dies in hurling accident.* And they wouldn't mean in the game *Hurling* either!

His assailant wiggled her derrière against his thighs, then tried to flip that mass of hair from out of her face.

"Bugger," the sexy voice muttered.

The sort of voice that made James think of fine Highland whisky, silk sheets and late nights. Only right now, he *really* didn't want such images intruding on his *pain.*

She tossed her hair over her shoulders. As the ache receded, James saw a red leather strap was around her wrist and there was a strain on it. Small wonder the collision went out of control. A *beast* was on the end of the lead.

"Cat...you'll be the death of me yet!"

James turned his head to eye the feline on the end of the leather tether. "Bloody hell—that's a Scottish wildcat! What idiot runs around with a wildcat on a leash? And one wearing an eye patch?"

"Half-wildcat," she corrected defensively.

She ceased trying to unwind the cat as her eyes locked

with his. She stared at him, transfixed, wonder in her voice. "You have lavender eyes."

James was ready to throttle her and she worried about his eye shade? "I have grey eyes," he snapped gruffly.

She sniffed. "Males. Most are colourblind. They're not blue or grey. They're lavender. Liz Taylor eyes. Oh, man, you're not wearing contacts, are you?"

"No, I only wear reading glasses." James stopped and felt for his eyeglasses in his shirt pocket. His *flattened* glasses. "Or used to."

"Oh, you broke your glasses?"

"No, *you* broke them...and *other things*...I think."

She wiggled again and turned to look at his legs, as if they were the part of his anatomy he referred to. Then she leaned forward to run her hands over his arms.

Finally able to focus, he stared up into a pair of witchy eyes. Dark amber with streaks of jade, they appeared green one moment, then transmuted to the color of whisky the next. All about him receded. He stared bound by them, unable to see anything else.

Part of his body proved it hadn't been damaged in the collision and pulsed to life under her shifting. "Scratch *other things* being broke," he muttered.

"I'm sorry. My beastie is hard to control."

His erection throbbed, insistent. James moaned, then chuckled. "Yeah, I know the feeling."

Shocked, she realized she sat on his aroused groin. "Oh!" Hazel eyes wide, she looked from side-to-side, searching for the best way to get up. "Sorry...really I am."

Witchy Eyes started to rise, but couldn't gain balance. James saw what would happen—she'd come down sitting on his face! He put his hands up to her thighs to stop the descent, but didn't count on her weight pushing downward to where his thumbs ended on her crotch.

Well, this is smart. She sits on my groin and I grab her—James groaned. He couldn't jerk his hands away or she'd tumble. Bloody hell, they didn't even know each other's names. What an introduction!

With a squeak, she grabbed the guide wire and straightened her knees, allowing him to scoot from under her. James sat up carefully so he didn't end up with him burying his face where his thumbs were.

She reeled in the long leash to a controllable length, then offered her other hand to help him to his feet. "I apologize—especially the glasses. Send me the bill. I'll replace them."

He rose to his six-foot height, glad she was tall, about five-seven, but not too tall. As Goldilocks would say, *just right* for him. She was pretty, no doubt, but something unique, a quality feline, drew him as he stared into those hazel eyes.

"Perhaps we should introduce ourselves?" He laughed as the huge cat rubbed against his leg like any ordinary housecat. "I'm James Douglas Kinloch."

She gazed at him, enrapt. "You have the most beautiful eyes."

He was about to suggest she'd enjoy staring at his beautiful eyes over supper, when enrapture morphed into shock—and maybe something *worse*.

"*James...Douglas...Kinloch?*" she repeated with loathing.

Bloody hell, the way she spoke his name you'd think she'd said Osama Bin Laden. "Yes." What else could he say?

"*James...Douglas...bloody Kinloch...*reviewer for *Money & Trends?*" she growled. "I'd like to know I have the right James Douglas Kinloch. But of course, you are. There could only be one despicable, *loathsome worm* by that name. The world couldn't stand two."

"Have we met?" James glanced to the side, hoping someone spotted them. While he'd truly love to jump her bones after all the bumping and grinding they'd just done, he began to fear he faced a crazed woman—with a one-eyed, Scottish wildcat, all three stone of him.

Her teeth flashed, but not in a grin. It was feral, what a cat wore just before pouncing on prey. "Met? Not face-to-face." Her countenance shifted to a magazine smile. "I'm a *follower* of your writing. You've quite the *penchant* with words. Ever considered fiction? You'd excel in it."

She moved so fast, male instinct to protect himself couldn't engage. Her knee connected with the part of a man that could fell the mightiest of modern day warriors. James crumpled to his knees, clutching his groin, trying not to puke. Down on knee level, he saw her feet and the cat's stalk off, only to hear her steps return behind him. He should've expected it, but occupied with writhing in agony, he failed to anticipate the kick to his arse.

"*James Douglas bloody Kinloch,*" she snarled.

This time her steps stomped off down the fairgrounds. The cat with the eye patch came pussyfooting back, dragging the red leash. Putting his feet on James' thigh, he stretched up and gave his chin a tongue bath. James managed to push him away, only to have the purring cat bump its forehead against his chin.

"Puss, this is going to be a *long* week."

Catlynne Falconer's cheeks burned with anger. "The nerve of the bloody man to have such beautiful eyes."

She'd envisioned James Douglas Kinloch—the man who trashed every one of her Scottish Romance novels over the past five years—pictured him as a dried up old Scotsman, with an expression like he sucked lemons! Never once had she imagined such a sexy, elegant man. Younger than her furious mind had conjured, Kinloch had blue-black hair that lay in wild waves. And those eyes. Wow! Never had she seen such *lavender* eyes! Most are too blue or grey. His were truly lilac. He was strong, lean, hard...yep...very *hard*.

Oh, why did James Douglas Kinloch have to be as sexy as his name? This man summoned visions of a tartan blanket over silk sheets, maybe a set of lavender ones matching those to die for eyes. He'd hit her senses with the power of a runaway locomotive, provoked her to want to kiss all his booboos and make them better. She wanted those beautiful hands on her, stroking her, squeezing...

"Bugger. I'm going to have an orgasm daydreaming about him and those eyes," she commented to the cat. Then she looked down and saw the silly beast wasn't with her. "Fu...dge."

She'd been so bloody turned on by the man, then hit with the bucket of ice water that he was that flaming reviewer from *Money & Trends,* she'd forgotten her cat.

"Well, nothing to do but find the pussycat before he eats Virginia Keller's teacup terrier. Blast."

The feline may be half-wildcat and sported a ridiculous black, pirate's patch, but he obviously was tame. After they had a *meeting of the minds,* James rather liked having the beast on the leash. Women kept their distance. He strolled down the fairway, checking out tents and booths with no fear of being ravished by Queen Victoria or a Lady Pirate.

Finding a vendor serving bangers and beer, he and the cat shared lunch. Lifting his mug for a drink, he spotted Witchy Eyes storming toward him. Dark auburn hair swirled about her shoulders, seeing her stand out in the crowd. A Pict warrior-princess out for blood.

Breaking off a chunk of the banger, he fed it to the fat cat. "I like watching her walk, Cat. She has world-class breasts. Very athletic legs, though I'd prefer she not use them to kick me. It's hard on a man's...*ego*. You have any idea why she hates me?"

The cat finished the num-num and meowed for another bite.

As she stalked up, James pretended not to notice her, but fed the beast his last bit of the sandwich. He stared at the jean-covered thighs, the lush hips and envisioned them wrapped around his waist as he drove his body into hers.

"Kinloch, you're one sick puppy," he muttered under his breath. Of all the women chasing him, ready to jump his bones, he'd developed a case of severe lust for the one who kneed him in the groin.

With a huff, she put her hands on her hips. "What are you feeding my cat?"

"My lunch. It's debatable if this critter is a cat. Personally, I think he's a small pony in a cat costume."

Snagging the red leash, she tugged. "Come, Jack."

"Jack? As in One-Eyed-Jack?" James suppressed his smile as Jack sat staring at him, ignoring her yanking on the red tether. "Mind telling me why you're dragging Jack around the Renfaire, Miss..."

Her body rocked with another huff, as amber eyes flashed daggers at him. "You may ask. Come, Jack." She pulled again on the strap, but the pussycat wouldn't move.

"Had lunch? Want a banger?" Kinloch signaled the waitress. "Jack and I want another, eh, lad?"

She blinked in shock, then composed her face. "Oh, yeah, it's a big hotdog."

"You're not Yank with that accent," he observed.

"Scot born, but I lived a big part of my life in the US until the last three years."

"Where do you live now?"

"Colchester."

James paused to give the order to the waitress. "Sit. Jack isn't finished yet. Isn't that right, Jack?"

The cat turned his head and meowed at her. Pursing her lips—delectable lips—she flopped down on the end of the bench. Witchy Eyes glared at him as the waitress returned with food, but said nothing until the woman left with the empty tray.

James broke off the excess and put it before Jack. "Mind telling me why you want to end my family tree? Often I affect women strongly, but I've never had one physically attack me, especially when I don't know her name."

He took a bite of the banger and was about to swallow when she spoke.

"You want my name, Mr. James Douglas Kinloch? Fine. My name—Catlynne Falconer."

James simultaneously choked on the hotdog and almost spit it out. Rising, she slapped him on the back—with a bit more strength than called for, James feared.

Small wonder. *Catlynne Falconer.* Surely, there was only one.

"Yes, Mr. James Douglas Kinloch, I'm the writer whose books you've shredded with glee. You've called me a sophomoric writer who must still wear Maryjane patent leather shoes, one whose stories are 'so cute it's painful.' Two of the kinder comments you've penned when reviewing my works. Every time sales of my books soar, you take great pleasure in posting your reviews—not only in *Money & Trends*, but on Amazon.com and Amazon.co.uk. My sales go down the tubes. After eleven books, I could sue you for loss of income."

James reached for his ale to dislodge the stuck bit of banger. With a forced swallow, the lump moved down his throat.

Catlynne Falconer. This vivacious lass with the flashing amber eyes and breasts he'd a hard time keeping his eyes off of was *Miz Hearts & Flowers?* She pens a rather original series about a pirate reincarnated as a huge cat. The beast went around solving murder mysteries and playing cupid to mismatched couples.

Bloody hell. Why hadn't he made the connection?

He stared at the mangy wildcat—her inspiration obviously. Explained why she had him here at the Renfaire. He recalled seeing her name on the program as one of the guest speakers, giving a talk on animals as characters in Romance writing. She'd dragged Jack along for *show and tell.*

What did one say to an author you'd taken great pleasure in harpooning? She was such a sensual writer. Her sex scenes had caused him to take more than one cold shower. Only she persisted in having mismatched lovers falling head-over-heels into happily ever after. When he reached the end of her books he felt he needed a shot of insulin to counter the overdose of *sweet.*

Well, best defense was an offence. He stared into her kissable face, raked his eyes down her made-for-sin body, reveling in every delicious curve, then slowly traveled back to lock eyes with her. "Pity. I guess the chances of me getting you into bed tonight just dropped by half."

She jerked up to her feet, acting as if he just asked her to go down on her knees before him and do the *wild thang.* The lass had a temper. Went with that auburn hair. Why did he find that so...ah...stimulating?

Catlynne shifted her stance, as if balancing her weight to one leg, prelude to delivering a stiff kick. James held up his hands, flattened palms to her. "First kick was getting acquainted. Kick me again and I'm going to turn you over my knee, Catlynne. Hmm, Cat," he growled. "Your mum named you well."

All sorts of images sprang to mind. *Here, kitty kitty.* He wondered if she'd purr when he stroked the curve of her spine with his tongue. Would she hiss and flex those claws when he'd enter her body with a sure thrust?

"Your mum named you after one of Scotland's greatest heroes. How did she muff it so?" she snapped.

"So, that means you won't sleep with me tonight?" James suppressed the grin fighting to escape. He wasn't usually a jerk, but he enjoyed teasing Ms. Catlynne Falconer. "I promise to make you purr, lass."

She drew back her hand to slap him, but he was quicker. He caught her wrist and yanked her forward, pulling her into his lap. Cat let out a strangled yelp. Before she closed her mouth, he kissed her.

Oh, man, did he kiss Miss Catlynne Falconer! Not a gentle first kiss, but with full pleasure and passion that erupted within him. Her lips tasted of tart lemonade. She wiggled, so he leaned her back, cradling her neck in his hand, the other on the small of her spine. His mouth molded hers, tilting for a better angle.

He couldn't ever recall enjoying a kiss as much. Catlynne stopped the squirming, her hands clutched his waist, hanging on. Her responses ran the gamut from resistance to acquiescence, then surprise, ending with her kissing him back.

James lost sense of where he was, until applause broke out around them. Recalling they were on the picnic grounds with about two hundred female writers, he reluctantly pulled back.

Dazed, Catlynne blinked several times, then grew aware of the hooting, whistling and clapping. Turning five shades of red, her eyes narrowed on him as she clearly considered slapping him again. She was furious. Even so, he saw the flash of desire threaded with confusion at the back of those whisky eyes. She nibbled on the corner of her kiss-swollen lips.

He leaned his head to hers and threatened, "Don't do it. Each time you do me bodily harm, I shall extract vengeance by kissing you senseless—no matter where we are."

"You...you...." she spluttered, at a loss for words.

He flashed a smile guaranteed to dazzle the ladies, then rose to his feet and executed a bow.

Catlynne dashed away from the area where the picnic tables were cordoned off.

James scratched Jack's head. "She left you again, beast. I think she does that just to have an excuse to come back and fetch you."

James tossed down a tip for the waitress, picked up the leash and started down the fairway with Jack. He began whistling an old *Blondie* tune, *One Way or Another*. "Yeah, I'm gonna get ya', get ya', get ya', get ya'."

Suddenly things were looking up.

Catlynne finished blow-drying her hair, then wound up the cord. Going back into the bedroom, she replaced it in her travel bag. She noticed the red blinking light on the phone indicating she had a message and had an idea from whom. Kinloch. He had Jack and wasn't answering her pages to return him.

Putting her fingers to her lips, she recalled how James Douglas Kinloch tasted. Her body started that low burning thrum that reminded he was an excellent kisser.

She was a little concerned. Jack didn't like men. And considering the scathing reviews Kinloch did for her books, she figured the man didn't like cats either. *This character—a cat mind you—is more annoying than a dozen Garfields rolled into one.* So she was uneasy about the beast of *Money & Trends* and her beastie paling together.

Going to the phone, she listened to the message. She'd called him seven times and demanded he return her cat.

The clipped Scot accent came across the recorded message. "Your cat? Mine now. Finders keepers, losers weepers." Then a click.

She imagined the self-satisfied smirk beneath the flashing lavender eyes. Knees feeling weak, she sat on the bed with a thump. A man like that was a heartbreaker. Worse, he was a bloody book reviewer.

Why suddenly were things looking so down?

Catlynne marched to the desk of the elegant, gold-tone foyer of the *Majestic Park Hotel* and addressed the desk porter behind the reception counter. "May I have the room number of Mr. James Kinloch?"

The young man sniggered. "Hotel policy doesn't permit giving out room numbers. You may leave him a message or I can ring a call through to him."

She gritted her teeth. Accepting the note pad, she scrawled, *return my cat or I shall have you arrested for catnapping.* Folding the paper, she pushed it at the man.

He lifted an eyebrow. "What? Not going to bribe me with a hundred-pound note? All the ladies wanting to get a message to Kinloch have funded my daughter's coming wedding."

"Much happiness on your daughter's nuptials, but I wouldn't spend one shilling on James Douglas Kinloch."

Spinning on her heels, she headed toward the ballroom. From behind her, she heard the porter say, "Methinks the lady doth protest too much."

"Would you look at that?" someone halfway down the row of tables gasped.

The cacophony of wolf-whistles and chuckles caused Catlynne's head to snap up from autographing her books.

Leanne Burroughs, author of *Her Highland Rogue* and owner of Highland Press, sat to Catlynne's right. Pausing, she leaned to Catlynne and pointed with the end of the pen. "I believe that's your cat, isn't it?"

Catlynne glanced down the crowded isle. Women stood in lines before authors to get their books signed. Suddenly, the interest wasn't in the tables where the books were displayed or authors busy autographing them, but at a ruckus behind them. The crowd parted so all could observe the man coming her way.

James Kinloch wore a black turtleneck sweater, stunning with that blue-black hair. What caused women to go on pheromone overload—he wore a black tartan kilt with purple in the plaid. Those pale eyes spotted her, then flashed with smug arrogance. Catlynne burned to slap the expression off his much too beautiful face. Torn, she watched as Jack bounced along, keeping pace with the man better than any dog could. Though she itched to bring the reviewer down a peg, her heart couldn't help but be touched by how man and cat had bonded.

"I found my Highlander hero for my next book." Leanne chuckled. "I'd take him home, but my Tom might not approve."

Catlynne repressed the urge to growl. "Trust me, you don't want him."

"Easy—I'm not going to arm-wrestle you for him."

Reaching for another book to sign, Catlynne had to tug the book from the fan's hand, as the woman was transfixed on the sexy man in the kilt. "Not what I meant. He's James Douglas Kinloch—a book critic."

"Ah, sigh. Just as well I have Tom, then. He's very supportive of my writing." Leanne watched the man draw near. "He does favor what I always imagined Good Sir James Douglas looking like. Can't you see him at The Bruce's side, claymore in his hands, fighting to free Scotland?"

Kinloch came directly to her table, scooped up Jack and

set him on the tabletop. He winked at the three ladies standing in line, then turned back to Catlynne. "Sorry, we're late. Jack couldn't decide what to wear and insisted on my bow tie."

Sure enough, Jack sported a tartan tie the same plaid as James' kilt. He looked adorable, but Catlynne was too gub-slapped to speak. The man was stunning, and yes, he did appear as if Good Sir James had come to life. As she stared into those pale lilac eyes, she felt lost to all around her.

"Awww...kitty does look like a reincarnated pirate," a Scottish lady waiting to have her books signed commented, petting Jack. "He's so huge. He must've been a braw and bonnie pirate in his other life."

James handed Catlynne the leash—a black one, then moved to set the boxes of books on the floor so he could use the chair. He pushed it to sit just to her right and a little behind her. "Did I miss much?"

Leanne cleared her throat loudly, holding out her hand. "Hello, I'm Leanne Burroughs. I write Scottish romances and I'm owner of Highland Press."

"Smart lass. I've heard good things about your quality books and the direction your small press is moving. Very positive for Romance Writers." James flashed a killer smile. Instead of shaking her hand, he kissed it in courtly fashion. "Please set aside copies of all Highland Press books for me so I can review them."

"*You'll be sorry,*" Catlynne muttered in singsong, so the words carried only to James and Leanne. "Trust me. I've been *blessed* with a Kinloch review for every book I've written. It's something every writer could live without."

"She thinks *moi*—a humble reviewer—hurt her sales," he confided with a wink.

Damn his charming rogue hide. Women had a hard time resisting melt down around a sexy man in a kilt with a burr in his voice. Add wavy black hair and lavender eyes and it was a lethal combination.

"I've come to make amends." He arched an eyebrow at the women suddenly lining up to get Catlynne's books.

Jack stretched out on the corner of the table enjoying the pets and adoration. Fixing on the leash, Catlynne asked, "What happened to his red one?"

James shrugged. "Red doesn't go with my plaid. We

stopped by the pet centre they have here. This hotel is a small city. I purchased a new leash and some treats. Also, he found a catnip mouse he *really* wanted. Do you know they even have babysitting service for pets or the super kennel where you can park them for a spell, say like later when we go dancing in the nightclub?"

"Dream on, Kinloch." Her reply was defensive, trying to keep him at arms' length.

Oh, but her heart, and Leanne's all-knowing stare, branded her a fool.

She was a coward. As the book signing broke up, the women mobbed the sexy man in a kilt. Catlynne used the confusion to slip away from him.

Hadn't mattered. James Kinloch would prove damn hard to avoid. Especially since he ended up with Jack again.

Early the next morn, before anyone was up and about, she slipped downstairs to relax by doing a few laps in the pool. When she came up for air, she spotted Jack laying on a chaise lounge smiling at her.

James dove into the pool with a backwash of water, then surfaced in front of her. She opened her mouth to berate him for causing the big splash, but the fool man kissed her. Kissed her until her toes curled and the water in the pool rose to boiling. She nearly forgot they were in the glassed-in pool and the dining room looked into it—until she heard a rap on the glass and glanced up to see Leanne Burroughs and Diane D. White waving at them.

That became the pattern for the next three days. Now, she was so confused she wanted to cry. She was falling for James Kinloch—hard. Yet, she had no idea how the arrogant man felt about her. Sure, he chased her like mad, but was he merely passing time at the convention, an affair he'd forget once he was back in Scotland? Until her next book came out and he had to write another review, that is.

Catlynne tried to push the fears from her mind as she stood in the nightclub with Leanne and Diane discussing new projects for Highland Press. A hush fell across the room as the first chords of a guitar and piano floated in the air. As it registered what the tune was, her eyes jerked up to see James standing across the room. Al Stewart's poetic *Year of the Cat* filled the air. Her gaze locked with James' and all about her receded to black.

Drawn to him, she walked away from Leanne and Diane without a word. He stood waiting for her to come to him, assured she would. A warlock conjuring her with a power she couldn't resist.

She didn't want to resist.

As she neared, she saw satisfaction in his lavender eyes. He opened his arms and she stepped into them. It felt like coming home.

That *terrified* her.

They swayed, not really dancing, just caught up in the magic of the moment. Al Stewart's beautiful song wrapped around them, cocooning them. Heat rolled off his body, the hint of cedar and bergamot of his cologne intoxicating. But the scent of the man underneath was even more lethal.

"Stay with me tonight," he whispered as he nuzzled her ear.

She looked up into the lilac eyes and nodded.

It was just that simple.

It was just that complicated. She'd taken the coward's way out.

At dawn, he finally fell asleep after making love to her all night. Drowning in those sensual images, peace eluded her. She leaned against his back, her hand stroking his beautiful arm.

She was in love with James Douglas Kinloch.

Fearing pain loving him could bring, she quickly dressed and slipped out of his room. Unable to face him, she hadn't even shown up for breakfast.

Thinking to distract the inner demons tormenting her, she'd joined Leanne and Diane in the crossbow demonstration.

Her mind not on the task, Catlynne struggled, trying to load the crossbow. Blasted thing wasn't easy to manipulate. There were several types, and naturally she ended up with one hard on her wrist. The crank that wrenched the bow into place required her to push with the power of her wrist.

"Ladies, the crossbow was an important development in

weaponry during the Medieval period. First hand-held weapon which could be used by an untrained man to injure or kill a knight in plate armour. The most powerful crossbows could penetrate armour and kill at two-hundred yards. The unassailability of the knight was at risk for the first time, taking the advantage from his hands." The instructor walked slowly along the line of women armed with replicas of the ancient weapons. "A crossbow contains a bowstring, which is held in place by a nut when the bolt is loaded and the crossbow is engaged. This is referred to as at *full cock.*"

This drew chuckles and baudy comments from the ladies participating in the class. One on the far end proclaimed, "Now *that's* what I'd call full cock."

"Hush, Marigold," Diane D. White, author of the successful *Tartan Cowboy* series, chided. She turned back to the others. "Ignore her, she's an erotica writer."

Catlynne knew without looking who had drawn the comment. Swivling her head, she saw James coming in their direction, that traitor Jack with him. For a cat that hated men, Jack sure bonded with Kinloch. Palies.

She'd fix him...*somehow.*

"You ladies have four types of crossbows. Pull-Lever, Push-Lever, Rachet," he nodded to Catlynne struggling with hers, "and Windlass." Taking pity on Catlynne, he paused and traded, giving her a 'baby version' about one-third the size. "Here, Miss, try the smaller one?"

She chuckled, trading with him. "My wrist thanks you."

"Careful. It's hair trigger. This smaller copy was an assassin's weapon. Easily hidden from view. Pope Urban II banned the use of crossbows against Christians in 1097, and the Second Lateran Council did the same for arbalests in 1139. The crossbow was seen as unchivalrous, a threat to social order. Ladies, aim at the target and gently release the trigger."

Just then, Virginia Keller's teacup terrier crawled out of her purse where she'd set it down to handle the crossbow. Yapping, it dashed in front of Jack. Big mistake. With a feral grin, Jack leapt, right on the mutt's trail. Jack's weight yanked the leash from James' hand, as the dog and the feline dashed onto the range just as the ladies were firing the weapons. James lunged in front of Catlynne, trying to snatch the leash to haul Jack back.

Virginia screamed, "My baby!"

She tried to go after the doggie, but the heel on her high heel snapped off, causing her to crash into Catlynne. The jarring caused the small crossbow to release its bolt.

Catlynne stared in horror. James had rescued Jack, but he now stood with a stunned expression—as a small crossbow bolt stuck out the right cheek of his arse.

"Bloody hell." James reached around and with gritted teeth yanked the small arrow out. Blood immediately soaked his pants. "I think someone better drive me to hospital so I can get stitches."

Taking the leash, Catlynne handed it to Diane. "Please, take Jack inside and tell the desk porter to have the sitter take him to my room."

Diane looked as if the Loch Ness Monster was on the end of the leash. "Me? You know I don't get along with kitties. He'd better not bite me."

Leanne laughed as she accepted the leash. "I love cats. Don't worry. Jack will be fine. Go with James."

James teased, "I think she shot me just to get even for all those bad reviews.

"I want her arrested," James demanded from his position on his stomach, where they just finished stitching him up.

Catlynne made a small gasp, staring at him with those huge hazel eyes. "I didn't do it deliberately, James."

The North Yorkshire Police Officer tried to maintain a stoic face. "There seems to be a question about whether Miss Falconer broke a law or not. There's a law still on the books which states it's legal to shoot a Scotsman with a bow and arrow every day of the week—except Sunday. Repercussions from William Wallace attacking York. Seeing as it's Saturday, by the letter of the law she didn't actually commit a crime."

"Why the bloody hell is that archaic law still on the books?" James demanded.

"It was an accident," Catlynne repeated, tears filling her eyes. "You cannot believe I did it on purpose."

"Accident or not, it's still not a crime. If she shot you on Sunday, then you'd have grounds to demand her arrest."

James shook his finger. "Ah ha! It's legal to shoot a Scot

with a *bow and arrow*. She shot me with a crossbow. That's not an arrow, that's a bolt. Arrest her."

"I need to check with the station to get a ruling on this." The officer scratched his head, clearly humbugged by the distinction. Shrugging, he left the emergency room.

Catlynne stood on shaky legs, coming to the end of the operating table. "James, why do you want me arrested? It was a series of dreadful mistakes, an accident. I didn't shoot you on purpose."

"Yes, you did." He reached out, took her hand and placed it to the centre of his chest. "Shot me straight through the heart and I shall never recover. You keep dashing about, have avoided me for the last three days. I hoped to have you arrested so I could post bond and get the judge to remand you to my custody. Then you, me and Jack could go home tomorrow."

"Home?"

"Aye, lass. Home."

"Oh, James!" Catlynne gasped and hugged him, smothering him with kisses.

"Easy lass, time enough to smooch once we get out of here." He kissed her slowly, deeply. "That's an aye to my proposal?"

"Oh, aye. I've always wanted my very own personal Scotsman."

He laughed. "It just struck me. How Jack brought us together. Like a plot from one of your books."

"Proper justice for all those horrid reviews. You fell in love just like a hero in one of my stories." Doubt shadowed her eyes. "You *are* in love, James, aren't you?"

"Ridiculously, deliriously, ecstatically, madly."

"Good, because I love you, too. Will you marry me in the kilt?"

James wiggled his eyebrows. "Aye, we'll have a Highland wedding. After, I'll even show you what a Scotsman wears under his kilt."

Gathering the green sheet around his hips, he sat up so he could kiss her properly.

"See, my books told you how wonderful love can be."

He pulled her against his chest holding her tightly. "I might've taken a little time for the *point* to be driven home.

But let's say, my love, I got it in the end."

DeborahAnne MacGillivray is the author of four books due out in 2006—
A RESTLESS KNIGHT, RAVENHAWKE, INVASION OF FALGANNON ISLE, and RIDING THE THUNDER.
Be sure to visit DeborahAnne's website
www.deborahmacgillivray.co.uk

Double Dare

by Michelle Scaplen

• *Delaware – It's illegal to get married on a dare*

Janie fed four quarters into the jukebox, her hands shaking as she pressed the buttons that would play her selection. *"You Shouldn't Kiss Me Like This,"* Toby Keith's ballad about a woman kissing her best friend, and the man so amazed by the kiss he finds himself feeling emotions for her he never felt before. Tonight she planned to put that theory to the test.

With the sounds of the opening chords filling the room, she walked up to Jake who sat at the bar with his business partner, Rick Mason, and tapped him on the shoulder. When she saw his face, she realized her mistake. He was never in a good mood when he spoke to Rick. But it was too late. If she didn't go through with this now, she never would.

"Excuse me," she said, hoping her voice didn't betray her fears. "Jake, may I speak with you alone for a second?"

Jake gave Rick a heated look, then flashed her a smile. "Sure, I'm finished here anyway."

She led him to the dance floor and before she lost her nerve, asked, "Dance with me?"

His arms went easily around her. Whether it was Jake beating up the boys who teased her in high school, or giving her moral support when she went on her first teaching interview, Jake had always been there for her. Even though he'd never admit it, he was the kindest man she'd ever known. How could she not be in love with him?

"Everything all right?" he asked, concern etched in his dark brown eyes.

She wrapped her arms around his neck and stepped into

199

his embrace. Jake stood over six feet tall, and if she meant to do this right she needed to move closer to him. "...*Cuz I'll just close my eyes and I won't know where I'm at, we'll get lost on this dance floor...*" The sweet lyrics rang in her ears. It was now or never! Janie stood up high on her tip toes, closed her eyes, leaned in closer, and kissed her best friend.

But he didn't kiss her back. Jake's mouth and eyes were opened wide as if in complete shock. "...*Spinning around and around and around...*" And that's exactly how it felt, as if the dance floor, not her and Jake, spun in circles. She pulled away from him, and beside the loud roaring of blood rushing in her ears, she heard the sound of everyone around her laughing and whooping it up.

Janie felt her face burn with embarrassment and saw the look of first shock, then pity on Jake's face. The tears would come, but she would hold them off until she was alone outside. Pulling away, she only stopped to grab her purse before she ran outside without looking back.

"Janie, wait!" Jake started after her. What the hell had just happened? One minute he sat arguing with Rick, the next he was being kissed by his best bud. "Janie!"

"Forget it dude, she's gone," Rick said from behind him with a slap on the back. He laughed. "That had to be the funniest thing I've ever seen."

"Screw you, Rick." *She must be hurting*, Jake thought as he tried to move away from Rick, but the dance floor was now packed as a fast paced 80's song played on the jukebox. "I've gotta find her."

"She'll be fine."

No she wouldn't. He knew she had about as much self-esteem as a pin. Sweet Janie, it must have taken all the strength she possessed to get up the nerve to kiss him. Kiss him? What the hell had that been about? "No, she won't be," he reaffirmed.

Mason put a hand on Jake's back and led him to the bar. "Just chill out a minute and have a beer." Rick signaled for the bartender and put up two fingers. "What are you going to say to her anyway?"

Jake shook his head. He hadn't a clue. "I don't know. Apologize?"

"She doesn't want to hear that," Rick said, then paused

and took a long pull on his beer after the bartender brought the two bottles over to them. "She wants to hear you're madly in love with her." He started laughing again, a sick drunken laugh. "She wants to hear you want to marry her."

Could that be? Janie Smith, the shy and slightly overweight girl he'd known since kindergarten was in love with him? "You're crazy."

Rick started to wobble out of his chair. The man was definitely drunk. "Ask her to marry you, she'll say yes. Trust me."

"No way," he replied. "It was just a kiss."

Rick put his arm around Jake's shoulder but he didn't know if it was a show of affection, or he needed to do it to steady himself. "Ask her to marry you." Then, with a grin added, "I dare you."

"Dare me? What are you twelve years old?"

"No man, just bored. I'm looking for some fun."

Rick and Jake owned First's Auto Body for six years, and Jake had been trying to buy him out for over five of them. They'd wanted to buy their own shop since high school. Jake was the brains behind everything, while Rick, or more precisely, Rick's father, was the money behind it. Now that Jake made enough money on his own, he wanted to run the place himself. He was fed up with his partner's laziness and unprofessional behavior.

"Come on, Rick. You've known Janie almost as long as I have. She doesn't want to marry me."

"Are you kidding? She's followed you around since I can remember."

Yeah, she had, but it'd always been all right with him. She'd never been like the beautiful, bone thin women he always dated, but she was smart, funny, and an honest to goodness friend. "Yeah, but that doesn't mean—"

"Ask her. I dare you. I know I'm right." Rick took another long sip of his beer. "You know what?" he said. "Let's make it interesting. You ask Plainie Janie to marry you, stay married to her for six months, and I'll sign those papers for you."

Jake didn't think about how this would affect Janie's feelings. He didn't think about anything but owning the shop full out. He put his hand out, Rick took it and gave it two strong pumps.

"Deal," they said at the same time.

Janie slammed her apartment door, threw her purse on the table, and fell onto the couch. She wiped the last of the tears from her eyes, willing herself not to let another one fall. All these years of a great friendship, and she'd thrown it away in a matter of seconds.

"So?" Donna, her good friend and roommate came out of her bedroom wearing a tattered bathrobe and fuzzy slippers. "How did it go? What happened?"

Janie leaned her head on the back of the couch and sighed. "How did it go? How do you think it went? I made a total ass out of myself."

"Oh honey." Donna was next to her in a second, then wrapped her arms around her. "I'm so sorry."

Janie pulled away, quickly stood, and walked into their tiny kitchen. "It's no big deal," she lied. "Jake and I will have a big laugh about it before you know it." Too bad Jake was probably already laughing about it now with his jerk-off of a business partner.

She took the tea bags down from the cabinet and turned on the kettle. Changing her mind, she turned it off again, then reached in the refrigerator and took out a beer. Maybe if she got good and drunk she'd forget this night even happened.

Donna followed her to the kitchen and sat in a chair. "Of course you will. I'm just sorry I couldn't be there with you tonight."

Janie sat next to her. "I know you weren't feeling well, don't worry about it." She took a sip of beer, then realized nothing was going to make her forget what happened. "I'm going to bed."

Two hours later, just minutes before she finally fell asleep, Janie heard the buzzing of the intercom. She quickly got up and answered it before it disturbed Donna. "What?" she asked, her voice rough from lack of sleep and too much crying.

"Janie, it's me. Let me in."

She froze and took a moment to calm herself before she pressed the button again. "It's two in the morning, Jake. Go home."

"I know what time it is. We need to talk," he called back, his voice as smooth and calm as always.

Might as well get it over with. "I'll be down in a second."

She put on Donna's bathrobe to cover her threadbare Mickey Mouse nightgown and walked down the flight of steps leading to the front door. When she saw him through the glass, she almost turned and ran back upstairs. God, he was so good looking, with light brown hair cut short and stylish. A strong, lean chest and thick muscled arms bulged through his black t-shirt. What had she been thinking when she kissed him? Did she think Mr. Perfect, Mr. Prom King would kiss her back, then admit his undying love for her?

When she didn't open the door right away, he knocked on the window. She took the last few steps to the door, opened it, and suddenly found herself held tightly in his arms as he passionately pushed his lips to hers. After the moment of shock, she relaxed and kissed him back.

She'd dreamt of this moment for as long as she could remember and it was finally happening. Jake Fielding was kissing her. On the lips, tongues dancing, bodies pushed together, kissing her. Her dreams were never this good.

He pulled away and caught his breath. "Marry me."

Janie stumbled back, but Jake's hand was quickly on her arm steading her. "What?"

"I've been driving around all night thinking about this. We've been best friends forever, have no secrets between us, and have a million things in common. Why waste our time looking for someone else, playing stupid mind games, going on date after date with the wrong person? Marry me, Janie. It makes sense."

"But you don't love me."

"Of course I do."

She shook her head. "I know you do," she said, "but it's not the romantic kind of love. It's not the kind where you think about me constantly, where you smile at just the thought of being near me, or where your heart beats faster whenever I touch you." *Not the kind of love I feel for him*

He let out a long breath. "But it's the best friend kind of love, and isn't that more important?"

"Well..." He pulled her into his arms again and kissed her more tenderly and she couldn't think of what she'd just been about to say. This time they were sweet little kisses with their eyes open, and she saw his were sparkling with affection.

She looked closely at his face, the bright lightbulb above them lighting every perfect feature, his perfect smile, his perfectly shaped nose, his perfect everything. She had to pull away from him when the realization hit her. "This is never going to work. I'm just me—Plainie Janie. I'm fat, and nothing special to look at, while you have women falling at your feet."

For a second she thought she saw a flash of anger on his face. "Have I ever once said anything bad about the way you look, Janie?

No, but he'd never said anything good either. She shrugged. "I guess not."

"Listen, Sweetheart," he said when he took her hand, "this could work. I really think so." Then he did something she would remember for the rest of her life. Jake got down on one knee and kissed her hand. "Janie Marie Smith, would you do me the honor of becoming my wife?"

Three weeks later Jake stood at the front of the church, his tie suddenly feeling too tight. "What am I doing here?" he asked his brother, Steve, his best man.

"Screwing up a perfectly good friendship."

Leave it to his brother not to pull any punches. "No, I'm not. It's all going to work out, you'll see."

"No, it's not. You're going to hurt one of the sweetest girls we know, and all because of a childish dare."

"It's not about the dare. It's about getting Rick out of my shop."

"Great, try explaining that to her six months from now, 'Gee, Janie, sorry about tearing out your heart and then stomping it into little pieces, but now I own my own auto body shop. We can still be friends, right?' Let me ask you something Jake. If you knew some other man was going to do this to her, what would you do?"

He'd probably beat the living tar out of them, he realized. "Shit," Jake mumbled.

"Yeah, shit is right."

But it was too late to do anything about it, because the organist began playing and everyone rose. He watched numbly as Donna walked down the aisle, then his six-year-old niece dropped flower petals with each careful step she took.

Then Janie appeared. The girl who helped him pass tenth

grade English, the girl who held his head when he threw up in the toilet the first time he'd gotten drunk, the girl who'd cried along with him when his father died. The woman who was about to become his wife.

He could see her nervous smile through her thin white veil. There was no way to stop the wedding without hurting her. And he cared about her too much to do that. *This won't be so bad*, he thought. If things didn't work out, they could remain friends afterwards, right? Maybe he could even tell her about the dare and she'd be willing to help him get Rick out of the shop and agree to a divorce if that's what they both wanted.

Of course, then he wouldn't be able to kiss her again, and he'd really loved those kisses. He never would have thought she could make his blood run so hot the way she did when her soft, sweet body pressed up against his. God, he was a selfish son of a bitch. Divorce her in six months? He'd be a fool if he did that.

It was a beautiful wedding, the reception went flawlessly, but now as they say, was the moment of truth. The beginning of their marriage.

Janie stood looking out on the balcony of the Bethany Beach hotel room shivering from the cool winter's air. Who was she kidding. The ocean breezes had nothing to do with her goose bumps. Very soon she'd be making love to her husband for the first time.

Jake had been wonderful throughout the whole ceremony, taking her cold clammy hand into his strong, warm one. He matched her every nervous smile with a reassuring one. And while her voice was a mere whisper while she spoke her vows, his was deep and sure.

During the reception when they danced their first dance to Toby Keith's song, Jake wrapped her in his arms making her feel warm and secure. He danced with her smoothly, and at the end of the song he dipped her back and kissed her wildly while their guests cheered him on.

Another thing that shocked her was when Rick had asked to dance with her. Jake, who she knew wasn't a jealous man, vehemently objected to it. It was fine by her. She wanted to save every dance for him.

Jake paced the room. What the hell was his problem? His wife stood outside on the balcony while he was inside. It was his wedding night for crying out loud, they should be in bed making love. And he wanted to make love to her—hadn't thought about much else all evening long.

His wife was Janie, not some model thin, stuck up snob that would judge everything he said, everything he did. She'd be kind and patient. Willing and accepting. He wouldn't have to make a move on her, or impress her with his charms. And that was why he was so nervous. Because for the first time in his life he was going to make love to a woman who meant more to him than a good time.

"Janie," he called out, "come inside. It's cold out there."

"Okay."

He handed her a glass of champagne that she placed on the table after taking a tentative sip.

He sat and patted the cushion next to him. "Sit." When she was beside him, he tucked a lock of hair that had come loose from it's pin behind her ear. She looked beautiful, he thought, then wondered if he'd said that to her tonight. Her skin glowed just as a bride's should, and her brown hair was piled on top of her head showing off her emerald green eyes. "We've been married for five hours, and I'm already a lousy husband. I should have told you when I first saw you walk down the aisle how incredible you look."

She looked as if she tried to hold back tears, and his heart lurched in his chest.

"No, I don't."

"Mrs. Fielding, are you calling your husband a liar?" When she shook her head, he said, "Good, are you nervous because we're going to make love soon?"

"Petrified."

God, he loved how they could be so honest with each other. "Me, too," he told her, "never more so in my life. But I know this is going to better than we've ever had with anyone else. Are you ready?"

She nodded and he took her hand and led her to the bedroom. After he flipped the light switch he asked, "Lights on or off?"

"Off."

"Alright." He switched the light off. "But next time we do

it my way, and I want to see you when I make love to you."

"But I'm fa—"

He stopped her words by putting his hand over her mouth. "If you say you're fat, I'm going right to my lawyer and get a divorce. Now, I'm going to kiss you and make you forget any insecurities you have." Before she had a chance to reply, he softly placed his lips on hers and felt her fears begin to melt away. His own fears quickly followed.

Everything after that was perfect. It was amazing to make love to your best friend. They laughed together when he couldn't undo her dress' zipper. They both tugged impatiently when his tie wouldn't go over his head. And the only shivering they'd done was because of pleasure and not fear.

He would never think of Janie as overweight again. She was curvy and soft. Her breasts were full and firm, and he made sure he gave both his full attention as he savored their sweet taste.

While deep inside of her, he felt complete. When she wrapped her legs around his, he felt desire. When he thrust his body and she met each one with abandon, he felt passion. And when she brought him over the edge into oblivion just seconds after he'd brought her there, he'd felt something he should have felt years ago. Undying love.

Five months of marital bliss. Janie still had to pinch herself every morning when she woke up in Jake's arms. Their honeymoon had been just a short weekend on the Delaware coast, because she couldn't take the time off of her kindergarten teacher's job. And when they returned, she moved into his three bedroom Wilmington home.

They fell into a pleasant routine. On weekends they either slept in late and read the paper together in bed, or got up early and went for a long drive to find a romantic place to have lunch. Weekday evenings were spent cooking dinner together, then snuggling in bed watching an old movie, or a classic television show. Their only arguments were about him leaving his shoes in the middle of the floor, or her forgetting to turn off a light when she left a room. It didn't matter much, since their arguments only led to making up, and making up led to making love.

This time, Jake had been the forgetful one. Janie walked

into the auto body shop with his lunch in her hand, when she heard loud voices coming from behind his office door.

"Just sign the damn papers, Rick," she heard her husband say.

"It's only been five months," his partner replied.

Her grandmother had warned her, never, never ever eavesdrop, but her feet wouldn't move. Her voice couldn't call out Jake's name, she couldn't even clear her throat to alert them of her presence.

"Dammit, Rick, it's close enough. I want you out of my shop."

"I dared you to stay married to her for six months, Jake, and I'm not signing over my half until then."

Suddenly every cell in Janie's body felt cold. Every moment of the last five months had been a lie. Every time he'd touched her, every sweet kiss he'd given her. Lies! She didn't know how long she stood behind the door, but she read the look on Jake's face when he'd opened the door. Guilt!

"Janie, how long—"

"Long enough." She threw his lunch at him and turned to leave.

She wasn't sure which was louder, the sound of Rick Mason's laughter or her husband's calling her name, but it didn't matter. She ran out the door and to her car before either one of them had stopped.

Later that night Janie went home. Not to the Wilmington house, but to her small apartment outside of the city. Donna waited for her with a warm cup of tea and friendly advice.

First came the tears. Then the men bashing. Finally Donna asked the inevitable. "What are you going to do?"

"I promised my Catholic grandmother a long time ago I'd never get a divorce. Silly, huh? But I can't stay married." Janie sniffed, battling another onslaught of tears.

"Oh, my God! I just remembered something." Donna flew out of her chair and went into her bedroom, coming out a minute later with a thick book in her hands. "Remember when I worked at the law office? Well, I remember reading in here that in the state of Delaware you can't get married on a dare. I thought it a silly law at the time, but now—"

"But he didn't dare me. Someone else dared him, is that the same thing?"

Donna flipped through the book, looking for the right page. Finding it, she said, "It doesn't specify here. All it says is that it's illegal to get married on a dare. Someone dared him, so you should be able to get an annulment. Is that what you want to do?"

Numbly, Jake stared at the papers on his lap. Janie had filed for an annulment. He let out a humorless laugh. Annulment—as if the past five months hadn't happened. The marriage had been consummated many, many times, but that wasn't the reason stated by her lawyer. It was all illegal because of that stupid dare.

He hadn't seen Janie in a week. When he called and she wouldn't come to the phone, he high-tailed it to her place only to discover she wouldn't come to the door, either. Being spring break, he couldn't even ambush her at school.

After neatly folding the papers, Jake placed them in the manilla envelope and put them in his glove compartment. The minute he received the certified letter, he'd driven to her apartment. Then he watched and waited for her to walk out the door and get into her car.

When she finally left, he didn't go after her. He waited for her to drive off and then got out of his car, walked to the door, and pushed the button under apartment 2C.

"Hello," Donna answered.

"Donna, it's me, Jake. I need to talk to you."

"Go away!"

"Just one minute." He ran his fingers through his hair and pleaded, "I promise. Please, Donna!" He had a plan and he couldn't pull it off without her help.

After a brief pause, he heard Donna reply a harsh, "Fine."

When Jake stood inside, he was met with exactly what he expected. The only thing worse than dealing with the woman whose heart you broke, was dealing with her best friend.

"You're an asshole!" Donna said when she'd opened the door.

Jake walked in. "I know."

"You're a really big asshole!"

"I know," he replied and then said, "but I love her, Donna."

"Real love, Jake?" she asked rightfully. "Not the 'hey

buddy thanks for helping me move' kind of love?

He didn't need a second to think about it. "No, it's the 'I hurt so much from missing her' love."

She studied him. He could feel her scrutinizing gaze and saw in her eyes the instant she believed him.

"We're going to Cape May this weekend," she said suddenly.

"I know. You always go during spring break."

"You won't make me regret this, will you?"

Jake gave Donna a reassuring hug and for the first time in a week he felt an ounce of relief. "Not for a minute," he promised.

It felt so good to finally be away, Janie thought. In town, she was reminded of Jake everywhere she went. No matter where, she was assaulted by either a memory of them hanging out together as friends, or spending time together as a married couple. So this year more than ever, she looked forward to her weekend in Cape May.

Donna booked them a room at The Camelot this year. The room had a stove and refrigerator, so it saved them money on dining out. They could spend it at the walking mall instead.

With her hands filled with grocery bags, she used her knee and a great act of balancing to unlock the door to their room. She pushed open the door and dropped her grocery bags the moment she saw Jake lounging comfortably on the bed. "Where's Donna?"

"She decided she'd rather go to Atlantic City this weekend."

Janie picked up her bags and placed them on the table. Great, what a turn-coat Donna turned out to be. "What are you doing here?"

He didn't move from his position on the bed. "I came to hand deliver the annulment papers. I signed them. They're over on the table."

She moved her bag and found the papers. It was what she wanted, so why did it hurt so much. "Thank you, you can leave now."

Still lying on the bed, he asked, "Did you know in Colorado it's illegal for a woman wearing a red dress to be out in public after 7:00 p.m.?"

"What?"

"It's true. I found it on this website the other day. And did you know in Georgia donkeys aren't allowed to be kept in bathtubs?"

She laughed at that one, couldn't help herself. "What does that have to do with anything?"

"Well there's a lot of stupid laws on the books, some so outdated it's not even funny. There are others about what you can't do with a farm animal that I won't even get into. Then there are those that tell you what you can or cannot do in the privacy of your own bedroom, but let's just say we won't be moving to Florida or California any time soon."

"We're not married anymore, Jake. We won't be moving anywhere together."

"This a great town, Cape May. I like it here," Jake continued as if she hadn't said a word. He stood up and walked into the kitchen. "New Jersey has it all, doesn't it? You have Atlantic City, and the beaches, mountains up north. And let's not forget it's the birthplace of The Boss and Old Blue Eyes. They do have their own set of ridiculous laws though. Can you believe you're not allowed to pump your own gas? Or that apparently in Trenton you're not allowed to eat pickles on Sunday. But you know what, I didn't find one law about getting married on a dare."

"Jake—"

"Come here, Sweetheart," he said before he wrapped his arms around her. Looking down into her eyes, he said, "God, this feels so good."

She tried to pull away, but his grip was too strong. Or maybe she didn't try that hard. All these years of being friends with Jake, of loving him from afar, and losing all that after he'd hurt her so badly, he still made her feel like the most beautiful woman in the world. "Jake you're not—"

"Not what? In love with you? I dare you to make me feel any differently." He gave her a peck on the lips. "I dare you to forgive me." He kissed her again, this time a brief second longer. "I dare you to tell me you don't love me anymore." Again, a longer kiss. "I dare you to marry me again, Janie. Because I am *so* in love with you. Like a friend, like a lover, like a wife—like hopefully the mother of my children some day. Like a man who couldn't bear the thought of living without you."

This time when he kissed her, he didn't stop until they were naked in bed. When he'd finished proving just how much he loved her, she asked, "What about the shop? Do you still have to own it with Rick?"

"Nah, I sold him my half instead. I'm going to open another one across town. I gave him a great deal on it though. I figured no matter how much of a jerk he was, if it hadn't been for him, I never would have married my best friend."

Be sure to visit Michelle Scaplen's website
www.MichelleScaplen.com

Faery Good Advice

by Jacquie Rogers

• *Auburn, Washington - Men who deflower virgins,*
regardless of age or marital status,
may face up to five years in jail

Shortly after the Frozen Time

Not a single soul had come into Virgin Freedom Travel all morning. I had more bills on my desk than fleas on a troll. The rent had been due a week ago last Friday. I stared at the ominously silent phone, hoping Auburn Bell hadn't shut it off yet.

My back ached and I'd have given my left faery wing to lean back on a pillow. Okay, *not*. I'm very proud of my wings—they're translucent and larger than most women's. Size *does* matter.

The phone rang and I snatched it up. "Good morning! Virgin Freedom Travel, Keely speaking. Where may I zap you?"

"Do you plan only virgin honeymoon packages?" a timid female voice queried.

"No, we also offer other honeymoon travel services that others, say, Purity Agency don't."

"Uh, is there an extra charge if, you know, you zap a bride outside of the Virgin Protection Zone and, uh, she's not a..."

"A virgin?"

"Uh, yeah."

"No extra charge, but you'd better be thinking about what you're going to tell your fiancé." I prided myself on my sensitive counseling abilities.

Click.

Okay, so I blew that one. I could have kicked myself.

Luckily, the phone rang again. I answered in my most polite and professional voice.

"My fiancée just called, but she forgot to give you my credit card number." A baritone voice oozed over me like syrup on a hot pancake.

Oh, my. I didn't want to tell him his fiancée hadn't actually booked a trip. And I sure didn't want to tell him why. "Your name, please? We have several associates and I'll find out which one worked with your fiancée."

"Tyler Grant." He sounded impatient, but I still basked in the sexy low timbre of his voice. "Listen, I'm busy, so just take my info and give it to the person who's booking the virgin honeymoon trip."

"But—"

End of basking. I grabbed a pen as he began rattling off his address and credit card number. He didn't give me his phone number, but I could get that off Caller ID if I needed it, which I doubted. "Thank you, Mr. Grant."

"Tyler."

"I'll give this to your fiancée's travel agent."

After he cut the connection, I leaned back and pressed the back of my hand to my brow in an effort to forestall an impending headache. I felt a doozy coming on.

I wondered why I ever decided to go into business for myself. Especially the virgin transport business, the trickiest of all. Auburn's city council had discussed striking the deflowering ban from its books, but doing so would put me and many others out of business. Thankfully, Auburn was still a Virgin Protection Zone, one of the few left in the United States.

The phone rang again. Instinctively, I reached for the handset, then hesitated, my wings twitching. I smelled trouble.

"Good morning. Virgin Freedom Travel, this is Keely—"

"I can't get married!" The young woman's panicky voice sounded shrill. She also sounded like Tyler's fiancée.

"Relax. Everything will be fine." I'm so good at this. I smiled to myself. "Not every bride is a virgin. Most men aren't that concerned about it."

She sobbed, then blew her nose.

I held the phone away from my ear for a moment of nose-blowing privacy. "I'm sure you can work it out."

"It's not that. It's, well, he's gone a lot..."

"And?"

She cleared her throat. "A *lot*. And, um, I'm going to have a...a baby..." The sobs overtook her again.

"And the baby's not his?"

"Yes! I mean no, the baby's not his. I can't marry *him*, because I'm going to marry Collin. Tell Tyler the wedding's off, that I'm, uh, sick or something."

Click.

A couple of aspirin would help a lot—and a shot of Jack Daniels.

The phone rang again.

After hoping for so long that the phone would ring, I suddenly didn't want to answer it. I glanced at the Caller ID. Tyler Grant. Big surprise.

"Good morn—"

"About that virgin honeymoon my fiancée booked, make it Cancun, Mexico, instead of Thailand."

"But—"

"And book dinner reservations at Riviera Maya."

"Tyler?"

"I have another call. Talk to you later."

Click.

I stared at the phone. For two cents I'd crush it.

The mailman backed up to the door and pushed his way in with his butt, sorting mail as he did so.

"More bills?"

"I just bring 'em. I don't send 'em." He handed me a stack of envelopes. "Have a good day." His sing-song voice trailed behind him, echoing throughout the room.

A good day, eh? I resisted the urge to whisk the whole darned mess of bills into the round file. The top envelope was from my landlord's attorney.

The phone rang again. Tyler. For a busy man, he certainly called a lot. "Good morn—"

"Have you booked the virgin honeymoon trip yet? I'm not about to get thrown in jail for five years over some technicality."

"No, sir, there's been a complication." As in, he wouldn't be deflowering any virgins in the foreseeable future.

"And that would be?"

"Mr. Grant, I think you should call your girlfriend."

"She said she didn't care where we went. Is there a problem with Cancun?"

I swear, this man could make a woman swoon with his voice alone. "No."

"Then book it."

"What dates?"

"Why, Valentine's Day, of course. For two weeks—the best hotel, the best restaurants, the most exclusive tours. Let me know which airline you're booking with. I have Frequent Flyer miles."

Click.

I sighed. My commission on a trip like this would be a nice chunk of change. I stared at the envelope from my landlord's attorney. I dared not open it. I knew exactly what he wanted—three months' back rent and the security deposit I'd never paid.

Tyler's trip would cover my rent—and the overdue phone bill, too.

But it wouldn't be right. I punched the Caller ID button and wrote down Tyler's number. He had to be told, even if his chickenhearted ex-fiancée wouldn't do it.

The phone rang before I worked up the courage to call.

"Ms. Smith?"

"Yes."

"Ms. Keely Smith?"

"Yes."

"This is Muffy from Auburn Bell." I could have bottled her cheery voice and sold it to Disney. "As I'm sure you're aware, your bill is overdue. If you don't have payment in our office before close of business this Friday, I'm afraid we're going to have to disconnect your service."

I bet that made her day. "Thank you, Muffy."

I sat back in my chair and stared at my computer. It sat on my desk, almost daring me to book the trip. A couple of keystrokes, a few measly clicks of the mouse, and voila! I'd have enough money to pay my rent and Muffy, too. But Tyler would pay for a solo virgin honeymoon.

We faeries take our word as our honor. The problem was, I hadn't said much. I rubbed the hologram tattoo on my forearm, hoping it would give me a hint as to what I should do. It didn't. His fiancée hadn't waited for an answer when she told me to give Tyler the news. As for Tyler, he'd done all the talking—and all the assuming, too.

So I booked the virgin honeymoon trip starting the next week, on Valentine's Day. For two. And watched the electronic funds transfer land in my bank account. A few more keystrokes and Virgin Freedom Travel's rent and phone were paid to current.

This called for a bagel with real cream cheese. Or Mylanta.

The phone—the one Muffy would no longer have the pleasure of shutting off—rang. Tyler, again.

"Good morn—"

"Whew! What a busy day. Did you get the trip booked?"

"Yes, I did."

"Good. I'll be over Friday night to check the itinerary."

"In person?"

"Do you have an objection to that?"

"No."

"Seven o'clock. I'll bring Chinese take-out."

Click.

I swore to teach that man to end a phone call properly or choke him until his eyeballs popped out.

It was Tuesday morning. Nearly noon, actually. I had three full days to book more trips and earn enough money to refund Tyler Grant's booking deposit. Actually, he'd have to stop talking and listen for once. In fact, I didn't really feel guilty at all. He'd insisted I book this honeymoon trip. *Insisted.*

In that warm-honey voice of his.

If he weren't so darned pushy, I'd be panting after him myself. That, and his humanness. I, of course, am saving myself for a faery man, not a vulgar human.

Not to mention the fact my parents would totally wig out if I told them I was in an inter-species relationship.

I spent the rest of the day tidying the office just in case Wednesday brought a flurry of customers banging down my door. I filed, vacuumed, and even cleared the top of my desk.

The phone rang a few more times. The first caller dialed the wrong number. The second caller booked a family vacation to Yellowstone. Although happy to help, that sort of trip doesn't net me enough money to make it worth my while. The third caller was a heavy breather. We get those a lot in my business.

Wednesday brought renewed determination that I would earn enough money to cover Tyler's commission should he cancel. Which he would, of course, since he had no bride at all, let alone a virgin bride. I called a few churches and talked to the pastors, trying to drum up some business.

Pastors had a pretty good lock on which brides-to-be were virgins. Many of them had recommended my services before and said they would happily do so again. Unfortunately, none of them knew of virgin brides who required a transport out of the Virgin Protection Zone. It took all morning to call the churches.

In the afternoon I resigned myself to calling Elvis wedding chapels. The ratio of virgin brides-to-be was smaller there, but I couldn't afford to pass up any lead.

Maybe there'd be a run on autumn weddings. The landlord and Muffy were temporarily mollified, but I still owed money for water, gas—and we won't even talk about American Express. (I fanned myself to keep from fainting.)

By Thursday I'd booked a few more small trips, but none that paid a decent commission. In truth, I barely made enough to pay my Crunchy Cheetos tab. I should have been a manicurist or something. People's nails grew during every season.

By Friday noon, I figured I'd be back in the faery world shortly after seven that evening, eating crow my parents would gleefully dish out.

I could hear their I-told-you-sos already. I should have met a nice fae man and had a bunch of cute little fae babies instead of running off to the human world to seek whatever I was seeking. While I still didn't know what that was, I wanted to succeed in both worlds.

At six o'clock I locked the front door, straightened my desk and went upstairs to my apartment. A quick shower didn't help me figure out an escape from my dilemma, but it did a whole lot for my state of mind. Showers are the most therapeutic device ever invented.

At 6:59 p.m. I headed downstairs, and at 6:59:59, a very

tall, broad-shouldered man stood outside the glass office door, rapping hard enough to vibrate the wall.

If I could design a man to fit his voice, he would have looked exactly like Tyler Grant—blue-black hair, defined eyebrows, and chiseled features that oozed manliness. I stared, then opened the door and stuttered my name.

"Nice to meet you, Keely."

As his hand grasped mine, warmth seeped in and up my arm. My stomach felt buzzy, like I'd gulped too much Perrier. And deep down inside, I felt a need I didn't quite understand. But I knew one thing—this guy could twitterpate a rock.

After a couple of deep breaths, I had enough poise to form actual words. "I'll get a vase for those flowers."

"That's not necessary." Tyler glanced at his Rolex. "Lettie should be here any minute now. She's quite punctual."

Not this time. It's amazing how the faster I needed my brain to work, the slower it went. He had a right to know Lettie wasn't coming; in fact, she was no longer his fiancée.

Tyler placed the bouquet on the credenza. "I'll go out to the car and get the Chinese food."

I stared at him, my mouth hanging open. Should I tell him he had no fiancée? What if he canceled the trip? I'd already spent the commission. The buzzing in my stomach turned into a hard knot.

He came back inside with two bags and put them on the desk. "I'm a little warm. Mind if I take off my coat?"

"Oh. No. Of course not."

He shrugged off his topcoat, revealing a T-shirt with a tie painted on it. He grinned and I thought I'd melt in a little pool at his feet.

"I don't stand on formality," he teased.

Then the most extraordinary mark caught my eye, one I'd never seen in the human world. His left forearm bore a septacle—not a dull colored tattoo like humans had, but an opaque design that looked three-dimensional. All the colors of the rainbow sparkled within. Very similar to my own tattoo.

Big-mouth me, I had to ask. "I love your tattoo. When did you get it?"

He studied me for a moment, his left eyebrow raised. "You're the first person who's ever noticed, actually. I don't know when I got it. My parents never mentioned it."

"It's very cool." I was tempted to show him mine. All members of our family sported the crest on their forearms. But humans couldn't see faery tattoos, so there was no point. And he couldn't be a faery because he didn't have wings.

"She should be here," he said, looking at his watch again.

I wanted to avoid talking about his phantom fiancée. "We might as well eat," I said, sounding as perky as Muffy. "There's no use letting the food get cold. I'll get some plates."

He took several boxes out of the bags. "Dang, they gave me plastic spoons instead of the chopsticks I asked for."

The smell made my mouth water. I looked over the banquet he'd spread out. "Mmmm, egg rolls, pork and seeds, moo goo gai pan—you brought the works!"

"Dig in." He chuckled, a low rumble that reached deep within me. "Nothing like a good meal to get my fiancée and me started on a long and prosperous marriage."

The mustard-coated pork didn't quite make it to my mouth. "What about a happy marriage?"

"Happiness isn't a variable. You don't marry someone you don't enjoy being around. Length of marriage, however, depends on luck and health. And while I'm currently prosperous, these things can turn on you in a flash. I might be living under a log next week. You never know."

He loaded his plate, then put a little back. "Better save some for Lettie."

"Who?"

"Lettie. You know, my fiancée."

"Oh, her. Yes." I swear, his gaze bore right through me. He liked what he saw, but being an honorable man, he hid it well.

He ate for a few minutes and then said, "You only brought two plates."

"Oh." No witty remark rattled around in my brainpan at the moment, so I had to wing it. "Maybe she got caught in traffic."

Tyler nodded once, took another bite, then dug his cell phone from his pants pocket. "I'll call her."

"No!" I had my hand on his before I knew it. My heart raced and my stomach tied in a knot. I couldn't let him find out he'd been dumped this way. He was pushy, yes. Abrupt, certainly. But something about him drew me and I couldn't be dishonest with him, no matter what the cost.

He tipped his head and raised a brow. "No?"

"No. Aren't you hungry?"

"Starved. I didn't have time to eat today, except for an Energy Bar on the way to the gym this morning."

"Eat hearty. Then we'll talk."

"About what?"

"Anything you want." And one thing he didn't.

His appetite was certainly healthy. I had to be patient while he consumed a major portion of the dinner. My food suddenly didn't seem so tasty. All I could think about was the heartache he would feel when I told him the bad news—and then the worse news.

"Lettie's still not here. Why don't you go ahead and show me the itinerary and brochures you prepared?"

"Let's not. Tyler, this isn't easy, but I have to tell you something."

Again he cocked a brow. I swallowed and rushed on before I lost my nerve. "Lettie isn't coming. In fact, she's not going on the honeymoon."

Tyler put down his fortune cookie. "But she insisted we get away even though she didn't care where we went."

"Tyler, there's no simple way to say this, but...she's marrying another man and having his baby."

His mouth gaped open. I hard a hard time not looking at his full lips—knew they could do real damage to a girl's defenses. At the same time, I could have kicked myself for my abrupt comment. Surely, there had to be a more diplomatic way of telling a man he'd been dumped.

But then he chuckled. Soon, he'd thrown back his head and laughed as if I'd told him the funniest joke he'd ever heard.

"You're serious?" he asked.

I nodded. "She called me the same day you gave me your credit card information."

"And you booked the trip anyway?"

After a deep breath, I told him the rest.

"So, you could cancel the virgin honeymoon, but you can't give my money back?"

"Not until Monday, and maybe not even then."

"I see."

"What do you see?"

"I see this is one of the happiest days of my life. I'm rid of a fiancée who didn't love me, nor I her. I met a beautiful woman with a sharp wit, and I'm booked on a vacation where there should be some great string bikinis."

My face flushed with sudden anger. I'd tormented myself with this for three days. Three days!!! And he was *happy*? "Why on earth did you propose if you didn't want to marry her?"

"Arranged marriage. My parents and her parents co-own a lumber mill. They wanted to ensure the business stayed in the family."

"And you went along with it?" I couldn't imagine such a forceful man being bullied into marrying anyone.

He shrugged. "My parents are good people. I'd do anything for them. Wouldn't you, for yours?"

I felt like a skunk. "No, I haven't done a single thing my parents wanted me to. But you know, I think I'm sorry for it."

He dabbed his mouth with a paper napkin. "In that case, I think we ought to go see a movie."

"I don't follow."

"Sure you can. Just stand up and follow me right out that door."

"And we need to discuss your method of ending phone calls."

A smile quirked the corner of his lips. "Right after you tell me your favorite color."

"Green." I rubbed my thumb against my fingers. "*Dinero.*"

"In that case, we should go to my house and watch 'The Color of Money' on DVD."

"Or to the theater. Move it, pal. I can't follow if you don't go out the door first."

Later that night, my head reeled at the turn of events. Tyler had asked me to visit his parents the next day. I'd refused. While he might be delighted with the way things worked out, they wouldn't like it at all. In that case, they wouldn't like me, either, which for some reason bothered me. So I'd talked him out of it.

I did, however, agree to go bowling. I'd never been bowling in my life. They have a dearth of bowling alleys in the fae world, I'm afraid. Like none.

The next day, I landed a huge account. A virgin bride-to-be who was the manager of Auburn Bell called—good ol' Muffy. The groom had grown up with the dot coms and had done quite well for himself. They'd booked a month-long trip to French Polynesia. My commission on the virgin transport alone would pay my rent and expenses for another six months.

By the time Tyler arrived to pick me up for our bowling date, I had the deal sown up, my office shut down, and my only pair of jeans on.

"Nice Wranglers." He took my hand. "Let's go."

The night ended too soon. I sat in the passenger seat of Tyler's blue Escalade, my arms tingling where he'd held them when he showed me how to hold the heavy bowling ball. His nearness now drew my molecules in his direction even though my seatbelt held me right where I was.

He pulled up in front of my office building and turned to me. "May I come in?"

The look in his eyes said that if I said 'yes,' it would mean yes to a whole lot more than him having a glass of wine—grave danger to him in the Virgin Protection Zone. "How about you have one glass of wine and then leave?"

"I'll take you up on the wine."

Somehow, I think I lost that round. Or won. Whatever. At that point I didn't know what I wanted. Tyler Grant attracted me like no other man, human or fae, ever had. But I couldn't stay in his world. No matter how my business turned out, I intended to return home eventually, and marry a man of my own kind.

Still, it wouldn't hurt to spend the rest of the evening with him as long as he didn't get too rambunctious. So I smiled and led him into my private apartment above the office.

As soon as we got in the door, he wrapped his strong arms around me and held me close. A man can't keep secrets at such proximity, I can assure you. He wanted me. I wanted him more.

I tilted my head up as he lowered his and our lips met. That first touch was hotter than Cinnamon Altoids. When I gasped, his tongue swept over my lips and into my mouth. I didn't know what to do. I needed his strength and pressed harder into him.

His low growl turned me on even more. The tattoo on my forearm began to glow, as did his. A quick caress of his back confirmed he had no faery wings, not even nubbins. I was disappointed, but didn't care as much as I had when I first met him. I ran my fingers through his thick hair and held his head so he could never stop kissing me. If I'd known kissing could be this good, I'd have done it much sooner!

He swept me off my feet and into his arms, breaking our kiss. I wanted him to kiss me again, but he started walking. I thought sure he'd head for the bed.

"The Virgin Patrol," I reminded him regretfully. "Five years in jail. You don't want that to happen over a moment of—"

He sat me on the couch. "Where are the wine glasses?" he interrupted, his voice ragged.

"Wine?" I couldn't remember ever discussing wine.

"You invited me for a glass of wine. So—glasses?"

I collected my wits, although I wasn't so sure I could stand yet. "In the cupboard to the right of the sink."

He brought two filled glasses, handed one to me, then sat beside me. "I need a virgin bride in order to go on the trip you booked for me."

I'm stared into his eyes, practically ready to jump his bones, even though I knew I absolutely couldn't do that, and he's worried about having a virgin bride? "No, you don't. But it's an expensive trip, so you might as well get your money's worth."

"I always get my money's worth." His gaze smoldered as he took my hand. "Go with me."

"What?"

"Go with me."

"Why would you even ask? We just met!"

He shrugged those hunky big shoulders of his. "I have the time off. I have a trip purchased. All I need is...you."

It seemed right. Wrong, but right. He short-circuited my common sense, but I was coherent enough to know I should delay this decision. "I'll let you know Monday."

"Only if you spend tomorrow with me. I want a fair shot at convincing you to take this trip with me."

"Are you thinking honeymoon?"

He took my wineglass and sat it on the end table. Then he

Faery Good Advice

turned to me and took me into his arms. "Whatever you give me, I want," his low voice rumbled in my ear. "And make no mistake about it, I want more."

He stood and pulled me to my feet. "I'm leaving now. You think about it. I'll be back at noon tomorrow." And he left.

The room seemed empty and my heart told me to chase after him and ask him to stay. But of course I couldn't. I'm a faery, and when we grant our love it's for millennia, not just seventy or eighty years.

My confusion hadn't subsided by the time he showed up on Sunday. But the moment I saw him, my heart did these funny little flip-flops and I felt warm all over. I wanted him more than anything, but was I willing to lose him after a mere seventy-or-so years? And then it came to me—the heartbreak would be worth the love if it were true and freely given.

But how could I tell if his love was true and freely given? Or mine, either? I'd never even been kissed before, so I couldn't call myself a great authority on the subject.

We spent a wonderful day together feeding the ducks in the park, sipping double-tall mochas—with whipped cream—at the corner Starbuck's, and watching a double-feature at the second-run movie theater.

Monday morning he called first thing. A shot of electricity gave me a shiver in all the womanly places when his name showed on the Caller ID. I answered, "Hello, Ty."

"Just thought I'd check in and see how your day is going."

I thought about the money I had in savings from Muffy's booking on Saturday. I'd never know the true reason behind Tyler's offer unless I told him I could refund his money. Did he do it for love or because he needed a companion?"

"Fine." I smiled. "I'm having a great day. You?"

"Me, too, especially when I'm talking to you."

Faery's honor and all that, I had to tell him. "Tyler, I just had a great deal come through. Since you don't have a virgin bride, I can now cancel your trip and refund your money."

Silence.

"Tyler?"

"I'll be right over."

My heart sank. He wanted his money back. I'd wanted so much for him to be the love of my life. Although I supposed it was for the best, him being human and all. Tears poured down my cheeks. I grabbed a tissue, wiped my face, then dabbed at the keyboard.

Ten minutes later Tyler crashed through the door. He pulled me out of the chair, hugged me close, and the next thing I knew, we were in a lip lock. I felt like a Hershey bar someone had left on the dashboard in August.

He finally broke the kiss.

"Do you want me to cancel the trip?"

Not fair. I was giving *him* an out. "It's not up to me."

"It's one-hundred percent up to you. I want you. All of you. I want you to be my wife and I want you to have my babies—at least two."

"How about puppies to start with?"

"I want puppies, too. They make great babysitters."

Tears welling in my eyes, I threw my arms around his neck. "Then I'll go with you."

On Valentine's Day, we married in front of the Justice of the Peace, and that afternoon we boarded the shuttle to the virgin transport station. The attendant gave us a bouquet of flowers and a bottle of champagne. "Follow me, Mr. and Mrs. Grant," she said, and led us to a compartment with two padded reclining chairs. We sat and buckled the seatbelts.

"This is it." Tyler squeezed my hand. "Our honeymoon."

The door shut with a whoosh. The attendant's voice sounded on the intercom. "Three, two, one, honeymoon!"

Darkness enveloped us, then sparkles, like pixie-dust, then bright light as if we stood on stage. The room spun faster and faster, then slowed to a stop.

I blinked a few times and looked around the familiar room. An overstuffed couch angled across the room, accompanied by several cushy chairs. Pictures of family members lined the walls and a big-screen television took up the end of the long room.

Tyler squeezed my hand, confusion filling his eyes. "Surely this isn't the hotel room you booked for us."

We weren't in Cancun, of that I was sure. "No, it's not."

"Then where are we?"

I took off my seatbelt and stood. "We're in my parents' house."

"Your parents?" He looked a bit baffled as he rose from his chair. "I'm happy to meet them, of course, but I had other ways in mind to show you a good time."

My dad walked in. "You'll have plenty of time for that."

I hugged him. "Dad, this is my husband, Tyler Grant." Turning to Tyler, I said, "This is my dad, Kelvin."

The two men shook hands and exchanged greetings. Dad hugged me again. "Your mother and I have been expecting the two of you."

"You have?"

"Yes, the Matchmaker said you'd find true love on the human earth, but not with a human."

"But Tyler is a human."

Dad shook his head. "Tyler, would you show me the tattoo on your forearm?"

Tyler frowned. "How did you know I have one?"

"Because all faeries have one." He looked at Tyler's. "You have the septacle of the Green Clan." Dad smiled and patted Tyler on the shoulder. "Your mother became gravely ill and had to return to the faery world or die."

Tyler looked confused. "My mother? But..."

Dad placed his hand on Tyler's arm. "Yes, son. Your real mother. She couldn't bring you with her at the time, so she left you with a human family she'd grown very close to. They offered to care for you—to love you."

"She's still alive?" Tyler looked shocked at the surprise news.

"She is, and you're the pride of her life. She's kept a very close watch on you all these years. I'll give her a call tomorrow."

I hugged Tyler and our tattoos glowed. "Oh Tyler, I'm so glad we found each other and you found your true home."

"This is bizarre." Tyler squirmed a bit. "My back is itching like crazy! What's happening?"

"Your wings are sprouting. They didn't before because they can only sprout in the faery world. Take your shirt off, son, you'll be more comfortable," Dad told him.

As Dad left, I helped Tyler with his shirt. I saw the first nubbins of his wings. I gently massaged them, and he groaned with pleasure.

"My human parents will be worried. I want to visit them as soon as soon as we finish our honeymoon."

"We can do that." His wings grew larger. "Tyler?"

Jacquie Rogers

"Hmm?"

"I love you."

He turned around and kissed me deeply. "Mrs. Grant, you're the love of my life, the light of my world."

Be sure to visit Jacquie Rogers' website and blog
http://www.Jacquierogers.com
http://keelysfaerygoodadvice.blogspot.com/

The Trouble With French Kisses

by Kristi Ahlers

• *France - It's illegal to kiss on railways*

Paris, France

Who would have guessed the country famous for its romantic city of Paris had a law regarding kissing on the public railways? Or, that said law would be enforced?

It amazed Hannah a country that had a kiss named after it would actually arrest people for sharing one. Unbelievable.

Hannah looked over at Damien and tried to find some humor in the situation they were currently in.

Sadly, sitting in a police station waiting to pay a fine for public displays of affection was *not* funny. At least not yet, but that could change...or not.

She was about to have a record, and for kissing no less. Well, to be fair, the kiss had been yummy—had been a kiss to beat all kisses. It would surely find a place in the *kiss hall of fame,* if such a place existed. But, had it been good enough to be arrested and embarrassed over? Well...maybe. All right, yes. If one really had to be arrested, it had definitely been good enough.

Hannah considered herself a good girl—she never cheated on tests, never cut class, always returned extra change when given to her. She tried to be kind to the elderly, kids, and animals. In other words, she played by the rules.

Except this one time, but to be fair she'd had no idea they had a law against kissing on the railways. After all, she was an American living in Paris. Damien, on the other hand, should have known better.

He claimed he had no idea such a law existed. He then made the mistake of pointing out he'd kissed plenty of other girls in front of the police without any repercussions. Nice, just what every girl wanted to hear after her toes had been curling, and she'd been in the process of melting into a puddle of...well it didn't matter now.

"I'm going to be deported. Shipped back to the States in shame. They're going to laugh me right out of the building when I show up for work again. That's if I'm allowed to even set foot in the store. You know, they do have standards, and I'm sure having their associates arrested for kissing isn't something they're going to overlook."

Damien looked over at Hannah and thought she'd never looked prettier. Her face was all flushed with a combination of humiliation and fear. "Hannah, it will be okay. I promise." Gently he reached over and brushed a tendril of her blonde hair away from her face. "They aren't going to deport you and you will not lose your job."

Hannah wanted to believe him, she really did, but she'd only known him a few short days. Days that had a much larger affect on her then she ever thought possible. She was in love, or at least as close to love as one can be before meeting the parents and extended family.

No, she knew Damien. He was a gentleman who considered her likes and dislikes, treated her to a wonderful first date, was kind to animals and had a sense of humor. Oh, and he kissed like no one's business.

In fact, Damien and his kisses had been true inspirations in several dreams she'd had over the past two nights after they'd hung up from their marathon phone calls.

Damien reached over and picked up Hannah's hand. Gently he stroked the top of her fingers. He'd waited a lifetime for the kiss they'd shared tonight. He wasn't going to let her get away. They were meant to be together despite the trouble they were in due to one of the hottest kisses he'd ever received.

No, this was one Frenchman that wouldn't let his heart walk away. He'd waited a long time for her. She'd been worth the wait, and one day they'd laugh about this. *One day.*

The Trouble With French Kisses

Five days earlier

"How do I get myself into these messes?" muttered Hannah as she hopped down the hallway of her apartment while trying to put on her shoes. She'd be late to work if she didn't get her act together fast. "Why can't I just say no?"

Chantal, her friend, looked up from her latest issue of *Vogue* and raised an eyebrow in enquiry. "And what mess would that be today, *mon ami?*"

Hannah blew the hair out of her face as she quickly glanced at her friend while putting on her coat. She wished she could lie around and read all morning, then proceed to wander down to a sidewalk café for Cappuccino and conversation. As luck would have it, she had to work for a living. She didn't have any hard feelings, as she enjoyed her work as an associate at *Louis Vuitton,* but every once in a while she'd like to just do her own thing.

"I just got off the phone with Emilie and agreed to go out tonight after work with her and her boyfriend."

"So, what's the problem?" Chantal asked as she stood and slipped into her shoes.

"It's a blind date." Hannah looked around the room searching for her purse and keys. "Where did I put my keys?" Frantically she started lifting the decorative pillows, looking for them.

"It's about time you started to see men, Hannah. After all, you've been living the life of a nun since you moved here. This is the *city of love* and *amour* will find you eventually."

"Yes, well, love will have to wait. I need to find my keys and bag."

Chantal walked over to the bench sitting in the hall and picked up the missing items. "Here's your bag. Come on, I'll give you a ride to work." So saying, she tossed them to her frantic friend.

With a smile, Hannah caught the small missiles and walked toward her front door. She really needed to get to work. She'd worry about the 'date' later, when she had time. She quickly shut and locked the door and ran after Chantal.

Hannah walked back to the stockroom for another signature monogram bag for what she considered the world's pickiest customer—for that day at least. Already the customer had inspected and rejected five beautiful bags. They were either too big or too little. Hannah kept thinking of 'Goldilocks and the Three Bears.' Hopefully, the *speedy bag* would be just right and, therefore, the winner. She'd be free to leave once she finished with *Goldie.*

Though always crowded, the store seemed more so today. She hurried around a luggage display when she ran smack dab into a very hard chest.

Immediately she felt arms come up and encircle her as she wobbled back, in danger of upsetting the display behind her.

"I'm sorry. I wasn't looking. Are you okay?" enquired a masculine voice in accented English.

Hannah dropped the bag she held and grasped the arms of her rescuer in order to steady herself. After making sure she'd remain upright, she looked up and met the most extraordinary green eyes she'd ever seen. The face that looked down at her was breathtaking.

He was gorgeous. His face looked as if it had been chiseled out of stone, but the cleft in his chin, combined with the sensual full lips and beautiful green eyes made him look striking rather then intimidating.

"Are you okay?" green eyes enquired once again.

Wetting suddenly dry lips, Hannah smiled slightly. "Yes, I'm fine. Sorry about that." Bending, she retrieved the bag she'd dropped trying to get her pounding heart under control. This was just too weird. She'd never experienced this kind of reaction to any man—ever. Perhaps that's what had been wrong from the get go with the few men she'd bothered to date. Go figure, she'd run into a man that could make her breathless when she was due to meet another man later that night.

"Well, I'm sorry as well. If you're certain you are quite fine now, I can see you have a not so very patient customer waiting for you." Green eyes nodded his head in the direction of Goldilocks.

"Um, yes, yes I do need to get back to her." Finally beginning to breathe normally again, Hannah found herself surprised once again at the tingling feeling of attraction surging through her a second time.

Green eyes' smile should have been tagged as a lethal weapon. With as much grace as possible, Hannah reluctantly left and made her way to the stockroom. She needed to get her customer on her merry way. Hopefully with a new bag in hand.

Damien continued to smile as he watched the pint sized Hannah as she made her way through the crowd. He'd been angling for an introduction for several weeks, but Emilie had been putting it off, saying she needed the right moment. Well, no one would ever call Damien Jacques *patient*. When he saw something he wanted, he went after it.

And he wanted Hannah.

Damien didn't consider himself a playboy, but he did enjoy the company of beautiful women. Lately though, his life seemed to be running in a predictable pattern he no longer found comforting. Something seemed to be missing.

He began to see his friends pairing off and finding happiness in relationships. In the back of his mind, he'd always wanted to marry and raise a family, but he'd never met the woman truly meant for him. Until he'd seen Hannah. Although they hadn't spoken until now, in his heart he'd known he'd found his match. He didn't understand why, but the little American spoke to his heart—and he was smart enough to realize it.

At thirty-five, he'd finally found his place in life. Now he just needed to be patient and wait for Hannah to realize they were meant to be together. Some might sneer at the idea of 'love at first sight' but Damien was proof it could happen. Tonight would be the beginning. He'd finally be introduced to the woman who would be his wife and the mother of his children.

Hannah stood in her bedroom changing for her big date when her phone rang. Walking around her bed while zipping up her dress, she made her way to the telephone.

"Hello."

"Hannah, are you about ready?" Emilie bubbled into the extension.

"Yes, but it would be helpful to know where we're going so I know if I'm dressed appropriately."

"What are you wearing?"

"My navy velvet sheath." One of Hannah's favorite

dresses, it made her feel sexy, while at the same time giving her a large amount of confidence. Although not understanding why, she felt she needed courage and confidence to get through the night.

"Perfect, you'll sweep Damien off his feet in that dress. We'll be by to pick you up in a quarter hour or so."

"Alright, I'll be ready. See you soon." After hanging up the extension, Hannah turned and took a good hard look at herself in the cheval mirror in the corner of her bedroom.

Never one to spend an inordinate amount of time on appearances, she was still like any other woman in the world when it came to wanting to look pretty. Granted, her self-esteem had been brutally ravaged a year earlier, but she finally seemed back on the right track.

Jason, her ex-boyfriend—who'd seemed perfect in so many ways—had proved to be nothing more than a snake 'dressed up handsome.'

Looking back, Hannah remembered things that had seemed off at the time, but had been cleverly explained. She should have stuck with her gut instinct, so to speak, and faced facts no matter how harsh they seemed at the time. It would have been a whole lot better if she'd opened her baby blues, instead of playing the clueless wonder to his Lothario. Unfortunately, hindsight being what it is, Hannah realized she'd allowed a handsome face to console her after the death of her parents.

Always close to them, she'd been understandably devastated when she learned of their fatal car accident on an icy stretch of Interstate Eighty up by Tahoe. Afterwards, Jason seemed the proverbial knight in shining armor, saying and doing all the right things. In other words, the man had completely reeled her in—hook, line, and sinker.

Keeping her head buried in the sand, she'd accepted his explanations when Jason made excuse after excuse for not spending time with her. When she came home early from work one day to find his car parked out front, she hurried inside—only to find him otherwise occupied with a startling redhead from down the street.

After the redhead departed in a huff, he proclaimed Hannah too uptight and said he wasn't in the market for a born again virgin. He topped off his speech by proclaiming he

The Trouble With French Kisses

probably could have handled the relationship if she'd been a tad more concerned with appearances.

It only took a few minutes to throw some things into a suitcase and head out without a backward glance—leaving the tarnished knight standing in the hallway with a throw pillow totally covering his privates. *A very small throw pillow at that.*

One thing led to another, and before she knew it she contacted her cousin, Emilie, in Paris. With the offer of a place to stay and encouragement from her aunt and uncle in France, she found herself accepting a job with *Louis Vuitton.*

After expediting her passport and filling out the proper papers, Hannah packed and left her past behind. She planned to start over fresh in a new city. This would be her chance to be what she'd always dreamed of being. Unfortunately, even after all this time, what or exactly who that was still remained a mystery.

Hannah walked down the hall to the bathroom and made the final adjustments to her hair. She thought her long, honey blonde hair with its corkscrew curls her best asset. She'd repeatedly been told other women envied the long tresses.

Quickly she spritzed herself with her favorite scent, then walked to the front room to straighten up a bit.

She loved her apartment. Only a few blocks from *Avenue Des Champs Elysses,* she had a breathtaking and interesting view. She loved to sit out on the second floor balcony and people watch, but for now she closed the view off with shutters she had for security reasons. Despite the fact she'd grumbled about going out, she actually found herself excited at the prospect.

After straightening her throw pillows and adjusting the blanket on the back of her couch, Hannah turned on a light so she wouldn't return to a dark place.

Lost in thought, she jumped when she heard the buzzer informing her she had visitors.

Hannah pulled open the door with a welcome on her lips only to fall silent the second she saw who stood there. Dressed in all black, *green eyes* appeared even more gorgeous now than he had earlier in the afternoon when she'd slammed into his rock hard body.

After a few seconds, the sound of someone clearing her

throat registered and Hannah pulled her eyes away from the handsome man in front of her.

"*Bon nuit,* Cousin." Emilie walked past Damien and pressed kisses to either side of Hannah's cheeks.

Hannah returned the greeting and did the same with Michel, Emilie's fiancé.

Emilie looked over at Hannah and noticed although she'd responded to their greetings, she'd barely taken her eyes off Damien. She thought this a good thing—a very good thing.

"Hannah, I'd like to introduce you to Damien Jacques. Damien, my cousin, Hannah Walsh."

"It's a pleasure to meet you, *Mademoiselle* Walsh." Damien picked up Hannah's hand and kissed the back of it.

"It's a pleasure to meet you as well," Hannah stuttered once Damien's greeting sank in. The night looked promising. Now if only she could manage witty conversation rather than impersonating a lackwit.

Emilie and Michel noted the smoldering attraction between Hannah and Damien. Sharing a sweet kiss, they both quietly walked out of the apartment leaving the two to follow— if they finally realized they'd been left behind.

They had dinner at *Moulin Rouge.* Hannah had wanted to attend the famous cabaret since she'd arrived in Paris, and the evening lived up to all her expectations.

The lively CanCan, the vibrant costumes, and the colorful sets left Hannah enthralled. The evening proved to be a dream come true, and for once she found herself glad she'd been unable to utter the word no.

Hannah had a hard time watching the performers, since her eyes had a tendency to drift in Damien's direction. Never before had she felt the breathless, heart pounding excitement she experienced simply by sitting next to this man. Having just met, he hadn't even kissed her, but still she felt the magnetic pull that proved to be a force unto itself between them.

She didn't give it a second thought when Damien put his arm around the back of her chair when the performance started. Nor did she think twice about the fact she actually leaned into it when a draft left her chilled.

Damien spent more time watching the expressions on Hannah's face than the performance on the stage. It surprised him how little it seemed to take to make this woman happy.

Life was all about simple pleasures, and he planned on making sure the smile currently gracing Hannah's beautiful face did so again and again. Would spending money be a delight on a person who didn't expect it automatically? Although he'd never before been fortunate enough to find someone who didn't know about his wealth, he honestly thought it might.

Loud applause for the talented performers brought him back from his mental musings. Entertainment over, people slowly stood and made their way to the cloakroom for their evening wraps.

Standing, Damien pulled Hannah's chair back and gently held her hand as they followed the crowd. Unconsciously he stroked her fingers, enjoying the connection no matter how small.

Hannah tried very hard not to melt into a puddle on the floor simply from his tender touch. She was in 'Hannah trouble.' Why was this happening? Especially after she'd promised herself to take things slow if she ever found another man she thought she liked. The man could prove to be a ratfink like Jason and here she practically purred in public, and over nothing more than him holding her hand. Pathetic.

The foursome finally made their way out onto the street and strolled down to the car park. The evening had turned cool, and Hannah shivered inside her light wrap.

Noticing her shiver, Damien didn't even think twice as he pulled her close to his side and wrapped an arm around her waist. The action was natural, as natural as breathing, and it lent an intimacy that proved comforting.

Emilie and Michel walked quietly ahead, absorbed in their own conversation.

The silence between Damien and her wasn't uncomfortable, which Hannah thought strange since they were practically strangers, but at the same time not. Never had she felt this level of intimacy and comfort with a man.

Hannah looked up into his face and smiled. "Thank you for dinner and the show. I've wanted to see it since I arrived here a year ago."

"I'm glad you enjoyed yourself." Without thought he pressed a gentle kiss to her forehead.

Slowly they walked along the crowed streets of

Montmarte, pausing now and again to allow someone to pass so they wouldn't have to separate.

Eventually they made it back to his car and he deftly maneuvered his way through the streets of Paris, dropping Emilie and Michel off at Michel's apartment before continuing on to Hannah's.

Suddenly shy, Hannah didn't want the night to end. At the same time, she didn't want to seem forward by inviting him up to her place. Feelings swept over her she neither understood nor felt comfortable handling on such short notice.

Damien pulled up and parked. He turned the engine off and got out, walked around and opened her door. Such a gentleman. When he held out his hand, Hannah gave him her keys. He unlocked the front door and opened it before following her up the stairs to her apartment.

"Would you like to come in for a little bit?" she stammered, unease clearly evident in her voice.

Damien smiled down at the little pixie in front of him. Truthfully he wanted nothing more, but he didn't trust himself to go slow, and based on what he'd gleaned from Emilie, slow was exactly what Hannah needed.

"No, I'd better not, although I thank you for the offer," he roughly whispered before he lowered his mouth to her upturned lips.

The kiss was gentle—little more than a mingling of breaths. Slowly, he placed soft kisses along her jaw line before he nuzzled her ear. He became intoxicated by her musky fragrance, a combination of woman and whatever scent she'd applied earlier in the evening. He brought his mouth back to her tender lips.

Hannah stood on tiptoe in order to draw closer to the velvety soft warmth of his mouth. His kiss felt delicious and she found herself lost in a myriad of sensations.

With regret, Damien pulled his mouth away from hers before he carried her to her bedroom and finished what they'd started.

Hannah came back to herself slowly. Never before had she been swept away by a single kiss. She felt his gentle touch on her face and looked up only to see the same look of amazement in his eyes.

"I know, *ma cour*, it is the same for me. Never before

you," he whispered. Placing another kiss on her forehead, he stepped back.

Hannah said nothing. There was nothing to say, or at least no words that came to mind to express how she felt. He'd called her his heart. Whatever had made him say that?

Damien smiled before he added, in a lower, huskier tone, "I'll see you tomorrow *ma petit.*" Then he turned and walked away.

Hannah closed the door and locked it before resting her forehead against the wood. "Yes, Damien, I might be little, like you just called me, but boy am I ever in big trouble," she whispered as she turned and made her way to her bedroom. Never before had her bed looked so big or so empty.

The Day That Would Live In Infamy

Hannah awoke and rolled over to see the sun shining. It was her day off and Damien would be coming home after a two-day absence.

The day after their first date, Damien had arrived with breakfast and then driven her to work. After kissing her senseless in the front seat of his BMW, he promised to pick her up after work.

Work had been vastly enjoyable that day. She enjoyed seeing the various visitors that came into the store. Her favorite had been the young Irish couple on their honeymoon. They told her, "We've never been in Paris before! We're from a lovely wee village called Adare. Have you heard of it?"

Hannah'd had to shake her head. Since her arrival, she hadn't been anywhere except Paris.

A broad smile had wreathed the groom's face. "Well then, you must be visiting us sometime soon. Once we return from our honeymoon, we'll be living in a small thatched house on the outskirts of town."

As Hannah rang up the sale, she could tell he relished treating his bride to a new bag.

By the end of the day she'd made several rather impressive sales, which went a long way toward her end of month totals. What a difference a kiss before work made!

Hannah walked out of the store and paused when she espied Damien leaning against his car. With a smile of greeting, she walked over. Though they'd only met the day before, she found it perfectly natural to offer her mouth for his welcoming kiss.

"How was your day?" Hannah asked as she sat in the front seat of the car.

Damien turned on the ignition and gazed over at her. "Better now."

When he smiled that devastating smile, Hannah felt a tingling sensation go clear to her toes. How could a simple smile be almost as intimate as his kisses?

"But, I do have some bad news," he continued. "Something has come up in Lyon that I must go and take care of. I should only be gone a day or two at the most."

Hannah laughed, relief flooding through her. "Is that all? For a second there I thought you were going to tell me you had a wife hidden away somewhere."

"*Non, ma Petite*, I have no wife. Not yet anyway."

Without thinking, Hannah reached over and gently stroked his face.

Damien grasped her hand, drew it to his mouth and placed a soft kiss into the center before folding her fingers over the moist mark.

"Why don't you just drop me off so you can go and get ready for your trip?"

For a moment Damien studied her intently. He didn't want to go, but he had several things he had to put together before he could leave for Gare de Nord. If he left now, it might be possible to make an earlier train, which meant coming back to this woman sooner. "I'll make this up to you, Hannah, I promise."

"There's nothing to make up, Damien. I understand. Really, I do." Impulsively she leaned over and nuzzled his neck, taking in his spicy, musky male scent before placing a tender kiss on his mouth. "Have a safe trip and if you get a chance, call me."

"Count on it." Before she exited the car, he gently wrapped his hand around the back of her neck and drew her close for a knee melting kiss. "I'll catch a taxi and come over once my train arrives in Paris."

Hannah shook her head. "Let me pick you up."

Peering steadily in her eyes, he tenderly traced her lower

lip with his fingertip. "I'd like that a great deal, Hannah Walsh." He gave her another quick kiss before he released her. He watched her give a jaunty wave before disappearing behind the front door. Carefully, he pulled out into traffic, eager to depart so he could return to this fascinating woman.

The next few days passed quickly. Hannah looked forward to Damien's evening calls. Over the course of their phone conversations, they learned intimate details couples the world over learn during a courtship.

Damien discovered Hannah had a weakness for dark chocolate, romance books, and bubble baths. Hannah learned Damien loved American football and thought the San Francisco 49ers were the team to beat. He loved snow skiing, and had spent a large portion of his growing up years in Northern California with his parents in San Francisco.

Closer now than they'd been before he left, Hannah was anxious to see him again.

When the hour finally grew near, she made her way down to the train station and found a place to park a few blocks from the platform where Damien's train would arrive.

When the train finally pulled in, she practically vibrated with excitement. Tonight would be *the* night. She just knew it!

As travelers pushed their way off the train and down the platform, Hannah caught sight of Damien. With a glad cry, she ran toward him and right into his wide open, waiting arms.

Damien clasped her close, holding her tight and taking in her unique scent. It felt like heaven having her in his arms. Though gone only a short time, he'd missed her while he'd been away. Next time business took him away from Paris, he'd make sure he had her with him.

Without thought to his environment, he drew her closer and pressed his mouth hungrily against hers. Not gentle, the kiss was all consuming, carnal. He made love to her mouth, sucking on her tongue and tangling his tongue with hers.

He could only think of getting them somewhere private—and quiet—where he could slowly peel off every item of clothing covering her sweet body.

Hannah felt on fire. She could think of no other word descriptive enough to express the feelings pulsing through her. Damien's kiss was delicious and like nothing she'd ever experienced before. The kiss sent shooting flames of desire through her body.

The clearing of a throat brought her back to herself along with the fact someone now tapped on Damien's shoulder.

They both reluctantly pulled apart only to see a frowning *gendarme* standing before them.

In rapid French, the police officer ordered them to accompany him to the station's office where they were directed to take seats and wait for a free desk.

Here they sat while getting ready to pay a two hundred euro fine for kissing. Hannah was mortified, but Damien seemed to think little of the fee.

They were finally called up to the counter. Papers were signed and money exchanged. And an important lesson had been learned. No smooching on the railways.

During a quiet drive back to Hannah's, Damien kept his hand possessively on her knee. No sooner were they behind the closed door when Damien had Hannah pinned to the door.

Gently he skimmed his fingers down her cheeks. When he spoke, his voice sounded tender, yet husky with emotion. "I don't want you to ever be embarrassed by our passion, Hannah." He brought his mouth closer, barely brushing her lips. "I dreamt about your lovely mouth. You gave me a precious welcome back gift—your passion, your heart." He brushed his mouth teasingly across hers. "*Je t'aime*, Hannah. I love you. " He then took fierce possession of her mouth. His kiss branded and claimed her as his.

With her breath sawing in and out, Hannah gazed into the face of the man she loved. Though she'd only met him a few days earlier, it felt as natural as breathing. She'd spent her life looking for this man, and she'd unexpectedly found him in Paris. She returned his pledge, "*Je t'aime*, Damien."

Damien smiled and lifted Hannah into his arms. With sure strides, he made it to her bedroom. The night and future were ahead of them. He smiled down at the woman in his arms, had no doubt they were going to be breaking the 'Kissing Law' frequently in the future. That was the trouble with French Kisses, you could never get enough of them, and in Damien's case, Hannah's kisses were priceless—and all his.

The Trouble With French Kisses

*Be sure to visit Kristi Ahlers' website
www.kristiahlers.com*

No Laughing Matter

by Patty Howell

• *Virginia - It's illegal to tickle women*

"All rise." The clerk of the court preceded the announcement "The Commonwealth of Virginia, Fairfax County Juvenile and Domestic Relations District Circuit Court of Law come to order. The Honorable Judge Judith Perkins presiding."

Amid a flourish of swirling black robe, Judge Perkins strode to her aerie of ruling and unlike any court in the land on this day in history, stood before the galleried audience. She slowly pivoted, lifting her eloquently manicured right hand and placed it over her heart. Facing the red, white and blue, star-studded flag of the freest Republic on the face of the earth, she strongly voiced in a rich contralto that echoed throughout the courtroom: "I pledge Allegiance..."

She glanced sideways at the strangers to the Court who began placing their own right hands over their hearts and conjoining voices to recite the Pledge of Allegiance.

Judge Perkins pulled the voluminous robe from behind her and assumed her seat on the highest family court in the county.

"Please be seated," she announced. She didn't have to look up to know spectators, court officials and the defendant did as she ordered. Rustling quickly subsided and the courtroom fell silent waiting for her to begin.

When she finally raised her gaze, signaling she was ready, the clerk of the court stood and called the first case of the day. "The Commonwealth of Virginia versus Cole Harris."

Mr. Harris, sitting at the defendant's table with his lawyer, Michael Byers, looked up at the judge. How would she rule concerning him today?

"Mr. Harris," the judge intoned, "please stand."

Cole did as she ordered. "Yes, ma'am."

"Good morning, Mr. Harris."

"Good morning, Your Honor," Cole said nervously.

Judith shuffled through prior record papers, although well aware of the charges being brought against this young man. She thought of Cole Harris as young, though he was actually in his mid thirties. After prosecutorial and defense attorney roles, she'd served on this bench for almost twenty years; however, on some days it seemed much longer. Offers of higher courtships had been extended, but she didn't have any higher aspirations than that of wife and mother, and soon to be grandmother. Plus she enjoyed the stability of her calling in this area of the country. This particular defendant had been before this court many times, all for the same offense. But this was the first time she'd be rendering a ruling in his case. She was the chief justice of the Fairfax County family court system.

"I assume you know why you're standing before me today, Cole?" she queried, relaxing the formality of the Court.

"Yes, ma'am, I do," Cole offered.

"And what are those charges?" she inquired, looking down toward the Summons of the Court and just as quickly glancing back at the man standing before her.

"Uh...ma'am...I believe the charges state I assaulted my wife."

"Do you believe you were assaulting your wife?" Judith peered down from her perch, unable to suppress the slight upturn on one side of her lip.

"According to Virginia's law, I was assaulting her, Your Honor."

The judge folded the file she had in front of her and held it up. "How many times have you stood before this Court, Mr. Harris, for these same charges?"

"Seven, Your Honor," Cole stammered. His heretofore strict posture seemed to be imploding, and his six-foot, two-inch frame took on the appearance of a much shorter man.

"Who brought the charges against this defendant?" she asked, straining to keep the annoyance from her voice from seeping through.

Stephen White, assistant county district attorney, leaped from his seat at the prosecutor's table. He'd been sitting there wondering where the judge was going with this line of questioning.

"Your Honor," White began, taking several steps toward the bench. "The charges have been brought by the Social Services Department of the County of Fairfax."

"And will that office be testifying before this Court today?"

"Yes, Your Honor, it will."

"Fine. Please be seated.

Shifting her gaze back to the defendant, she said, "Cole, it doesn't please me to see you here facing these same charges. I thought the last time you stood before this court there was an understanding you'd make certain this matter didn't come up again."

Attorney Byers, who'd been standing aside his client during the querying, raised his hand.

Judith admired Mr. Byers. He wasn't like other lawyers who thought they had the power to superimpose themselves upon the Bench just by opening the gaps in their faces and spewing forth words. His manner was authoritative without being offensive and he was extraordinarily polite. What other lawyer would raise his hand for permission to speak? She knew of none.

"Yes, Mr. Byers? You have something to say to this Court?" she asked, leaning back in her chair.

"Your Honor...if it pleases the Court, I would like to state that there have always been extenuating circumstances surrounding my client being taken into custody for the offenses he's said to have committed."

"Objection," Prosecutor White shouted, leaving his chair, right index finger extended to the ceiling.

Objection? Judith blinked and did a double-take, looking at him quizzically, not sure she'd heard correctly.

"Uh...alleged offenses, Your Honor." The prosecutor lowered his hand and resumed his seat.

The defense attorney glanced from the judge to the prosecutor, then back to the judge and shrugged his shoulders. "Well, they're hardly alleged if the perpetrator of the offenses admits to them," he stated, wondering why on earth a prosecutor would refer to the offenses as alleged. Wasn't it usually the purview of the defense to question the charges?

Judith returned her astounded expression from the prosecutor to the defense attorney. "Overruled. Please continue, Mr. Byers."

"Of course, Your Honor, thank you. As I was saying, my client never meant to dismiss this Court's earlier rulings and recommendations. But, I believe we will be able to prove my client's innocence even though he admits to breaking the law."

"That's a rather ambiguous statement, so I'll have to take your word for it at this point. Proceedings on this case are now open and I'll hear the case at this time."

Nodding toward the clerk of the court, Judith waited for the courtroom to clear of all people not wishing to witness the current hearing. Lawyers and their clients who awaited other hearings stood and exited the court. All but a few family members and a handful of curiosity seekers decided they'd rather be elsewhere and vacated the courtroom.

The most evident member of the audience was the defendant's wife, Kathryn Harris. She sat in the first row, behind and a little to the right of her husband, so that just by slightly turning he could view her pretty face and familiar, supportive smile. Judith noticed the loving eye contact made by the couple. Two well-behaved young children flanked their mother, who'd been granted permission for their attendance in the courtroom. Mrs. Harris had explained she wanted them to witness their country's judicial system in action.

"Order," the clerk of the court pronounced to the last few who were settling in their seats.

Judith called for the prosecutor to begin. "You may state your case for the record, Mr. White."

"Thank you, Judge Perkins. The Social Services Department of the Commonwealth of Virginia, Fairfax County brings charges against the defendant, Mr. Cole Harris, in the matter of gross abuse to his wife, Kathryn Harris. This defendant has had these charges leveled against him on six prior occasions, Your Honor, and he does not appear to have benefited from counseling sessions rendered free of charge to him by this Court."

Prosecutor White looked from his notes to the judge, as a

sneer bracketed his lips. "The State will show through the testimony of two witnesses, Your Honor, that Mr. Harris did willfully and without concern for his beloved wife, bring her to a convulsive state by breaking the law of this Commonwealth."

Judith waited a few seconds for the court reporter who was recording the proceedings. "Very well, Mr. White, you may call your first witness."

The court clerk looked down at his records and said loudly, "The Court calls Cecelia Ling to the stand."

The doors at the back of the courtroom swung open and a petite Asian woman stiffly walked down the aisle and entered the arena. She minced toward the witness stand and climbed into the box. Turning toward the audience, she was approached by the clerk. "Please raise your right hand and state your name."

In slightly broken English, the woman uttered, "My name Cecelia Ling."

"Ms. Ling, do you swear to tell the truth, the whole truth, and nothing but the truth, so help you God?"

"I do," Ms. Ling replied.

"Please be seated," the clerk of the court ordered.

Approaching the witness, Mr. White began, "Ms. Ling, could you please state your profession for the Court?"

"Yes. I a Fairfax County social worker."

"And in serving your duties, Ms. Ling, did the crime committed by this defendant, Mr. Harris, come to your attention?"

"Objection. Leading the witness," Mr. Byers interjected.

"Please rephrase your question, Mr. White," Judith recommended.

"Right. In performing your duties, Ms. Ling, how did the crime committed by the defendant come to your attention?" Mr. White mimicked.

"I in my office one day, 'bout two month ago, when I get telephone call from Elizabeth Monroe."

"And who is Ms. Monroe, Ms. Ling?" the prosecutor's sonorous voice boomed out as he rocked forward on the balls of his feet, staring at the witness as if willing her to remember her lines.

Ms. Ling jerked to attention in her seat. "She sister to Mrs. Kathryn Harris."

"So, the sister of the wife of the defendant called you?"

"That correct."

"Did Ms. Monroe inform you at that time of the perpetration of the crime against her sister?"

"Objection...again, leading the witness." Michael Byers didn't like objections, but he also didn't want the defendant to be run roughshod through the court. Plus, keeping the prosecutor on his toes was part of the game.

"Mr. White," the judge pleaded, "please format your question so the answer isn't implied therein."

"Yes, Your Honor." He returned his attention to the witness stand. "Ms. Ling, why did Ms. Monroe call you?"

"She call to say her sister being abused by her husband. Could she come to see me in person and talk?"

"And what was your response?"

"I tell her okay. Come see me. She come and I take statement about the defendant, sitting at that table," at which point Ms. Ling threw a skinny finger in the direction of Cole, "abusing his wife."

The prosecutor's glare and slight headshake caused the witness to quickly retract the extended digit and hide it in her lap. It became evident to the entire court that she should have waited for him to ask her to point out the criminal. Snickers erupted throughout the room, but just as quickly subsided with one hammer of the judge's gavel.

"Would you please state for the record what Ms. Monroe told you after coming to your office?" Mr. White asked, ignoring the spectators and clearly trying to regain control of the courtroom.

Judith was impressed when Michael Byers looked at her, but decided not to object because of 'hearsay.' He knew he'd be overruled, since the woman was an expert witness. It told her volumes about the defense counsel's moxie and integrity in the courtroom. The man was a no-nonsense lawyer.

"She say she visiting with sister and brother-in-law. They invite her to dinner. After eating, everyone sitting around, enjoying themselves. They watch movie. Some comedy Ms. Monroe bring to sister's house. But Ms. Monroe say her sister not find movie funny. Then her husband also say it not so funny." Ms. Ling stopped talking and looked from the prosecutor to the judge and back again to Mr. White.

"Go on, Ms. Ling," the prosecutor prompted.

"Then Ms. Monroe tell me that her sister, Kathryn Harris, say out loud, 'I'd just as soon Cole tickle me as to continue watching something called comedy that not make me laugh.'"

"And those were Ms. Monroe's exact words?" Attorney White queried, knowingly shaking his head.

"Exactly...I know this cause I write words down and memorize them for testimony today."

"Thank you, Ms. Ling," the prosecutor hurriedly said. He didn't want the judge lingering over that comment and arriving at the conclusion this witness's testimony was blatantly rehearsed. "So, on the basis of this discussion with Ms. Monroe, you decided to bring charges against the defendant, Mr. Cole Harris?"

"That right. No should break the law," Ms. Ling prejudged, ending her dialog.

"No further questions, Your Honor," White rejoined, taking his seat at the prosecutor's table.

"Mr. Byers, your witness," the judge said.

Michael stood. "No questions of this witness, Your Honor."

"Very well. Mr. White, please call your next witness."

The clerk of the court stood. "Will Ms. Elizabeth Monroe please take the stand?"

The guardian of the courtroom opened the heavy, solid oak door to receive Ms. Elizabeth Monroe. Dressed to optimize her assets, a well-endowed young woman strutted the distance to the witness stand.

She was sworn in by the star-struck, tongue-tied court reporter.

The prosecutor stood, approached the witness stand, and guided her through the paces of corroborating expert witness Ling's testimony.

Satisfied the witness had supported the major points, White proceeded to put the lid on his case. "Ms. Monroe," he queried, "why did you report the incident that occurred at your sister's house to Ms. Cecelia Ling, in her capacity as a social worker?"

Emitting a little huff, Ms. Monroe sat forward in her chair. Licking her brightly glossed, red lips, she practically spat, "He's been warned before about this type of behavior, yet ruthlessly continues to ignore the Court's rulings. He has—unmercifully in my opinion—tickled my sister until tears ran down her cheeks and she couldn't stop laughing! I have witnessed his actions time and time again, and believe such behavior is intolerable. The man should be thrown behind bars. And, to make matters worse, his own children were standing right there watching while he did this to their mother."

"No!" Mr. White exclaimed, feigning surprise and shock. "In front of his own children? Ms. Monroe, do you believe you could correctly gauge—by the expressions on the children's faces—their reactions to this unconscionable conduct?"

"Objection," Mr. Byers intervened from the defendant's table. "It hasn't been shown that this witness is trained in child psychology and capable of forming an opinion on child behavior."

"Sustained," Judith agreed. "However, I will consider her comments in light of the fact she has no specific training."

"Well then, in your opinion, Ms. Monroe, what were the children's reactions?" the disgruntled prosecutor asked.

"I found it appalling," Ms. Monroe replied, the look of disgust openly visible on her face. "They looked like they would have loved to join in and take part."

"So, what you're saying, Ms. Monroe, is given the opportunity, these young, impressionable children—seated in the audience—would have jumped right in and participated with their parents in breaking the law?"

"I definitely believe that to be the case, sir." She slapped her hands, one on top of the other in her lap.

"That's all for this witness, Your Honor," the prosecutor said, but his facial expression clearly indicated he wished there was a way to extend his conversation with her.

"Mr. Byers?" Judith turned from the prosecutor and looked appraisingly to see if there was going to be a cross examination.

"Yes, thank you, Your Honor." Michael Byers jotted a few notes on a pad on the table, then stood and approached the witness.

Without preamble he said, "Miss Monroe, would it be fair to state you do not particularly like your brother-in-law, Cole Harris?"

Flummoxed, Ms. Monroe's eyes widened in surprise. She didn't know quite what to be indignant about—the attorney's address of 'Miss' or his matter-of-fact statement about Cole.

"Miss Monroe?" Mr. Byers prodded, turning his back on her as if indicating he didn't truly care what she answered.

"I'm sorry, that was a rather abrupt question," she stated, trying unsuccessfully to smile demurely to those in the courtroom, particularly the judge.

"Yes or no would be a sufficient answer," he said, turning back to face her.

"Okay. Yes," she said, not caring that her voice had gone up an octave or two.

"Yes, what, Miss Monroe?"

"I do not particularly like my sister's choice in husbands."

"*Husbands*, Miss Monroe? Why, has your sister had more than one you didn't like?" the defense attorney asked, cutting his eyes away from and then back to the witness.

"No, he's the only one she's had," the witness testified, wishing she hadn't mentioned it.

"Do you have a husband, Miss Monroe?"

"Objection, Your Honor. Irrelevant and no lead-in to this line of questioning. The witness is not on trial," the prosecutor railed.

"Mr. Byers?" the judge queried, a hint of a smile threatening to pull at the corner of her mouth.

"I intend to show relevance, Your Honor, and the witness, herself, raised the line of questioning by bringing up *husbands*."

"I'll allow it," the judge ruled. "Please answer the question, Ms. Monroe."

"No," the witness said flatly.

"No, you're not married, or no, you won't answer the question?" Mr. Byers taunted.

A nonplussed look came over the witness' face. "No, I'm not married," she said, trying desperately to control her tone.

"I'm always amused at how people become terse when they don't wish to respond," defense counsel offered, his eyes twinkling in merriment.

"Objection. The defense is badgering the witness," Mr. White bellowed, practically knocking his chair backwards as he jumped up.

"Mr. Byers, mind your manners," the judge intoned, a smile edging her lips.

"Yes, Your Honor." He turned back to face the witness stand. "So, Miss Monroe, you have no husband at present. Have you ever been married?"

Wringing her clasped hands, the witness eked out, "Yes."

"Please let the record indicate Miss Monroe said yes. In fact, let me get right to the point and state for the record that the current witness has previously had four husbands. All of them whom she divorced. She has no children." Giving the woman a dismissive glance, he faced the judge. "Those are all the questions I have for this witness, Your Honor," he said, returning to his chair.

Directing her attention to the prosecutor, the judge queried, "Do you have any further witnesses, Mr. White?"

Remaining in his seat, the assistant D.A. responded, "No, Your Honor. The prosecution rests."

"Very well." She then addressed the defense attorney. "Mr. Byers?"

"Yes. I have one witness, Your Honor." He nodded to the clerk of the court, who called, "Kathryn Harris, please take the stand."

Standing and leaning over to whisper something to an older woman sitting on one side of the children, Kathryn Harris patted each child on the shoulder. She kissed their cheeks and proudly made her way to the witness box. Assuming her place, shoulders back and chin raised, she stood as she was sworn in by the clerk of court.

The defense attorney approached his witness. "Mrs. Harris, has the testimony you've heard by the two previous witnesses been stated correctly?"

Leaning forward toward the microphone, her bright blue eyes wide and twinkling, Kathryn Harris smiled. "I believe it has."

"Do you mean to tell this court you consider your husband is guilty of abusing you as stated in the charges brought forth by the prosecution?" the smiling attorney questioned incredulously. He began to walk slowly back toward the defendant's table.

"Oh, no, Mr. Byers," Kathryn said, as she watched Cole's lawyer casually lean against the side of the table. "Regrettably, my husband did indeed break a law. But he did not abuse me."

"Would you please explain your answer for the benefit of the court, Mrs. Harris?"

"I'd be happy to, sir. My husband likes to amuse me, not abuse me," she stated, smiling in the direction of the defense table, her love for the defendant obvious in the spark in her eyes.

Kathryn's thoughts traveled back in time, to when she'd first met Cole. She turned to address the judge. "Your Honor, it's probably not relevant, but may I beg the court's indulgence for a few minutes?"

At the judge's nod, she turned to face her husband and continued. "I met Cole when I worked in the drive-in teller's cage at a local bank. It was a few minutes before closing and no one had been through the line in more than ten minutes. I'd started tallying up my drawer's receipts for the day and wasn't exactly paying attention to the drive-though. Even though extremely tired, I jumped in surprise as the well-tuned, sixties muscle-car purred thunderously to a halt under the portico. My exhaustion quickly dissipated as I found myself dazzled by the most incredibly piercing, sky-blue eyes that stared up at me through my tinted, bullet-resistant window. And, as if that weren't enough, the man's smile completely disarmed me."

Kathryn twisted around to face the judge. "Your Honor, love at first sight was something I'd scoffed at for years, as my easily smitten girlfriends fell from one romance to another. Despite their wandering affections, I'd always told myself, *'When it comes along, I'm sure I'll recognize it.'* And 'it' had just pulled up to make a deposit." Her eyes swerved back to her husband. Tears welled in them as she remembered that happy day.

Returning from the momentary reverie, she continued, "My sister, whom I forgive for her poisoned approach to life, has always been jealous of the love my husband and I have for each other and for our children. Because of that, she has repeatedly taken advantage of an antiquated law on Virginia's books, six times previously in fact, to try and harm our unity. I'm not sure why she has such a bitter outlook on life and love. In addition, I've actually tried to discover the background of the law that states it's illegal to tickle women. However, while

I've been unable to trace its origins, I do know I'd certainly like to change it. Maybe the framers of the law had the same misguided reasoning as my sister and were unhappy with their own lives. Whatever...the law needs to be rescinded and stricken from the books."

Both children in the front row gave a little wave toward their mommy, who in turn waved back. The older woman, now sitting between the two children, hugged them tightly into her sides.

"I've heard enough," Judith said, exasperated over the day's events. "Would the attorneys please approach the Bench?"

She addressed both lawyers sotto voce. "I've reached my decision in this matter." Turning to the prosecuting attorney, she leveled her gaze. "Mr. White, if you entertain the idea of bringing a matter of this type based on some archaic law into my Court again, I will ensure you face contempt charges. I should think you and your office would have matters far more important than entertaining frivolous antics brought by mentally deficient busybodies. You may return to your tables," she said in dismissal, her eyes taking in both men.

Banging her gavel, she addressed the entire assemblage. "It's my opinion this matter has no merit. Therefore, I'm dismissing the charges against Cole Harris. Furthermore, I'm having his otherwise perfect record expunged of all previous charges, these being the only reasons for prior arrests. Additionally, although I do not have the jurisdiction or authority to repeal a law, silly or not, I'm putting Mr. and Mrs. Harris in touch with a newly elected Virginia state senator who will, hopefully, begin steps to have this law removed from the books of this Commonwealth."

Banging her gavel one final time, she pronounced, "Case dismissed."

Kathryn Harris descended the witness box and tearfully rushed into the open arms of her adoring husband. Cole wrapped his arms around her and pulled her toward him. He kissed her tenderly on the lips and then gently tweaked his fingers into her sides, causing her to giggle. She had to bury her head into his chest to keep from bursting out in joyous laughter.

Judith Perkins smiled to herself as she watched the overt

affection displayed by the young couple. Yes, this antiquated law needed to be changed, and with the dedication these two had to each other, she had no doubt they'd give it their all to get the law repealed some day—just as they appeared to have given their all to each other through the years.

She rose, exited the courtroom and headed back to her chambers. Sighing, she removed her robe and hung it on a rack in the corner; it had been a long, stressful day. Suddenly smiling, she knew exactly what she planned to do now. She was going home to spend a quiet evening with her husband, watch a movie, and as this young couple had chosen to do—she was going to tickle her husband until they both fell into bed laughing.

Thank God there was no law against that!

Be watching for Patty Howell's future website

Them's Fightin' Words

by Leanne Burroughs

• *Georgia - Mules may not roam around unsupervised*
- It's illegal to swear over the telephone

Georgia, 1924

Jake Major pulled his pick-up to a screeching halt to avoid hitting the mule ambling across Riverend Road. How the devil did that infernal female get away with letting her blasted mules wander the countryside? The sheriff knew full well it was illegal for her to let them roam around. Why didn't he do something about it? His temper boiled. He was tired of people molly-coddling her.

Well, I've had it. He couldn't take driving down this road one more day and having to stop for *Lady* Samantha's mules. The woman thought herself too good to accept a date from him, but it didn't faze her to break the law day after day.

Putting his green, Buick truck with its varnished dash, in reverse, Jake looked over his shoulder and steered it back down the highway until he came to the dirt road leading to the widow's property. He ignored the posted 'no trespassing' sign and headed up her tree-lined drive.

The Wayside Christmas Center, as it had been dubbed after Samantha married and moved there, was a beautiful piece of property. Had been a beautiful estate when he'd grown up here, too. He'd been too young to appreciate it at the time, had just taken it for granted. When Samantha's husband, Jethro, had been alive, the place had been lively year round. He'd heard about its success all the way over in Atlanta.

257

Samantha had loved everything then—especially Christmas—and his brother, Jethro, had built several buildings for her on their land, each and every building to Samantha's exact specifications. She'd turned each small building into her vision of the North Pole—from reindeer barns, to elf carpentry shops, to Mrs. Santa Claus' bakery. Jake smiled at all he'd been told. He had no doubt Samantha Felicity had been one bossy bit of goods when she watched the replica being raised!

Samantha had been a whirlwind back then. Busy keeping the farm going, maintaining the upkeep of each building, teaching Sunday School every week, helping with bake sales, and serving on the library board. Seemed no function or charity passed without her having a finger in. *Volunteer* should've been her middle name.

All that changed the day Jethro died. Now she went nowhere, barely spoke to anyone.

Enough is enough, Jake fumed.

Parking before the stoop of the white frame house, Jake shut off the truck's engine. He was about to open his door when Samantha appeared on the porch. A lump formed in his throat at the sight of his family home and the woman he'd once loved. He'd always planned on it being him sitting on that porch and rocking away in the big wooden chairs as they watched the sun set together. It hadn't happened that way though.

"What part of 'no trespassing' didn't you understand, Jake Major? I painted that sign myself. It's big enough even *you* couldn't possibly have missed it."

Jake leaned out the truck window as his eyes took in everything about the stubborn woman. No shoes. She'd probably been sitting in her living room reading. Unwanted memories flooded his mind, of her sitting in the corner of the sofa, bare feet tucked under her while she read those silly nickel romance novels she picked up at the *Woolworths*. She liked the ones filled with lots of history, saying they transported her to another time, another place—she who'd never left the state of Georgia. Stories set in Scotland were her particular favorites. Her eyes had sparkled when he teased her about them.

Her blue eyes didn't look pleased to see him now.

Jake noticed a few loose curls managed to escape the pins

she used to keep her hair in that severe style he couldn't stand—a tight bun on the back of her head. Like some old granny-woman. The stray wisps softened her appearance despite the glower she flashed him.

"I didn't come all this way for you to contrary me, Samantha Felicity. One of your blasted mules wandered out on the road— *again*." He narrowed his eyes, hoping to intimidate her.

In response, she cocked a brow as if to say, 'So?'

"I'm warning you, *Sa-man-tha*. If you don't keep those stupid animals within your fence line, I'll not be responsible for anything that might happen to them."

Samantha just smiled. "You'd never hurt an animal so don't threaten me with nonsense. I know you too well."

Jake glowered. "It's a pity you only remember that when it's convenient."

Placing her hand on her hip, she ordered, "Start your engine, Jake, and turn that truck around. I don't want you here. If you don't leave, I'll call Sheriff Moss."

"Go ahead Samantha Felicity—"

"Quit calling me Samantha Felicity. You know I hate that. You always called me that to aggravate me. Please leave. You delivered your message about my animals. We have nothing else to say."

"I have plenty to say," Jake groused, unable to hide his annoyance. "You just won't listen."

"No, I won't," Samantha said, her tone hurt. She turned to head back into the house, hastening up the steps. "Good day, Jake."

Before he could utter another word, the door closed soundly behind her.

"Shoot!" Jake ground his gears into first and floored the pedal, lurching the truck forward and sending a shower of gravel towards Samantha as he headed out the drive toward the main road.

Up the road stood the blamed mule he'd almost run into earlier. Jake knew he should get out and send the animal packing back to Samantha's property, but he was too aggravated.

How can one lone female be so blasted stubborn? Well, they say pets take after their owners!

The next day, young Carl Perkins had just been getting into his delivery truck when Jake pulled up at the grocery.

"Hey, Carl," Jake greeted the teen.

"Hey, yourself, Mr. Major."

"Where you off to this time of day?"

"The Mule Lady called in an order, and Pa wants me to deliver it." He looked torn. "I get a good tip every time I go out there, but I hate driving so far for one delivery."

The words popped out of his mouth before Jake's brain was engaged. "I gotta go right past her place, Carl. Want me to deliver them groceries for you?"

The lanky youth's eyes brightened. "You wouldn't mind, Mr. Major? I'd be beholdin' to you." His face swiftly fell. "Nah, on second thought, I'd better not. Miz Major always tips *real* good. I'm takin' Amy Simmons to the Saturday night social. Wanted to buy her a corsage.

Jake smiled. "Tell you what, Carl. I see no purpose in you driving all the way out there. How about I tip you now and then I'll collect the money from Mrs. Major?"

"You wouldn't mind?" Carl's face lit up once again, causing the dimples in his cheeks to deepen.

"Honest. You just put all them groceries in the back of the pickup while I get what I came to buy. I need to put a question to your pa."

"You want what?" Seth Perkins said after Jake ordered the rolls of barbwire.

"You heard me. I'm tired of Samantha's mules getting out on the road every day. I plan on stringing up barbwire to keep them inside her property."

"She won't cotton to the likes of that," Seth warned, shaking his head.

"I'm sure she won't, but then there ain't much she does cotton to nowadays. She's holed up in that house, and has for all intents and purposes, quit living."

"And you think riling her is going to help?"

"Something's got to get a reaction out of her. Since Jethro's death she's closed herself up in that house and refuses to see just about everybody."

"I don't know, Jake. I think you're just stirring up a

hornet's nest." Seth shook his head again, but went to the back of the store to get the barbwire.

Reaching the white, wooden house with its huge wrap-around porch, Jake put the truck in park, got out and slammed the door. With a defiant glare toward the front door, he grabbed the boxes of supplies from the truck's back and started up the steps.

"Carl, is that you?" Samantha called from inside the house. "Bring the supplies on in if you don't mind. I'm feeling a little poorly today."

Jake swore. The woman stayed out here alone with no one to check on her. What would happen if she ever got really sick?

Opening the door, he headed to the kitchen.

Samantha stood at the sink, doing dishes. She didn't bother to turn around. "Thanks, Carl. Money for the order and your tip are on the table. Tell your pa thanks for filling my order so quickly."

"Everyone always trips all over themselves to do exactly what you want, don't they *Mrs.* Major? Permits you to play a hermit out here."

Samantha swung around, soapy dish water dripping from her hands. Seeing Jake, she grabbed the counter for support, pale as if she saw a ghost.

She grabbed a towel from the counter to dry her hands. "How dare you come into my house like some...some...thief?"

"Used to be my house, too. I grew up here, remember?" Jake countered.

"I should call Sheriff—"

"Go ahead. Be sure to tell him you're reporting me for delivering your supplies."

"My groceries? What—"

Jake lifted the boxes as if to draw her notice to them, then dropped them down on the tabletop. "Carl was busy. I offered to save him the trip."

"I...oh...well..." Samantha couldn't seem to find the words. "You needn't have put yourself out. I could've waited for Carl to deliver them. I—"

"I know—you don't need my help. You've made that abundantly clear this past year." Jake grabbed the dish towel out of her hands and threw it toward the sink. "You don't need anyone's help. You'd rather stay out here and shrivel up and die—like Jethro."

"How *dare* you talk to me like that? Jethro was my—"

"Husband. I know. A saint of a man, perfect in every way. You've told me often enough since I came back."

"He—"

Jake raked his eyes over Samantha. "Never mind. I've delivered your stuff. Now I'm leaving. You can go back to hiding from the world."

Taking long, angry strides, he stormed outside and to his truck.

Reaching the main road, he had to swerve to avoid one of her blasted mules when it dashed out of the woods, the truck coming to a halt in the ditch. Jake hit his hand against the steering wheel.

"Enough, Miz Samantha, Mistress of the Mules!"

Arriving at his house fifteen minutes later, he snatched up the phone.

"Libby, this is Jake Major. Get me the sheriff."

"Is everything all right, Mr. Major? You sound awfully upset."

"I *am* upset, Libby. Connect me now."

"Yes, sir, Mr. Major." A short time later Jake heard Libby talking with the sheriff's secretary, Darlene Mackelhenney.

"Is the sheriff there, Miss Darlene? I have Jake Major on the phone and he sounds mighty riled."

"I am riled, Libby. And don't talk about me like I can't hear you."

"I was only trying to help, Mr. Major."

Jake heard the petulance in Libby's voice and felt like a worm for snapping at her. "I know that, Libby. I'm sorry I yelled." This conversation was getting him nowhere. "Miz Darlene, is Sheriff Moss there? I need to speak with him."

"Why yes, he is, Jake. Is everything all right? Libby said you sounded upset. Can I do anything for—"

"Miz Darlene, I want to speak with Sheriff Moss," Jake said, interrupting her. "Now."

Darlene's voice chilled. "Don't have to shout at me, Jake Major. Here's Sheriff Moss. Your mama—bless her soul—raised you with better manners than that. She'd a washed your mouth out with soap."

Before he could apologize—*again*—Mickey Moss' calm voice came across the wire. "Moss here."

"Mickey, this is Jake. I want you to go out to Samantha Major's house and arrest her."

Sheriff Moss almost choked on his laughter. "You want me to what?"

"You heard me. I want the damn woman arrested right now. She's as much a pain in the arse as her mules are. They're out on the main road every single day and I'm tired of it. One sent me into the ditch just now."

"Have you tried talking with your sister-in-law, Jake?"

"The fool woman refuses to listen—about anything. I want her arrested—now. She breaks the law every day by letting those blasted mules run free. Somebody's gonna get hurt if you don't put a stop to it."

"It's not one of my high priorities, Jake. Mules running around unchecked doesn't have the same importance as keeping drunks and thieves locked up."

"Well, it should," Jake roared indignantly. "What if some of those fancy tourists from up toward Chimney Rock came through there? One of them ends up in the ditch and they'll get their rich daddy to sue the pants off Miss Majors and the town both."

"Mrs."

"What?"

"Mrs. Majors. You called her miss."

"Have you lost your mind? You're talking labels when I'm demanding the woman be arrested? As a town councilman, I order you to arrest the mule-headed woman—no pun intended. She's a damn nuisance."

"Stop cursing, Jake. You know Miz Libby eavesdrops on all calls. Can't be having you offending her delicate ears." The sheriff stopped chuckling. "You're not funnin', are you? You really want your sister-in-law tossed into jail over a mule?"

Jake forced himself to stop gritting his teeth. "The damn woman's forced me to do it. The front wheel of my truck is pretty messed up. This is beyond nuisance factor and into property damage."

"All right, Jake. If you're sure that's what you really want, I'll go arrest her."

"Good," Jake shot back.

The sheriff assured, "I'll go do it shortly. I have one other stop to make first."

"I don't care how many stops you have. Just see that female is arrested."

A half-hour later, the sheriff pulled into Jake's driveway. Not seeing Samantha in the truck, Jake rushed out the door. "What are you doing here, Mickey?"

"Came to arrest you, Jake," he replied, suppressing a grin.

Jake's eyebrows shot up. "You're what?"

"Arresting you."

"Are you deaf? I told you to arrest Mrs. Major—not me."

"And I have every intention of doing just that. Only, I have to arrest you, too. You swore over the telephone—three times. Miz Libby complained about it. I warned you."

"I swore over the...are you daft? The woman drove me to frustration and you're going to arrest *me*? Surely, even Miz Libby can understand that?"

Mickey just stared at him.

Mickey guided Jake inside and into one of the two empty cells in the small office.

Darlene stared with mouth agape, but quickly snapped up the receiver to tell Miz Libby the sheriff had just arrested Jake for swearing on the telephone.

Sheriff Moss turned and started back toward the door.

"Where are you going, Mickey Moss? Don't you *dare* leave me in here! This nonsense has gone on long enough. Let me out of here." Jake rattled the bars.

The sheriff winked at Miz Darlene and left the building.

"You're here to do *WHAT?*" Samantha couldn't believe her ears.

"A complaint's been lodged against you, Miz Major. Sorry, but I have to arrest you."

"I have absolutely no intention of going anywhere with you, Mickey Moss."

"Now, Miz Samantha, don't make a fuss. You don't want me to haul you down to the courthouse in handcuffs do you?

You know Miz Darlene will be on the telephone to Miz Libby, and within fifteen minutes every old biddy in Goose Creek will know about it."

"Handcuffs..." Samantha blustered.

"Yes, ma'am. Now come with me, please."

A scant half hour later, Samantha was ushered into Sheriff Moss' office under the watchful eye of half of Athen's-Clarke's residents.

She rounded on him as soon as the door closed behind them.

"Mickey Moss, I have never been so humiliated in my life. How dare you treat me like a common criminal in front of the whole town? Why, I won't be able to show my face again as long as I live."

Sheriff Moss' eyes met hers. "What difference would that make, Miz Samantha? You've already shut yourself away from the world. There's little else you can do to avoid townfolk."

"Well, I never..." she huffed.

She spun away from him. Only then did she see the room's other inhabitant. Her eyes narrowed as she swung back to the sheriff.

"What's *he* doing here?"

"Had to arrest him, too, ma'am. Ain't had such a run on our cells since I became sheriff." He started to move her toward the barred cell.

"Run on cells? Sheriff, there's only two of us."

"Yes, ma'am, and the judge ain't gonna take kindly to having to listen to so many trials."

"Trials? Mickey Moss, have you lost your sanity? Surely you're not going to have me appear before the court because my mule wandered off my property."

"Don't rightly know, ma'am. Depends on the person who lodged the complaint against you."

Samantha narrowed her eyes and glared at Jake. "I know *exactly* who lodged the complaint."

"Yes, ma'am, I'm sure you do." He placed the key in the lock and swung the cell door open. "Now, if you'll just step inside, I believe we can turn the tide on this rampant lawlessness."

Dazed, Samantha stepped inside the cell before it dawned

on her she was in the same cell as Jake. Too late, she heard the lock click. She spun to face the sheriff. "Mickey Moss, open this door. I will not remain in the same cell as this...this...this miscreant."

"Now don't be cursing me, Mrs. Major. That'll only make things worse for you."

"Curse you? I swear—" she began.

He wagged a finger at her. "I just warned you not to swear."

"You can be so pigheaded at times. You know perfectly well I didn't—"

"Have a seat, Miz Major, and calm yourself. You might as well make yourself comfortable. You're not going anywhere for a spell." He headed to his desk and placed the key to the cell in his desk drawer, closing it firmly. "I'll send Miz Simmons over later with a mite of food for you both." Tilting his hat to the side, he opened the door before turning back to face them. "You know Elizabeth makes the best chicken and dumplings in the county. And she had carrot cake for dessert earlier today. You'll love that if she still has any left. Anyhow, it's late now, and I'm plum tuckered out. Takes a lot out of a body arresting two people in one day. I'm gonna head on home for the night. I'll see you both in the morning."

"*Morning*? Mickey Moss, you come back here right this instant," Samantha shouted as the sheriff firmly closed the door behind him.

Samantha rounded on Jake. "This is all your fault."

"My fault? I sure as perdition didn't ask to be arrested." He sat on the narrow cot and glared at her. "If you'd kept your blamed mules on your property, I wouldn't have lost my temper."

"What do my mules have to do with the price of tomatoes?"

"I almost crashed my truck into one when I left your property today. I was so blue blazes mad at you, I almost didn't see it until it was too late."

"And?" she prodded.

"I went home and called Moss. I lost my temper and cussed at Mickey for not taking the situation seriously. You know Miz Libby..."

She nodded. "She listened in on the call."

"And then complained. Moss claims there's some law on the books that says it's illegal to swear on the telephone."

"Well, I never—"

"That's right—you never do anything anymore. You've shut yourself away from the world. I can see you running from me, but why avoid everyone else?"

"Don't flatter yourself, Mr. Major. I'm not running from you. I simply have no desire to see anyone. Since Jethro died, I prefer being alone."

"Criminy, woman, you're twenty-four years old. No one quits living at twenty-four."

Samantha arched a brow. "You're such an expert on life? The four years you have on me taught you everything you need know?" She left her spot by the cell door and approached him as he sat on the cot. She poked her finger into his chest. "Let me tell you something, Jake Major, you don't know anything about anything."

Jake sat still on the cot, his eyebrow lifted in a challenge. He didn't stop her from poking him. Raising his eyes to hers, he said softly, "I know we loved each other once."

Backing up, Samantha's eyes widened. She tried to swallow over the lump forming in her throat. "I never—"

"Don't lie. You buried your feelings, but I'd bet my last dime they're still there."

"I..." Samantha turned and walked back to the cell door. "I don't wish to speak about this. Please refrain from—"

"Telling the truth? Samantha, I think it's time we got everything out in the open. We've both kept our feelings buried too long—and it hurts." He came up behind her and placed his hands on her shoulders, turning her to face him. "Talk to me, Sam."

Tears welling in her eyes, Samantha tried to wiggle from his grasp.

He didn't release her. Instead he leaned closer.

She felt his breath on her face. Recognized his scent—soap and leather. A scent she'd never forgotten. Her mind slipped back to the first time she'd smelled it—the first day they'd walked to school together. He could've ridden his horse, but once he saw her walking along the side of the road, he'd dismounted and kept pace beside her. He'd done that every day until he graduated the small school. Although she knew he often thought her a pest at times, they'd been inseparable.

She'd fallen in love with him the first time he'd bent to pick a small dandelion and handed it to her. A silly weed. To her it was the most beautiful flower she'd ever seen.

A tear slid down her cheek as she remembered the day they'd met behind the small one room schoolhouse. He'd held her close and she'd leaned her head on his shoulder. She'd wanted to stay like that forever. But she couldn't. She'd come to tell him good-bye. Came to tell him she'd accepted his brother Jethro's proposal.

It was the day her world had ended.

Hurt, he stormed away from her—left town the next day. Stayed gone the entire five years she'd been wed. He'd only returned ten months earlier to attend Jethro's funeral.

She'd thought he'd leave again. Prayed he would. He hadn't. Every time she turned around, he seemed to be in town, always trying to talk to her. She couldn't face him. Unable to bear the questions in his eyes, her response had been to turn and flee. That's when she stopped going to town. It was easier to stay home than risk running into him. She couldn't face him.

It hurt too much.

Jake led her to the small cot, pushed her to sit. Instead of joining her, he paced the small cell with the restlessness of a caged animal.

When Samantha didn't say anything, he stalked back to her.

She averted her face, but he cupped his hand and placed it lightly under her chin, forcing her to look at him.

"Why, Sam? You owe me that. After all this time, tell me why you married Jethro instead of me." He released her face and gently rubbed the back of his knuckles against her cheek. "Blast it, woman, you knew I *loved* you. I planned to marry you as soon as you graduated from school."

Samantha closed her eyes. All the old memories washed over her—of Jake holding her hand as they walked to school. Of him holding her closer than he should at the Saturday night social each week. Miz Burnside had always had a fit over that. She'd even complained to the town father's one time, but they'd done nothing but talk to Jake.

He'd told her afterwards, "They said I needed to not hold you so close. Seems some of the old women in town don't like it. Especially that old biddy Burnside. Hell, no wonder no man ever wanted her. Her face looks like she sucks lemons."

They'd laughed about it—and had ignored the warning. Samantha hadn't cared what Miz Burnside thought. It felt good to be in Jake's arms, and she had no intention of stopping him. She planned to stay in his arms forever.

Then Jethro returned from the war.

Although he tried to maintain a normal life, everyone could tell he was sick. His skin had the pallor of the chalk in Miz Tschorn's classroom. Samantha had seen him in town one day and he'd come over to talk to her.

After that, her life had changed.

She looked up at Jake and wanted to cry. Wanted to throw her arms around his neck and beg him to forgive her. That could never happen. As her mother used to say, "You've made your bed, Samantha Felicity Owens. Now lie in it." Of course, at the time Samantha had done nothing worse than steal apples from Mr. Jacobs' grove, but she knew she'd be in for it when her pa came home. The look on her mother's face told her that.

Six years ago, she'd *made her bed.* She'd accepted Jethro's proposal—and she'd have to *lay* in it the rest of her life.

"Jake, please. It'll do no good to talk about it. What's done is done. Let it rest."

Jake crouched before her, his hands steepled almost in supplication. "I *need* to know why, Sam. The question burns in my gut every day, every night. What did I do to make you stop loving me?"

Samantha gasped. Before she gave thought, she blurted, "Jake, no. I never stopped loving you." Her hand flew to her mouth, too late to recall the words.

Eyes wide, Jake stared at her. "Then why? Hellsfire, woman. Why did you leave me?"

Tears rolled down Samantha's cheeks. Jake caught them with his finger. He reached into his pocket for a handkerchief and gently blotted the tears.

"Jake, I..." She stopped. Could she do this? Could she tell him the truth after all this time? Even if she did, it wouldn't fill the longing in her heart. The painful hole he'd left the day he stormed out of town. She caressed the side of his face with her fingertips, the face she so loved. "Jethro needed me, Jake."

"*I* needed you," Jake growled in anguish.

Samantha shook her head. "It wasn't the same. You were strong, healthy. I knew you'd go on to find someone else to love—to marry." She gulped. "I didn't want you to, but I had no choice. And *I'm* not the one who left. You left town the very next day. We never heard anything from you in all the years you were gone."

Jakes' eyes narrowed. "What do you mean you had no choice? Did my brother compromise you? Did you have to marry him?"

Samantha gave a weak smile. "Nothing like that. When he came back from the war he knew he was dying. It's why they discharged him early."

"I knew he was sick. What does that have to do with the price of beans?"

"Don't you see? He needed someone to take care of him? He needed—"

"A nurse. We could have hired someone from the city. Ma and pa left us enough money."

"He didn't want a stranger looking after him. He wanted to be around people who cared for him."

"*Cared* for him? Don't you mean loved him?"

Samantha drew in a breath and lowered her dark, silky lashes. "No, Jake. I never loved Jethro. I cared for him, but never loved him. He was like a brother to me—just as he was your brother."

"You never loved—?"

She raised her head, unflinching under the probing eyes. "No. He was kind to me. Before his health deteriorated completely, he built the Santa's village for me. He said your dad taught him carpentry—joked you always used to bug him about helping. Said you were a downright nuisance at times."

Her eyes drifted to a distant place. Jake doubted she actually saw anything. "He wanted to do something for me so I'd always remember him. He felt the tiny village would be all this town had left of him once he died."

"But you closed it up. I came by and saw it after the funeral. It was newly painted then, but you never let anyone on the property after that."

"I couldn't. After I saw you at the funeral, I...I needed to keep that part of him for myself for awhile. To remember what he'd done while we'd been married. I needed to feel..."

"What?" Jake prodded when she didn't continue.

"Needed to feel I wasn't betraying him."

Exasperated, Jake rose and began to pace the room again.

"Samantha, that's ludicrous. You can't betray someone who's dead."

She bit her lower lip as tears welled in her eyes, threatening to fall. "You can when you realize your entire marriage was a lie. Admit your heart had been elsewhere."

Jake was afraid to breathe. Did she...could she...possibly mean what he hoped? Though hesitant to voice his thoughts, he walked back to the small cot and knelt on one knee.

His fingers gently caressed her cheek. "Where was your heart, Samantha?"

Tears spilled over and ran down her cheeks. "You took it with you the day you left town."

Jake drew in a sharp breath. "Then why in the name of all that's holy did you leave me? Why did you marry Jethro?"

"Because I owed him my life."

"You what? What nonsense are you—"

It was Samantha's turn to try and calm Jake. She placed her hand on his shoulder and leaned so close, stroking the thick eyebrow with her thumb, trying to ease the frown.

"When I was a very little girl, I used to sneak away from Mama and go down to the fishing pond. One day I saw a baby duck flounder. Trying to rescue it, I got a stick and tried to reach out to drag it to shore." She stopped and closed her eyes. When she opened them, Jake was rising. He moved to sit beside her on the cot.

"I fell in—and couldn't swim."

He placed his arm gently around her shoulders and drew her close. "How old were you?"

"Five."

Her eyes locked with his, begging him to forgive her—to somehow understand why she'd done what she'd done.

"I screamed, but kept going under the water. Suddenly I heard splashing in the water and strong arms pulled me to the surface. Sobbing, I threw my arms around his neck as he moved cautiously to the embankment. It was your brother. He saved my life, Jake. If not for him, I'd never have met you."

"What does that have to do with why you married him?"

"When Jethro returned from the war, he was dying. They'd told him in the army infirmary he wasn't responding to treatments."

"What did he really die from? The death certificate stated heart failure, but I never really believed it."

"Syphilis. They'd apparently tried cupping while he was overseas—you know, where they use that thin metal rod to try and break up the infection." She shuddered at the thought of the procedure. "He said it hurt like Hades and hadn't helped at all—even after going through all that pain."

Jake's eyes widened. "He must have been miserable at the end. I've heard stories of men who suffered with it through the war."

Samantha nodded her head. "He was. All I could do was try to make him comfortable."

"But I still don't understand—"

"I saw him in town one day a few weeks after he'd returned. He invited me to Mr. Moore's ice cream shop. He makes the best hot fudge sundaes in town, so I went. While there, he told me he needed my help. Reminded me of how he'd saved me once, and would I return the favor."

"Damnation! He didn't."

"Yes, he did, and I felt too beholden to him to say no. He insisted I not tell you, but he asked me to marry him and stay with him until he died." She closed her eyes against the pain.

"I had to, Jake. I..." She choked back a sob.

Jake drew her into his arms and she laid her head against his firm chest. Oh, how she'd wanted to do this all those many years ago.

"It's alright," he crooned against her hair. "We can make it right now."

"It can never be right. I hurt you—and I'm sorry."

"Yes, you did, but it can be right. You can marry me now. Be my wife for the rest of our lives."

"I can't," she wailed. "I can never undo all the things I did wrong."

"Them's fightin' words, woman. Don't *ever* again tell me

you can't do something. You can—and you will. I won't let you run from me again."

"But—"

"But nothing. If Sheriff Moss agrees to release us tomorrow morning, we're going to head straight to apply for our marriage license. I hate the thought of that blood test, but we're going to do it first thing." He placed his fingers beneath her chin and lifted her head. "And before you tell me you can't have children, let me assure you I don't care. It will be just you and me for the rest of our lives. We'll grow old together and sit on our porch and rock in those chairs Pa built – just like I always dreamed."

Samantha turned her head away, but Jake saw the flush creeping up her cheeks.

"I don't know if I can have children or not."

"You didn't have any in the five years you and Jethro were wed. It's clear—"

Interrupting him, her cheeks turned even redder. "We didn't have any children because we never..." Clearly embarrassed, she couldn't continue.

Jake's eyes widened in sudden understanding.

"You and Jethro? You never...in all that time...you never..."

Samantha pursed her lips and shook her head.

"No."

"Why not?" he asked bluntly. He'd experienced such a shock at her words, he didn't think to temper his words.

"Because he...couldn't."

Jake's eyes widened in understanding. "The syphilis?"

"Yes."

"But he tried?"

"No. He was afraid I might contract the disease, too. That's how he caught it—over in Europe."

A smile crossed Jake's face and he pulled Samantha close. "So you've never...?"

A blush rose to her cheeks. "No."

Lowering his mouth against hers, Jake brushed her lips with the lightest touch. Wrapping his arms tightly around her, he lifted her easily into his lap.

"Feel *that*, my love?"

Samantha's eyes widened, clearly shocked by his rampant

arousal.

"Three days, Samantha. As soon as the waiting period for the marriage license is over, I'm dragging you before the preacher and you're going to be mine. We have a lot of time to make up for. I plan to love you until you start to live again. You'll be so content you'll want to share your joy with the entire town—the way you used to." He reached up to brush away a wayward curl, rubbed it between his fingers.

"Is all of you this soft, Samantha?" He leaned forward and murmured against her ear, "I always wondered. I thought about you every day I was gone. Your memory haunted me. I plan to find out, you know. Plan to learn everything about you—just as I'll teach you everything about me."

He wagged his finger in front of her face. "You'll not be doing it out of any warped sense of loyalty like you did with my brother."

He saw the smile lighting her eyes. "And why are you so sure I'll wed you, Mr. Major?"

Jake wanted to shout with joy. It was probably the first time she'd joked since Jethro's death. Yes, this woman was his, and he planned to make her live again. Had every intention of making her happy for the rest of their lives.

"Because you love me." He looked deep into her eyes, suddenly unsure again. "You do, don't you?"

His heart soared when she nodded her head.

"It's the only reason to ever marry someone, Sam. Love. We both made mistakes in the past, Sweetheart, but we have every day of the rest of our lives to correct that mistake. I thank God for granting us the second chance."

As he looked around the small cell, a grin crossed his face and his eyes glinted with merriment.

"Why, I might even invite Mickey Moss to the ceremony."

Samantha frowned. "I shall never speak to that vile man again. He locked us up—"

"Exactly. He's smarter than either of us give him credit for. I have no doubt he locked us together to make us talk to each other and admit what everyone else in this town probably already knew." He brushed his lips against the ridge of her ear.

"That we still love each other?" she whispered.

"Yes—and to think it took some blasted silly laws to make us come to our senses. Maybe they weren't so silly, after all.

They obviously served a purpose in the past." His eyes held hers and he saw all the love she'd tried so hard to keep hidden from him. "They certainly served one now."

Leanne Burroughs is the author of two books,
HIGHLAND WISHES and
HER HIGHLAND ROGUE.
Both books are available at Amazon.com
Visit Leanne's website at
www.leanneburroughs.com

I Swear

by Michelle Scaplen

• *New Jersey - It's against the law to use profanity*

"Oh, Cheryl, that's too funny. Let me hear another," April asked her friend, after she told her about the law against racing horses on the New Jersey Turnpike. They were sitting at Cheryl's cubicle in the Raritan Press building looking up ideas for April's next story. Cheryl wrote the movie reviews, while April wrote fluff pieces for the local newspaper. April didn't mind admitting to that. She enjoyed writing the kind of articles one would find in the community section of the paper, the kind people could read to put a smile on their faces after flipping through the front pages and reading about war, corruption, and the Mets' third straight loss.

Cheryl scrolled down on the computer. "Oh, this one is great, and right here in Raritan. Can you believe this? Apparently it's against the law to use profanity." It was another in the list of silly laws that was on the website Cheryl had found.

Each state had them—laws that had been on the books since the time a town probably was established. Laws so outdated they wouldn't apply in today's time. "No profanity, huh?" April sat up straighter in her chair, her mind instantly buzzing with ideas. "I can only imagine your brother, Ethan, trying to impose *that* law."

Ethan Winters. Blond hair, blue eyes, and one hundred percent man. And one hundred was probably the number of hearts he's broken, April concluded.

"He'd have to arrest the whole damn town—oops I said damn. Does that mean I just broke the law?" Cheryl asked with a laugh.

"With the way everyone swears around here, I doubt

anyone is going to turn you in. But how does that sound for an idea for an article? I'll write about how profanity is now an acceptable form of communication and can be heard on school playgrounds, or how even eighty-year-old grandmothers who get their hair done once a week at the beauty salon swear all the time, too. Of course, I'll need to research this."

She started by borrowing her six-year-old niece as a decoy, and spent the next afternoon watching and listening to children at the playground. Sixteen, April counted. Ten of the *F* word, three *S* words, and three other words she wouldn't even repeat. Little boys swore, thinking it the funniest thing in the world. Some teenage girls cursed into their cell phones, and then there were the two stressed out mothers who used them while fighting with their toddlers when they'd pleaded to go down the slide just one more time.

The next morning she went to the hair salon to have some highlights put in—all in the name of research, of course. Not because she hadn't done anything new to her hair in the last year. While she waited for her hair to process, she hid behind a *Star* magazine pretending to be interested in what Brad and Jennifer were up to this week. April was surprised at what she'd heard. Women as old as her grandmother used four letter words just as frequently as the children she'd witnessed the previous day.

Even though she was thirty years old, she remembered a time when people censored their words before they spoke. Children said words like doody or poopy instead of the four letter words they used now. She'd never heard her grandmother swear in her own home, never mind in public. Had profanity become such an acceptable form of language nowadays that nobody considered censoring what they said anymore?

Working on the story made her realize how guilty she was of the *crime*. She forced herself to put a dollar in a can at home every time she swore. She decided she'd use the money to buy the fantastic boots she'd seen in a store window. Though ashamed of her lack of restraint, if she kept it up, at this pace she'd have the boots by the end of the month!

April couldn't remember where she'd seen it, but sometime in the past she'd read an article that brought up the question, if you swear all the time, what do you say when you're *really* angry? She thought long and hard about this and it made sense to her. And it didn't say much for people's self-control if they had to say 'shit' just because they found no close parking spaces at Walmart, forcing them to walk an extra fifty yards—even though the weather was sunny and warm. And if that were the case, whatever would people say when their cars broke down on deserted highways in the middle of the night during a snow storm?

It had started out as a joke, but suddenly the tone of her article grew more serious. After all, everybody swore. You heard it wherever you went. She wondered how anyone could possibly have a law against it. Surely it had to be unconstitutional. But, after researching and listening to all the profanity coming from everyone's mouths, April thought maybe the citizens of her town should clean up their language. Three days later, her article was printed with a more substantial tone. And April had never been more proud of her work.

"You have to print a retraction!" Ethan demanded, clearly startling April. Her back was to him as she thumbed through a filing cabinet searching for something. She turned, and a brief smile touched her full pink lips before she walked away from him through Raritan Press' offices. He slowly walked behind her, enjoying the way her hips swayed with each step she took.

"I'm sorry. Did someone call the cops?" she teased, her tone mocking.

Ethan came straight from working the midnight to eight a.m. shift. He'd kept his uniform on hoping to intimate, and maybe even impress, April while he asked for her help. "Yes, someone called the police! Fifteen times in the last two days! You know what they wanted? They wanted fine, law abiding citizens arrested. And it's all because of your damn article."

April sat at her desk, looked up at him and tsked. She actually had the audacity to wag her finger at him and say, "tsk, tsk." Her attitude didn't help his already bad mood. She might be the cutest woman in the state of New Jersey, but since the day he'd met her, she'd done nothing but drive him crazy.

"I'm sorry Ethan, I can only print a retraction for something that isn't true, and I checked my facts thoroughly before printing the article."

Ethan ran his fingers through his hair. "Well there has to be something you can do." The edition with her article hit the stands over the weekend. He always skipped over the headline news to read April's articles first. He'd laughed when he'd read her ridiculous article that it was illegal to swear in their small New Jersey town. But it was no longer a laughing matter after the calls kept coming over the radio.

"I was called over to Mom and Pops' Diner for a domestic disturbance yesterday," he explained. "Turns out Pops wanted Mom arrested because she told him his chicken salad tasted like shit. The woman is seventy-five years old! I think she's earned the right to say anything she wants to. And by the way, I've tasted the chicken salad, and it does taste like..."

When she wagged her finger at him again, he bit back the four letter word. Instead he asked, "How am I supposed to arrest someone for using profanity, April?"

"Well I guess..." April began to say before her telephone rang. She held up a hand to him indicating he should wait a minute. "April Rose," she said into the phone. She paused for a moment and Ethan saw her green eyes light up and a smile brighten her face. "Yes, yes, of course I can be right there."

When she hung up the phone, she quickly got out of her chair and headed for the door.

"What's going on?" Ethan demanded.

"Can't talk. I gotta go. That was CableNewsJersey on the phone. They want to interview me about the article."

Furious, Ethan followed her out to her car. "You can't do that!" he shouted. "The whole town watches that station. How am I going to do my job if I'm answering ridiculous calls when there are real crimes going on in this town?"

April stopped just as she reached to open her car door. Her short red hair blew recklessly in the wind. "Ethan your problems stopped being mine a long time ago." Without another word, she got in the car and drove away.

That left nothing else for Ethan to do except get in his car and follow her.

"This is going to be fantastic," Tina Long, the show's host and producer bubbled as she walked onto the stage.

April sat in her chair, trying not to fidget. The bright lights from above probably were melting the make-up that was caked on her face. *This is so not going to be great.*

Seeing Ethan stalk into the studio after April, Tina had come up with a plan to tape a debate between 'the journalist and the police officer.' Ethan sat smuggly across from her, looking as cool and as handsome as could be. *She wanted to smack him.*

"My notes," Tina said, walking back off the stage. "Where the fuck are my notes?" she asked her assistant who frantically looked through some papers, obviously fearful of her boss.

"You think you're funny, don't you?" April leaned close to ask Ethan.

"Yep, I do. Now do you think I look better with my cap on," Ethan asked, placing his police cap on his head, "or off?" He removed it from his head with a killer smile on his face.

"You're not going to win this debate," she said, ignoring his question.

"Oh I think I will." He settled his cap on his lap. " I happen to know I'm very good at riling you up and making you do and say things you never meant to. I know I can get you so frustrated they'll have to beep out all the naughty words you say."

A few choice words came to mind, but she bit her lip instead. "Yeah, riling me up never was a problem with you was it? It's the kissing and making up you never quite figured out."

Ethan looked at her with the devil in his eyes and lowered his voice to a sexy whisper. "I happen to remember many times I was *very* good at kissing and making up."

April remembered those times as well. They'd argue over silly things, most of which she couldn't remember now. But she could relive every passion-filled night in vivid detail. He'd say he was sorry, or she'd apologize, then they'd kiss and fall into bed.

Except for that last time—when neither of them would admit to being wrong.

"You're impossible!"

Ethan Winters had a beautiful grin—and he turned it on her now.

"I know you are, but what am I?"

"Is that how you plan to win this debate, by acting like a

child?"

"Nope."

And he didn't.

He spoke eloquently and like a true professional. He stated his reasons the law was outdated. "Phone calls to the police station by women who are fed up with their husband's language has wasted taxpayer's money and the police force's valuable time."

April thought she didn't do so bad herself. Without sounding prudish, she explained, "Vulgar words are heard everywhere. Even at the diner or grocery store—whether you want to hear the words or not. No one considers the sensibilities of those around them. And what about our children? They repeat things their fathers say, and other children pick up on it." Turning to stare directly into Ethan's eyes, she said, "And although I believe the law shouldn't actively be enforced, I believe controlling our language is something the citizens of Raritan should think about."

Ever aware the camera was rolling, Ethan asked her, "And do you practice what you preach?" He smiled, looking like the cat who'd just eaten the canary.

"I'll admit I've been guilty of using profanity, but since doing the research I've cleaned up my vocabulary." She narrowed her eyes, but pasted a smile to her face. "What about you, Officer Winters? How are your manners? Do you set a good example for our town?"

"Certainly," Ethan replied. Although most people who didn't know him wouldn't have noticed, April watched his left eye twitch as she caught him in the lie.

"Really?" she said, hoping to get some good final words in. "You could go a day—or a week—without using one word of profanity?"

She noticed a veil of sweat break out on his forehead. Smiling, she doubted it was only from the heat of the cameras. Finally, she'd gotten Officer Calm nervous!

"Uh, yeah, sure I could. Longer than even you."

"I'd love to see that," April replied dryly.

"Yes, yes. I would love to see that as well." Eyes alight with excitement, Tina Long looked confidently into the camera and asked, "How about you, New Jersey, wouldn't you love to see which one of our guests slips up first? Perhaps while the whole state watches."

Suddenly April became very nervous. Tina seemed to be the type of woman who looked for her shot at fame. She was very aggressive and eager. April could only imagine what was running through the woman's mind.

It had been two days since Ethan had been locked in April's house. Under different circumstances, that would have been something he'd have been excited about. But with cameras set up in every corner, in almost every room, and with microphones carefully placed throughout the house, Ethan was on the verge of a nervous breakdown.

Although both he and April had tried to object, April's editor thought it a great promotional idea, while the mayor thought it would help the police department's image. "Now just behave yourself," the mayor had warned.

So for the past two days, Ethan and April were forced into Raritan Township's version of a reality show. Cameras were everywhere in the house but the bathroom, and they were also free to use the back yard without being watched. Too bad it'd been raining since he'd arrived.

The footage would be chopped up into little pieces and thirty minutes of it a day would air in prime time until one of them slipped, with of course any swear words being bleeped out. Ethan was tempted to look directly in the camera and say "fuck you," just to end this, but he was a competitive soul being the youngest of four brothers and one sister, and giving in just wouldn't do.

Living with April took some getting used to. Especially while he had to spend his nights on the couch, when there was a perfectly comfortable bed with a soft warm body in the other room. He missed sharing that bed and his life with her. Living under the same roof, and not being able to share everything made him wish for things he feared he'd never have, and he felt trapped because of it.

He'd just have to make April annoyed enough that she'd say something wrong first, otherwise he feared he might just have to grab her and kiss her senseless whether thousands of people were watching or not.

Ethan flipped the next page of the outdoor life magazine he brought with him. Out of the corner of his eye he watched

April work on her computer at the kitchen table. She must be going as stir crazy as him. He had to end this! He started to hum, a tuneless high pitch hum that would push anyone over the edge.

April continued tapping away at her computer. Next he tried to annoy her by rapping. *"April's gonna give up...I know she's gonna give up...pttt ptutt pstt tutu...April's gonna give up I know she gonna give up...pttt ptttput pstttut..."* She turned around and smiled at him, then continued her work.

That smile was almost worth it all. And Ethan had to wonder if he was more upset that he had lost his freedom or because she wasn't paying him enough attention. When they dated, almost two years ago, April would always smile at him and look at him with her beautiful green eyes as if he were her moon and her stars. They only dated for nine months, but they'd been the best nine months of his life.

April signed off and closed her computer. She was in the middle of her next article, writing about what it was like being locked in a house with a man who pushes all your buttons. But she couldn't concentrate anymore when she started thinking about some of the good buttons he would push on her, too.

Like while they were dating, and she had a bad day and wasn't in the mood for being foolish, Ethan would take her to play miniature golf and had her relaxed and smiling by the second hole. And after being stuck in a relationship with a workaholic New York Times journalist who managed to find time for two other girlfriends on the side, it felt good to have a man who made her happiness his number one priority.

Then there were the times when she was on the phone with her mother, listening to all her put downs. Jake would give her a back massage, then rain gentle and enticing kisses on her neck. It frustrated the heck out of her, but God it felt good. And that's why it hurt her so badly when in the end she learned she couldn't trust *him* either.

"You hungry?" she asked, hoping food would help her brain focus. "I can make us a salad."

Ethan walked into the kitchen and opened the refrigerator. "You made breakfast, I'll make lunch." He took out some ingredients, chopped up some vegetables, and threw them in a pan. Soon a delicious scent filled the room.

She stood next to him as he cooked. "I forgot you were such a great cook. What are you making?" Standing close, she realized he smelled delicious, too, and it had nothing to do with the mushrooms and onions he had sizzling in a pan.

"Omelets," he replied, "nothing against your cooking, of course, but the oatmeal you made for me this morning didn't quite do the trick. Now get out of my kitchen and let me cook."

April obeyed, although she was tempted to argue with him. She wondered if he was looking to start an argument with her, knowing it would lead her to either swear at him—or kiss him. Besides, she was standing too close, and her mind trailed back to when he used to make breakfast for her and served it in bed.

Ethan placed the plates and a pitcher of orange juice on the table and sat down across from her. "How's your article coming along?"

She swallowed her mouthful of eggs and frowned. "Not so good," she admitted. "I'm trying to write about our captivity, but my mind keeps going off the subject."

"You know, you could solve your problems by just saying one little four letter word and this whole thing would be over."

"Or you could."

"Yeah, but then I might lose my chance at winning you back." He smiled at her, but she didn't know if it was because he was joking or serious. She didn't know which one she wanted it to be. *If only she could trust him.*

Since she couldn't think of a clever or witty reply, she rolled her eyes and kept eating.

Afterwards she cleaned up the dishes and went back to work. Still the right words wouldn't come to her. She kept thinking about what he said about winning her back, and she wondered if maybe she should let him...that's when she felt something soft strike the back of her head.

April picked up the balled-up piece of paper off the table and threw it away. "Stop it," she said. So he threw another one at her. "Stop it, Ethan, I'm trying to work." He threw another. "Ethan you are such a pain in the...oh I get it now...sorry buster not happening. You're such a pain in my tushy."

"And what a fine little tushy it is," Ethan smiled and threw another one at her. Frustrated because she was enjoying his game, April began to throw them back. She moved into the living room towards the couch he lounged on and fired at close range. Before she knew what had happened, he grabbed her and had her on top of him, and his bright blue eyes were filled with mischief—and something more sincere.

Slowly he leaned his head forward, moving in for a kiss. Her body shivered and she instantly felt his reaction to her position, and she shivered again. She began to melt the moment his lips touched hers. It'd been two years since she'd felt his warm lips...his sweet tongue, his gentle hands framing her face. And it felt like they'd never separated. So perfect, so right.

So many cameras watching them!

"Holy..." Ethan was about to say holy shit because he was at a loss of any eloquent response after such an amazing kiss, but he caught himself in time. Plus, April had quickly shot off of him and was frantically straightening her disheveled clothing, breaking the mood.

"Ethan, the cameras," she said in a whisper. "We can't do this."

"There's no cameras in the yard, or the bathroom, how about..."

She was going to curse, he could tell, but she stopped herself in time. When she noticed his smile, her eyes lit up in anger. God he loved the way she looked when she was angry. "Is that what this was all about...you were trying to get me to swear at you...you, you...butthead!"

"No! No," he said, now standing an inch in front of her, "that's not what that was about...listen April..." Ethan looked directly into a camera and shook his head. "Come on, let's go outside." He gently took her arm and when she remained still, he said, "To talk, April, to talk."

The rain continued to beat down heavily. They stood close together under the small overhang. Because he couldn't help himself, he bent and kissed her again. She was reluctant at first, but once she gave in she was pure fire in his arms. The rain was loud, but it was the perfect soundtrack for his raging emotions.

"We're not talking," April said when she broke their kiss.

"No," he said before possessively taking her mouth again. When he stopped an eternity later, he asked nearly out of breath, "God, we are so perfect together, why did we ever break up?"

She turned away from him, then wiped the rain, or was it tears, from her face. "Because you cheated on me."

"I did not cheat on you!" Ethan replied enunciating each word.

"And then you lied about it!" April pulled open the sliding glass door and walked back inside.

Luckily Ethan didn't follow her. April had a feeling he was taking advantage of the privacy and was cursing a blue streak. She kind of felt that way herself. She felt like an idiot letting him back into her heart like that. Just a few kisses from Mr. Smooth and she was ready to plan her wedding. Idiot.

He could deny that he cheated all he wanted, but April knew what she'd seen. And he still hadn't come up with a reasonable explanation for why his ex-girlfriend's car was in his driveway at two o'clock in the morning, and still again at nine a.m.

She hadn't been stalking him. Knowing he was working the late shift and would be home early in the morning, she'd stayed up all night and drove over wearing nothing but a rain coat, with a bottle of wine in the front seat. When she saw his ex's car in the driveway, she pulled over and went to the door, but at the last minute chickened out. She couldn't bring herself to go to the house and confront them. Instead she went back to her house and cried herself to sleep.

Shaking off the bad memories, April made herself a cup of tea and sat back at the table staring mindlessly at her computer. A minute later she heard Ethan walk inside, then a few minutes after that heard the sound of the shower running.

Good, this was her house, he should be leaving her alone. While left alone at the computer, April did some on-line shopping, buying those boots she'd seen, figuring she deserved them. Nothing like a new pair of boots to help repair a broken heart. If only that really were true, she thought as she wiped away a tear stuck in the corner of her eye.

Ethan dried himself off from his frigid shower and swore into the mirror. What a fuckin' idiot he was, thinking they could pick things up where they'd left them two years ago. No matter what, she still couldn't trust him. And that hurt more than he was willing to admit.

I Swear

Cheat on her? What a joke! He was in love with her, the very idea of cheating on her was ludicrous. Yet she wouldn't believe the truth anyway. He knew she'd been hurt terribly by her ex-boyfriend. His sister, Cheryl, had told him all about the moron who broke her heart, and she'd warned him before she introduced them.

"Don't hurt her," his sister demanded the night of the blind date. Well it wasn't actually a blind date. Ethan had seen April a few times before he begged his sister to set them up. He knew he was crazy to believe in such things, but it really had been love at first sight for him.

He was a police officer, made it his job to notice everyone in town. Then one day while driving around, he noticed his sister walking down Main Street with the prettiest redhead he'd ever seen. He nearly hit the car in front of him when his heart lurched in his chest from just looking at her. Ethan spent the next few weeks looking everywhere for her, he'd found her going in the grocery store, the movie theater, and the pet shop.

After getting dressed, Ethan went to the couch he claimed for himself the past two days...and two painful nights and sat down. "Why don't you have any pets?" he asked her out of the blue.

"What?" she asked, turning and looking at him curiously.

He surprised her. Good. "I saw you one day, before we started dating, and you went inside a pet store, but you don't have any pets. I've always wondered about that."

"I thought you'd never seen me before the night of our first date."

"Yeah, I did a few times around town. I saw you with Cheryl once and asked her to fix us up. Why don't you have a pet? You seem to be a cat person to me."

"I'm not sure what you mean by cat person," she said before joining him in the living room, sitting in the chair across from him. "You asked Cheryl to set us up? I didn't know that."

"Of course I did. I fell in love with you the minute I saw you." He didn't add that he never fell out of love—let her figure that out herself. "You don't even have a fish or a hamster."

She sat silently for a moment, and he expected her to reply to his declaration of love, but instead she finally

287

answered his original question. "I interviewed the pet store owner about why people insist on dressing their dogs up like people...not one of my most interesting articles."

Ethan watched April fidget in her seat. She was nervous, she could never sit still when she was nervous.

They both spoke at the same time. "I never cheated on you," and "Are you hungry?"

"No," he replied answering her question. "My ex-girlfriend, I won't say her name with all these cameras and microphones, was at my house because she was afraid. Her boyfriend at the time had hit her, gave her a black eye and some nasty bruises. I'm a police officer, she came to my house asking for advice and for help. I talked her into going to the station and filing a report. She was in no shape to drive, so I asked one of my friends, another cop, to pick her up and drive her down there. That's why her car was there."

"Why didn't you tell me that?" *He loved her? From the minute he saw her?* April's heart pounded wildly in her chest. All this time wasted.

"I couldn't. I promised her to keep it a secret, and well...I kinda hoped you'd trust me enough to know I'd never cheat on you. I was so madly in love with you, April...I still am. You gotta believe me—I'm saying it in front of all these cameras." He sat on the couch, just watching her with such love and emotion in his eyes. "Say something, Honey, I'm dying here."

April stood up, looked directly at one of the cameras and said loudly, "Fuck, damn, shit!"

The look on his face was priceless. She reached for him and pulled him up and led him outside. The rain had finally stopped and the sun began to peak through the clouds.

"What...what was that all about?"

"I want those cameras out of my house, I want you all to myself. I love you, too, Ethan. I never stopped. I'm sorry I didn't trust you. Can you forgive me?"

He wrapped his arms around her and kissed her. She was dizzy by the time he stopped. "I'll forgive you on one condition."

"What?"

"Marry me, soon, and forever."

"I will if you promise to never stop riling me up."

"Oh baby, I don't only promise to, I'll *swear* to it."

I Swear

Be sure to visit Michelle Scaplen's website
www.MichelleScaplen.com

Something Rotten This Way Comes

by Cissy Hassell

• *North Carolina - If a man and a woman who aren't married go to a hotel/motel and register themselves as married, according to state law, they are then legally married*

"Look, mister, you're either going to help me or you're not. Which is it going to be? Don't waste my time!"

Natalie was livid. She'd come all this way on a recommendation from her brother. And *this* is what she got. Unkempt. Unshaven. A definite lowlife, she decided. Even so, there was a dangerous element lurking in his dark eyes that made her shudder. Maybe this was the kind of man she needed to find Audrey. Nevertheless, when she got her hands on her brother, she was going to hurt him bad if this was another one of his silly jokes.

She eyed the man who sat at the table pouring another shot of Jack Black into a glass, tossing it down his throat like water and wondered what Justin had been thinking. It wasn't like him to steer her wrong. But this! This poor excuse for a man was supposed to be a professional private eye. Instead, he looked like something the cat thought about dragging in but decided it wasn't worth the effort.

Deliberately, Johnny reached for the pack of Marlboros lying on the table. He'd promised himself he wouldn't take another drag of the nasty things, but this babe stretched him to the limit. He took his time lighting his cigarette, studying her through the blue smoke he blew out as she planted her palms on the table where he sat. She was hissing like some bad-ass alley cat. He took a deep drag just to irritate her, his lungs welcoming the nicotine it had been deprived of.

He poured another Jack and downed it, lifting a brow in enquiry. Angry. Nervy. He wondered what other qualities dear Justin's sister possessed.

When Justin had called him, filling him in on the details of his sister's friend—that she'd disappeared from the face of the earth—he was just doing an old buddy a favor. They'd gone through four years of college together, then endured the rigorous studies of law school in each other's company. They'd both gone on to working at prestigious law firms. But something had happened along the way.

It was Johnny who had faltered. He'd been crazy in love and popped the question way too soon. They were to have a short engagement, then one day his lady love went missing. All evidence had pointed to a kidnapping. For days, he'd desperately turned over every rock he could find, then two weeks later found his bride to be willingly ensconced in a hideaway cabin in the hills of Tennessee with her new husband.

Devastated, he began to drink, relying on a temporary fix of amber liquid to drown his pain. He lost his job, then somewhere along the line, Justin had rescued him and put him back on his feet. For that he was grateful. Knowing he no longer wanted to practice law, Johnny became a private detective as his career alternative.

And now this walking dream needed his services.

He'd learned a long time ago to stay away from women this gorgeous, especially ones with angry eyes that burned him down in consuming flames of fire. Under other circumstances, if she wasn't his best friend's sister, if she wasn't so damned stunning, he'd jump her bones the first chance he got.

Natalie eyed him with disdain. The phrase *Something Rotten This Way Comes* marched through her mind like good little soldiers. Now, here she was putting her life and that of her friend's in the hands of a perfect stranger, one whose personal appearance left a lot to be desired. But what choice did she have? She had to find Audrey. She was in danger and needed her help. Natalie was sure of it.

Johnny pushed back a chair with the toe of his boot. "Sit, little lady, and tell me again why you think your friend's in trouble."

"Weren't you listening to me at all? She was supposed to

meet me three days ago. We'd planned a getaway together to Oak Island and she didn't show. That's not like her."

"Note?"

Natalie gave him a blank look. "What?"

"Note. Did your friend leave a note?"

"No, she didn't leave a note. Kidnap victims don't, you moron." She didn't want to think about what could've happened to Audrey by now. It was too much to wrap her mind around.

"Runaways don't either, Doll Face."

Natalie stiffened. "You will kindly address me as Natalie or Miss Case."

"So, I take it you're not married?" Good, Johnny thought. Maybe after this little game played itself out, he'd ask her out, brother or not, and see where it took them. Great eye candy, that was for sure.

Natalie dropped her head, silently screaming at the incompetence of the male species—all except her brother, of course—and even he was questionable now. This was not the time for a man to hit on her. Especially one that reeked of liquor.

Of course, he'd probably clean up good, given his good bone structure and all those angles and shadows on his features. Any other time she'd give him a second look. Maybe. He was attractive. Sort of, she amended. In a rugged sort of way.

With a shake of her head, she thrust those thoughts from her mind. Now was definitely not the time for *that*!

"No. I am *not* married. I don't see what that has to do with anything."

"Just wondering how we'd do this, you know, have a working relationship if there were a jealous husband on the scene to complicate matters."

He could've said she misunderstood his every word. He could've said the devil made him do it. He could've said a lot of things, but all he wanted to do was prod and poke until he got the reaction he was looking for. He stared her straight in the eye, raised one eyebrow and then wiggled both suggestively.

Instantly, Natalie was on her guard. She didn't like the way this was going at all. How could her brother possibly be a friend to such a degenerate? Her eyes narrowed and she clenched her jaw so tight she thought her teeth would break.

"What's that suppose to mean?"

Johnny searched for just the right words so she wouldn't get suspicious. He didn't want to tell her the real reason for such a comment. He couldn't tell her his body was doing back flips from being within breathing distance of her. He couldn't tell her all the things that crossed his mind that he'd like to do to her. He couldn't tell her he was hotter than a blazing inferno just by looking at her.

There would be a big problem if he did. She'd probably pick up the bottle of Jack and crack his head with it, wasting half a bottle of the delectable whiskey in the process.

Then there was the brother. Justin would definitely commit murder if he ever found out what way his mind was going. He'd play this one by ear, he decided.

"You haven't really thought this out, have you?"

"I beg your pardon?"

"Beg all you want, sweet cakes. It's your dime."

It took all her strength to keep from grabbing the bottle of whiskey and bashing it over his head. She raked her gaze over his features, flipped them over what she could see of his body and let him know without a doubt, she found him wanting. Even so, her instincts were screaming that he had the strength of character and wherewithal to do the job she needed done. There was a look about him that kept her standing, waiting for him to make up his mind.

Finally, she sat in the chair he'd indicated. It was then Johnny noticed shadows under her eyes, worry within their depths. His stomach knotted with regret. He was a sucker for a woman who had heart.

"Look," she began softly. "I think we got off on the wrong foot. I really do need your help. Please consider helping me. *Please.*"

It was the last please that really got to him. He'd already decided to lend his services, but the silent plea hanging on the edge of that one word clinched it.

Then she had the audacity to look so damn beautiful he literally lost his breath. His whole body felt like it had been hit by a Mack truck, throwing thoughts in his mind he had no business thinking about. She made him think about making love into the wee hours of morning, waking up all tangled arms and legs, bodies warm and snuggly from sleep and starting all over again. She could take him places he'd never been...places he'd willingly go.

"Johnny? Is something wrong?" She placed her hand on his forearm to get his attention and drew back quickly. Just that slight touch burned her fingertips, sending a shiver dancing up her arm chased by a streak of blazing heat.

"No," he muttered. Where was his mind? This was not the way to conduct an investigation. "I'll need to know what your plans were. Where were you to meet? Where was she coming from? Did she fly in? Drive? Take the train? Bus? Start there."

"Okay." The relief she felt made her lightheaded. He was going to help. That was all that mattered at the moment. "We were going to meet at the Wildflowers Inn last Friday. We rented a villa on the beach for a week. She was driving down from Ivanhoe...starting Thursday morning. I don't get an answer when I call her home phone or her cell phone."

"How about work?"

"They told me she was on vacation and wouldn't be back until the following Monday."

He considered the information for a moment. "I'll need to go down there and see what I can find out. Maybe backtrack. I'll leave this afternoon. Give me a number where I can reach you at all times, preferably your cell."

"Wait just a minute! You're not going anywhere without me!"

Johnny looked at Natalie like she was crazy. "You're kidding, right? Tell me you're kidding."

"No, I am not kidding. I've got to go. Audrey might need me."

"Then why in the hell are you asking for my help if you're going anyway? You'll just be tagging along where you have no need to be."

"Justin said you were the best private detective on the planet. I need your expertise. You know what to look for. I don't. I've got to be there if something—"

Johnny heard the pain in her voice and cursed himself for being such an easy mark. He relented. "Okay. But let's get one thing straight. You will *not* interfere with what I'm doing, no matter what."

Natalie nodded her compliance.

294

"And one more thing. You'll do what I tell you. Understand?"

She nodded again, feeling very much like a small child. She didn't say a word for fear he'd change his mind.

"Come on. Is your car here? Where are you staying?"

"I took a cab. I'm staying at the Cape Cod Inn."

"We'll pick up your things, check you out and be on our way."

It was all done with swift and measured precision. Some time later, as she watched the landscape fly by in flashes of green, she hoped Audrey was all right. Even though Johnny drove like a speed demon, the drive from Ivanhoe to Oak Island seemed hours long. She must have lost her mind to be doing this, to be handling this emergency in this way. She was only going by what Justin had told her, that Johnny was the best. She certainly hoped so. She didn't want anything to happen to her friend.

Finally, Oak Island came into view. Traffic was minimal, thank goodness. Johnny hadn't said more than five words to her in the few hours it had taken to drive down. She'd sneaked glances his way every now and then. With each passing glance, she found one more thing that piqued her interest. His hands, for one. Nicely shaped, nails blunt cut, nice long fingers. She wondered how they would feel on her skin. Would they be gentle, a little rough, perhaps? Would he linger over certain parts of her body as those long fingers took a long, slow slide wherever he cared to caress? She grew warm, sucked in a small, but steadying breath to wipe all that away. It didn't help in the least.

Johnny pulled into the parking lot of the Wildflowers Inn and turned off the motor. "Whatever I say, you keep quiet and go along, understand?"

She stared at him, a protest on her lips, but was stopped by the way he looked at her. He reached out and twirled a strand of hair around his fingers. He tugged. She followed. His lips brushed hers. She never knew she could feel so needy. She felt the twist of it grow into something larger. The strangeness of it all made her body grow rigid. He felt it and pulled away, corralling his own needy hunger.

"Come on." The growl was low and deep. Husky.

Rattled, Natalie followed, her lips still tingling from that slight brush of his mouth against hers, her body still humming from his touch. She tried for righteous indignation, but it was nowhere to be found.

Inside, she found Johnny talking to the desk clerk. Flirting was more like it, she grumbled silently. The young woman appeared to be about twenty-one years of age—if that—fresh-faced and very attractive. Natalie's own twenty-nine years suddenly seemed old. Next to the sweet, young thing, she felt like an old rag mop that had seen its better days.

"This is the little woman," he crooned, wrapping his arm around Natalie's waist and pulling her to him. "Been married only a month, we have."

Natalie balked. Married to this moron? She opened her mouth to tell him so, but clamped it shut at the warning look he gave her.

"We'll be spending a few days, see what's here, maybe run up and down the coast. Say, a friend of ours was supposed to meet us here. Can you check your records, see if she got tired of waiting and checked out? Hey, maybe she left a message."

He winked at the desk clerk, her youthful features welcoming his subtle flirting. "What was her name?"

"Audrey Wright," Natalie supplied. "I—that is—we were supposed to meet her here a few days ago."

Johnny took advantage of the situation and kissed her on the nose. "We kinda got side-tracked."

He wiggled his eyebrows outrageously and Natalie thought he was the most disgusting man she'd ever met. Then she felt his warm breath on her cheek and her body was seared with a blazing heat. She was tingling from so many things she didn't know what to do first. Pull away? Stay and let the heat burn her to a crisp?

All that was taken away in the next breath. His mouth was on hers, shocking her system yet again. He was gentle, but firm. Demanding, but persuasive. Possessive. Hot. Sweet. Too many things for her mind to comprehend. Too many to fight against.

Johnny didn't know why he was kissing her like this in plain view of the desk clerk or any one else for that matter. He'd been teasing, or so he thought. Then the first thing he knew, her mouth was under his and she was kissing him back, sending all his senses into a tailspin. She tasted damn good and he wanted more. She was just so soft against him, sinking into him like she belonged there. That was a feeling he hadn't felt in one hell of a long time. He liked it, wanted it to last. More than just a moment. More than just a day. Maybe a lifetime.

Suddenly, he shoved her away. A lifetime? To be shackled to the same woman for a lifetime? How crazy was that? What the hell was he thinking?

"I think you guys better take these room keys, Mr. Rotten, before you do something you're not supposed to. I'll check our records for your friend and let you know, okay?"

Johnny grinned sheepishly, picked up the key cards, grasped Natalie by the wrist and pulled her along after him. Outside, he heard her laughter and stopped abruptly.

"What's so funny?"

"I can't believe your name is really Johnny Rotten."

"Yeah, so what?" He'd been ribbed his whole life about his name, thought about changing it, but what was in a name anyway?

There must have been a little imp on Natalie's shoulder urging her to goad him. "Tell me, Johnny, are you rotten to the core? Are you the bad apple? Bad to the bone, perhaps?"

Johnny growled and walked away, listening to her laughter following him. He grinned despite himself. He liked her sense of humor. He liked way too much about Natalie Case. She sure got under his skin in a hurry. Started him thinking about what ifs and nonsense like the future—with her in it, no less.

One thing was certain, she'd be a hard woman to forget. He let his imagination run free as he moved, let images form— of hair laying across a male chest, its strands curling possessively around fingers entangled in its softness. *His* chest, he realized, with a swift shock to his senses. What he was imagining was her, Miss Natalie Case, in his bed. The surge of desire was so strong he nearly turned around to taste her mouth again.

It was a struggle to keep his feet moving forward. The force of it took him by surprise. It was so not like him to be affected by a woman. He'd schooled his emotions to take a dive under the wire of retreat whenever one piqued his interest.

He needed to find her friend and get the hell away from this babe in sheep's clothing. She was already digging under his skin and making herself right at home. If he wasn't careful, the next place he'd find her would be in his heart.

Natalie watched him go, then reluctantly followed, wondering how she was going to survive being in such close confines with the man. She needed to focus, to train all her thoughts on Audrey.

She moved through the open door of the motel room and sighed with relief. The bathroom door was closed and the shower running. She was granted at least ten minutes reprieve, she hoped. The stress of the day bore down on her in a rush. Bone-tired, she plopped down on one of the double beds and laid a weary head on a pillow. In moments, she was fast asleep and didn't hear the creak of the bathroom door as Johnny exited.

He moved quietly to the space between the two beds and stared down at her. She lay with palms together under her cheek, sleeping like she hadn't a care in the world. His heart did a triple flip and thudded against his ribcage like angry surf against the seashore. Desire sprang hot and heavy. He was glad she was asleep. He didn't know what would happen if she woke and found him with the hardest boner he'd ever had in his life.

Heavens above, what had he gotten himself into this time? He needed another shower. A cold one this time.

"It's been a week, Johnny."

She was ever so tired of this man. Not only was he stepping on her last nerve, but being in the same room with him day after day was taking its toll on her emotions. From sleepless nights to erotic dreams. From watching him parade around without a shirt exposing rock hard abs to the play of rippling muscles across his back, she'd been done in. The sooner she got away from him the better. She was having thoughts and feeling things she never should feel about a man with a name like Johnny Rotten. He had to be bad news. Bad boy news.

What was that song? *I'll show you how a real bad boy can be a real good man?* Just the implication of that sent her nerves skittering like a Mexican jumping bean. She wanted to hold onto something tight. It was already proving to be a wild ride.

"I've canvassed the whole island, Natalie. It's not that big and I've found nothing. We'll have to start over, maybe go to Ivanhoe, track her movements there. Start at the beginning instead of the end."

Before she could begin her tirade on his incompetence, her cell phone rang. A prickly sensation skipped along the nape of her neck. Justin. What the heck did he want? She was a little put out with him anyway. There was no time like the present to give him a piece of her mind.

She flipped it open. "I've got a crow to pick with you, brother."

Justin sighed. She was always so volatile, this sister of his. "Before you do, Audrey's here."

"Audrey?"

"Yes, Audrey, dear sister. No cloak-and-dagger stuff, no pervert waiting in the shadows, no slasher wielding a switchblade. Audrey is here safe and sound. Hold on, I'll get her."

Natalie twisted the phone cord through her fingers while she waited. This couldn't be happening, she thought, trying to convince herself she hadn't spent the last few days with Johnny Rotten for nothing.

"Natalie! Hi, Hon, how ya' doing?"

"Where the hell have you been? I've been worried out of my mind about you. Why didn't you meet me? Why didn't you call me?"

"Hold on there, Hon. I've been at Myrtle Beach. Tried calling several times to let you know my plans had changed. Sorry to make you worry."

Natalie blew out a breath of resignation. There was no talking to this woman. She didn't operate on anything but slow speed. "Okay. Let's start at the beginning by you telling me what happened. And we'll go from there. Why didn't you show up?"

"I was on my way, see," Audrey explained. "I had this flat tire and no spare. So, I was rescued by the most gorgeous man I've ever seen in my life. He changed my tire, we got to talking, lost track of time and one thing led to another. I am now Mrs. Derek Thorpe!"

"What!" Knees weak with shock, Natalie sat down hard on the chair closest to her. "You're married?"

"Yeah. How 'bout them apples, huh?"

"You're...married?"

"Yes, Hon, I'm married. Be happy for me."

What could she say? "I *am* happy for you, Aud. Are you sure this is what you want?"

"Damn sure, Sweetie. Have you ever met someone and knew immediately that they were your destiny? That they were who you've been waiting for all your life? That it was meant to be?"

Natalie glanced at Johnny, felt a blast of recognition in Audrey's words, then instantly dismissed it as nonsense. There was no such thing as love at first sight.

"I can't say I have, Audrey. But, uh, I'm glad for you."

"Good. Gotta go, Hon. Derek is waiting. Ta-ta."

Natalie sat with the phone in her hand, stunned at the turn of events. Johnny stripped it from her palm and replaced it on the cradle.

"So, I take it your friend is fine and dandy?"

"I'm gonna kill her," she decided from delayed reaction. "I worried for days and days. I've had visions of her being kidnapped, abused, slashed to pieces and murdered. And, dammit, there's not a cotton-pickin' thing wrong with her! Married! Of all the damn things she could do, she goes and gets herself married!"

"That's not such a bad thing, is it?"

He'd been thinking a lot about the chains of the institution of marriage ever since Natalie marched boldly to where he'd been sitting, planted her hands on his table and demanded his help. At first, he thought she was just Justin's scatter-brained little sister, but she filled out those jeans with such delicious curves and delectable shapes, his mouth watered. He wanted to drink in her charms, taste those lips and plunge his fingertips through that mass of lush dark hair. Yes, he could definitely agree he'd been moved by much more than lust. There was something about Natalie Case that scrambled his heart as well as his brain. He wanted to know more, see more, touch more.

Before common sense could kick in, he pulled Natalie to her feet and captured her mouth. It was all heat, hunger, greed. Breaths came in gasps and pants. Hands roved, explored, caressed.

Natalie didn't know what hit her. She was hot—cold. Lightheaded. Weak-kneed. And swept with the most glorious pleasure she'd ever felt in her life. So much so she couldn't think. Couldn't resist. Couldn't do anything but feel.

He tried to break free, but she tugged him into the fire. When he finally regained control, it was all he could do not to throw her down on the bed and ravish her. It's what he wanted to do. He must be absolutely out of his mind. The immediate crisis was over and it was time to wash his hands of this little number.

She drew in a ragged breath and pushed at his chest, asking herself what the hell she thought she was doing. She gave Johnny an angry glance, grabbed her bag and threw what contents she had inside.

"Let's go," she ordered in a shaky voice. She had to get away from him. Either that or she was going to jump his bones, right there and then.

Johnny followed her out the door, went to checkout and returned to his car. Natalie waited, fuming, he could tell. Well, let her stew. He wasn't a damn bit sorry he kissed her. Given the first chance, he'd do it again in a heartbeat.

Later, Johnny dropped her off at her apartment. Once inside, Natalie threw her bag against the wall, watched it bounce and hit the floor. She should call her brother and tell him exactly what she thought of his friend. But all she wanted right now was a good night's sleep. Heaven knew, she hadn't had one in days. She showered, dried quickly, flopped down on the bed and promptly fell asleep.

It had been a week now since she'd last laid eyes on Johnny Rotten. He wouldn't let go of her, even in her dreams. Her fingertips itched to touch him, her arms ached to hold him, her heart filled with longing.

The doorbell rang as she dried her hair. She was in no mood for company. She was still in a snit at the whole world over the incident with her so-called best friend and the audacity of getting married without her knowledge to a perfect stranger. Still a little more put out at Justin for his part in the Rotten debacle. If it was her brother thinking he could walk right in and be instantly forgiven, she was going to bash him over the head with the first object she laid her hands on.

Except it wasn't her brother. It was Johnny Rotten.

"What do you want?" She knew she was being rude, but she had no qualms about doing so. The memory of his kiss still haunted her. She'd never forgive him for that.

Johnny held out a document. "Just making it legal, my love."

Her antennae went up in full force. What was he trying to pull now? She grabbed the envelope out of his hand and ripped it open. She scanned the contents and laughed. She flipped the paper with a finger.

"What the hell is this?"

"It's our marriage certificate, Sweet Cakes."

She glanced down at the official document, knew it was the real thing by the seal in the right hand corner. She slapped it against his chest and let it go. He caught it as it fell.

"You are out of your ever-loving mind!"

"No, I'm not, Natalie. There's an old law that states if a man and a woman who aren't married go to a motel and register themselves as married, they are legally married."

Natalie looked at him like he'd grown two heads. "What kind of asinine joke are you trying to pull here? There's no such idiotic law and you are so full of crap, it ain't funny! Get out of my house!"

Johnny put his hand on the door she tried slamming in his face. "Call your brother."

Natalie stomped away in a huff, snatched the phone off the hook in fury and punched in Justin's number. The answering machine came on and upped her threshold of rage another notch.

"You answer the phone this minute, you jerk. I want to talk to you now!"

Justin heard his sister and wondered what had her in a snit. Something had set her off and he was going to get the brunt of it from the sound of the anger riding her voice.

"Hey, Sis, what's up?" he answered cheerfully, hoping to dampen her temper a bit.

"What kind of friend did you hook me up with, Justin? Do you know what that moron jerk is trying to do?"

"I'm sure you're gonna tell me," he mumbled, knowing he

might as well be spitting in the wind.

"That...that jerk is saying we're married!"

"Well, did you? I mean, you were together for a week, after all. What did you do all that time anyway?"

"Justin! How can you say such a thing to me? I wouldn't marry that man if he was the last man on earth!"

"Nat, this is getting us nowhere. What exactly did he say to make you think you were married?"

"He's spouting a bunch of nonsense about some old law that states *if a man and woman who aren't married go to a motel and register themselves as married, they're legally married.* It's crap and you know it!"

Justin wanted to laugh, knew if he did, Natalie would march right over and be in his face. And that he didn't want, not when her anger was on the same level as a raging inferno. Now he had to figure out a way to make his sister happy. God knew, if she wasn't happy, she wouldn't allow anyone around her to be either.

"Nat, calm down a minute, will you?"

"Don't tell me to calm down, Justin. I am not married to this slime ball. Granted, we checked into the motel as Mr. and Mrs., and granted we stayed together for a whole week. But that doesn't mean we're married."

"Let me ask you this, Natalie, before you explode. Why in the world would a man like Johnny say such a thing? What's he going to gain by it?"

Her eyes burned from frustration. This was *not* happening to her. "You'll have to ask *him* that question!"

She thrust the phone in Johnny's face, barely missing his nose. He just grinned and kissed her on the nose.

"Hey, there, Justin. How's it hanging?"

Justin ignored his remark and got down to business. "Johnny, what the hell do you think you're doing? This is my sister you're messing with and I don't take too kindly to that. Do you want me to come over there and beat your face in?"

Johnny ignored him right back and got down to his own business with what he came for. "My intentions are honorable, Justin. You're a top-notch attorney. Read up on old laws that are still on the books. You'll see."

"That may be, but that doesn't explain why you're doing this to Nat...why you're claiming you two are married. What's going on?"

Johnny locked his gaze with Natalie's and opted for
nothing but the truth. "I've fallen in love with your sister,
Justin, and want to marry her. It was the only way I could get
her attention. She'd have refused me any other way."

"Hmm. Well, have you asked Natalie how she feels? Does
she love you in return?"

"Don't know. I'll let you know."

Johnny replaced the phone, keeping his gaze on Natalie.
"Well?"

"Well, what?"

"What do you say, Natalie? I love you and want to marry
you. Will you?"

"So, it's true then?" She gulped in air, tried to steady
herself, to calm her racing heart. She so wanted it to be true.
"We're already married by that insane law?"

"I won't hold you to it, Love," he said gently. "But I'm
dead serious about marrying you. From the moment you
walked up to me demanding my help, you had me. I want to be
with you, share my life with you. I want it all. House. Kids. The
whole domestic bit. And I want it with you."

Natalie was speechless. She wanted to shout with joy, but
her vocal chords were frozen. She wanted to scream, *yes, yes,
yes,* but the words wouldn't come out. She wanted to throw
herself at him, but her body wouldn't move.

Johnny felt like he'd been hit by a giant fist in the gut. She
wasn't saying anything. She didn't love him! Dear God, he'd
never counted on that. He could have sworn she returned his
feelings. He'd felt her surrender, felt the heat, the passion.
He'd felt her hunger, her need, the fire.

He turned away, an ache in his chest the size of the planet
that was crushing his heart. How could he have been so
wrong? He had to get out so he could breathe.

Natalie watched him go, disbelief finally releasing her
from the chains that held her tight. "Where do you think
you're going?"

His hand fell away from the doorknob and he turned
back. "There's nothing for me here, Natalie. I poured out my
heart. I understand you don't love me."

Before she could say a word, he was out the door like a
shot. He wanted to get as far away as possible. It hurt too

much to be here.

Stunned, she watched him go. Finally her brain kicked into gear and she moved with the speed of a rattlesnake striking a victim, grabbing the marriage document from the floor and racing after him. He was already in his car, turning the key, motor springing to life when she got there.

She placed her body in front of the car, daring him to drive forward. When she didn't move, he rammed the gearshift into park and slid out of the car. He held her gaze as he walked straight up to her, trying to intimidate her by his size, his height. She was having none of it. She didn't back off, didn't even flinch.

"Get out of my way, Natalie. I said I wouldn't hold you to that marriage. It may be a marriage in the sense we were booked into that hotel as man and wife, but I release you from it. Tear it up and we'll forget the whole thing."

Natalie saw a thread of pain pass over his features before he squelched it. It hurt to know she was the cause of it. She tapped the document against his chest and met his gaze head on.

"No, I won't tear it up. And, no we won't forget the whole thing. We're married in the eyes of the law, Johnny Rotten, and I'm holding you to it. How can you be such an idiot! Of course, I love you! Of course, I will marry you—for real this time."

Johnny stared at her in bewilderment. "You love me?"

"You can be so dense, Rotten. Yes, I love you. I want to marry you. I want the whole nine yards, the whole enchilada, all of it. House. Kids. Sharing a life with you until we're old and gray, sitting on the front porch in our rocking chairs."

Johnny drew her close and just held her. The planet-sized ache that had crushed his heart now clogged his throat with emotion. "I love you so much, Natalie."

"You better," she warned. "With a name like Johnny Rotten, you'd be hard pressed to find someone else who'd put up with you."

"Then just remember that when something rotten this way comes, he means business."

"I'll remember."

He crushed her to him wanting to find the right words, serious words. He wanted to tell her there was no one else in the whole world that moved him liked she did. And there would never be anyone else in the world he would ever love. He wished for soft words, meaningful words, something to convey what he was feeling.

He settled for letting her know through his kiss. He moved his mouth over hers, pouring everything he felt into her. She felt it, reciprocated and returned his love.

Cissy Hassell is the author of
THORNS, A KNIGHT THIS WAY COMETH,
THE SAME LOVE TWICE,
NOWHERE, THE BRINGER OF RAPTURE, and
DECEIT TIMES TWO.
Be sure to visit Cissy's website at
www.cissyhassell.com

In A Pickle In Connecticut

by Diane Davis White

• *Connecticut - In order for a pickle to officially be considered a pickle, it must bounce*

"You call that a pickle?" Janis Jones looked at the limp green thing lying on her plate. "This wouldn't pass for a pickle where I come from."

"You wouldn't know a good pickle if it jumped up and bit you in the butt," June Jones retorted, staring hard at her sister. "And we come from the same place, if you'll recall."

"Yeah, but Mother had me first, which means I got the best of it." Janis used her old, childhood argument against the other woman with a gleam of malice in her eyes. "I got the brains, the beauty...the ability to tell a good pickle from a bad one—"

"Oh please," June interrupted, whipping her hair back with a shake of her head. "We're identical twins, so you didn't get more of anything than I did."

"Except I got everything first, so I got more of it."

"Really? Only thing you got more of was a big mouth."

"Quiet!" Ramona Jones glared at her daughters. "We're getting down to the wire. Deadlines for entering the pickling contest this year at the fair are looming, and I want you both to concentrate. Three of the judges are bachelors who are well off."

"Mother, a pickle judge is not my idea of a good catch." June winked at Janis.

Ramona ignored the comment. "An attorney, an entrepreneur and the owner of the largest dairy farm conglomerate in six states are going to judge this year's competition."

"While I admit their professions sound solid, it's the man that counts," Janis argued. "What good is a wealthy dairy farmer if he can't dance...or isn't romantic?"

"You won't know anything about any of them if you don't get the pickles just right." Ramona sighed in exasperation, eyeing her girls warily. "You do want to make good marriages, don't you?"

"Yeah, sure, Mom." Janis smirked at June. "Someday... when I can *produce* the perfect pickle. You know...one that bounces."

"You are twenty-seven years old and it's time you got married and *produced* some grandchildren for me," Ramona stated flatly. "I may not be around forever, and I'd like to see my daughters settled in good marriages before I die."

"Mom, you're forty-five years old, for gosh sakes. Stop pulling the old age bull on us. You got married so young you just *feel* old."

Janis lifted a pickle from the plate. With a dramatic lift of an eyebrow she declared, "This is not a pickle. It's an abomination."

"It's a perfectly good pickle," June retorted. "Anyone can see that."

"It doesn't *bounce*," Janis replied. Lifting the pickle between thumb and forefinger, she held it over the plate and dropped it. The pickle landed with a thud, not bouncing even a little bit. "See? If it doesn't bounce, it'll never get a blue ribbon."

"I agree. This batch is not the quality we want," Ramona intervened. "Let's start a new batch."

The twins groaned in unison.

"Hop to it, ladies." Ramona tightened her apron strings and started pulling ingredients from the cupboard. "Time's a wasting."

Three weeks and several dollars worth of wasted ingredients later, Ramona stood in her untidy kitchen beaming at her twins. "I knew you could do it if you tried."

"It won't stand against Muriel Potter's sweet jerkins," Janis—ever the voice of doom—retorted. "Do you honestly think we've got a winning pickle?"

"It bounces," June snapped as she lifted one of the prize pickles over a small saucer and dropped it. "See? It's perfect. Bounced not just once but twice."

"It only bounced once and just a little," Janis complained, looking at their mother for confirmation.

"This batch is blue ribbon quality." Ramona whipped off her apron and hung it behind the pantry door. "Now, let's decide what you girls are going to wear to the fair."

"That's a damned silly law," Peter Parker stated unequivocally. "Damned silly."

"It *is* a law, however," Mister Jenkins—their instructor— stated firmly. "We judge our pickles by their bounce as well as their taste and crispness."

"I'm with old Pete here," Rufus Turner said, slapping the object of his admiration on the back hard enough to make the man struggle to catch his balance. "That law don't hold vinegar." He snorted at his little play on words. "Vinegar, get it?"

"Yes, we surely *all* get it Mister Turner," Jenkins stated in a long-suffering tone, waving a dismissive hand. "Now, next thing to remember is the crispness. If a pickle is too crisp, it's hard on the teeth, and if it isn't crisp enough...well, you have to tear it to get a bite, which is also hard on the teeth. On the table are four pickles. I want each of you to take a small bite of each one and tell me—"

"Hey, by the time this contest is over we'll be pickle sick, for sure," Adam Truman interrupted. "I'm saving my pickle taste buds for the real thing."

"You have to know what you're doing. Now each of you promised to learn the pickling business—at least the tasting part—in order to judge this contest. Please, no more foolishness."

"How are we going to stand tasting pickles a week from now if we have to keep tasting them now?" Peter looked slightly rebellious. "I only agreed to this to get free advertising for my new housing tract."

"As for me," Adam said loftily, "in my bid for the Attorney General's office I need as much favorable publicity as I can get. Lot's of exposure at these county fairs." He ran a finger around his collar as though it were too tight. "Kissing babies and glad-handing the locals can win a lot of votes."

"Well, then let's consider the sum parts of a perfect pickle," the instructor interjected hopefully. "If we can just concentrate on the ideal pickle quality, then you can get your wish."

"Yeah, *I* agreed because you said the Jones Twins were entering and I want to give one of 'em a blue ribbon and get a kiss." Rufus planted his feet wide as he interrupted the nervous little man. "I've got two dairy farms needing my attention right now and the other twelve soon will, no doubt. Let's cut this lesson stuff short. I know a good pickle when I taste one."

Adam turned his head slightly, eyeing the dairy farmer with mild interest. "Who are these twins anyhow? I haven't seen a woman worth looking at since I got here."

Rufus answered with a grin. "The Jones Twins are the best looking gals this side of heaven. But Janis now, she's the prettiest and I have plans for that one. Yes, indeed."

"I see," Adam said. "So you plan to gain her affection by allowing her to win the contest?"

"Sounds like a plan to me," Rufus answered with a big grin. "A real nice plan." Then he frowned earnestly, shaking his head. "But only if her pickles are worthy, of course. Wouldn't be right to cheat another lady out of the prize."

Rufus craned his neck, peering out the window. "Uh oh, here they come. Look at that, will you?"

All three men stared out the casement at the vision of the Jones Twins. Peter gave a low whistle, Rufus grinned even wider, and Adam ran a hand over his short-cropped hair as though to smooth it.

One of the twins glanced at him, and Adam swallowed hard. Clear, light blue eyes stared into his with the intensity of a freight train rolling over him. His heartbeat went crazy, his hands began to sweat and his feet moved of their own volition, heading toward the door. Bent on introducing himself to the loveliest woman he'd ever seen, he barely registered the look of anger on the dairy farmer's face.

"Hey, that's Janis. You stay away from her," Rufus called, following close on the other man's heels. "I've been tryin' to get an introduction to her for weeks."

"Hold up guys. Wait for me." Peter, enraptured by the soft swell of perfection that was June Jones' lips, tripped over his feet as he hurried to catch the other two. His concern was getting himself in the path of the other twin—the one who was slightly shorter, whose hair was a long, lustrous mass of ebony waving in the breeze. Darker and sleeker than the other twin, her skin was perfection, her smile radiant. Peter edged past Rufus and Adam, planting himself firmly in front of the girls.

"Hello, ladies," he said in what he considered a smooth, sexy voice. "I'm Peter Parker." He let his eyes drift over June's face, then trail downward over her long, elegant throat then back again to linger on her lips.

"Adam Truman, at your service." Adam edged himself close to Peter, leaving Rufus slightly behind.

"Rufus Turner," the dairy magnate offered, pushing both men aside with his considerably large shoulders. Standing dead center, he looked from one twin to the other. "I own Turner Dairies. Largest Dairy conglomerate in five states," he added, puffing up like a bullfrog calling to its mate. "You must be Janis," he said, his eyes bright with excitement as he stared at the slightly taller, lighter complexioned twin.

The ladies glanced at each other, then at the three eager-looking men directly in their path. Shrugging in silent communication, they looked back at the male objects blocking the sidewalk.

"I am," Janis offered with a twinkle in her eyes. "How do you know my name?"

Rufus' face went hot with a blush at his own boldness. "Been hearing about your legendary beauty."

June turned her attention to the other two men, batting her long sooty eyelashes in what she hoped was a provocative manner. "And who did you say you are?"

"Adam Truman, Attorney at Law, at your service," Adam offered, along with his hand. When June took it, he nearly jumped in surprise at the surge of electricity that sparked from her touch. After all, it was the other twin that had caught his eye. This one's eyes were a darker shade of blue, only perceptible—he was certain—to one who enjoyed the minutest details of life.

Peter, not to be outdone, edged forward, eyes still glued to the magnificent lips he so wanted to kiss. "Peter Parker."

He held out his hand, practically dragging her fingers out of Adam's grasp, earning himself a dirty look and a subtle shove from the tall attorney. "I'm the developer for the Sunnyside Golf and Country Club and housing tract up on the hill."

"Ah, yes." June smiled at him, squeezing his hand slightly before letting go. "The entrepreneur."

"Well, I guess you could say that." Peter, like Rufus, felt a blush heating his face. He almost scuffled his feet like an adolescent on a first date.

"Are you ladies going shopping? In need, perhaps, of someone to carry your packages?" Adam peered at them hopefully. The other two men appeared likewise.

"Actually, we're just on our way to get more ingredients for our pickles. The packages are rather heavy...if you're offering to carry?" June kept her gaze on Adam, causing Peter's heart to plummet with regret.

"Ah...pickles?" Adam looked wary and disappointed. "You're entering the competition at the fair?"

"Why, yes, as a matter of fact, we are," Janis affirmed. "Why?"

"I believe the rules preclude us from engaging in any sort of fraternization with anyone entering the pickle competition," Adam explained in a regretful voice.

"Yeah. We can't be seen with the contestants," Rufus admitted sullenly, regret filling the gaze he locked on Janis.

"Oh my goodness, you're the judges, of course," June said in counterfeit surprise. "The gossip would be rampant if we actually won and everyone thought we'd been...well, *consorting* with you."

"I believe the term is collusion," Adam offered, voice saturated with regret. "So, I guess this is goodbye for now. Good day to you, ladies."

All three men stepped back and allowed the luscious Jones Twins to pass. As they made their way down the sidewalk, Janis couldn't resist looking over her shoulder and winking at Rufus. She laughed delightedly when the man blushed to his roots.

"Don't encourage them," June scolded her sibling. "We want to win the contest, but I don't see any need to acquire a husband along the way, despite our dear mother's ambitions."

"Hmmm...you're right, of course. But did you see the

shoulders on that dairy farmer?" Janis waggled her eyebrows. "That's enough to give a girl a heart attack."

"A heart attack?" June snorted in disbelief. "I don't think your *heart* has anything to do with it."

"So you say." Janis pouted, her lips drooping prettily. "You didn't exactly let go of that attorney's hand. The other fellow had to pry it loose."

"Hey, girls!" Their cousin, Annabelle Jones, hailed the twins from the doorway of the *Crimp and Curl* beauty parlor. "Are you planning to introduce me to those handsome men you were just talking to?"

Cousin Annabelle was a flirt who had no scruples at all when it came to stealing someone else's man. June thought about that as she formed her answer. "Annie, don't be silly. We don't know them that well."

"Well, there are three of them and only two of you." Annie stepped out the door of her mother's shop. "I think that shorter one with the blazing blue eyes is soooo cute!"

"Ah...that would be Peter Parker, the entrepreneur," June said. "He's the developer for the Sunnyside Golf project."

"They're also the judges for the pickle competition at the fair," Janis informed their cousin. "Therefore, they're off limits."

"Not to me," Annie said. Craning her neck, she sent a dazzling smile to the gorgeous triple dip of testosterone standing in the middle of the walk about a half block down. "I'm entering the fruit compote competition this year." She wrinkled her nose at the twins. "You two are actually going to enter those awful pickles of yours in the contest?"

"There is nothing awful about our pickles," Janis defended, though not with much enthusiasm. She, too, felt their pickles were less than blue ribbon.

"Well, I think we'd better do some collaborating with the judges if you hope to win anything at all," Annie said in her usual forthright manner. "You won't win any other way."

"We don't want to collaborate," Janis protested. "It would be dishonest."

"The truth is," June said with a wry smile, "*they* won't collaborate with *us*."

"You already asked them to give you favors?" Annie looked aghast, despite the fact she'd suggested it in the first place. "Oh my."

"No," Janis almost screeched. "It's just that when they found out we're entering the contest that lawyer said—"

"And the dairy farmer backed him up," June interrupted.

"Said what?" Annie preened at the men, who continued to stand in the middle of the sidewalk watching them. "I can't imagine them caring about such things." She wiggled her fingers in a coy wave in the general direction of the testosterone trio.

"Said they couldn't carry out packages because it would be considered collusion and that was fraternizing and that's not allowed." June answered in one long breath, her eyes straying to the tall, lanky form of the lawyer in his elegant Italian cut suit.

"That doesn't mean they can't be influenced," Annie said dismissively. "Heck, any man who would stand on the sidewalk for twenty minutes in this heat just to look at you isn't beyond duplicity."

"I don't know," Janis said slowly. "I wouldn't want that dairy farmer...ah, Rufus? I wouldn't want him to think I'm dishonest. Although he wasn't happy about the rule." She smiled slyly. "I could tell that much. But he wouldn't go along with anything against the rules. He's not that sort."

"How do you know what sort he is?" Annie shook her head. "You need a good dose of reality, cousin of mine. You read too many romance novels. Men are men...no better or worse than they ought to be."

"Okay," Adam summed up what they'd learned in a patient, if annoyed, tone. "So if a pickle doesn't bounce like this one, it's disqualified automatically?"

"Exactly!" Jenkins beamed at Adam like he'd just won the spelling bee. "And that keeps collusion to a minimum."

"How so?" Rufus rolled his massive shoulders as though that would give him the answer more quickly.

Peter—not wanting to be thought less intelligent than the lawyer—answered for Jenkins. "Pickles that bounce are usually pretty good tasting. While pickles that don't bounce usually aren't. So, nobody can play favorites to a pickle that doesn't bounce, leaving the best pickles in the running."

"Just so!" The stuffy Mister Jenkins clapped his hands

together with a pleased smile. "Now, on to the more intricate minutiae of the perfect pickle."

"How much more of this *minutiae* do we need to learn?" Rufus asked impatiently. "I've got to get to dairy number four as soon as possible. Got problems there, you know."

"Just another few minutes. And then there's the final course the day of the fair." Jenkins didn't look pleased to be interrupted. "You'll bear with me another few moments, Mister Turner?"

"I guess," Rufus agreed grudgingly. Then his attention was diverted and he failed to hear another word as he gazed out the window at the double vision of delight crossing the street with another, fair-haired young woman. Contemplating the slightly rounder curves of Janis as compared to June, he then measured them against their wide-hipped blonde companion. Janis won, hands down.

Rufus sighed unhappily at the necessity of turning down a chance to spend time with the object of his fantasies. But later, perhaps. After the competition. Of course, if one of the twins didn't win, his chances of furthering his acquaintance with her would be crushed.

"...as you will recall. Is that not correct, Mister Turner?" Rufus turned at the sound of their pickle-mentor's voice. He was caught red-handed, but bluffed it out, as was his way.

"Yeah, that's right." He eyed his watch. "Can we go now?"

"I suppose. Just as long as you realize this contest has to be completely aboveboard and appear as such. No staring at prospective contestants, that sort of thing." Mister Jenkins let his gaze cut to the window, the view of the strolling ladies nearly gone as they disappeared around the corner.

"Now what will we do?" Janis wailed. Wringing her hands, she looked to Ramona for guidance. "It doesn't bounce anymore."

"That's because it had time to settle and absorb the overabundance of vinegar brine. I told you girls—"

"Oh, Mother, it's hopeless." Janis sniffed back a tear. "We're not going to win any blue ribbon."

"No matter, girls." Ramona rolled her eyes at the ceiling. "I don't give a hoot about the *ribbons*. I want you to catch the *men*, don't you understand?"

"I'm not sure any of them are suitable," June said defensively. "Just because you want us married to someone with money—"

"And the ability to help you give me grandchildren," Ramona inserted smugly. "All those young men look quite capable of fatherhood to me."

"Really, Mother," Janis wailed. "You are just too crude."

"Crude? I think not." Ramona patted her daughter's creamy cheek. "Let's get on with this. The next batch needs more sugar, less vinegar. And be careful about the boil. Not so long this time."

"Are you suggesting we do something dishonest?" Adam sat up straighter in the booth of the coffee shop. "Do you realize I'm an attorney?"

"Yes, and I realize that you're running for Attorney General next year." Annie smiled cat-like and let her hand trail down the side of her ice tea glass in slow motion. "And you, mister... ah...Turner? Do you think it's dishonest to find my cousin's pickles blue ribbon worthy whether they are or not?"

"Absolutely," Rufus answered quickly. "I won't be a party to such goings on."

"Neither will I," Peter chimed in, though in truth, he didn't sound as convinced as the other two judges.

"All I'm asking is that my poor little cousins get a fighting chance at the ribbons. Their mother," she leaned closer to Peter in a confiding manner, "my aunt, is very set on them winning this competition. She's driving the poor things nuts. Year after year she puts my dear Janis and June through the ringer over the pickle competition. It's not fair, but what can I do? They just have to win, don't you see?"

"What does she care if they can cook a pickle?" Peter looked surprised. "It's cruelty."

"It's stupid, is what it is," Rufus concluded roughly. "I wouldn't have poor little Janis slaving over a hot batch of pickles. She's too delicate for such."

"And those pickles they produce," Adam chimed in. "It's rumored the judges quit last year and that's why we were invited. They swore they'd never touch another Jones Twin pickle."

"I'm going to help them with that this year." Annie leaned even closer to Peter, pleased when he didn't move away. "I've stolen my mother's secret pickle recipe and I'm going to copy it for the girls. But, of course," she frowned slightly, "that won't make them the best pickles on such short notice. It takes years of practice. But they will bounce...and truly, that's all that counts at the moment."

"It is?" Adam tore his eyes away from her hand stroking the ice tea glass. "I don't see how bouncing pickles have anything to do with it. Either they taste good or they don't."

"It's the rules," Peter reminded him. "If the pickles bounce, we can at least pretend to like them best."

"And if they don't bounce, we can't even consider them," Rufus concurred unnecessarily. "So? What's the big deal? Get your mother's recipe to them, and we'll do the rest. Just make sure the pickles bounce."

"Ah...then you *will* help me...ah...us...them." Annie slid out of the booth, her smile brilliant, her eyes shining with triumph. She didn't care so much if her cousins won the competition, but she had taken advantage of the opportunity to get closer to the blue-eyed entrepreneur. And the way things looked, her aunt might just get her wish after all. Both the dairy farmer and the attorney seemed very interested in June and Janis.

"I didn't say that. All I said was I'd consider a pickle that meets the criteria," Adam qualified. "I'm not going to cheat...not even for the most beautiful pair of eyes..."

He trailed off, realizing he'd just copped out on himself. Grinning ruefully, he shook his head. "All right. I'll admit to a small amount of collusion...but only if they bounce."

Peter followed Annie out of the booth. "May I walk you home, Miss Annabelle?"

"I suppose so, Mister Parker. Being as I'm not a pickle contestant, it should be alright." She smiled at him with just a hint of mystery.

Peter's heart flipped clean over in his chest at the sight of that feline smile. He grinned at the other two men, tossed a few bills on the table to pay his part of the meal and took Annie's hand. "Later, guys."

"Such a crowd!" Ramona looked around in delight. "There will be so many here to applaud my girls. She squeezed the twins, who stood to her either side of her. "I can't wait to see the look on Jenny's face when you win."

"We don't know for sure we'll win," Janis protested modestly. "Just because those damned pickles bounced this morning doesn't mean they will in an hour. Remember the last batch?"

"Never mind the last batch. With Jenny's recipe, we'll be sure to win...I mean you, of course." Ramona smiled at first one then the other twin. "You make me so proud." She lowered her voice, eyes fixed on the three judges coming onto the platform. "Just remember to put your best foot forward and make those judges notice you. June, did you lotion your hands like I said? Let me see."

June stood still under her mother's scrutiny as the eager woman prattled on about the virtues of soft skin, soft voices, demure demeanor and so on. She smiled and nodded in all the appropriate places. It might be 2005, but her mother's sense of what was appropriate was stuck in 1965.

Lawyer Truman looked better to her every minute— especially with the thought of escaping her mother's constant smothering. *Anyone would do right now,* June screamed inwardly. *Anyone at all.*

Janis, in an effort to distract Ramona and give June a break, squealed and jumped. "Mouse!"

"Oh-my-God!" Ramona did a little skip and hop in her effort to avoid the creature. "Where?"

"There!" Janis could hardly contain her laughter as she pointed to a non-existent mouse. "He's running between Mrs. Johnson's feet."

"Oh, Laura! There's a mouse." Ramona hopped over to her friend, Laura Johnson. "Watch where you step!"

Within seconds there was a calliope of screaming women hopping around in circles shouting, "Mouse!"

The scene was comical from where Adam stood on the podium. He scanned the women until he spied June and Janis standing back and laughing hysterically. They didn't seem at all afraid. In fact, they looked conspiratorial. He couldn't help the smile that tugged at his mouth.

"Will you just look at those two?" Rufus came up beside

him, nodding in the direction of the twins. "They aren't afraid of no silly mouse, are they?"

"No," Adam managed to choke back a laugh. "They certainly don't seem to be."

"You'd almost think they knew something everyone else didn't, huh?" Rufus furrowed his brow, suspicion lighting his eyes. "You don't think they'd deliberately start a rumor?"

"I wouldn't doubt it for a minute." Adam let his laughter out finally, joined by Rufus, whose deep bellow of mirth caught the attention of Janis who waved at him, winking as she had that day on the sidewalk.

"I'm sorry, Miss Jones. This pickle is just plain limp. And no pickle at all according to the law," Adam said solemnly as he laid the fork down. "I truly am sorry."

"Oh." June's eyes filled and her mouth trembled. "That's alright, Mister Truman."

Adam felt like the world's biggest heel as he watched her walk away, shoulders slumped. But what could he do? The pickle didn't even come close to bouncing. And he was sort of glad, judging by the smell. It probably tasted like kerosene.

"Miss Jones, this is the best danged pickle I ever tasted." Rufus lied through his teeth, crushing the chunk of pickle as rapidly as he could to get it down his throat before it scorched his palate. He saw Adam looking at him with raised brows and he shrugged. What could he do? The damned thing bounced. Nothing to do then but taste it. Good grief, he needed a cold brewsky to wash down this vinegar and kerosene mess. Trying not to cough and choke, he chomped away, swallowing at last. "Water," he rasped. "Quick."

"Miss Muriel Pennworthy is our winner," Peter announced loudly, one disbelieving eye on Rufus. "Never have I tasted a better pickle in my life." Relieved that he had no stake in who won or didn't, Peter was happy to hand the blue ribbon to the elderly spinster. He leaned down to peck her cheek and was rewarded by applause. Grinning foolishly, he escorted the winner off stage and made a beeline for Annabelle.

"My hero," she breathed, leaning up for a kiss. Peter obliged happily.

Adam stood there, wishing he could follow the dejected

June, but unable to get his feet to move. There were too many people milling around and he'd lost sight of her. Now, he'd never be able to tell her how much he'd like her never to make pickles again...after they were married.

"There she is," Rufus exclaimed, correctly surmising Adam's searching gaze was for the other twin. "Run on, lawyer-man, and catch that gal before she gets away."

"You think so?" Adam was off the podium before the words had left his mouth.

"Rufus?" Janis looked up at the man who had dared swallow one of her awful pickles and declare publicly that it was the best danged pickle he'd ever eaten.

"H...hello." Rufus was still having trouble with the aftermath of the pickle. His throat burned terribly, making speech something he'd rather avoid.

"May I buy you a cold glass of beer?" she offered apologetically.

Not trusting himself to speak, Rufus could only nod as she led him down the steps and away toward the brewery wagon where ice cold Pabst was being served straight from the keg. Mouth watering at the thought of the icy brew, Rufus let go of Janis' hand and boldly threw an arm across her shoulders. Janis merely leaned into his embrace and they marched on together.

"Well, I think purple and silver are the best colors," Janis mused as she sifted multiple colors of silk ribbon through her fingers.

"No. Purple is just too, too crude," June argued. "I say silver and moss."

"Ugh!" Moss isn't a bridal color." Janis glared at her sibling.

"Now, girls. If you can't agree, I'll just have to choose for you." Ramona stood over her twins, hands braced on her hips. "Don't make me have to do that."

"Moss is fine with me," Janis said hurriedly.

"I like the purple. It will do just fine," June said at the same time.

"I think all three," Annie chimed in. "Purple for royalty, moss for evergreen and silver for...silver for just being beautiful." She smiled at her two cousins and beamed at her

320

aunt. Happy in the knowledge of the two-karat diamond on her finger, she knew she'd be next to wed.

"Do you think Rufus will like those pickles as well in fifty years as he did last month?" Annie's eyes twinkled with mischief. Everyone knew he'd nearly choked to death to get that pickle down...but he surely wouldn't admit it to anyone.

"It won't matter," Janis answered. "When we made our wedding vows up, Rufus added a codicil to mine. At least that's what Adam called it. I have to promise never to make pickles."

"Well, I never," huffed Ramona Jones. "That's awful." Still, she couldn't stop a burst of laughter. "Even Jenny's recipe was no help to my girls."

"Hush auntie," Annabelle looked around cautiously. "Mom would skin me alive..."

"Well, for my part, I promised Adam I wouldn't even *buy* pickles at the store," June added her two cents worth. "He says with my pickle taste, I'll wind up with the worst pickles on the shelf."

"Well, I say we get back to the matter at hand," Ramona said, picking up a moss green doily. "Are you sure you like this for a wedding color?"

The church was filled to brimming with the entire town turning out to see the 'pickle queens' wed. Ramona sat in the first pew, alternately crying into her lacy kerchief and smiling at the crowd behind her. Her girls came down the aisle, settled into their respective places and a hush fell over the crowd as they began their vows.

The minister cleared his throat and looked at the two couples, eyebrows raised as though getting ready to do a down stroke and begin the orchestra.

"Do you Janis take this man to be your lawfully wedded husband?"

"I do, and I promise never to cook pickles again as long as I live."

"And do you June, take this man to be your lawfully wedded husband?"

"I do, and though I may shop till I drop, I will never purchase pickles as long as I live."

The reception in the park after the ceremony was a glorious success, except several guests were heard to complain that there wasn't a pickle or a bit of relish in sight and they had to make do without.

Be sure to visit Diane Davis White's website
www.dianedaviswhite.com

Single Girls Can't Jump

by Jacquie Rogers

• *Florida - A special law prohibits unmarried women from parachuting on Sunday or she shall risk arrest, fine, and/or jailing*

Sunday afternoon—Julienne Bay, Florida

I snapped my cell phone shut and yelled to my sister skydivers, "Guess what? Reporters from three radio stations and both the English and the Spanish newspapers are waiting for us at the landing site!"

"Huzzah," yelled the women. One of them patted me on the back. "You're the best, Shelley."

Not exactly the best, but I did get tired of fighting a silly law on Florida's books that says it's illegal for unmarried women to parachute on Sundays. So I gathered a few of my sister skydivers and talked them into participating in a little civil disobedience with me. They all too happily agreed.

On the tarmac, I called the police and gave the dispatcher my name and address, as requested. Then I got down to business. "In defiance of Florida law, a group of unmarried women is skydiving onto the beach at Julienne Bay."

"That's against the law?"

"Yes, unmarried women can't jump on Sundays and we want the silly law repealed."

"I'll inform the nearest officer, but be aware your call is not priority."

"Please, we need someone to arrest us. The legislature isn't listening."

"Yes, ma'am."

All six women gazed at me expectantly. "We can only hope they'll send someone. The dispatcher wasn't exactly enthusiastic about our cause." The ladies groaned.

I pumped my arm a few times and yelled, "Let's do it!"

An hour later, all seven of us had leaped from the plane, deployed our chutes, and were floating toward the designated landing site. I was the last one out of the plane and quite far above the rest. As the wind whipped my hair and we neared the earth, I spotted the TV camera crews and two radio station vans parked on the road separating the swamp from the tiny strip of beach sand. And a patrol car! The ladies pointed to it and looked up at me. I gave them the thumbs-up.

The six of them landed and I was only a hundred feet in the air when a great rumble exploded into a vicious roar, like thunder except it didn't stop. A mighty wind caught my chute and sent me flying sideways. I tried to make adjustments, but to no avail.

The beach sped by in a blur and my heart stood still from fear. It looked like I was going to bounce. Buy the farm. Push up daisies. The wind pushed me inland with so much force I could barely breathe, and then my back slammed into a tree. The blow forced the air out of my lungs and all grayed into black.

The air smelled different somehow. Just to make sure, I took another sniff. I didn't smell the freedom of the ocean breeze, the pungent claustrophobia of the swamp, or the vanilla comfort of my apartment. Probably a hospital. I had over a thousand jumps without an accident, until now. This one freaked me out.

Being a woman of great courage, I peered through my left eyelashes. The pink walls weren't at all clear, but this definitely didn't look like any hospital I'd ever seen. I took another breath and dared to open both eyes. The room looked blurry in the darker pink corners and around the door. An elderly woman with curly blue hair sat in a chair that looked like it came from *The Jetsons*. Dang, I bet they sent me to the loony ward.

"I'm glad you're awake, honey." Her voice sounded sweet as pie. "Do you remember your name?"

"Shelley Clark. What hospital is this?"

"Hospital?" She giggled. "You're in jail."

"And you are?"

"In jail, too." She dabbed at her hair. "But not to worry, my Kael will bust us out of this joint in no time."

"Kael?"

"My boy. He's a handsome lad. Daring, smart—you know, all the things a man should be." She sighed and looked forlorn. "Yes, he's nearly as handsome as his father was." Then she patted me on the arm and grinned. "He'll like you. He's a sucker for curvy women with long, auburn hair."

Actually, I was a little concerned about the 'busting out' part of her previous statement. "I need to be here. I planned to be arrested for civil disobedience. Some friends and I are trying to get a law changed."

The old lady clasped her hands to her heart. "Oh, I knew it, you're one of ours!"

I didn't think so. Nevertheless, I needed a few details. "What jail am I in?"

"The Julienne Bay City Jail. It's quite nice, don't you think? I much prefer it to the bigger city jails, or, heaven forbid, the state prison."

"You've been in them all?" I'd seen the Julienne Bay City Jail. It wasn't pink and it sure wasn't this size. I wondered if maybe I was off my rocker.

The lady nodded. "Every one. Some of them a dozen times."

"Who *are* you?"

"Ginger Gibson. I'm a professional rebel and founder of the Scofflaw Society."

"Oh, my." I settled back on my cot and pressed my hand to my forehead. "What law are you protesting now?"

"The one that says it's illegal to tie an alligator to a fire hydrant. We don't have fire hydrants anymore so I had to tie it to the police chief's porch swing. That got his goat." Her eyes danced when she giggled.

"What do you mean, no fire hydrants?"

Ginger stared at me. "Why, honey, have you just fallen off a turnip transport? We haven't had fire hydrants for seven hundred years. In fact, only historians know what they are."

This woman babbled nonsense. I stood slowly, still feeling a bit woozy, and took a moment to get my bearings.

The bright pink room had no visible means of illumination. I touched the fur around the door and was forced back a step somehow.

"You can only get through the door if you're ten degrees hotter or colder than a human. Haven't you ever been in jail before?"

"No." And this whole business gave me the willies. "Seven hundred years without fire hydrants?"

"Yes, I think the last ones were removed in the twenty-fourth century."

Twenty-fourth *century*? That pretty much blew my socks off. "But you do have alligators."

"Oh yes, they're one of the few animals that survived the Purging War in the twenty-sixth century. Some of them still live in the wild. But don't worry, Kael will keep you safe."

At that moment all went black. I thought I'd passed out again, but I heard shouts. Ginger squealed, "He's here! I knew Kael would be here soon."

A hand gripped my wrist like a vice. "Come with me." The voice was low and commanding. I stayed right where I was. "Lady, you're going to run out of oxygen in exactly two minutes and fourteen seconds. Are you coming?"

Put in those terms, it behooved me to go along with the show. I didn't cotton to the idea of becoming a fugitive, however. I ran behind Ginger, who could really haul ass for an old lady.

"Stay within the force field," Kael said. "It disguises our body temperatures."

I couldn't see a force field. I could barely see Ginger, and I couldn't see Kael at all, so how he expected me to stay within its bounds was a mystery. We ran for a couple of minutes, finally into the light of outdoors. The bright sun nearly blinded me.

We ran on a raised path over jagged limestone and saw grass. I began to breathe heavier, still not recovered from my earlier skydiving 'bounce.' You'd think little old granny would lag a bit, too, but she seemed as fresh as a bunny. A broad-shouldered man with black hair tied back in a queue led the way with purposeful strides. Kael. His mama got it right—he was very handsome and daring.

"Little missy here isn't feeling well, Kael," Ginger told her son.

He looked back. "Sorry." He stopped and grabbed me as I ran into him. He lifted me, cradled me like a baby, and continued running toward destination unknown. Heck—*year* unknown.

"Incoming!" Ginger yelled.

Kael fell to the ground, covering me with his body. It was a whole new meaning of 'incoming.' Oo-la-la!

"Quit wiggling," he growled as he pressed my body harder with his.

"Now Kael," his mother said, "you have to make allowances."

"She's going to make us dead if she doesn't hold still."

I froze just as an explosion blew water, sawgrass, and rock debris fifty feet into the air.

"Good, they don't know where we are." The low rumble of his voice and the touch of his lips on my neck distracted me. Here we were about to die and I'm concentrating on his lips. But he meant life to me at that moment. Handsome, virile life. I don't think I've ever been so hot for a guy in my life.

"This is ridiculous," I muttered.

"Wanna trade mothers?" Kael offered, misunderstanding me completely, thank heavens.

"No, yours is too much trouble. She has a good sense of humor, though."

Ginger saluted us with her third finger. "That's what they say about the ugly girls."

Another explosion blew up to the right of us and Kael pushed me down again. "Quiet, you two," he hissed. "They're getting closer."

"Get a move-on, sonny. My knitting circle is at five and we're going to be late as it is."

I felt warm and secure with Kael's overly muscled body covering mine. While his warmth made my insides tingle, his mother remained completely exposed. "Why aren't you protecting your mother, too?"

He snorted. "From what? She has her own portable force field—disguises it as blue hair. Everyone thinks she's old, but she's really only 147."

"147?" Another explosion sounded, farther away, and I flinched. "What year is this?" I finally had the nerve to ask.

"3006, all year long."

That's what I was afraid of.

"You must be a re-enactor. I'd like to know how you replicated your jumpsuit so well. It looks so authentic you could've raided a museum."

Ah, if he only knew. "It's a long story. I don't have any other clothes, though."

"The Scofflaw Society can fix you up. We have everything a person needs in reserve."

Ginger tugged on Kael's sleeve. "This is neither the time nor the place to have a little chit-chat. Let's get out of here."

The explosions had stopped. Ginger sprang to her feet and headed for the cypress swamp. Kael ran after her, still holding my hand. I did my best to stay on my feet, running as fast as I could.

The dark, dank swamp closed in around us. A large bird, a brown and white speckled limpkin, cried its wails of despair, echoing my own thoughts. Ginger and Kael slowed to a walk, each studying the trees with great concentration.

I didn't dare speak. Somehow I felt the importance of silence and the power of the unsaid word. Soon, Kael pointed at his mother to stand back. With a running leap, he kicked a branch. Birds flapped their wings in panic. The branch swiveled instead of breaking—a secret entrance! But to what?

Kael motioned us to follow him. The dark hollow of the tree had black goo glistening on the sides and I took care not to touch it. The acrid odor made breathing unpleasant at best.

As we trod the meandering path, I wondered what had become of my parachute. The police must have arrested me and taken everything. All I had to my name was the jumpsuit and boots I wore. No wallet, no helmet, no equipment. I wondered if skydiving on Sunday was still an illegal activity for an unmarried woman. After all, I did wake up in jail. I must have been arrested for something.

Ginger patted my arm. "You're safe now. We're in the Natural Habitat Zone. The police can't follow us in here."

I wondered if the zone was similar to a national park or a game reserve. Then again, why didn't the police have jurisdiction?

"In here," Kael said, pointing to a path that branched to the left. "This path takes us to my transport. We'll be home soon."

"Home?" My stomach knotted as if I'd been gut-shot. He had no idea just how far from home I was. "I have to get home."

"Where do you live?"

"Uh, Tampa Bay."

"I've been there many times. Don't worry, you'll be there by dark."

That remained to be seen. I didn't have any idea whatsoever how I'd get back to the twenty-first century. "I don't think it would be a good idea for me to go to my house. What if the police are waiting for me?"

"Good point. I live right here in the glade. You'll be safe at my house."

"I knew you'd find a reason to take her home," Ginger muttered, then winked.

"Mother!"

She giggled. "I'm delighted. She's a rebel just like we are. Did you know she skydived on a Sunday and she's *unmarried*?"

"Nooooo." His tone was unnecessarily sarcastic, in my humble opinion. "Are you matchmaking again, dear Mother?"

"Of course. You're sixty-eight years old and it's darn well time you started a family."

Sixty-eight? The guy didn't look a day over thirty.

We came up on the transport, an aerodynamic vehicle with no wheels, but a silicon bottom. "Does it hover?" I could have slapped myself when I saw their questioning looks.

"That's generally how you get from point A to point B." Kael peered into a retinal reader and the door opened. He motioned me to board, which I did, and Ginger followed. Kael slipped into the cockpit and we all fastened our shoulder harnesses.

"Drop me off at the Scofflaw Rec Center," Ginger directed. "My knitting circle has probably already started."

"What do you knit?" I wondered aloud.

"The usual stuff—laser gun scabbards, pocket protectors for explosives..." She sent a sidelong glance toward Kael. "Baby booties, things like that."

I was still contemplating her definition of 'usual stuff' when Kael ejected Ginger in her personal pod and sent her into the swamp. "Now maybe we can have some peace and quiet."

I laughed. "Ginger is a delight."

"I'm glad you like her, but she can be a real pain."

I ventured a guess on the source of his discontent. "Baby booties?"

He let out a low groan. "You got it. In the last year or so she's been impossible."

"Don't worry, I promise not to attack you."

"I wouldn't mind." He grinned, and darned if he didn't tempt me. Sorely.

A loud whistle followed by violent trembling of the transport jerked the harness straps tightly to my shoulders and pinned me back in the seat. "What's going on?"

"They've spotted us. We're hit."

"Oh, rats."

"More like alligators. We're going in." He sounded like he was taking a Sunday spin instead of guiding a diving transport.

"And snakes?" I shuddered.

"Water moccasins. Hold on." I watched him wrestle with the controls.

I'd much rather be eaten by an alligator than attacked by a water moccasin. "I thought you said the police didn't have jurisdiction in the swamp."

The transport bounced on the tops of the cypress trees, losing parts and pieces here and there. Vegetation swept past the window and I thought it best not to look.

"They don't. Bounty hunters."

"For me?" Surely there couldn't be a large bounty on me from breaking such a silly law.

"For me. I'm wanted for several successful jailbreaks."

I suspected that. "Uh, do you have a survival kit in here?"

"Yep, but we're close to the Scofflaw Museum—we'll go there."

Branches clanged on the side of the transport. It behooved me to keep my mouth shut so Kael could concentrate. While I didn't mind jumping out of perfectly good airplanes, I did *not* want to wade in the mucky swamp, dodging icky reptiles that wanted to poison and/or eat me.

The transport bounced this way and jerked that way,

practically jarring the fillings out of my teeth. The bottom of the craft screeched, probably scraping rocks. Finally, the vehicle settled to a stop, about twenty degrees out of kilter.

Through my mental fog, I heard Kael unbuckle his shoulder harness. "Let's get a move-on!"

I fumbled with my own buckles and freed myself. Kael helped me out of the transport. Oh, how I didn't want to walk through the swamp! But I didn't want to get blown up, either.

Kael held me around the waist and I leaned into him, as if I could borrow some of his strength and lower the ick-factor. The swamp creepy-crawlies didn't seem to bother him at all. I shivered, and he held me tighter.

"How far to the museum?" I asked, mustering all my bravado.

"Less than a quarter of a mile. We have plenty of daylight, don't worry."

Criminently! I hadn't even thought of mucking around this spooky place in the dark. "And the bad guys?"

"You know those explosive pocket protectors my mother knits? I have one—and what goes in it. So don't worry."

He helped me from high spot to high spot. His legs were long enough to take them in one stride, but I had to jump. "Good thing we're in the dry season."

I didn't answer, conserving my energy for walking, jumping, and wading. And avoiding all creatures great and vile.

After several minutes, Kael stopped and pointed through the dense foliage. "There's the museum."

I was never so happy to see a building in my life. "Let's go." I would have led the way, but creatures, both slithery and large-toothed, abounded between the museum and us. I gripped his hand tighter.

We had only forty or fifty feet to go when a transport swooped down, guns blazing. We dove inside an alligator hole. Golden eyes peered back at me. I gulped and tugged on his sleeve. "Kael, a Florida panther!"

More gun blasts ricocheted off the trees and rocks. "Duck!" Kael pushed me down with his body. The panther, in his fright, leaped over the top of us in his effort to escape. Kael grunted. "Damn, he used me for a launching pad." He let me up and I saw blood dripping down his back. "I don't know how maneuverable I'll be. Let me keep the bounty hunters busy while you get into the museum. Once you're in, you'll find a stash of weapons inside a closet right behind the admission desk. Get them, then start firing at the transport while I run to the building."

"Gotcha." Leaving him there made me uneasy, but sitting in an alligator hole waiting to be blown up by the bad guys or eaten by a reptile sounded even less appealing.

"Go now!"

I popped out of the alligator hole and leaped from high spot to high spot to the walkway surrounding the building, where I picked up speed and ran like the devil was after me. By the time I got to the door, I heard an earthshaking explosion. I turned just in time to see the bounty hunters' transport crash into the swamp—right by the alligator hole where Kael hid.

At first I worried they might have killed him in the accident, but then he ran away, two men chasing him. I burst through the museum door and scrounged for the weapons, grabbing as many as I could carry. When I got back outside, I saw the two men escorting Kael into the swamp, his hands tied behind his back.

I had to save him!

No way was I going back in that swamp, though. Not knowing the land, it would be foolhardy for me to even contemplate it. Frantically, I searched for an alternative. There it was right on the first floor of the museum—a twenty-first century airboat! A sign indicated the airboat had been lovingly restored and was operational.

Great, but how about fuel? In back of the airboat was a transparent box labeled 'Hazardous Liquid' with a fuel can labeled 'Gasoline' inside. Someone had processed the gas just for this airboat. I grabbed the nearest hard object and smashed the box. An alarm sounded.

The fuel can was full! After filling the airboat's tank, I shoved the weapons on the deck, opened the museum's double doors, and started the engine. It took off at the first shot. I was ecstatic. A miscue or ten later, the airboat and I finally made friends and we headed in the direction I'd seen the bounty hunters drag Kael, wounded, into the icky swamp.

I hoped 3006 had some slam-bam antibiotics, because Kael would need them for those panther gashes on his back, and who knew what the bounty hunters would do to him. The more I thought about them capturing him, the madder I got. He was a good man—he loved his mother and he was undoubtedly kind to small animals, not to mention he made me hotter than Tabasco in August.

Branches, vines, and unidentifiable slimy things smacked me as I slalomed through the trees and other obstacles. After a few minutes I spotted the three men. Kael's strength seemed to be flagging. With his hands tied, blood running down his back, and the men poking and pushing him, he struggled to maintain his balance.

I cut the engine to idle and took out one of the weapons. I'd never held even a handgun before, so my competence with futuristic firearms wasn't optimal. I could, however, fake it.

"Hold it, or I'll blast all three of you!" Just to punctuate my point, I fired into the trees. Branches and splinters flew everywhere. The captors ducked behind the trees but Kael didn't move a muscle and didn't seem at all afraid. I scared myself, actually, but then I felt powerful.

One of the bounty hunters shot back. "Quit firing, woman!"

Meantime, Kael broke their hold on him and ran toward me. I sprayed the trees over his head, hoping I didn't hit him. By the time he reached the boat, he collapsed. I dragged him on deck, revved the engine, and took off toward the museum.

Now, that's where being directionally challenged is a handicap. I had no idea where we were, let alone where the museum was. And Kael had lost consciousness. So we meandered here and there. After a few minutes I released his wrist restraints and shook him. "Kael! You have to wake up now. Kael!"

"Quit yelling. I'm awake—always have been." He sat up and shook his hands to get the circulation going again. "How'd you learn to operate this thing?"

"You've been faking it?" If he didn't look so pathetic, I'd have whapped him upside the head. "My brother has an airboat. I'll explain later. But for now, we're lost and nearly out of fuel, so if you wouldn't mind, tell me how to get back to the museum."

"We're closer to my house, and it's safer, too." He studied the terrain. "Turn a little to the west."

"If I knew where west was, I wouldn't be lost in the first place."

"To the right."

"Thanks." We got to his house with only about a gallon of gas to spare. I hoped that would get us back to the museum so we could return the airboat.

I dressed his wounds—a couple of the scratches were deep and I worried that they had severed muscle—and applied antibiotic ointment he had in his medical kit. "Leave your shirt off so the ointment can dry," I advised. Okay, so I enjoyed the view. He had not an ounce of flab, but sported six-pack abs, great pecs, and defined biceps.

"Hungry?" he asked.

"Sure." But not necessarily for food. I couldn't get enough of looking at his chest.

His house amazed me. Heating, cleaning, and cooking systems ran by thought processes. He wanted hot chocolate and a sirloin steak, the food creator beeped and there was a cup of hot chocolate and a steaming sirloin. Amazing. He asked me what I wanted. What the heck, I went with lobster tail and real butter. In a jiff, the food creator made it. I'd never have known the lobster wasn't caught off the coast of Maine that afternoon.

We sat together, our thighs touching. I could barely breathe for wanting him, let alone eat.

Kael had no such problem. Soon, he pushed his empty plate away. "So, tell me how you got that authentic jumpsuit and why you can run an airboat like you've been doing it for years."

"Do you have an open mind?"

"Do I need it?"

"Yes." I dabbed the napkin to my lips and leaned back. "I have the jumpsuit because I was skydiving on the Sunday before Valentine's Day in the year 2006. I bashed into a tree, and the next thing I knew, I was in jail with your mother. So that's that part of the story. I know how to drive an airboat because my brother runs airboat swamp tours and I've driven for him many times."

"A thousand years ago?"

"Yes. *Two*-oh-oh-six."

He contemplated for a moment. I knew time-travel was a

difficult concept to process—I wasn't even used to the idea yet. To give him a little time, I changed the subject. "Are you feeling all right?"

"No." His eyes turned dark, which sent a warm shiver deep inside me. "A man like me needs a woman like you."

There was no arguing that. I'd wanted him the moment I'd heard his low, sexy voice in the Julienne Bay City Jail. He pulled me into his arms. I started to wrap my arms around him but remembered his wounded back, so was careful not to touch him there. He laid a kiss on me that could have started a fire out of ice cubes in Antarctica. I melted into him, touching his tongue with mine.

"Are you hurting?" I asked, desperately wanting to continue, but not if he were in pain.

"Mmmm, yes, but you make me feel so much better." He deepened the kiss. His arms and chest felt muscular and solid. So safe. I thought I'd sprout wings and float. I wrapped my arms around him and rubbed his back.

Then I realized there were no wounds. None! I broke our embrace. "Turn around."

"Huh?"

"Turn around!" Sure enough, he had no open wounds and not even a visible scar or mark of any kind. "Why...you don't have any wounds at all!"

"Of course not. You applied regeneration cream on them. What did you expect?"

That shut me up. I had no idea what to expect, nor did I have a clue as to how society functioned. I was lost. "I need to go back to my own time."

"No, you don't."

"Yes, I do. You don't understand."

"I understand that I want to get to know you better." He nearly melted me with the passion in his eyes. "A lot better."

"Yoo-hoo! Kael!" Ginger knocked on the door, peering through the window.

Kael sucked air through his lower teeth and growled, "What do you want, Mother."

She let herself in. "Have you started making my grandchildren yet?" She set her bag on the couch and handed Kael a package. "Here, I knitted you another pocket protector for explosives. Oh, and I reported the bounty hunters and they

were arrested for property damage. They bailed themselves
out of jail, but not before they bought you a new transport."

"Thanks. I didn't expect they'd pay so quickly." He
opened the package and took out the pocket protector. Pink
booties fell on the floor.

He glared at her.

She shrugged. "A girl can dream." Then with a dramatic
flair, she asked, "Was I interrupting anything? I hope so!"

"We were checking out the Sunday before Valentine's
Day, 2006."

"Oh, I've already done that. Miss Shelley Clark, 28, was
killed when her parachute slammed her into a tree while she
was skydiving to protest the Florida law prohibiting unmarried
women from parachuting on Sunday." She pressed a button
on her watch and two images appeared in thin air. One was a
photo of my accident (totally gruesome and turned my
stomach), and the other was a picture of my jerk ex-boyfriend
and me. "It seems she matches our Shelley."

"Who's that?" Kael demanded, pointing to my ex.

"Not anyone I want to see again."

He visibly relaxed. "I'm sorry about your accident."

There's nothing quite like the sick feeling you get when
you see your own death announced in the newspaper. "So
there's no going back. If I managed to travel back to 2006, I'd
be dead."

"That's about the size of it." Ginger clapped her hands
together. "But the good news is you can marry Kael and make
my grandbabies just as soon as you get ID!"

Kael put his arm around my waist. "Don't listen to my
mother."

"Ginger, did Florida repeal the law?"

"Oh, no. It's still on the books. We'll protest it next
Sunday if you want."

"I don't have a parachute."

"Yes, you do. I stashed it when they brought you in. The
stupid paramedics had no idea what your gear was for, and
while they were busy regenerating your tissue, I got it all. It's
at my house as we speak."

"Paramedics were there?" I had no memory of them at
all.

"Oh yes, you had a crushed skull and over thirty other

broken bones as well as scrapes and cuts. They regenerated your teeth, your tonsils, and an ingrown toenail while they were at it." She picked up her bag. "Well, toodle-oo. The Scofflaw Society ladies are having a male stripper at our midnight poker party."

After Ginger left, Kael let out a long-suffering sigh. His arm was still around my waist and he pulled me a little closer. "You know, she does have a few good ideas." He kissed me, caressing my sides so close to my breasts I could hardly bear it. "I don't know about grandbabies right at this moment, but practicing sounds good."

It sounded *very* good.

Three days later, Kael came home with an odd-looking gun. "Roll up your sleeve."

"Why?"

"So I can inject this ID chip in you."

I couldn't work up a lot of enthusiasm for this Big Brother device. "What if I refuse?"

"That's your prerogative, but we can't be married until you're legally identified."

"I wasn't aware we were getting married. You haven't asked me yet."

"I couldn't ask you before because we couldn't be married anyway." He kissed me on my nose. "But you have your ID now so I'm asking you. Would you be my wife, keeper of my heart, partner to my soul?"

After a long, slow, wet kiss, how could I refuse? "Yes!"

He injected the ID chip. "It's fake, you know."

Kael strode into the Scofflaw Society ladies' poker game carrying his three-year-old daughter. "Would you ladies mind babysitting?"

"Of course not," came a chorus. One lady asked, "Where are you going at this hour?"

Another lady elbowed her and said, "Ginger's at it again, and who knows what Shelley thought up this time."

Kael handed his daughter to the woman who last spoke. "Shelley bailed out of a transport with only a parachute on her back, but the police wouldn't arrest her because she's no longer unmarried." He chuckled. "So she and my mother tied an alligator to the mayor's desk. Caused quite a stir." He put the diaper bag on the poker table. "I'll be back in an hour or so."

Be sure to visit Jacquie Rogers' website and blog
http://www.jacquierogers.com
http://keelysfaerygoodadvice.blogspot.com/

Double, Double, Toil & Trouble

by DeborahAnne MacGillivray

• *Scotland- Trespassing on someone else's
land is legal.*

"Now she's done it!" Cian Mackinnon glared at the chain
across the road, furious it prevented him from driving to the
castle the back way. He considered putting the vehicle in low,
rev the engine until it reached high torque, then smash
through the chain. His luck—it'd only mess up the front of his
Range Rover. "The witch has no bloody right to stop me from
using the driveway."

Aye, he could use the front entrance to Castle
Dunnascaul. It'd mean backtracking several kilometers. Add to
the fact, the road leading to the front door wasn't really
drivable—needed grading and filling in with gravel—his mood
was *not* cheerful. A gale loomed on the horizon. A sensible lad,
he wanted no part of getting caught on the old cliff road when
high winds howled like *The Bansidhe*.

Gillian Grant played the bitch simply because she bought
into the centuries old feud between her family and his. Didn't
matter she spent half her life in the States. Nor did the fact
neither of them had been raised in the castle have bearing on
The Troubles. He was a Mackinnon and she was...hmm...*a
bitch.*

A damn sexy bitch, he admitted, but a pain in the arse
when it came to the castle. What did he expect? She was a
Grant. Their motto surely was *Stubborn to the End*. Living up
to her name, she'd upped the ante by placing a chain over the
back drive to prevent him from taking it.

The Mackinnon-Grant War was about to heat up.

Disgusted, he climbed out of the Rover and stomped down the winding driveway to her quaint, thatch cottage. As he neared the whitewashed, two-story structure, he saw the picture window curtain flutter. She'd been watching, expecting the confrontation when he discovered the chain.

The front door squeaked open and she stepped onto the stoop, arms crossed, a glower upon her face. If she ever stopped frowning, she'd be a damn fine woman. Neatly braided, her dark blonde hair snaked over her shoulder, around her full breast and past her hip. Always in the prim braid, he'd never seen that mass of hair loose. If just once she'd let down her hair—literally and figuratively—he feared she held the power to bewitch him until he didn't ken down from up.

From the day they'd sat in the solicitor's office and heard the will, relations between them had been anything but cordial.

The bone of contention—a five-hundred-year-old castle.

Castle Dunnascaul once belonged to Gillian's family. *Once* being the key here. When Bonnie Prince Charlie pulled his stunt in 1745, trying to claim the throne of Scotland for his father, Clan Grant remained Royalists. Supporting the lost cause, Gillian's branch blithely marched to their doom. Oddly, though most Mackinnons were *out* for Charlie—showing no better sense than the Grants—his particular sept of the Mackinnnons refused to rally to the Stuart's standard. After Culloden, Dunnascaul had been confiscated and given as a reward to Malcolm Mackinnon, his great-grandfather, thirteen odd generations back. Despite the Grants being attainted, they held tight to the burning hope one day they'd regain the castle.

Tempers cooled over the past century. Controversy again flared when Gillian's grandmother, Anne Grant, began an affair with his grandfather, David Mackinnon. Cian didn't know the story, why if they were so in love they didn't each divorce and marry, ending the feud. But no. They'd scandalized both clans, indulging in a lifelong affair. Tongues wagged for decades.

The castle's ownership became a rub once more when Anne died of pneumonia. Supposedly, David promised Anne on her deathbed Dunnascaul would return to her family on his demise. Several witnesses swore he'd vowed this. For years, the Grants waited for David *to stick a spoon in the wall* so the ancient castle could revert to its *rightful* owners.

Last month, when they met at the solicitor's for the will's reading, Gillian anticipated Dunnascaul would be hers. Shock came when they learnt it passed to Cian. Only the thatched cottage on the southern boundary was left to Anne's granddaughter. Not uttering a word of protest, and with a defiant tilt of the chin, she accepted the keys and took possession of the thatch. Since then, she'd plagued him at every turn.

"You trespass, Mackinnon." She tugged the shawl around her shoulders.

"Aye, I am. I wouldn't be troubling you, Gillian Grant, but someone foolishly put a chain across the driveway."

"It stops trespassers. You have a drive to Dunnascaul."

Cian ran his eyes over her. She was an eyeful, not some skinny model-type, but a woman with flesh shaped to please a man. Shame she looked like she'd sucked lemons. "You know what you need, Gillian Grant?"

That stubborn chin jutted higher. "Save your chauvinistic patter, Mackinnon."

"Chauvinistic, she says." He huffed. "You thought I'd say you needed a good shagging—and I won't deny that might be the source of your sourpuss moods. What I was going to say, Gillian Grant, is you need turning over my knee and given a good paddling."

She snapped, "You and what man's army?"

"I don't need assistance, lass." He stepped up on the concrete porch, invading her space. "A pleasure it'd be to demonstrate it. If you'd rather, I could help in the shagging department...just to improve your disposition."

Gillian took a step backward, caught herself, clearly not about to let his taller frame intimidate her. Composing her face, she glared at him with regal bearing. "Shouldn't you hie yourself off. You've a wee bit of a drive back to Dunnascaul and a storm's coming."

Since it neared Winter Solstice, *night* came in the middle of the afternoon. It would be pitch-black before he reached the castle if he took the front drive. With the storm coming, he had *no* intention of navigating that kidney-busting driveway.

"You cannot close access to the road. You may have been

raised as a Yank, but surely you know simple trespassing isn't a crime in Scotland."

"Only if the trespass doesn't—"

"Destroy crops, inhibit the property's regular use or invade privacy. Since I do none of those things, you cannot prevent me from using the drive."

"The driveway's mine. Your grandfather—liar that he was —left the cottage and ten acres surrounding to me. Freehold."

"I care less if the Pope blessed your Freehold. You can't stop me from using it."

She smirked. "I just did."

"Och, you shouldn't have said that, lass." He winked, then spun on his heels to head down the drive.

Over his shoulder, he saw her watching him. The smug expression fell off her face. Calling after him, she moved to the edge of the small porch. "What are you doing, Mackinnon?"

He swung around, walking backwards. "Guess you'll have to watch, lass."

"Mackinnon!" She raised her voice to carry over the rising wind.

He shrugged. "Can't hear you!" Jauntily, he jogged to his truck.

She didn't leave the stoop. She must be getting chilled, but stayed observing as he reversed the Rover until the tail backed up against the chain.

Getting out, he snagged a rope from the back and uncoiled it. Wrapping it around the chain, he then secured it about the boat hitch. Whistling, he scooted behind the wheel and shifted the Rover into gear. Watching the rope play out in the rearview mirror, he saw Gillian on the stoop, hands on her hips, furious as it grew clear he planned to yank the chain and the posts out.

Precisely what he did. Completing a U-turn, he sped down the drive to park. Hopping out, he untied her chain, then dropped it clanking at her feet. "Yours, I believe?"

"OOOooo, bloody Mackinnon!" She seethed. "I'm calling the constable."

"Go ahead, ring up Hamish Abercrombie. While you're at it, lass, tell him you limited the access. You'll end up fined."

"OOOooo, beast," she growled.

He shot back, "Vixen."

342

"Ogre."

He laughed. "Witch."

Her brown eyes blinked. "Did you call me a bitch?"

"No, I called you *witch*."

"Why would you call me witch?"

"You must be one."

"Why would you assume that?"

"Because all I can think of doing is this." Tossing good sense to the wind, he grabbed hold of her shoulders and yanked her to him, taking her mouth with his in a bruising, no-holds-barred, mother-loving, knock-your-socks-off kiss.

He must've lost his mind! Or maybe felt surge in his blood what his grandfather felt for Gillian's grandmother all those many years.

To his surprise, Gillian kissed him back! She leaned into him, her mouth softly opening under his, as though she couldn't get close enough. Inside his skin wouldn't be close enough!

She tasted of lemon drops and rain.

Rain? It registered the sky had opened up while they stood kissing, as if neither of them wanted to stop.

His sane side said he was nuts to kiss her, even more of a fruitcake for standing in the rain when they could take a few steps into the coziness of her thatched cottage. Only, instinct warned the instant he broke the kiss, her presence of mind would return and she'd probably deck him. It'd be worth it.

Gillian stepped back, blinking tear-filled eyes. "Wh-why did you do that?"

"Seemed the thing to do." Reaching out, his thumb gently stroked the curve of her cheek. Crippled by grinding hunger, his eyes traced over her face, memorizing every line, mesmerized to the point he couldn't speak. Shrugging, he pulled his hand back to massage the centre of his chest where a tightness lodged. Off kilter, he was unsure what possessed him, other than he dreamt of kissing her for the last month—of doing a lot *more* than kissing her.

Gillian put the back of her hand to her well-kissed lips, her eyes accusing. "You think since my grandmother was easy for your grandfather, that I'm easy, too? That history can repeat itself?" She pushed the door open, glaring as if he were akin to a snake. "Think again!"

She slammed the door so hard the glass of the picture window rippled with vibrations.

"There's likely one thing my grandfather and I agree on—a Grant woman is *never* easy." Sighing, he shook his head and returned to the Rover.

Gillian followed the taillights bouncing across the burn and up the steep hill to Dunnascaul. Absentmindedly, she ran her thumb over her mouth, tasting *him* on her lips. A hint of cinnamon overlaid upon Cian Mackinnon's own unique flavour. Her mouth tingled from his possession. Wow, he just didn't kiss—*he kissed*. A slow burn licked at her body.

Never had she been willing to forget everything. Not once had she wanted a man to the point you could only see *him*, everything about him blurred to grey.

In spite of all, she *so wanted* Cian Mackinnon.

Too bad the Mackinnon men were heartbreakers. Oh, they vowed fancy promises, but weren't there when it counted, never one to keep their word. She mustn't forget that. Hadn't her mother drummed it into her brain how David Mackinnon disappointed her grandmother time and again? Hadn't he even broken his deathbed oath to Anne, leaving the castle to Cian instead of willing it to her granddaughter?

Curse fickle Fate! Oh, why had they met in a solicitor's office instead of some romantic setting—moonlight, tropical breezes and slow dancing on a shadowy balcony? They'd sway to the soft music, their bodies so close, luxuriating in the heat that rose between them. She closed her eyes, savoring the power of the vision.

"Instead, I'm trapped by this blasted feud. His grandfather pledged to my grandmother on her deathbed. He broke it. I gave one to my mum on hers. I keep my word—unlike bloody Mackinnons. Mum said it's left to me to see the castle was back in the family...my duty." Sighing, Gillian frowned at the cat lying by the fireplace. "Don't know why I talk to you. You might as well be a stuffed toy, Basil."

The brown and grey tabby snapped his tail, as if that was all the recognition she deserved. *Nothing* stirred Basil. The laziest cat in the world, if he more than twitched his tail three times in a day she needed to mark it on the calendar.

"Oh, Gran, I wish I could talk with you, learn why you

loved David Mackinnon with such a passion you'd trust the lying, conniving..." Feeling futility, she shrugged and headed to the bedroom to change into dry clothes.

It was spooky, living in the small thatched cottage where Anne and David carried on their lifelong, torrid affair. Their love *permeated* the house, lending her imagination flights of fancy at times, as if she heard bubbly laughter in another room. Sounds lovers might make.

After taking possession of the fairytale cottage, vivid erotic fantasies plagued her. At first, she passed them off as *residual memories* of Anne and David, seeing her grandmother at the age she was now. One night, after a particularly gripping fantasy of a man making love to her before the fireplace, she'd awoken in shock. The woman in the images was she, and the man was David Mackinnon's arrogant grandson, Cian. Ever since, she'd worked to keep a shield between them.

Her mother, Maeve, had resented David Mackinnon, and for more than the centuries old Grant-Mackinnon feud. She'd abhorred Anne never loved Maeve's father, blamed David for ruining Anne's marriage. Gillian shivered. Her mother had been a bitter person, and in that dark coil tried to control Gillian's every thought. In ways, Gillian supposed Maeve succeeded. Why else couldn't she let go Dunnascaul hadn't been returned to the Grants?

In her heart, she feared there's a part of her too much like Anne, waiting to rise to the surface. Cian Mackinnon got to her on too many levels. Made her want to forget the past, all the old hatreds...*and just love him.*

If only he didn't plan to ruin the castle. For a price, Blue-haired Go-Ins would queue up for twice-weekly tours, and May through August he'd throw open the doors to paying guests. A ruddy hotel! No respect for the history, the heritage! Dunnascaul should be loved, reverenced, not exploited.

Buttoning her jumper, she sat in the chair by the fire. Basil yawned and shifted closer to the flames. "You're right, you silly feline, the heat feels good."

Gillian placed her feet on the ottoman and pulled the soft plaide over her legs. Maybe dreams wouldn't come if she slept in a chair.

Gillian rested peacefully, but Basil lazily lifted his head and yawned a meow to the shadowy figures of the two people standing by the chair. The woman raised a finger to her lips in shush, warning the cat not to awaken the slumbering woman. Anne gently stroked the dark blonde hair, so like her own when she was the same age.

Sins of the fathers...how many generations must this silly feud go on?

"Gillian favours me, does she no'?" she asked the distinguished man at her side.

"Aye, almost as bonnie as you were..." he cleared his throat, "are."

"Och, you're eyes fail, David Mackinnon. She's prettier than I was at that age." Anne once more touched her granddaughter with such love, with pride.

"Got bigger knockers, too." He winked when Anne pulled a face and punched his arm. "Cian is a lucky lad. If he just wakes up and smells the roses."

"I dinnae recall you complaining I lacked." She huffed playfully.

"Now, lass, I dinnae say you were lacking, just she has a wee bit more than you. Males notice these things. I may be dead...but I'm no' blind."

David Mackinnon saw, indeed, Anne's grandchild was a comely woman—perfect lass for his braw grandson. Only, no one was lovelier than his Annie—never was, never would be—even though grey threaded the golden hair and lines crinkled the corner of her eyes. Smile lines. Well, he'd given Anne plenty to smile about over the years. Heart heavy, he acknowledged he'd brought her ample sorrow, too. Still, he loved her with a passion that defied time. Loved her as the years placed its stamp upon her elegant countenance. No one was more beautiful than his Anne.

"She's a lovely lass, a bonnie match for my Cian."

"You're a sly one, David. You promised Gillian would get the castle. She loves it, will care for it, protect it."

He patted her on the shoulder. "Trust me. It shall work out."

Hope sparkled in her eye as tears welled. "Do you really think—?"

"Trust me, Annie, everything shall come out right. Our love will see the dream come true."

"The woman's barmy." Fergus gestured wildly with his hands. "No bloody reasoning with her. None of us can budge her."

"What did you expect? She's a Grant," Cian pointed out, climbing into the Rover while Fergus shoved himself into the passenger's side.

Curious, Cian wasn't sure what to anticipate. After dragging down the chain, he knew Gillian would one-up him in some manner. Bloody witch wasted no time pulling an end run.

He shifted into low gear as the Rover splashed through Dunnascaul Burn, then he pulled off the side of the drive. He noticed vehicles parked on the carriageway, emergency blinkers flashing. The crew of men milled about at the mouth of the drive, clearly keeping their distance from the crazy woman.

At first, he didn't see Gillian. Then he spotted her. Aye, she was barmy. "Only a bloody Grant would pull such a stunt," he growled, climbing out of the driver's seat and slamming the door.

Wearing a determined expression, Gillian lay across the drive. A claymore clutched in her hands! He wondered how she missed indulging in the theatrical touch of painting her face with blue woad.

"Coward," she hissed at Fergus. "Figured the worm ran to the bloody Laird of Dunnascaul to whine about me."

"Gillian, you'll catch a cold laying in that muck." Cian hid his smile. The lass had spunk.

A fat cat slowly waddled up, licked Gillian's cheek, then with an exhausted sigh, slid down to lean against her shoulder.

"That's the most moth-eaten, overweight pussycat I've ever seen." Cian snorted a laugh.

"Don't insult Basil," she snapped.

Cian knelt down to scratch the kitty's chin. "Aye, he looks insulted. Basil, tell your mistress she's cold lying on the damp ground. Why her teeth chatter." As he pulled his hand back, the cat stretched to maintain contact. He leaned so far, then sort of went *thump*—face down to the ground. "Gor, is he dead?"

Her cheeks jerked in suppressed laughter. "No, that's

Basil. Any exertion takes a toll on him, poor dear."

Rubbing the cat's chest showed Basil rumbled in a deep purr. "Like your silly mistress, you don't have any more sense than to lie in the middle of the muddy drive."

"We're committed," she huffed.

"No, but you *should* be." Cian glanced to the men he'd hired to put in the new patio. "She won't use the sword on you. She's a Grant. It's all bluff."

"Bluff?" she spluttered.

Fergus the foreman shrugged. "She threatened to charge us with gang rape."

"She's a *bloody* Grant." Cian shook his head. Reaching down, he picked up the limp cat. "Someone take the pussy and put him in the house."

"He ain't goin' to bite me, iz he?" Fergus accepted the seemingly boneless animal.

"Look at him...he probably doesn't have any teeth left," Cian assured.

"Eh, watch the beastie, Fergus, he might gum ye to death," one worker called, sending the others into gales of laughter.

Standing up, Cian loomed over Gillian. Snapping his fingers he ordered, "Give me the ruddy claymore. No one believes you'll run them through."

Gillian unsteadily waved it at him, hard for a woman to control the long sword from that prone location. He wrapped his hand around the pommel and jerked her to a sitting position. Ridiculously, she tried to yank it out of his grasp. While she struggled with the sword, he leaned forward and scooped her up around the waist, then deposited her on her stomach upon his left shoulder.

"Mackinnon, you horrid beast! Put me down!" When she wiggled and almost toppled off, she changed her tune. "Don't drop me!"

The crew applauded. He considered taking a bow, but figured that would push Gillian too far. "Gentlemen, start your engines."

Cian put a balancing hand on Gillian's derrière and started toward the house. Workers sped by in their vehicles, followed by the flatbed truck loaded with creek rock. He met Fergus coming out of the thatched house as he was going in.

"I put kitty by the fire. You sure he's all right, lass? Never saw a cat that limp before," he worried.

Pushing on Cian's back, she raised up so she could see Fergus. "Oh, that's Basil. He tends not to bestir himself unless necessary."

Cian set her on her feet, spun her around, and with a swat on her muddy covered arse, pushed her toward the bedroom.

Bedroom. He moaned. Last night another of those damn erotic dreams visited him. They began after he'd met Gillian and continued nightly. Shaking with need, he'd awoken, his head pounding, covered in sweat. Unable to stay in bed, he jumped up and paced like a caged tiger, pausing to stare down the hill at the thatched cottage, willing Gillian to come to him. So the *last* thing his libido needed was to couple *Gillian* and *bedroom* in the same sentence.

"Get out of those muddy clothes, lass."

"Who gave you leave to order me about, Cian Mackinnon?" Gillian swung around, her chin tilted in a to-the-manor-born style.

Cian smiled and slowly walked to her. "Lass, you get that perfect arse into your room and out of those damp clothes or−"

"Or what?" Eyes flashing, she glared.

The corner of his mouth tugged into an arrogant smile. He could feel it. "Or I'll strip you buck naked and−"

Gillian shot into her room like a bullet. She hesitated, staring at him with big brown eyes, before slamming and locking the door.

With a chuckle, he walked to the fireplace, knelt and added peat bricks. Life around Gillian was never dull, he admitted.

Nudging the pussy with his foot to make certain the fuzzy thing still lived earned him a tail snap. "Basil, you're the most worthless feline I've ever seen."

Basil yawned.

Once the fire's warmth spread, he ambled into the kitchen and washed the mud from his hand where he'd swatted Gillian. Finding several blends of *Brodies*, he selected the silver tin of Edinburgh tea mix and then set the kettle boiling.

As he laid out shortbreads, Gillian came in. Wearing a

wary expression, she watched him pouring tea. He got the impression she wanted to say something, but hesitated. Fine, he could break the tension.

He sat the cup and saucer before her. "What did you hope to accomplish, lying in the drive so my workmen couldn't get to the castle?"

Glaring at it, she finally pulled the chair out and flopped down. "Guess I didn't think it through."

"What's wrong with me repairing the castle?" he asked, stirring his tea.

"Fixing the castle is marvelous. Making it a tourist trap is so..." She gestured with her hands, "mercenary. Dunnascaul is part of my heritage, part of *your* heritage."

"Allowing Go-Ins twice a weak for a tour and tea or putting up a few tourists during the summer won't ruin it," Cian countered.

"Have you seen what they've done to Urquhart Castle? It's disgusting." Gillian shuddered.

Cian nodded. "I'm not doing anything like that. I'm merely trying to repair the place before it falls down around my ears. I hope to restore it, with my money, blood, sweat and likely a few tears."

"Why turn it into a hotel?"

"It's a monster of a castle, Gillian. I've tried counting the rooms and lose track. Over seventy-five rooms, twenty-three bedrooms. There's enough to have two wings for guests and still keep the rest as a private residence. Neither of us was raised there, but we both hold a deep love for Dunnascaul, want what's best for it, to see it survive."

"Restore it, Cian, but drop plans for the hotel," she pleaded.

He glared into the tea as if the answer might be found floating there. "If you dropped the Grant-Mackinnon feud, you'd understand. The hotel is the only option left—"

"You'll ruin it, being greedy—"

Cian's anger flared. "Damn it, Gillian. Don't you think I want the castle repaired and not put up with a bunch of Yank tourists poking about?"

"Then why?"

"Use your mind, lass. The same reason my grandfather didn't leave you the castle, despite promising your Gran—

money. *The lack of it.* You've done nothing but huff and glower since you learnt the castle wouldn't be returned to the Grants—"

"He promised—"

"Aye, he did. He also comprehended you wouldn't have enough money for taxes. Then what? You'd sit in the castle while the roof leaks like a sieve? I've money. Not enough to see the castle saved. Am I to sit in that bloody monster while it crumbles around my head?"

Her face brightened. "What about the treasure?"

"Och, you buy that cock 'n bull story?"

"No story. They couldn't take it with them. Cumberland's men would've gone through their belongings and stolen anything of value. They *had* to hide it in the castle."

"I've heard the legend. We all have. Why my back pasture is full of holes. Why vandals and potholers broke in, ripping out walls and floorboards in Dunnascaul, searching for treasure. You stubborn Grants wanted a last laugh on the Mackinnons. They started nonsense about a fortune in gold and gems hidden inside Dunnascaul. For centuries they've sat on their arses and laughed while Mackinnons ran themselves ragged, trying to find that blasted gold."

Gillian put down the teacup. "If you'd only believe, I bet we'd find it."

"We?" he prodded, with an arched brow.

"Yes, we."

Cian eyed her from behind hooded lids so Gillian couldn't tell what he thought. She had to focus on the argument, not get lost in those beautiful pale eyes that were neither green nor blue, but aquamarine, shade of the water around the Isle of Lewis on a bright sunny day.

"You, me and that dilapidated excuse of a feline?" He chuckled as Basil waddled in.

Gillian touched his hand, then yanked hers back as a blush tinged her cheeks. "If we applied ourselves we'd figure out the riddle."

Cian's long lashes flicked over those mesmerizing eyes as he stared at the hand she used to touch him. "The riddle says none shall see the gold until the castle once more is in possession of a Grant."

"Why your grandfather should've left Dunnascaul to me.

I'm the last Grant from the attainted Dunnascaul line."

He nodded. "I'm the last of the Mackinnons that Dunnascaul was given to after Culloden." Though he placed no value in it, he knew the riddle by heart.

> *Until a Grant comes home to*
> *Dunnascaul,*
> *Secrets remain unearthed.*
> *Some search far afield.*
> *Some smarter look closer to*
> *hearth.*
> *Clever is the lad or lass who can*
> *wisely riddle, to see something*
> *others cannot...right in the middle.*

Gillian leaned forward to close the distance between them, putting a hand on his thigh for balance. "Surely, it cannot be that hard."

A lowly male, blood rushed from his brain and went south at the touch of her fingers on his leg. He struggled to focus, wanting to reply, *yes, it could be that hard.* With effort, he dragged his mind from below his belt. "Who says the Grants haven't found the treasure centuries ago?"

She laughed. "We might not have told the Mackinnons, but you can bet if a Grant discovered the treasure, they'd have bragged to other Grants. The treasure waits for us to discover it."

As he stared into her brown eyes, he felt like a warrior of old, ready to slay dragons and to topple kingdoms just to win his lady's smile. Hell, if she was underfoot, rummaging through his castle, it'd give him time to build a bridge over the centuries of hatred that lay between them.

He exhaled resignation, feeling this lass just slipped a ring through his nose. "When do we start?"

With a small squeal of glee, Gillian wrapped her arms around his neck and kissed him. Not a peck, but a big thank you smooch. Seizing the moment, he wasn't letting her go. He wrapped an arm about her waist and dragged her across his lap. Cradling her, he savored the taste of tea and lemon, nibbling her soft lips, using his tongue to outline their seam until she opened for him. Images of sending the tea and biscuits crashing across the room while he took her on the oak table flooded his mind.

Hell, they wouldn't disturb Basil!

Her perfume was a hint of jasmine and heather. It did nothing to mask the scent of the intoxicating woman underneath. Man had lost many animal instincts, depending too much on sight as a primary input to his brain. Only, as he held Gillian, something dark and primeval rose within his blood, of a man wanting to claim his mate.

Pulling back, he stared into the amber eyes, caught in the wonder of Gillian. He was lost. No hope for rescue.

As he drank in the image of her silken hair, he wanted to see it loose. Reverently, he slipped off the elastic band and untwined the coil of the honey-coloured braid.

Cian admitted being pole-axed. Shifting his fingers through the golden mass, mesmerized, he figured this was the *real* treasure of the Grants.

Exhausted, Cian dropped to the sofa before the massive fireplace. For a week, Gillian and he searched Dunnascaul from top to bottom. He still lacked an accurate room count. This time he blamed Gillian. Somewhere around forty-to-fifty, he became lost, watching her body move, the way her braid brushed against her derrière as she rapped on walls, how her eyes often were upon him as much as searching out a hiding spot for treasure.

Gillian came in, an on-the-rocks glass in each hand. She handed him one and gently clinked her lead-crystal tumbler against his. "Cheers, Mackinnon."

"Sorry, lass, I warned there's no gold." He wasn't saying I-told-you-so as much as admitting defeat.

He never believed in the treasure. It would've been nice to find the cache. He could undertake a total restoration of Dunnascaul instead of piecemeal efforts he planned over the next few years. What irritated, he felt he'd let Gillian down by not finding the hidden fortune for her—old warrior's instinct to slay dragons for his lady.

"Sorry, I put you through all this searching." She leaned against him, staring into the fire. Slowly, her eyes roved about the huge library. "I love this room. The heart of the castle. I like how the platform runs around the second level, leaving the room open. What a beautiful place this will be decorated for Christmas."

The vision shimmered before his eyes, of evergreen and holly with Mackinnon and Grant tartan ribbons lining rail of the upper level. Over where the stairs turned ninety-degrees, the tallest tree imaginable would be tucked up in the curve. More importantly, he saw Gillian, mistress of Dunnascaul, hosting an open house Christmas tea for the Blue-haired Go-Ins, wrapping gifts for under the tree, or tying a tartan bow on Basil.

Making love with him before the fireplace.

"So, you're back to Blue-hairs trooping through the castle twice weekly," she grumped.

He wrapped an arm about her, shifting so they stretched out on the soft sofa. Leaning his head against hers, he kissed her temple. "Would that be such a hard life, lass? Sharing the history, the wonder of Dunnascaul for a few hours. Rest of the time it'd belong to us."

Her hand holding the glass trembled. "Us?"

Basil waddled over and tried to hop onto the sofa. So fat, he landed on his belly, hind legs kicking in the air. Cian leaned over and grabbed him. "Yes, us. You, me and this worthless furball."

"Are you—?" Gillian paled.

"I am." He took the glass from her hand and set it on the coffee table next to his.

She jumped on him. He laughed, liking how her body felt draped over his. Wrapping her arms around his neck she kissed him hard. He kissed her back. She tasted of the Malt Whisky, tasted of Gillian.

"Two ways this can go, lass, fast and wild or slow and torturous." He nibbled along the curve of her neck. "I'm thinking slow..."

She sighed. "I'm up for suggestions."

"*Up* for suggestions? Hmm...so am I, lass." He smiled, but then yelped.

Gillian frowned. "Cian?

He shifted to pull the fat cat out from under him. "We're squishing this moth-eaten excuse for a pussycat. Why didn't he fuss before?"

"That's Basil. Only imminent suffocation could make him

stir."

Dropping the fat feline on the floor, Cian took hold of Gillian and rolled so she was under him. "Ah, have you where I want you, lass, wanted for the past five weeks. Five weeks gives a man a powerful hunger. One that could take a lifetime to satisfy. Is that a yes, *cushla mo fuil?*"

"*Pulse of my blood...*" Gillian echoed the translation in wonder. "Oh, aye. You know—"

"Right now there's not enough blood in my brain to know much of anything, lass." His grin felt wicked. "My hand is up under your sweater and I'm heading to *first base* fast. You should ken better than to expect a lad to think at times like that. Shush, and kiss me. You just said yes to a marriage proposal."

Basil twined around the legs of the man. Leaning his arms on the balustrade, running around the second level of the library, her David watched the couple sleeping on the sofa below. Anne's eyes lit as she studied the man and animal. Fondly, she recalled owning a dilapidated pussycat just like this one, recalled when the pet died and how she cried. David had been there, holding her, rocking her through the night.

She smiled to think much of her still lived on in her granddaughter. As David lived on in Cian. The love she saw growing between these two bode well for the Mackinnons and Grants. Peace between the two Dunnascaul clans would reign, first time in over two centuries. Cian would give her Gillian beautiful babes. The castle would ring with laughter and love.

When she linked arms with David, he asked, "Where did you disappear to, mo gràdh?"

She leaned her head against his. "My love? Do you ken that never stops making my heart flutter? After all these many years?"

"Same as when you tell me you love me forever." He rubbed his shoulder against hers. "Told you the lad would see the real treasure of the Grants, that Gillian would get the castle. I promised."

"Aye, you just didn't tell me she'd get Dunnascaul—and Cian."

"They're the best of you and me, lass. They were destined

355

to come together. With Maeve carrying her off to the States to spite you, I needed to play cupid in my fashion." His eyes roved over her face. "You dinnae answer, lass, where did you go?

Anne smiled, but a glint of sadness flickered over her countenance. "I needed a moment alone."

He sighed and slid his arm around her. "Out with it, Annie, it's too late in our sojourn to keep secrets."

"It's just..." She exhaled a sigh of regret.

"What, my bonnie lass?"

"I envy them. They have it all before them..." A tear sparkled in her eye. "They'll have each other in a way we never did."

"We loved each other, Annie Grant, don't be forgetting that. We had responsibilities we couldn't walk away from. No matter what life threw at us, we always had our love." His chide faltered. "Oh, Annie, we have so much more than many people ever have. I would've loved for you to be my wife. You wouldn't leave John Grant and I couldnae leave poor Janet. The cancer destroyed her over time, but by then you decided it wasn't right to take Maeve from her father. Life wasn't fair with us. Seldom is life fair."

"It comes full circle."

He gave her a squeeze. "Aye, with a Grant in Dunnascaul, part of the riddle's fulfilled. Maybe they'll find that ruddy treasure."

Anne pushed away her sadness. "Do you think there's really a treasure?"

"I believe Cian agrees with me—the real treasure of the Grants is their women."

Gillian woke, the chill of the library touching her as she shifted.

Mrs. Cian Mackinnon. Hundreds of Grants must be rolling in their graves. Divinely happy, she wiggled her toes, then scooted her body against Cian. Oh, think of waking up every morn wrapped in those beautiful arms! Who needed a fireplace blazing when she could cuddle to this sexy bod?

The lids lifted over those sea-green eyes, a lazy half-smile spreading across Cian's sensual mouth. Cian pulled her under him, his weight pressing her down in the soft sofa. His hot mouth nibbled along her collarbone, and up the column of her neck, sending prickles of sexual anticipation snaking over her skin. As he latched onto her earlobe and sucked, she about melted.

Tilting her head to the side to give him better access, her unfocused vision half-saw the portrait of the braw Highlander in a kilt over the fireplace. Cian's ancestor two-hundred-years ago. Breeding ran true, for Cian could've posed for the painting. Beautiful Mackinnon men.

Something attracted notice at the edge of her peripheral vision. With Cian's hands moving on her body, it was hard to pinpoint what bothered her. It would be too easy to surrender to the power he wove around her. She finally pinpointed it.

The scroll of the stone fireplaces. There were seven saucer-sized discs across the face of the mantle. Each depicted a scene of Highland life, all related to harvest themes. The one in the centre showed men drinking. Underneath, was the word *Meadhoney*. Mead was made of honey, so it struck her as odd to have it said in that fashion. Wouldn't it be two words?

"Cian?"

"Hmmm," he murmured as he slid down her body, chaining kisses across her stomach.

"Why would they paint mead and honey together as one word?"

"What?" He raised his head. "You're asking a man with his tongue in your bellybutton to hold a reasonable conversation?"

"Put your randy thoughts on hold, Mackinnon, I'm on to something." She tried to sit up, but he pinned her to the sofa with his weight.

The sexy man flashed a killer smile. "No, I am *on* to something." He slid his hand around her breast, cupping it. "Something I find absolutely amazing."

She slapped his hand. "It thinks you're amazing, too. But I need your mind in gear and not on shagging me."

Cian sighed and sat up as she slithered out from under him. Pulling a grumpy face, he ran his hand through his hair as Basil tried to drag his tonnage onto the couch. Holding his palm up to his mouth he blew into it, then made a face. "Think it was the dragon breath, Basil?"

"Basil's not much of a conversationalist." Feeling the

chill since she wore only Cian's T-shirt, she dropped a couple peat bricks on the fire and poked it. Then she rose to examine the tableau. Just a carved scene of men drinking from horns. "Why *meadhoney*?"

Lifting Basil on the sofa, Cian patted the kitty. "Woman's gone barmy on me again. Mead is made from honey. What's the deal?"

"Why *one* word?"

Shrugging, he came to stand beside her. "Lass, you in nothing but my T-shirt is more than my poor beleaguered brain can handle. Besides, I don't think about anything until I've had my tea."

"Cian, this is important. Think. What is middle in the Gaelic?"

"Basil, now she wants me to converse in the language of warrior kings." He chuckled as Basil laboriously rubbed against his leg.

"Cian!" she growled. "*Some smarter look closer to hearth. Clever is the lad or lass who can wisely riddle, to see something others cannot...right in the middle.*"

"Gor, she's henpecking me already and I haven't gotten the ring on her finger. *Mead—*" He paused as the reality hit him. "*—hon.*"

"Precisely. It was there all the time. Right before their eyes. It was soooo simple. *Meadhon* means *middle*. This is the centre tableau. The room is the centre of the castle." She leaned over examining the bottom rim. "Cian, look. There's a tiny groove here. You have a flat-headed screwdriver we can use to pry?"

Sliding into his shirt, he tossed her slacks to her. "Hide that tush if you want me to concentrate on treasure hunts. Don't get your hopes up lass," he cautioned, not wanting to see disappointment in her brown eyes.

"I'm not, but this is the only one with the groove. They told us *right in the middle of the hearth.* So simple. Everyone expected a difficult puzzle to solve. Told you I was good at riddles!" She shimmied into her black trousers, excitement nearly more than she could contain. "See, Basil, these hardheaded Mackinnon men needed a Grant lass in possession to figure it out."

Gillian shook her head as Basil keeled over in one of his

death-faints. Pushing him aside with her foot, she examined the plate-size carved, green marble. There were no grooves on the other six and they appeared mortared in place.

Cian returned, shirt still not buttoned. If he thought she was distracting in just his T-shirt, she found it near impossible to concentrate on ancient riddles when flashes of that wonderfully sculpted chest tantalized her with visions of giving him a tongue bath. She buttoned the two lower ones, earning a kiss. Well, she left three undone. It'd be a sin to hide that chest completely.

"Sorry, lass, no having your wicked way with me. I think you solved the Grant's Riddle." He held up a foot-long screwdriver. "I think this'll do."

Gillian chuckled. "That thing's obscene."

"Stand back, Gillie, I'm very good with my *tool.*" Scooting the limp cat to the side so he had room to work, he frowned. "I see pussycat's playing dead again."

"The excitement's too much for Basil."

"Breathing's too much for Basil." He inserted the screwdriver and used it as a lever. "I feel it give, but it's not coming out. Damn, I thought we were on to something."

"Ye of little faith. Let a Grant at it. It was under your Mackinnon noses and none figured it out." She saw it wiggle in place, but it wouldn't let go. She'd hoped they'd pry the face off and out would pop the treasure. "It jiggles."

"So does that sweet arse of yours, but it doesn't detach either." Sitting on the arm of the sofa, he watched her. His brow furrowed as he considered the problem. "Maybe it doesn't come out."

"Then why wiggle?"

Coming to the mantle he examined it. "Okay, right or left, lass?"

She shrugged, "Deasil."

He rotated it to the right until he felt the groove settle into a slot. "By damn...watch."

He gradually pushed the whole disk inward, recessing into the mantle. They heard a scraping sound, but couldn't tell where it came from. Cian looked at Gillian to see if she pinpointed the source of the noise. She shrugged. The disk stopped, didn't sink any farther into the marble mantle.

"Now what?" she asked.

Cian stepped back to look at the fireplace to see what he was missing. "You're the great unriddler."

Putting her hand on his bicep for balance, she leaned over to look up at the underside of the deep hood of the mantle. "It sounded like maybe from inside here. Look...isn't that a crack? Give me the screwdriver."

"Mitts off my *tool*, lass," he joked, kneeling down until he was beneath the mantel. Inserting the flat of the blade into the crack, he pried. "It's moving—"

There was a pop, and instantly, gold coins rained from the mantle.

"Bloody hell." Cian yanked her back as the fireplace spewed hundreds of large gold coins like a berserk slot machine.

Gillian jumped up and down and hugged him, thrilled they'd found it. "Cian, we did it! We found the Grant's treasure!"

"No Blue-haired Go-Ins?" He picked up a coin, examining it front and back.

Gillian chuckled. "Actually, after spending this past week exploring the castle, I decided opening part to guests isn't such a bad idea. Dunnascaul is something rare, magic. Wouldn't hurt to share that for a few hours."

Cian glared at the coin. "Might be good you feel like that."

"Why? What's wrong? We found the treasure. No telling how old those coins are. Their weight in gold is worth a fortune, but old coins should go to auction for collectors. No telling their value."

He held a gold coin between his fingers flipping it. "We found a treasure, but not the Grant's cache. The date on the gold Louis is 1740."

"I don't understand."

Cian reached up in the hidey-hole dislodging more coins. "Your Yank raising is showing its head, lass. The French sent £4000 in gold Louis coins to the Bloody Bonnie Prince. Only when they arrived on the shores of Loch nan Uamh to deliver the four chests, they couldn't find anyone to give it to. Supposedly, they just left the gold on the beach. You think the Mackinnons and Grants hunted for the Grant's fortune. All of Scotland has hunted for centuries for Charlie's gold. The government will snatch this up. We'll get a finders fee.

Certainly will give the Go-Ins something to natter about."

"Cian, the finders fee won't be small change. Can help with repairs—"

"I found something else." Cian pulled his lower arm from the hole, his hand holding a small chest. He rubbed his thumb across the dusty metal crest that adorned the top. "'ello, 'ello, I think this is the Grant's booty. Your family's crest."

"Maybe the Grants hid their treasure with Charlie's."

With a playful grin he held up the screwdriver. "We're about to find out."

"Down, *Toolman*. Let's try this before you destroy a piece of our history."

She removed the delicate chain from around her neck, then carefully pried apart the heart-shaped locket. Inside was a small key. Holding it up, she fit it into the lock on the box. Her hand shook as it finally gave in the lock and the key turned. "Gran gave me the locket, when I was seventeen. Passed down through the Grant women. Said it'd hold the key to my heart's desire."

Moving to the table, Cian spilled out the contents. Large gems of every colour twinkled in the light. Basil tried to hoist himself up to the table to see what was going on, but only succeeded in looking as if he did chin-ups. Cian laughed, picked him up and put him on the table. Immediately the cat seized the idea the pretty toys were there for his enjoyment and batted a large yellow stone like a hockey puck.

"Careful, Basil. You're due to keel over any second," Cian teased.

Gillian snatched the stone away from the cat at the instant he sent it sailing off the tabletop. "Watch it there, Puss. Oh, Cian, they're...beautiful. Prepare for a little I-told-you-sos."

"They're beautiful lass. But basically worthless. These are garnets of various shades, citrine, beryls. Semi-precious stones. They were likely worth a lot to them, but not much today." Cian's eyes reflected his fear she was disappointed.

Gillian leaned to his kiss. "Oh, don't know about being not worth much. I think this citrine Basil used as a hockey puck would make the most beautiful engagement ring, and this green garnet would be a gorgeous pendant. Cian, we found not just the Grant's treasure, but Charlie's treasure. Our Blue-hairs will be so excited. Think what a great PR tag it will make when we advertise our vacation package."

"Lass, as long as I have you by my side I can face a whole herd of Blue-haired Go-Ins."

He leaned to kiss her, but there was a loud thump on the table.

"Basil," they said in unison, then slid their arms about each other.

The cat lay sprawled in the middle of dozens of semi-precious stones, purring.

The library was dim, lit only by firelight. Its orangish cast lent a magical glow to the room, fading into deep shadows. Anne patted the snoring kitty, still resting on the table in the midst of gold coins and the glittering gems.

"You're a silly beastie, Basil," she said in a whisper. Her eyes took in the couple drowsing on the sofa. Oh, but David's Cian was a braw and bonnie lad. Perfect for her beautiful, valiant Gillian.

David approached, just behind her shoulder and placed a hand on her back. "Mo gràdh, why do you fash? I thought you'd be happy. Cian and Gillian will marry soon. The castle shall fare well in their care. People will come from all over the world to see where Bonnie Prince Charlie's treasure was found. All is settled and well, isn't it. Did I no' promise you, lass?"

"Oh, aye. It's all so perfect. Dunnascaul is in their safekeeping. Gillian and Cian are a beautiful couple, their love grows stronger every day. He'll give her beautiful bairns..."

"And?"

She forced a smile, her hand still rubbing the purring body of the silly pussycat. "You were never one for letting me hide from realities, David Mackinnon. That can be damned annoying at times."

"Stop avoiding the answer."

"He'll give her beautiful bairns, but we won't be here to see them."

"Och, Annie, where do you think we'd go?" He lovingly took her into his arms, cradling her head to his shoulder.

"But you said once our duty was finished we'd—" Anne

362

looked up into the face she loved, willing to follow him into the fires of Hell.

His chest vibrated with the soft chuckle. "Annie, lass, you and Glennascaul are Heaven."

DeborahAnne MacGillivray is the author of four books due out in 2006—
A RESTLESS KNIGHT, RAVENHAWKE, INVASION OF FALGANNON ISLE, and RIDING THE THUNDER.
Be sure to visit DeborahAnne's website
www.deborahmacgillivray.co.uk

Dude Looks Like A Lady

by *Kemberlee Shortland*

• *Carmel, California - A permit is required to wear shoes with heels higher than two inches*

"I can't believe I let you talk me into this," exclaimed Pam. She watched Maisie applying the finishing touches to her costume.

It was bad enough she was being forced to dress as a man, but that costume came complete with funny pants, hose and garters, a hideous powdered wig and a hat with so many feathers she felt like the ostrich they came from.

"Don't be such a stick in the mud," said Maisie. "Stand up straight and let's get this cape on you."

Pam suppressed a groan. "Really, Maisie. Why can't *I* dress as Marie Antoinette? I would rather have been dressed as her poodle than Louis XVI," she continued to grouse. Maisie just laughed. "Tell me again why you and Jake didn't sign up for this. Why me?"

"Because Jake doesn't have the legs for it. And I seriously doubt Louis ever carried a child other than in his arms." Maisie stepped back and waved both hands in the direction of her enormous belly.

"Okay, you have me there. But you could have at least introduced me to Marie Antoinette. Even the real Louis got to meet his bride before they wed."

"We would have, but Hank didn't arrive until late last

night and there wasn't time this morning. When you're ready, we'll find him and I'll introduce him personally. You'll like him. He's a real sweetheart."

Pam wasn't convinced this would work. The charity costume contest was for couples, and she'd never heard about Hank until last week. She didn't see how they could pull this off.

The contest itself was simple. The event was being staged in the gardens of La Playa Hotel and each contestant had been given a room in which to prepare, which was where Pam and Maisie were now. Each couple dressed as a famous romantic couple in history and paraded up and down a catwalk. The twist was that each couple had to wear the other's costume. The audience would vote by donation for their favorite couple. All donations were going to each couple's chosen charity. The couple with the highest donations would win the contest.

Easy.

Yet, Pam was anything but at ease over the whole affair. She couldn't remember ever being so nervous. She'd be in full costume; no one would recognize her. She hadn't met her 'date' yet, and once this was over she'd never see him again. And the money would go to charity.

So why was she so nervous? She normally enjoyed crazy stunts like this.

But something didn't feel right. The last time she'd heard the name Hank, she'd been kicking his sorry butt out of her apartment. She'd left San Francisco after that and never heard from him again. She knew nothing about this Hank, but was certain there had to be more than one Hank Higgins in the world.

"Don't look so glum." Maisie's voice cut through the fog in Pam's mind, handing her the walking stick. "It'll be over in a couple hours."

"Says you."

Maisie just laughed again. "Yes, says me. Now, turn around and look in the mirror."

The image staring back at Pam was eerily male. Eerily overstuffed, froufroued and pompously male. She'd always thought her features were feminine, but now she wasn't so sure. She couldn't remember the last time she wore so much satin and lace...outside of her bedroom sheets that is.

"I can't believe I let you talk me into this," said Hank Delacroix, teetering where he stood, glaring down at the man he'd considered his friend—Jake Hennessey. "Man! How do I get myself into these things?"

"Don't be such a pansy," Jake taunted. He safely stood to one side of the hotel room and watched fellow officer Anita Lopez work on Hank's costume. He knew Jake had been thrilled when Anita offered to help. Of course, it came at a cost — a month of babysitting. Jake agreed because he was desperate for the help, and with Maisie about ready to drop, he figured he'd need the practice.

"Easy for you to say. You're not the one dressed in your mother's best curtains with a poodle on your head."

Jake's laughter didn't make Hank feel any better. Yes, he'd promised to participate in the charity event and to wear a costume. But he had no idea it would be a dress and ridiculously high heels.

"Dude!" Hank pleaded. "Can't I at least ditch the treads?"

"'Fraid not. Besides, you have terrific legs. I might have to ask you out myself when this is over." To add insult to injury, Jake blew him a kiss. Hank's fists balled at his sides. It was a damn good thing his friend had situated himself across the room.

Anita stepped down from the chair she'd stood on to work on his wig and glanced between the two men. "I can leave if you need some private time." She knew she added salt to his wounded male pride. "And you do have great legs. Mmm... mmm...mmm!" she murmured, lifting the hem of his gown.

Jake put his hands on her shoulders. "Down, girl. You're a married woman, or have you forgotten?"

Anita faced him, one eyebrow raised. "I've got three spawn of the Devil at home. How could I forget? And I won't forget our deal either!" Facing Hank again she said, "Let's see you walk in those shoes. You don't want to break your neck out there."

"No, man. There's only one neck I want to break." They both turned toward Jake, who gulped audibly.

A moment later Hank was sauntering dramatically around the room. "What do you think?" Jake and Anita were in deep discussion. "Well?"

"You're a natural," said Jake.

"And gorgeous to boot," added Anita. "You're gonna kick ass."

Hank looked at himself in the full-length mirror. He definitely wasn't the man he'd woken up as this morning. Gone were his rumpled dark hair, morning scruff and more importantly, his manhood. Now, he had to be the tallest damn transvestite in Northern California. He had to be close to eight feet tall.

Who knows? I could really have some fun with this. After all, he spoke French, thanks to his Parisian mother. And no one knew him here. Carmel was a long way from San Francisco. His fellow 49ers would never see him like this.

Hank suddenly locked gazes with Jake, as if spying a lover across a room, and strode over as seductively as possible. He stepped behind him, drawing his painted fake-nailed fingertips around Jake's shoulders. Then, leaning close to his friend's ear, he whispered with his best feminine French accent, "*Je vous trouve très sexy. Voules-vous coucher avec moi ce soir?*"

Anita burst out laughing, but Jake's face went noticeably white, his voice gravely serious at Hank's offer to sleep with him. "That's not funny, man."

"Revenge is a bitch and so am I," Hank said victoriously, adjusting the massive fake breasts in Jake's direction.

There was little time when Pam met her partner backstage. They were up next, and Maisie and Jake had been ushered away quickly after brief introductions.

Pam raked Hank from head to toe. He had to be the tallest drag queen she'd ever seen. Boldly, she lifted his hem and spotted his six inch heels. Craning her neck to look at him, she said, "I hope you've got a permit for those."

She wasn't sure what was more shocking—the balancing act he did with the grossly exaggerated wig on his head or that he looked so much like a woman in the extravagant gown. Pam wasn't a tall woman. She'd always been comfortable in her averageness. Now, she felt like a tiny mouse beside a very large cat. A cat whose eyes narrowed intently with what she thought might be active interest.

Maybe he's gay—like the couple standing near them. Maybe a woman dressed as a pompous ass turns him on. She swallowed hard at the thought. She couldn't wait for this to be over. Her stomach twisted in knots. And something familiar about Hank rankled.

"*Il fait beau de vous rencontrer, cherie.* Emm... It eez nize to meet you," Hank said delicately, translating as he dipped into a graceful curtsey. The huge bell of his skirt almost knocked the next couple off their feet. She smiled apologetically at the couple—Romeo and Julio. She lifted an eyebrow at their take on Shakespeare's classic.

Hank leaned into her, now with the voice of a man. "*Vous êtes sexy dans ces bas que. La jarretière donne m'à une dur-sur.*" He gave her a green-eyed wink that seemed familiar. And were her ears playing cruel tricks on her? Did Hank just say she was giving him a hard on with her stocking garters? Suspicion planted a vigorous seed in her mind.

"*Vous êtes une telle secousse!*" She'd surprised him by calling him a jerk in French. She should have called him worse for what he'd said to her.

"Don't lose your head, cherie. I was only teasing." Hank liked this woman. There was something familiar about her, too—something that awakened memories he thought long-buried. Memories of the love he'd lost that left a gaping hole in his heart. But this wasn't Pam. She was long gone. Didn't Maisie say her name was Anne?

Hank looked her up and down. She was a fair Louis XVI. Beneath her make-up, he could tell she was quite pretty. And if her legs looked as good out of those stockings as they did in, he definitely wanted to make nice with her.

He peeked through the curtains at the couple on the catwalk. "They're a lame excuse for Anthony and Cleopatra. She walks like a girl and he has no boobs." When Anne leaned over, he caught the scent of her perfume and his imagination started working again.

"Their costumes are very good though," she finally said.

He let the curtain drop and looked down at his partner. "Not as good as ours." He gave her a smile he hoped appeared earnest and searched her face for something he couldn't name.

Her lips twitched and mirth reached her brown eyes. "Not as good as yours anyway."

"Hey, your costume is terrific. I already told you how

excited I'm getting." She lifted a brow at his reminder, but didn't reply.

Just then, the main curtain swept aside and Anthony and Cleopatra returned backstage. They grinned as if they'd just won an Oscar.

Hank grasped Pam's hand to draw her attention. He was startled by the tingle that warmed him clear to his toes. He shook off the familiarity as coincidence. "Let's give them a performance they won't forget."

"If you can manage to stay on your feet and don't lose that bee's nest, I'll be happy enough."

Hank was happy to see Anne fall into her role as the pompous French king. He admired the way she postured, tilting her nose up and sneering at the peasants. She used her walking stick with flare.

Then he spotted half his team in the front row and nearly lost his balance. Who the hell told them he was here? He spotted Jake and knew instantly. The man was cruising for a bruising and Hank was just the man for the job. He took his teammates' heckling in stride and fell into his guise as France's most notorious queen, gazing sensually to the men, plumping his fake boobs in their direction and swishing his bell skirt with great effect. He made a few French jibes in their direction, laughing at their ignorance, and gave them his best shit-eating grin.

Their turn was coming to an end and Anne moved in beside him to take his arm in hers. She gazed up at him, waving her walking stick over the audience and asked in a very good accent, "Antionette, vat shall ve do viss deez pez-awnts?"

Hank slowly cast his gaze over the people around the catwalk then replied, "*Laissez-les manger le gateau.* Let zem eat cake!"

The audience burst out laughing, clapping and cheering. His teammates stood and shouted "Hoo hoo hoo's" while pumping the air with their firsts. He let Anne guide him backstage.

She was a good sport. He couldn't help but like her. He couldn't wait to get out of this get-up so he could meet her as the man he really was.

Once the curtain fell closed behind them, Anne practically ran from him. He sniffed his under-arm. Unlike the

French, he believed in bathing daily, so he wondered what made her run off.

Pam rushed across the garden, heading for her room to change and go home. She had to get away. Hank unnerved her. He reminded her of times better left forgotten, and the resulting broken heart.

Midway across the garden someone grabbed her arm and spun her around. She wasn't sure who attacked her, but she certainly hadn't expected an eight-foot French queen. She was awed he'd moved so fast in his heels.

"Wait." Hank practically slammed into her when she stopped so suddenly. He straightened his wig, which listed to one side. His gaze never wavered from hers though. "Where are you going?

"Home."

"You can't leave yet. They're going to announce the winners soon."

His damn voice. Every time he opened his mouth she heard Hank Higgins, but the face beneath the make-up wasn't his.

"You accept the prize for both of us." She smiled encouragingly, hoping he'd leave it at that.

"No can do. They'll want both of us."

Her shoulders slumped. "All right. What are we supposed to do before then?"

"I don't know. But I need to use the john and I don't know where Jake is. I'd be eternally grateful if you'd give me a hand." The way he phrased his request left a lot to be desired. He had a killer smile and his mascara-caked eyes were sincere.

"I'll help, but I draw the line at the dress. You can *handle* the rest on your own."

The bathroom was roomy, but his gown took up most available free space. He'd removed his heels so he didn't have to aim from so high. Anne stood behind him, holding up the front folds of fabric so he could manage to do his business. She shifted and he caught the scent of her perfume again.

"Obsession."

"What?"

"Your perfume. Obsession. I like it."

370

"Are you done yet?"

Hank heard impatience in her voice, so he finished up and took the fabric from her hands. She couldn't get out of the bathroom fast enough.

"We better get back out there or we'll miss the announcements." She didn't look at him.

He wedged himself sideways through the bathroom door. "Okay, but you'll have to help me put my shoes back on. I can't bend over in this wig. It was hard enough holding the wig with one hand while I—"

"I don't need details." She knelt quickly. "Lift your hem." He did and felt her cool fingers grasp one foot to slide on the first shoe. When he stood up on it, his wig brushed the ceiling light.

She gasped when she lifted his other foot. He looked down. She was flat on her ass, leaning back on her hands and glaring up at him, angry. Before he could ask what was wrong, she was gone.

There was no way he could catch up with her. He heard the announcer call the last couple to the catwalk, so he made his way in that direction, gazing over the tops of the people he passed looking for her.

She wasn't at the staging area, but Jake was. "Hey, buddy," called Jake. "I've been looking for you."

"I had to use the john. Anne helped me. But she ran off and I can't find her. Have you seen her?" he asked.

"Anne who?"

"Anne...Louis the sixteenth?" He rolled his eyes.

Jake's eyes snapped open. "No, man. Her name is Pam. Pamela Howard.' Hank teetered on his heels and felt himself list to one side and knew it had nothing to do with the heavy wig. "You okay?"

Hank blinked several times to clear his head. His heart began to pound, but he couldn't seem to catch his breath. "Yeah."

"Do you know her?" Jake looked noticeably bewildered.

Hank didn't have to lift the dress' hem to see the tattoo on his ankle. It was small, but had caused so much trouble in his life. He'd gotten it the day before their wedding. The thought of a piece of paper and rings at the ceremony just hadn't been enough. He'd wanted something permanent, so he'd gone to Fisherman's Wharf to the city's best tattoo artist and had a pair of interlinking hearts put on his ankle with their initials in the center of each heart.

He'd known it was bad luck to see the bride the night before the wedding, but he had to be with her. His body craved contentment only she could satisfy.

When she'd seen the tattoo, there had been war. She told him their marriage could never work if he kept secrets from her. A tattoo was a big decision. One he certainly couldn't have made on the spur of the moment. If he kept this from her, what else would he keep from her? So she threw him out of her apartment and slammed the door in his face. No matter what he said, she wouldn't let him in. She'd turned on the stereo and cranked up the volume so she couldn't hear him.

He never believed she'd leave him standing at the altar alone. They'd planned a small courthouse wedding with just a pair of witnesses from both sides. He should have known when her witnesses failed to show. If he'd only kept the tattoo a surprise until after the wedding.

He grunted. If he'd only talked to her before he got the tattoo. She was right. He would have been upset if she'd done something to her body without telling him first. He wanted to tell her he was wrong, but when he went back to her apartment that afternoon, still in his tux, she was gone. His mind reeled at how quickly she'd managed to clear the place out. The only remaining item was a box of his things, all replaceable. On top of everything was her engagement ring.

Hank's eyes stung as the memory flashed through his mind.

"Yeah, I know her," he said bitterly. "She left me standing at the altar."

"Jeeeezus."

Hank hated to ask, but he had to know. "Is she married? Kids?"

"I still don't know much about her. She's been over a few times, but I always disappear after dinner. I've never seen her with a guy. I don't think she even dates. She works and comes to our house."

"I gotta find her." They had to talk. It had been five long years and he'd never stopped loving her. He'd dated, but rarely slept with his dates because they weren't Pam. He was

Dude Looks Like A Lady

frustrated, in pain, and now he was pissed off.

"Don't look now, but here she comes with Maisie," Jake warned.

Hank whipped around so quickly his wig almost came off. It reminded him of where he was and how he was dressed. This was no time for a confrontation. He had to get through the awards announcements, then they could talk so they could settle this once and for all.

Straightening his wig, he tried to compose himself enough to get through this. But when Pam stepped up beside him he caught the scent of her perfume again and almost swept her into his arms to carry her away.

Jake's nudge drew his attention back to the speaker who loudly announced the winners.

Third place went to the two young men, Romeo and Julio. Second place went to a geriatric Adam and Eve. Honorable mention went to Anthony and Cleopatra.

"And our first place winners are Pamela Howard and Hank Delecroix as France's notorious monarchs, King Louis XVI and Marie Antoinette!" The announcer stepped back and let Hank and Pam take their places on catwalk. This time, Pam's distain was real. She held her nose in the air, her spine stiff and refused to look at him.

He suddenly felt like the fish out of water he was. He looked around the audience who was on their feet cheering. His 49er teammates whooped and made catcalls. For the first time since starting out the day, perspiration beaded his skin.

The consummate clown when he was nervous, he leaned down toward Pam, and in a grief-stricken feminine French accent, he said, "My love, vee are about to meet Madame Guillotine. Before I die, I must haff von last kees." She gazed up at him, wide-eyed. "Vee haff been apart for so long, cherie. I long to taste your leeps upon mine for von last time."

Before she could protest, Hank lifted Pam into his arms, pulling her off her feet, and covered her lips with his. She fought, but he refused to her go. She gave in and let him kiss her. The sound of the crowd faded into the back of his mind. For years he dreamed of having her back in his arms. Now that he had her in a place she couldn't easily escape, he poured all of his frustration into his kiss.

The judge placed his hand on his shoulder and Hank was

373

forced to pull away. He'd worked himself up and was glad of the billowing gown. He wanted nothing more than to throw Pam on the runway and have his way with her, to remind her of how good they were together. But this wasn't the time or the place.

He reluctantly set her back on her feet. Her cheeks flamed as she looked around her, then raced off the catwalk. He needed to follow her. He couldn't lose her again.

With dramatic flare, he waved his hand and shouted, "Farewell, cherie. Vee veel be together again soon!"

Alone in her room, Pam was showered and dressed in her own clothes—a dark blue wrap-around dress with short matching blue heels. She smoothed her freshly blown dried honey-brown hair away from her face and looked in the mirror. Her eyes were still red and puffy from her tears. There was nothing she could do about that. She just wanted to go home.

Maisie said she would take care of the costume, so she left it on the bed. She gathered her things and opened the door.

Hank leaned against the balcony railing. He'd showered and changed, too—tight denims, black boots and a white shirt, the top three buttons of which were open to reveal a small tuft of chest hair. Gone were all remnants of the make-up. His slightly long dark hair waved back from his tanned face, his green eyes shining.

If the last five years didn't stand between them like a brick wall, Pam would have stepped into his embrace. His kiss awakened long-buried emotions that reminded her just what a great kisser he was. No one else she'd met compared to him... in any way.

He casually stepped into her room and closed the door behind him, leaning against it and making it obvious she couldn't leave.

She backed away from him and moved to the other side of the bed. When she reached what she considered a safe distance, she cast him a sidelong glance. "I suppose we better get this over with."

Hank said nothing. She felt like he stripped her with his gaze. She was well-familiar with the look. Subconsciously, she laid the flat of her hand over her stomach to calm the butterflies.

She couldn't meet his gaze, but he didn't say anything, which made her more nervous. "You came here to talk, so talk. Otherwise, please leave. I want to go home." When she finally looked at him, he hadn't moved. His expression had darkened considerably though. She knew that look, too. She was surprised he still stood by the door and hadn't leapt over the bed.

"Say something, damn you!" she cursed.

He finally reached into his back pocket and tossed an envelope on the bed. "You didn't stick around long enough to get your half of the prize. Ironically, it's only good for a couple, so I thought you'd like to have it. I don't need it."

His deep silky voice penetrated her defenses and she strove to rebuild them. "Wh-what is it?"

He chuckled lightly. "A weekend for two in this hotel, all expenses paid."

"What makes you think I can use it?"

"I'm not seeing anyone. A beautiful woman like you must have guys falling all over themselves trying to get a date. Maybe you can ask one of them. It'd be fun." She heard strain in his voice at the mention of other men.

Her chest tightened when he said she was beautiful. He'd never called her that before. Pretty, yes, but never beautiful. Her resistance crumbled a bit more. She straightened her spine to shore up her defenses.

"It's a wasted prize then. Give it to Jake and Maisie," she told him, trying to keep her voice from cracking.

"They won't have time to use it for months. Go on. Take it. Stay alone, but let the hotel pamper you. You deserve it." Pulling another envelope from his pocket, he tossed it onto the bed on top of the first. "And I think you wanted to see this."

"See what? I don't remember asking you for a damn thing."

"It's my permit...for the heels. I might be stupid about some things, but I did know I needed a permit to wear those ridiculous heels."

Her lips quirked, remembering her ex-lover in those shoes and the dress. Now that she was fully aware of *who* he was, what he'd done almost vanquished her anger with him.

Kemberlee Shortland

She couldn't let him do that to her. She turned fully toward him. "What is this all about, Hank? You came here to talk, so talk."

"I came here to give you our prize." She saw him rake her with his eyes. "And to look at you."

"You've had your look, now get out."

"Not yet." He stepped away from the door and moved around the bed to where she stood. "Sit and talk with me. Give me the chance to apologize that you never gave me five years ago. Please, Pam. I deserve at least that much."

Pam flipped her gaze away from him, remembering how angry she'd been that night. She never had let him apologize—just kicked him out and shut him out of her life. She'd been very young then. They both had. Maybe they'd grown up enough since then so they could talk like adults.

The only chair was in the dining area near the door. Her only option was to sit on the bedside unless she wanted to push past Hank or crawl over the bed.

One thing she knew about Hank was that he was honorable. If he said he just wanted to talk, then he would. He was a clown in public, always gregarious and funny. Today had been a testament to that. But privately he was the consummate lover, a perfect gentleman, his every action and word from his heart. Even when they argued.

Knowing this about him, she lowered herself to sit on the edge of the bed. Hank relaxed noticeably, but he stayed where he was.

"I'm listening."

Hank ran his fingers through his hair. She longed to do the same. Instead, she clasped her hands together in her lap.

He chuckled lightly to himself. "Now that I have you where I want you, I don't know what to say."

"I'm sure you'll think of something. If you don't, I can go."

A moment later, Hank sank to his knees and sat back on his heels. She felt his gaze burn a path across her body, then cast his gaze toward the floor.

She couldn't help wondering if he was on his knees to bring them level with each other while they talked, or if he was on his knees to beg. Either way, it brought them closer and the scent of his cologne punched a hole in her heart.

"Well?" After a brief silence her voice was barely a whisper.

He rubbed both hands across his face then looked up. The moment their eyes met, Pam's defenses collapsed. Hank's eyes glistened and pain etched across his strong features. His lips drew tight, trying to maintain his control. She felt her own eyes well with emotion, but she didn't dare move.

"Oh, Pam." He buried his face in his palms once more. His shoulders shook.

"Hank," she started. Suddenly, everything that happened paled in significance to Hank breaking down like this. In all the time they'd ever known each other, she'd never seen him cry.

She didn't know what to say. Without thinking, she ran her fingers through his hair. Hank buried his face in her lap and wrapped his arms around her hips. "I'm so sorry. God, I'm sorry."

He came here to be a man and apologize, not fall to pieces and cry like baby. Hank thought he'd never see Pam again, let alone have the chance to talk to her. Now that she was within touching distance the words wouldn't come. He'd practiced for five long years and now he was speechless. Frustration, anger, heartache, hopelessness...all his emotions crashed against each other and he snapped.

Then she touched him and memories of her hands on him flooded his memory and he longed for the comfort only she could provide.

When he looked into her eyes he saw them brimming with unshed tears. Her fingers slid from his hair to his cheek and he turned his face into her touch, kissing her palm.

He squeezed his eyes shut and murmured, "What do I have to do for you to forgive me? Just say the word and I'll do whatever you want. But please, tell me we can try again. I've been so lost without you."

He felt her shudder, then tears spilled over her cheeks. Her lips trembled, her chin quivered. He would like nothing more than to kiss her until she shivered in passion rather than sorrow.

"Maisie reminded me every argument has two sides. I was wrong five years ago and I've paid for my mistake every since. I thought I was angry with you, but I was really angry with myself," she said. "I had no right to be such a shrew."

Hank thought his heart would explode with hope. He couldn't move. He focused all his attention on every word she spoke.

"When I saw you today, everything you did reminded me of the Hank I once knew. My heart recognized you through all that make-up and hair." She wove her fingers through his hair once more, causing him to revel in her touch.

"Everything about you, your laugh, your smile, your eyes, your clowning around in that costume all reminded me of you.

"I've been angry for five years for throwing away a life I could only dream of for such a little thing. I should be the one begging your forgiveness."

"Then we're both at fault, because I should have talked to you first. Ah, Pam. I'm really sorry."

"Me, too."

He smoothed the tears from her cheeks with the backs of his fingers. "Where do we go now?"

"Maybe we can start here."

She drew him up between her knees and kissed him. Sweetly at first, then she stole his breath. When she pulled away, he smiled and told her, "That's a very good place. I'm sure we can think of a few more."

He rose and slid across the bed with her in his arms. He intended to start with kissing every inch of her. When he finished, he'd begin again. When he finished kissing her, he had five years worth of fantasies to catch up on.

Maisie and Jake stood on the balcony outside of Pam's room. Jake leaned toward the door. "I don't hear any yelling," said Jake.

"That's because they're making up. Come on, let's go home." As they crossed the garden, still thronged with people, Maisie asked, "I'm confused. Why did Hank change his name?"

"He didn't. His full name is Henry Delacroix Higgins. When he joined the 49ers, he got tired of the guys making wisecracks about his name being the same as that guy on Magnum P.I. He thought Hank Delacroix worked better for his macho football image."

"Is it true what they say about football players shaving

their legs?" asked Maisie, remembering Hank's great legs. Jake nodded. "If they didn't shave, the tape would stick to the hairs." Maisie's confused look made him chuckle. "There's a lot you need to learn about football, babe."

We invite you to visit Kemberlee Shortland's website
www.kemberlee.com

Susan Barclay

A Ray for Mary Jo

by Susan Barclay

• *Arkansas - It's against the law to kill*
any living creature

Mary Jo applied a swift, sure pass of Paradise Pink lipstick, pressed her lips together, and blotted them with a tissue.

Her mother was right. Clint was gone, and the time had come to move on. She sighed as she walked from the powder room into her bedroom to put on her uniform. Pink button-up sweater over a pink tank top, white knee-length skirt, neutral pantyhose, and low heeled, black shoes. As the proprietor of the café, even she had a dress code, albeit a little more flexible than the rest of the staff's.

Naming the café had been a bit of an ordeal. Her Uncle Howard had suggested calling it The Merry Widow's Place, but Mary Jo's mother, Millie, had squelched that. "Ain't nothin' merry 'bout bein' a widda," she'd said eloquently, speaking from experience. Indeed, it would only remind Mary Jo, and might even sound like she was advertising for a new husband. However, Millie's own proposal had been "Coffee, Tea, or... Cake," and Mary Jo thought that idea was as flawed as her uncle's. Everybody knew the common phrase was "coffee, tea, or me," and Mary Jo had no intentions of being on the menu.

After much back and forth discussion, Mary Jo finally set her foot down. "I really appreciate your interest, y'all," she'd said, interrupting, "but I've already decided. I'm calling it The Mary Cake Coffé." A hushed silence followed her declaration, then everyone had started speaking at once.

"You mean, The Merry Cake Café?"

"No, I think she said the Mary Kay Café."

"Mary's Cake and Coffee! I love it, girl – you shore got a

380

way with words!"

"Mary Kay? Couldn't you get in trouble for that? Wouldn't it be like goin' against brand name or something?"

Heaving a sigh, Mary Jo scrawled a few words on a large piece of cardboard. "Shush, y'all," she'd said, holding up the sign. It's spelled this way—'The Mary Cake Coffé'."

"Well, now, don't that beat all," her cousin, August, had shrugged. "I don't get it."

But Mary Jo didn't give a hoot what anyone else thought. It was The Mary Cake Coffé, plain and simple. Mary for her name, Mary Cake because of the play on Mary Kay – and cake was her specialty–and not only was Coffé a high falutin' allusion to coffee or café, but *coff* was an archaic past participle of the verb 'to buy'–which she hoped a lot of people would be doing at her shop. Mary Jo loved words as much as she loved cake.

Six years ago, she'd have laughed if anyone told her she'd be a Mary Kay rep. Wasn't that for *old* people? She was only twenty-one, for heaven's sake! But neighbors had been moving out as Mary Jo and Clint moved in and Jenny had come right over to say "hi." She'd suggested Mary Jo pick up the Mary Kay clients Jenny was leaving behind. "Think about it," she'd said. "You've already got the right first name."

Mary Jo had laughed. The idea! Still, she'd taken Jenny's list of customers, just to be polite. And when weeks of loneliness and isolation followed as Clint kept busy learning the ropes at his new job, she'd finally called Jenny's MK supervisor and registered as a bona fide vendor. It hadn't made sense for her to look for any other kind of work. She'd needed flexibility since they planned to start a family, and it was a great way to meet people in a town as foreign to her as democracy to Cuba. Clint had joked, "Honey, we sure ain't in Arkansas anymore." Indeed, 'Bastin' was as far from Arkansas as Mary Jo could have ever imagined.

Working for Mary Kay had been Mary Jo's salvation. She couldn't count the number of women she'd met, and a few of them had become close friends. She'd needed friends after the accident. Even five years later the nightmare continued to play out before her in waking dreams.

Clint was home from work early for a change. With the

baby due in three weeks, both were on pins and needles. At this advanced stage, Mary Jo didn't feel much like cooking, so Clint picked up a prepared meal from their favorite deli on his way home and dinner sat on the table. Even though it smelled good, Mary Jo couldn't eat more than a few bites.

"I can't wait for the baby to come, can you?" she asked between nibbles.

"Mmm," agreed Clint. "I'll bet she's beautiful, just like her mother." Smiling, he reached over and rubbed Mary Jo's back.

"Or handsome like his father," she grinned.

The phone rang just as Clint poured their tea, and he jumped up to get it. "Hello...Oh, hey Mark...Uh huh...Uh huh...Sorry to hear that, buddy. Sure...I'll be right over...Bye." He hung up. "Sorry, Mare," he said. "You okay if I go over to Mark's for a little while? Crisis time."

"Sure, honey," Mary Jo replied. "You go on ahead. I'll page you if I need you."

Clint smiled, leaned down and kissed her on the lips. "I'll be back before you know it," he promised.

But it was a promise he'd never keep. On his way home, a driver too drunk to even see him, killed him. Clint's body lay shattered on the ground surrounded by a scattered bouquet of flowers she'd never receive. In shock, Mary Jo went into premature labor that night and, in that time between dusk and dawn, brought their son into the cold world.

Millie came out at once, but had to return home to Fayetteville after a month. Mary Jo's friends rallied around, helped with the baby and the chores, saw her through the investigation and the inquest, and finally helped her pack for the move back home. It had been a draining nine months and Mary Jo didn't know how she would have managed without their kindness.

A voice broke into Mary Jo's meditation. "Mama?"

"Yes, Jabez, I'm coming," she replied. She tugged on her sweater, squared her shoulders, and pasted on a smile. Her son needed her.

She'd finished reading *The Prayer of Jabez* just before Clint's death, when the tiny book had been sweeping the nation. Mary Jo felt it a fitting name for her own son, because she'd given birth to him in pain. The pangs of labor, yes, but even more, the pain of death and loss. The pain of being without a father. Maybe God would bless her son, bless her Jabez.

"Let's go, Sunshine," she said to him now. "I've got to get you off to Grandma's house and myself to work."

"I'm all dressed, Mama."

"Yes, Jabez," she whispered, feeling a rawness in her throat. "You're such a good boy."

Millie smiled warmly for her grandson, but when he turned his back, she eyed Mary Jo pointedly, her eyebrows raised. "That boy needs a man in his life," she mouthed.

Mary Jo nodded and mouthed back, "I know." But she thought, Uncle Howard's a man! August is a man! She knew what her mother meant, though, and sighed. Time to get on with it. Pulling out of Millie's driveway, she steeled herself for what must come.

Mary Jo's staff had been telling her for weeks that Ray, one of Fayetteville's finest, had the hots for her. "Look," said Ella, who helped out at the counter, "he used to come in during the morning crush and get lost in the crowd. He's figured out the downtime so he can see you."

"You should see how moony-eyed he gets whenever you walk out from the back," teased Janine. "He's spent oodles of money here just waiting for the chance to talk to you."

Mary Jo decided today, Officer Ray would get his chance.

For the next couple of hours, she found herself too blessed busy to think about it. She kept herself and three other staffers occupied. 7-Up, Red Velvet, and Amalgamation cakes; Mississippi Mud, pecan, and peach pies; along with a variety of cookies and other sweets were made fresh every morning before the café opened. Mary Jo kept lunch simple. Three kinds of sandwiches–but no fried catfish, it's too smelly–coleslaw, and cornbread were the staples. To drink, people could chose from sweet tea, hot tea, coffee, and the usual soft drinks.

With the kitchen under control, Mary Jo checked the dining area. It held about a dozen small tables, each with a pink cracked-ice laminate surface and chrome legs. The chrome chairs had pink vinyl backs and seats. Certainly not a man's café per se, but Mary Jo had known the men would come. Once their girlfriends, mothers, and wives brought her goodies home, they'd have to come themselves. She knew her desserts were irresistible.

The menu and prices were neatly printed on a huge chalkboard on the wall behind the counter. The menu holders on the tables contained Mary Kay catalogs. Mary Jo made sure each holder held the current issue. Her regulars looked forward to thumbing through the pages, marking their choices, and filling out their orders while they drank a Cheerwine soda and ate one of Mary Jo's yummy concoctions. One evening a week when the café closed, Mary Jo ran sessions on skin care, makeup, and spa treatments for her Mary Kay clients. Combining her two businesses proved very profitable. She'd built a good life for herself and her son.

The café opened at 8:30, two and a half hours after her arrival. Someone always waited outside for Mary Jo to unlock the door. A little jingling bell announced the entrance of the first customer and every customer thereafter. Soon a happy hum and steady rhythm of activity swept through the café. The wait staff ensured coffee cups were topped up, while the girls at the take-out counter had a stream of people to serve. Every once in a while a pleasant lull settled in, allowing everyone to catch their breath before the next onslaught.

During one such quiet period Ella poked her head into the kitchen, getting Mary Jo's attention. "He's here," she hissed. No need to elaborate—everyone knew who *he* meant.

With a deep breath, Mary Jo wiped her hands on the apron she wore, untied it, and tossed it down on her worktable. Checking her image in a mirror by the door leading into the restaurant, she tucked a stray hair behind her ear, trying to calm her racing heartbeat.

Janine kept Ray waiting, pretending to rearrange some cream puffs behind the glass. Mary Jo walked over to Ray's table, hoping he couldn't hear the pounding in her chest. "May I help you?" she asked, trying to sound nonchalant. Her hands were as cold as ice. Raising her eyes to meet his, she couldn't help noticing how handsome he is in his uniform. His cap lay on the table and she took in his thick, wavy brown hair. His jaw was square, with a cleft in his chin. Above it, his lips looked ready to laugh, a straight—but not sharp—nose, and twinkling blue eyes. Her mouth dry, Mary Jo pressed her lips together.

"Yes, thanks," he answered with a smile, exuding confidence and ease. "I was hoping to get a slice of your famous Mississippi Mud Cake. Unless you'd make some other recommendation?"

"Well, I'm rather partial to the Red Velvet myself."

"Great!" exclaimed Ray. He peered over her shoulder and hollered to Janine, "Two slices of Red Velvet, one medium coffee, black, no sugar..." He turned back to Mary Jo who, startled, slumped into a chair across from him. "You like coffee?" he asked. At her wordless nod, he turned his attention to Janine again. "And another coffee. I assume you know how your boss likes it." Ray leaned across the table. "I don't usually have the pleasure of such lovely company on my morning break," he said with a grin. "You don't mind joining me?"

Mary Jo shook her head no, still at a loss for words. *Doesn't let the grass grow under his feet, does he? Sees an opportunity and jumps on it.* Not sure if she liked that about him or not, she looked at him more closely. "Say, don't I know you from somewhere? Other than here, I mean?"

Ray smirked and raised a brow. And that one expression gave him away completely.

"Ray Laramie," she said aloud. Former star forward of the Razorbacks. Interesting. Hometown hero turned cop?

His grin captivated her. "Don't hold it against me," he said. "I'm really a nice guy."

Janine set their coffees on the table along with two slices of cake on white ceramic plates. Ray hoisted his mug, saying, "Cheers!" and waited for Mary Jo.

"Cheers!" she said weakly, raising her cup.

Taking a sip of coffee, Ray set it down, and leaned forward again. "So, tell me about yourself, Miss Mary Cake Coffé. By the way, I really like that–*coff*–archaic past participle of the verb 'to buy.' Clever."

Mary Jo blushed and smoothed back her hair. "Not many people know that," she said. "I'm impressed."

"I guess most people don't think of football players as terribly articulate," he said with a shrug. "But I'm pretty good with an etymological dictionary...among other things. I actually majored in English and Criminology."

"Wow." *Now who's inarticulate*, she thought. "Quite a

combination."

"But enough about me," said Ray. "I really like your café. Tell me how you got started."

So Mary Jo found herself talking about Clint, their dreams cut short, Jabez, and the return to Fayetteville. How her family had given her plenty of time to grieve, but finally forced her to take a look at her situation, and to determine what she planned to do about it. "Mary Kay, cake–it just seemed like the answer. And it has been. It's been very good," she concluded. She hadn't noticed it while talking, going on and on, but now she felt a bit embarrassed by the intensity of his gaze. "But enough about me," she murmured, lowering her head. "Tell me about Ray Laramie, post Razorbacks."

He did. As he talked, Mary Jo found herself more and more drawn to him. And it seemed they had a lot in common. Not only did she find him attractive, but intelligent, funny, and modest. For the first time in a long time, Mary Jo smiled so much it hurt.

Finally, Ray pushed back from the table. He looked at his watch and grimaced. "I'd better get back to work before they fire me," he said. Janine, wiping down the table next to them, overheard and handed him his bill. "I don't suppose I can put this on my tab," he said, grinning and pulling his wallet from his back pocket. "I really enjoyed your company, Mary Jo."

"I enjoyed yours, too, Ray."

He stood up and put on his police cap, pressing it forward on the brim. "Listen," he said. "Can I ask one more thing of you?"

"Of course," Mary Jo said rather coquettishly, thinking he meant to ask her out – maybe to dinner or a movie.

"I need a birthday cake. I can pick it up today after work, before the café closes."

Caught off guard, Mary Jo simply said, "Oh, yes, I can save you a cake."

"I need it to say, 'Happy Birthday, Josie,'" said Ray. "Is that okay?"

Mary Jo blanched, but quickly regained her composure. "Sure, Ray, I can do that." Her fingernails dig into the skin of her palms. "Have a nice day." She turned her back on him and, staring straight ahead, marched into the kitchen. Once the door closed behind her, she leaned against it and covered her eyes with one hand. Taking her hand away, she saw the kitchen staff staring at her. Mary Jo glared, and they returned to their work with unusual focus.

"Lindy Lou?" she snapped.

A slight girl with long hair tied back and tucked under a hairnet raised her head cautiously. "Yes, ma'am?"

"Please save a cake for Officer Laramie and write 'Happy Birthday, Josie' on it. Okay?"

"Yes, ma'am," the girl said meekly.

Out of sight of the others, Mary Jo berated herself vigorously. Her first foray back into the world of dating, and look where it got her. Fool! Idiot! Why had she ever listened to those simple girls who worked for her? *"I don't usually have the pleasure of such lovely company on my morning break,"* she mimicked. Of course not! He's always *here* on his morning breaks—he gets his 'lovely company' on afternoon and evening breaks somewhere else. With someone else. A woman named Josie.

What had ever made her think, even in her weakest moment, someone like Ray Laramie could fall for a nobody like her? Frumpy uniform, child-bearing hips. Used to glamour and sophistication, Ray could get anybody he wanted.

She and Jabez would make out just fine on their own. Look how well they'd been doing already. Uncle Howard and August and the other men in her family would just have to step up to the plate a little more. Take Jabez fishing and to football games—do all that guy stuff a boy needed to grow up big and strong. Just don't ask her to go on the prowl anymore. It was too humiliating.

Mary Jo avoided the staff for the rest of the day and decided to miss Ray by leaving work a few minutes early. "Lock up for me, Janine," she commanded without looking at her.

As she hopped into her Passat and opened the sunroof, Ray drove up in his squad car across the street. Mary Jo shifted into gear and pulled out of her spot. In a sideways glance, she caught sight of Ray's upraised hand, an expression of curious bewilderment on his face. She almost laughed aloud. *Serves him right.*

Too early to pick up Jabez without questions, Mary Jo decided to give the car a good run. Farmington wasn't too far from Millie's, but a ways from the café. She'd have plenty of time to clear her head and decide how she'd get Millie off her back.

As she eased onto the highway, she glanced in her rearview mirror. A few car lengths behind her she saw a police car. Surely not Ray's? He wouldn't have had time to pick up and pay for his cake and to chase her down, would he? And why would he want to? *Josie's waiting for him, and it's her birthday. With any luck, he'll get to see her in her birthday suit.*

Mary Jo snorted. Why did she care anyway? Good grief, she hardly knew the man! They only spent forty-five minutes together. Her hopes had just been too high. Her staff had set her up to think Ray was nuts about her when the only reason he'd come in day after day was for a slice of her Mississippi Mud Cake. *She* was the nutty one – believing with the others that it meant something more. Unexpectedly, a tear escaped and trickled down her cheek. She wiped it away impatiently with the back of her hand.

Glancing in her rearview mirror again, she saw the police car still there, but couldn't tell if it was Ray or not. She pulled into the passing lane to get in front of the Jeep ahead of her. The squad car pulled out, too. Mary Jo felt a twinge of nervousness. What would she do if it turned out to be him? Why wouldn't he just leave her alone? She glanced down at her speedometer and noticed she'd been doing the speed limit, but panic caused her to press down on the accelerator. The tears kept coming—unbidden. Her soulmate had been killed and left her raising their son by herself. Hadn't she been through enough?

But today, before Ray asked for Josie's cake, when they were just talking, she'd felt something she hadn't felt in a long time. A flicker of hope. Only to have that hope snuffed out before it had a chance to burn brighter. Well, it was just cruel.

The overhead lights of the pursuing car flashed. Mary Jo glanced down at her speedometer and saw, through her tears, she suddenly had gone twenty miles over the speed limit. She had no doubt she was in trouble now, but finding herself loathe to stop, she kept going. She slowed at the turnoff for Old Farmington Road, though. Ray, or whoever drove the car behind her, followed her down the off ramp. The siren blared loudly. He's determined, she'd give him that. Mary Jo exhaled loudly, put her turn signal on, pulled onto the shoulder, and came to a halt, shutting off the engine as she did so. The police car pulled in seconds later.

Mary Jo bowed her head over the steering wheel as she heard a door open about twenty-five yards away and the crunch of footsteps on gravel. Suddenly something large and bright green flew in through the open sunroof and fluttered near her head. Jolted into action, Mary Jo screamed. Her arms flailed wildly at the thing as she shuddered and shrieked.

Through her terror, she heard Ray's voice as he ran towards her vehicle. "Mary Jo! Mary Jo! What are you doing?" He sounded angry.

Still batting at the as yet unidentified creature, now in her lap, Mary Jo swung her car door open. Prevented from opening it fully by Ray's body, she gave the door a hard shove, pushing him backwards. As she sprang forward out of the car and stood up, a praying mantis fell from her legs to the ground. It twitched, and Mary Jo raised her foot to finish the job.

With quick instincts, Ray grabbed her ankle.

"Let go of me, Officer Laramie," she yelled, "or I'll have you charged with assault." Remembering her tear streaked face, she hoped he didn't notice. "That...*thing* gives me the creeps. It attacked me!"

Ray released her, but inserted himself between her and the mantis. "You may not know this, Mary Jo," he said softly, "but it's against the law to kill any living thing in Fayetteville."

Mary Jo looked at him in disbelief. "Huh? You've got to be kidding me. Why are you doing this to me, Ray? You don't even know me!"

"You're right, Mary Jo, I don't really. But I thought I was starting to," he replied. "Why did you take off on me like that, anyway?"

Mary Jo felt ready for a fight. She backed off a bit to get a better vantage point. "Why, what was I supposed to do, Ray? Wait for you to pick up your girlfriend's cake at the café so I could be sure her name was spelled right? It was spelled right, wasn't it?"

"I don't know, Mary Jo. I didn't pick up the cake. I came to find out what was wrong with you. And...what do you mean, my girlfriend?"

"Yoo-hoo!" Mary Jo snapped her fingers in front of his face. "Hel-lo. Your girlfriend? Josie – remember?"

Ray laughed, infuriating Mary Jo. She pushed him with little effect. Ray tried to muffle his laughter, but his heaving shoulders betrayed his amusement.

"What's so funny?" she barked, frowning.

Ray wiped his eyes, trying to get hold of himself. He looked her in the eye, put a hand on her shoulder. "I'm sorry," he said, "I should've made my order clearer. Josie's not my girlfriend–"

"Oh, I get it," Mary Jo said, cutting him off. The light of understanding dawned, but she felt extremely foolish, and didn't want to give in yet. "She's your wife."

"No, Mary Jo. Not my wife." Ray's voice sounded so husky she hardly dared to look at him. When she did, his eyes were filled with tenderness. "Josie's my niece. I promised my sister I'd pick up a cake from your shop for her birthday." He slapped his forehead. "Man, am I gonna be in trouble. I'm supposed to be there right now."

Mary Jo grimaced. "I'm sorry, Ray. I jumped to conclusions." She sighed deeply. "I shouldn't have done that. And now I'm late picking up my son. But what about that?" she pointed at the green object of disgust now lying dead on the ground a few feet away. "And what about the speeding? I'm sure you've got to write me up."

"Mary Jo? Can we start over?" He reached out hesitantly, and when she didn't move, stroked the side of her face.

"I don't know, Ray," she answered honestly. "You're a police officer and I've broken the law twice today already. Are you sure you should be thinking about dating a felon?"

They heard a sound behind them. A dark-eyed junco swooped down and started nibbling at the mantis. Mary Jo made a face and looked away.

"Looks like you've got a friend," teased Ray. "There goes my evidence..."

"What about the speeding?" she asked, turning to him with a smile.

"Well, you *were* being pursued," he offered. "You didn't know my intentions were honorable. You do have the right to protect yourself."

A Ray for Mary Jo

"Okay, Ray," nodded Mary Jo. She sighed heavily and it felt like a burden had been lifted. "Let's start over. Let me make it up to Josie. I'll go pick up Jabez, then go back to the café for the cake and some other goodies. We'll meet up with you at your sister's place—if you'll give me her address?"

"Oh, you already know it," said Ray. "And I don't think you need to worry about the cake, though. She's probably already taken it home. I mean—I was supposed to pick it up, but that was just an excuse to invite you along."

Mary Jo shook her head as if it was stuffed with cotton batting. "I don't understand."

"Your best waitress," smiled Ray. "She's my sister... Janine."

Mary Jo's jaw hung slack as she stared at him wide-eyed. She felt like shoving him again, but he pushed her chin up to close her mouth before dropping his lips to hers. A long kiss followed, and her resistance faded as he pressed her close to his body. At last he pulled away and looked at her, drinking her in.

"And, Mary Jo, honey, just in case you were wondering— there might be laws against speeding and killing, but there ain't no law against love."

Be sure to visit Susan Barclay's website
www.susan-barclay.ca

We hope you've enjoyed NO LAW AGAINST LOVE. While the authors believe the laws they have written about are still on the books in the states and countries listed, the validity of that is only as good as information provided on the internet and in various books. Whether they actually are or aren't, we hope we've provided you with enjoyable stories.

We invite you to watch for NO LAW AGAINST LOVE 2.

Check our website frequently for future Highland Press releases.

www.highlandpress.org

Printed in the United States
44384LVS00003B/76-111